PETER ROBINSON

Bad Boy

HODDER

First published in Great Britain in 2010 by Hodder & Stoughton
An Hachette UK company

This paperback edition published 2011

1

Copyright © Eastvale Enterprises Inc. 2010

The right of Peter Robinson to be identified as the Author
of the Work has been asserted by him in accordance with the
Copyright, Designs and Patents Act 1988.

A CIP catalogue record for this title is available from the British Library

A format paperback ISBN 978 1 444 70963 6
B format paperback ISBN 978 0 340 83697 2

Typeset in Plantin Light by Ellipsis Books Limited, Glasgow

Printed and bound by CPI Group (UK) Ltd, Croydon, CR0 4YY

Hodder & Stoughton policy is to use papers that are natural, renewable
and recyclable products and made from wood grown in sustainable forests.
The logging and manufacturing processes are expected to conform to
the environmental regulations of the country of origin.

Hodder & Stoughton Ltd
338 Euston Road
London NW1 3BH

www.hodder.co.uk

'Brilliant! . . . Gut-wrenching plotting, alongside heart-wrenching portraits of the characters who populate his world, not to mention the top-notch police procedure. This one will stay with you for a long time.'
Jeffery Deaver

'Riveting'
Marcel Berlins, *The Times*

'Robinson writes with gusto . . . his tale cracks along at a satisfying lick, with splashes of dark humour along the way.'
Metro

'A master class in the organisation of narrative.'
Independent

'A murderous psychopath presents Alan Banks with the most intensely personal challenge of the maverick detective's storied career. Superbly cinematic from the beginning to the explosive finale, this would be a thrilling movie.'
Joseph Wambaugh

'Excellent . . . Robinson deftly integrates Banks's personal life with an acute look at British attitudes about police, guns, and violence in this strong entry in a superb series.' *Publishers Weekly*, starred review

'Robinson writes solid, tense, police procedurals that depend on good plots, accuracy and the genuine likeability of the central character, Alan Banks. I would highly recommend *Bad Boy*.' *www.eurocrime.co.uk*

'After 18 tales of the fiendishly good DCI Alan Banks, the bestselling author delves into his leading man's past. For die-hard fans [*The Price of Love*] explains how Banks came to be in Yorkshire and how he got his mysterious scar. For the rest of us, it's the start of a beautiful relationship with the novelist's extensive back catalogue'
Shortlist

'Inspector Banks. A man for all seasons, he knows that often the clues to the answers he seeks can be found in his own troubled soul'
Michael Connelly

'Banks is one of the most fully drawn figures in this genre of fiction'
New York Times

ALSO BY PETER ROBINSON

Caedmon's Song
No Cure for Love

Inspector Banks Novels

Gallows View
A Dedicated Man
A Necessary End
The Hanging Valley
Past Reason Hated
Wednesday's Child
Dry Bones that Dream
Innocent Graves
Dead Right
In a Dry Season
Cold is the Grave
Aftermath
The Summer that Never Was
Playing With Fire
Strange Affair
Piece of My Heart
Friend of the Devil
All the Colours of Darkness

Short Stories

Not Safe After Dark
The Price of Love

To Sheila

I

By the end of August, the waterlogged Yorkshire country-side was a symphony of green and gold under a blue sky scribbled with white clouds. Heaven only knew how the farmers had managed to mow and bale the hay, as the rain seemed to have been falling for days without end, but somehow they had succeeded, and their neat straw cylinders dotted the fields. Bright tractors ploughed in the stubble and turned the earth a dark fecund brown. Smells of the recent harvest and of the coming autumn chill mingled in the mild air. On the moors, the purple heather was in bloom. By the roadside, swallows gathered on the telephone wires preparing for their long flight to South Africa.

Annie Cabbot wished she could go with them as she drove the last few miles to work that Monday morning. A few days on a game reserve would do her the world of good, photographing and sketching giraffes, zebras, leopards, lions and elephants. Then perhaps a tour of the Winelands, a taste of fine Cape Town cuisine and nightlife.

But it was not to be. She had exhausted her entire holiday allowance for the year, apart from a few days, which she planned to use to create occasional long weekends between now and Christmas. Besides, she couldn't afford to go to South Africa; she would be hard pushed to pay for a mini-break in Blackpool. Lucky swallows.

The traffic came to a halt about half a mile from the big roundabout on the southern edge of Eastvale, and when Annie finally got close enough to see the fender-bender that was causing the delay, she was already late for work. A patrol car had arrived at the accident scene, so she felt she could safely leave the uniformed officers to deal with the obvious case of road rage between the two drivers, who were standing by their cars shouting at each other, fists raised. Traffic wasn't her department.

Annie made her way through the increasingly built-up and busy streets around the college, where a few late summer students strolled across the green to morning lectures, rucksacks slung over their shoulders. From there, she cut down a long narrow street of three-storey red-brick Victorian houses, mostly converted into student flats, over to Market Street. When she reached the market square, she took the narrow lane between the buildings and parked at the back of the Tudor-fronted police station. She said hello to a couple of officers she recognised standing outside sneaking a quick smoke break, then swiped her card in the slot on the back door and entered Western Area Headquarters.

A couple of people greeted her when she walked into the Major Crimes squad room. Geraldine Masterson, their new probationary detective constable, told her that Winsome Jackman and Doug Wilson – known to most of his colleagues as 'Harry Potter' owing to his uncanny resemblance to Daniel Radcliffe – were already out interviewing witnesses to last night's hit-and-run on the Lyndgarth Road. The incident had left two teenagers in hospital and one no doubt very shaken driver holed up at home, just waiting for the knock on the door, wishing he hadn't had that one last drink for the road.

Annie had hardly made a dent in the accumulated paper-work when her phone rang. She put down her pen and picked up the handset. 'DI Cabbot.'

It was the desk sergeant. 'Someone to see DCI Banks,' he said. 'A Mrs Doyle.' There was a moment's pause while the sergeant apparently conferred with the visitor, their voices muffled. 'Mrs Juliet Doyle,' he went on. 'She says she knows the DCI. Says it's urgent.'

Annie sighed. 'All right,' she said. 'Send her up. Might as well have someone show her to DCI Banks's office. It's a bit more private there.'

'Will do, ma'am.'

Annie closed the thick folder of crime statistics on her desk and walked down the corridor to Banks's office. The few occasions she had been in there recently had unnerved her even more than her brief visits to his cottage to water the plants, take in any parcels and flyers and make sure all was well. Banks's absence seemed even more palpable in the cool silence and the slight musty smell of his office. His desk was empty except for the computer, which hadn't been switched on in ages. A CD player/radio combination stood silent on one of his bookshelves next to a couple of tattered Kingsley Amis paperbacks he'd picked up from the second-hand book-shop in the market square a few days before he had left. Annie moved the computer monitor aside so that she would have an unobstructed view of the person sitting opposite her. A young PC knocked at the door and showed the woman in.

'I thought this was Alan's office,' Juliet Doyle said. 'It has his name on the door. Who are you? I don't mean to seem rude, but I specifically asked to see Alan.'

She seemed nervous, Annie thought, her movements jerky and bird-like as she took in the sparse room. 'DCI Banks is on holiday,' Annie explained, standing up and extending her hand. 'I'm DI Annie Cabbot. Can I help you?'

'I . . . I don't know. I was expecting Alan. This is all so . . .' Juliet fingered the chain around her neck. A heavy gold-and-jade pendant hung from it in the lightly freckled cleft between her breasts. She was probably in her mid-forties, Annie guessed, smartly dressed, her clothes definitely not from any of the shops you would find in the Swainsdale Centre, more likely Harrogate or York, wavy blonde hair with dark brown roots, tasteful make-up, still attractive, and not concerned about showing a little cleavage. Her skirt was a modest knee-length, legs nicely tapered beneath it, and she wore a tan suede jacket in an elegant hourglass cut. Annie wondered whether she fancied Banks, whether there had been something between them.

'Please sit down,' Annie said. After a slight hesitation, Juliet perched at the edge of the chair opposite her. 'Is it anything I can help you with, or was it something personal?'

'That's why I was hoping to see Alan,' Juliet went on. 'You see, it's both, really. Oh, this is *so* difficult. When will he be back?'

'Not until next week, I'm afraid.'

Juliet Doyle seemed to consider this for a few moments, still fidgeting with her chain, as if debating whether the matter could wait that long.

'Would you like some tea? Coffee?' Annie asked.

'No, thank you.'

'I can't help you if I don't know what it's about,' Annie went on. 'You say it's both police business and personal, is that right?'

Juliet nodded. 'That's why it's so hard. I mean, Alan would *understand*.' She had shifted her attention from the necklace to the chunky diamond ring on the third finger of her left hand, twisting it around and around. Her fingernails were bitten low and painted pink.

'Why don't you try me?' Annie said. 'Just tell me what the problem is.'

'Alan would know *what to do.*'

Annie leaned back in the chair and linked her hands behind her head. She felt as if she were in for a long haul. 'Perhaps you could start by telling me exactly what your relationship is with DCI Banks?'

Juliet appeared startled. 'Relationship? We don't have a relationship.'

'I simply meant how you came to know one another.'

'Oh, that. I see. Yes. I'm sorry. We're neighbours. Were.'

Annie happened to know that Banks had no neighbours anywhere close to his Gratly cottage, so she assumed that Juliet Doyle was referring to the past, perhaps when he had lived on Laburnum Way, about a mile down Market Street from the police station. But Banks hadn't lived there for ten years. Had they kept in touch all that time? Was there something she was missing? 'When was this?' she asked.

'When he and Sandra were still together. I still think it's so tragic that they parted like that, don't you? Such a lovely couple.'

'Yes,' said Annie, whose only experiences of Sandra had been humiliating and more than a little frightening.

'Anyway,' Juliet went on, 'we were friends and neighbours. That's why I thought he might be able to help me.'

'Mrs Doyle,' said Annie, 'if this is a police matter, you really should tell me. Are you in some sort of trouble?'

Juliet flinched as if she'd received a surprise tap on the shoulder. 'Trouble? Me? No. Of course not.'

'Then what is it?'

Juliet scanned the office as if she suspected Banks were hiding behind a filing cabinet or in a cupboard. 'Are you *sure* Alan's not here?'

'Positive. I told you. He's on his holidays.'

Juliet twisted her diamond ring again and let the silence stretch. Just when Annie was about to get up and show her the door, she blurted out, 'It's about Erin.'

'Erin?'

'Yes. Our daughter. Mine and my husband's, that is. Patrick. He sent me. He's stopping home with Erin.'

'Is Erin in trouble?'

'I suppose she is. Yes. You don't know what they get up to, do you? Do you have any children?'

'No.'

'Well, you wouldn't know, then . . . It's too easy to blame the parents, the way they do in the papers and on television. But when you just don't know . . .' She let the sentence trail.

'I'm going to ring for some tea,' said Annie. The good old English panacea, she thought, as she picked up the phone and asked for a pot to be sent up, a nice cup of tea. This was clearly going to take some time, and if Juliet Doyle didn't need a cuppa, Annie certainly did. Maybe they'd bring chocolate digestives, too, if she was lucky.

'Erin lives in Leeds,' Juliet said. 'In Headingley. Hardly a den of iniquity, you might say, but you'd be surprised.'

'Like most big cities, it can be a dangerous place if you're not careful,' said Annie. 'But I must tell you, we're North Yorkshire. If the problem is in Leeds, then you need to—'

'No, no. That's not it. You don't understand.'

Of course I don't understand, Annie thought, gritting her

teeth. I'd have to be a bloody mind-reader to understand. 'Tell me, then,' she said.

The tea arrived. A welcome interruption. No chocolate digestives, though. Normally, Annie would have asked or made some sort of comment to the young PC who brought in the tray, but it wouldn't do to take up a petty issue like the lack of chocolate biscuits with Juliet Doyle sitting opposite her.

'Erin's a good girl. I think she must have fallen in with a bad crowd,' said Juliet, accepting the cup Annie handed her, adding milk and sugar with slightly shaking hands.

'How old is she?'

'Twenty-four.'

'Working?'

'Yes. As a waitress. It's a nice restaurant. Very upmarket. Down in The Calls, with all those fancy new boutique hotels and waterfront flats. And she makes decent enough money. But even so . . .' She shrugged.

'It's not what you expected for her?'

'Not with a good upper second in psychology.'

'Times are hard. Perhaps she's just waiting for the right job to come along.'

'I'd like to think so, but . . .'

'What?'

'Well, I think she's more likely been wasting her time. It's been two years now since she got her degree. She took a gap year before she went.'

'Does she have a boyfriend?'

'As far as I know she still does,' said Juliet. 'Not that we've met him, or even that she's told us much about him. Mostly we keep in touch through phone calls, texts. You know what the young are like. The last thing they think of sometimes is visiting their parents unless they need something, or it's a special occasion.'

'Young people can be very secretive,' Annie agreed.

'She's a grown woman. I was married when I was her age.'

'But times change,' said Annie. 'Kids aren't so quick to leave the nest these days.'

'Erin's not a parasite, if that's what you mean. She was happy enough to get away from home in the first place. Couldn't get out fast enough. That wasn't the problem.'

'Then what is?' Annie said, close to the end of her patience. She was beginning to think that this was some sort of domestic matter, and she was starting to feel resentful that she was left not only to do Banks's job while he was away, but handle his personal problems, too. 'Why are you here? What did you think Alan could do for you?'

Juliet's back stiffened. 'He'd *know* what to do, wouldn't he?'

'About what?' Annie knew she was almost shouting, but she couldn't help herself.

'About the gun,' said Juliet Doyle, head bowed, speaking so softly that Annie could barely hear her. 'She has a gun.'

'Tell me how it happened.'

Detective Superintendent Catherine Gervaise was sitting on the edge of her desk with her arms folded, and the way she towered over Annie and Juliet Doyle made Annie feel as if they were two truant schoolgirls brought up before the headmistress. Gervaise could have that effect when she wanted. Annie had her notebook open and her pen in her hand, waiting. No matter what action the situation warranted, there was likely to be a lot of red tape ahead, and she had to get it down right.

'I was dusting and cleaning her room,' Juliet began. 'Honestly, I wasn't prying. Erin was downstairs watching breakfast television. I like to keep a neat and clean house, and it was my morning to do the upstairs, so I didn't see any harm in it.'

'So Erin still lives at home?' Gervaise asked.

'No. As I told Ms Cabbot here, she lives in Leeds.'

'Would you give us the address, please?'

'Of course.' Juliet gave an address in Headingley and Annie wrote it down. She knew the area and recognised the street name.

'What is she doing in Eastvale?'

'She . . . she didn't really say.'

'What did she say?'

'Just that she needed to come home for a while. I thought she might have split up with her boyfriend or something.'

'Did you ask her if she had?'

'Yes, but she just told me to mind my own business. She isn't usually so rude. We brought her up to be polite and respectful to her elders. But she's upset. I thought if I left her alone, she would tell me what was bothering her eventually. She usually does.'

'Are you very close?'

'I wouldn't say *very* close, but I like to think that we are close, yes, that she feels she can talk to me, tell me anything. That's why it was such a shock, finding the gun.'

'What do you know about her boyfriend?'

'Just what she told me on the phone, really.'

'What's his name?'

'Geoff. I don't know his last name. They only use first names, don't they?'

'How long has she been going out with him?'

'About six months.'

'Do you think he's been a bad influence on her?'

'Quite the opposite, really. From what she says, he's a nice lad, and he's done very well for himself, not like her usual scruffy student types. And I must say, I've noticed a great change for the better in her appearance on the few occasions I have seen her since they've been together.'

'Like what?'

'Her dress sense, for a start. Her whole style. Much smarter. For so long she dressed like a typical student, but she turned up for her dad's birthday in a nice summer frock with a lovely heart pendant around her neck. She never used to wear jewellery unless it was the cheap kind, plastic coloured beads and the like. She's had her hair done, too. You can tell she went to a good hairdresser. It's a professional job.'

'When was this?'

'Thirtieth of July'

'Do you know what this Geoff does for a living?'

'He's in sales and marketing. That's all I know. And he's got a company car. A BMW.'

'Sounds like a good catch,' said Gervaise. 'What was Erin like when she came back home? What was her state of mind? You said she was upset.'

'Yes. She seemed distant, distracted. Quiet and withdrawn.'

'Is that like her?'

'No. She's usually quite normal, when it comes to conversation and such. Always has been. Cheerful. Quick to smile. Gregarious, even. But this time she's been acting like a hermit, staying in her room.'

'Did she ask you for any help at all?'

Juliet frowned. 'What do you mean? What sort of help?'

'Financial, emotional, medical. Anything. Could she be in trouble?'

'You mean *pregnant*?'

'It's a possibility,' said Gervaise. 'Though that wasn't what I meant specifically. Would she have been able to talk to you about something like that?'

'I'd like to think so.'

'How long has she been back here in Eastvale?'

'Since Friday morning. We kept her room. Always. Just as it was. Well, tidier.'

'Lots of parents do that,' Gervaise said. 'It offsets the sense of loss when their children leave home. Sometimes it's hard to let go.'

Annie knew that the superintendent had two children of her own, though it was hard to imagine it at the moment, as she perched there in her pinstripe skirt, buttoned-up jacket and crisp white blouse, all business.

'Yes,' said Juliet.

'Did you get the impression that this time it's more than a passing visit?'

'Definitely.'

'And is this the first time she's come to stay for any length of time since she left home?'

'Yes.'

Gervaise paused. 'Now, about the gun you found on top of the wardrobe,' she went on.

'It was near the back, where you couldn't possibly see it unless you stood on a chair or a stepladder. It was wrapped in a tea cloth. I suppose she thought it was safe up there. I mean, she doesn't really think about housework or anything like that.'

'It would have been if it hadn't been for your thoroughness,' said Gervaise. 'You did the right thing coming to us, Mrs Doyle.'

'I don't know,' Juliet said, shaking her head. 'My own daughter. I feel like such a . . . Judas. What will happen to her?'

Annie had deeply conflicted feelings towards Juliet Doyle at that moment. On the one hand, the poor woman was turning in her own daughter, and she must be going through hell. Whether Juliet was aware of it or not, Annie knew there was a mandatory five-year sentence for possession of a handgun, and the courts tended to be strict in its application, though there had recently been some complaints about overly lenient judges. Perhaps they would take special circumstances into account for a young woman with no prior record, but however forgiving they were, Erin Doyle was looking at a prison sentence of some sort, rather than probation or community service. And she would come out with a criminal record. Juliet probably didn't suspect this. Still, Annie reminded herself, as yet they had absolutely no evidence that Erin Doyle was guilty of anything.

'It's a very serious matter,' Gervaise went on. 'Guns are dangerous weapons, and the more we get off the streets the safer our towns and cities will be.'

It was the party line, Annie knew, and Gervaise was clearly trying to make Juliet feel more at ease with her betrayal, feel like a right-thinking citizen. But Annie sensed that Juliet Doyle was getting seriously worried now, and beginning to regret that she had come. She was probably thinking that she and her husband could have dealt with the whole mess themselves, disposed of the gun, chucked it in the river, given Erin a good talking-to. In a way, Annie thought, she was right.

For a mother to take such a step was almost inconceivable to Annie, no matter how much police policy encouraged it, or how much, as an officer of the law and a campaigner against gun crime, she was supposed to applaud it. While a part of her admired Juliet's sacrifice to duty, to the greater good, another part of her felt disgust for what the woman was doing. Though Annie had never raised a child herself, she didn't think she would be capable of betraying her daughter. She was certain that her own mother never would have done such a thing, though she had died when Annie was very young. Her father would have given her a stern talking-to and thrown the gun in the sea, but he would never have turned her in to the police, either. But, she reminded herself, Juliet Doyle had come here asking for Banks's help. No doubt she had hoped that he would be able to deal with the matter unofficially, off the record.

'What happens now?' Juliet asked.

Gervaise moved away from the edge of her desk and went to sit behind it. She didn't seem quite so imposing there, and Annie felt the atmosphere lighten a little. 'There are procedures to be followed,' Gervaise said. 'Where is the gun now?'

'In the kitchen. Patrick has it. We didn't think it would be a good idea for me to carry it in the street, and I must admit the idea made me very nervous.'

'And your daughter?'

'She's with him. We agreed this was the best way. They would stay at the house. I would come here and talk to Alan, ask him to go back with me, but . . .'

'Yes, I understand that DCI Banks was a neighbour,' Gervaise said. 'Don't worry, we're all professionals here. We'll deal with this just as he would. I know it's much more pleasant to have a familiar face around in a situation like this, but we all want the same thing. First of all, are you absolutely certain it's a real gun? You have no idea how many people we get reporting replicas or ball-bearing guns.'

'Patrick said it is. He used to belong to a gun club, many years ago, after grammar school. I don't know about such things.'

'Did he also happen to check if it's loaded?'

'He says it is. He handled it very carefully.'

'Good,' said Gervaise. 'Did he unload it?'

'No. He said it was best to leave it as it was, not to contaminate the evidence.'

Wonderful, thought Annie. Another one been watching too many episodes of *CSI.* A loaded gun. Now they would have to bring in the Firearms Support Unit for certain. It would have made more sense, and been much safer, if Patrick Doyle had unloaded the gun. Annie also knew that most people rarely act sensibly during crises. After all, how often do you find a loaded gun in your daughter's bedroom?

'Did he happen to mention what kind of gun it is?' Gervaise asked.

'He said something about a semi-automatic. Can that be right?'

Annie knew very little about firearms, but she knew that a semi-automatic used a removable magazine to hold cartridges, rather than a cylinder. It usually held several rounds of ammunition, and it fired one shot each time you pulled the trigger.

'So when you left the house,' Gervaise went on, 'your husband and daughter were in the kitchen and the gun was on the table?'

'Yes.'

'Still wrapped?'

'Patrick wrapped it up in the tea cloth again after he'd examined it, yes.'

'What state of mind was Erin in then?'

'She was upset, obviously. Angry. Tearful. Frightened.'

'Did you ask her who she'd got the gun from?'

'Of course. But she wouldn't say.'

Gervaise pursed her lips and thought for a moment, then she glanced at Annie and stood up. 'Thank you,' she said to Juliet Doyle. 'I'm going to ring for someone to take care of you for the time being while we deal with the problem of the gun. That has to be our priority, you understand. We need to get that loaded gun out of your house and into safe keeping, and there are strict procedures we need to follow.' She picked up the telephone and talked to the officer on the front desk.

Juliet looked pleadingly towards Annie. 'Will you stay with me?' she asked.

'I'm afraid I need DI Cabbot,' said Gervaise. 'She's the only other senior officer I have here at the moment. But don't worry, I'll make sure you're nice and comfortable with WPC Smithies in the canteen.'

'Can't I go home?'

'Not just yet,' said Gervaise. 'Not until we've cleared the premises of the firearm.'

'But can't I go with you?'

'I'm afraid not,' said Gervaise. She touched Juliet's arm. 'Don't worry. I told you, you'll be well taken care of.'

'Can I ring my husband?'

'Sorry,' said Gervaise. 'It might seem petty and silly to you, but we can't allow any contact until the matter is settled and the firearm is safely in our possession.'

'But what harm could it possibly do if I talked to my husband?'

It could do a lot of harm, Annie thought. It could precipitate an argument between father and daughter in the house, for example, and with a loaded gun lying on the table and tempers no doubt already stretched to breaking point, that could prove fatal. But before Gervaise could answer the question, assuming she was intending to, WPC Smithies knocked at the door and escorted a reluctant Juliet Doyle to the canteen.

Gervaise beckoned Annie to stay. 'We'll do this by the book, Annie. I don't want any guns on my patch, and I certainly don't want any accidents with them due to haste or negligence. Is that clear?'

'Yes, ma'am,' said Annie. 'Want me to log the incident and call in an Armed Response Vehicle?'

'Yes. And get one of the DCs to run a check on the Doyles, especially the daughter. Everything seems hunky-dory on the surface, but find out if we've any cause for alarm. I'll ring ACC McLaughlin and he'll no doubt get in touch with the Deputy Chief Constable. I also want to arrange for the Leeds police to search Erin's house. I hardly think she's an arms dealer, but we'd better cover it. Let's get this in motion. The longer we delay, the more chance there is of something going wrong.'

It wasn't the first time Annie had witnessed an armed police raid. She had been involved in two of them in London a few years earlier. The first had gone smoothly, but the second had been a disaster. Shots had been fired and two men had been killed. This time, she felt much stranger, being just down the road from the police station, across from Banks's old suburban semi. It all seemed so ordinary. A black cat picked its way through a flower bed; people passed by the end of the street with their shopping and paused to see what was happening.

Annie sat silently in an unmarked police car with Detective Superintendent Gervaise and waited for the Armed Response Vehicles to arrive. She almost wished she smoked. It would be something to do to help pass the time. Instead, she just gazed out at the bay-windowed semis with their low walled gardens, pebble-dash and trim lawns, and she realised she found it hard to imagine Banks ever living here as a family man. To her, he had always been very much a lone figure, even when they had had their brief romance. Now she couldn't fathom him at all. Something had changed in him, something fundamental had broken, and she wasn't sure whether it could ever be mended.

Two Volvo T5s parked at the junction with Market Street. Each Armed Response Vehicle from the Firearms Support Unit comprised two Authorised Firearms Officers, or AFOs, in full Personal Protective Equipment, carrying PR24 batons, rigid handcuffs and CS spray, in addition to Glock sidearms and tasers. They would have Heckler and Koch MP5 carbines locked in the boots of their Volvos, along with an array of other lethal weapons.

Laburnum Way was a cul-de-sac about a hundred yards in length, so their arrival effectively cut off the street. Two patrol cars were parked at the far end. People were already watching at their windows.

The four AFOs had already been briefed on the layout of the house, as provided by Juliet Doyle, should they need to effect entry. They didn't expect to have to do that, however, as Patrick Doyle and his daughter knew where Juliet had gone, and they were expecting a police visit.

Annie thought one of the team members was a woman, but it was hard to tell behind all the body armour and equipment she was carrying. Another car pulled up and Mike Trethowan, the Firearms Cadre's superintendent, also wearing full PPE, spoke briefly with his officers then came over to join Annie and Gervaise.

'Any change?' he asked.

'None,' said Gervaise. 'According to our information they're just sitting there in the kitchen waiting for us to arrive.'

'And the kitchen is where?'

'Back of the house. Down the hall, door off to the right.'

The superintendent sniffed the air, nodded and went back to his team.

This wasn't a firearms hostage situation or a fatal shooting. So far, nothing had happened, and the procedure was a simple one. As it didn't appear that anyone was intent on using the firearm, and the situation was more or less under the control of the girl's father, the uniformed officers would knock at the door and shout for Patrick and Erin Doyle to come out. Once they appeared, they would be asked to hand over the weapon in question and step away. It was simply a matter of being on guard and of using the usual extra care and caution around firearms. The house was certainly quiet enough from the outside.

Things started to go wrong right from the start, when no one answered the door. Because of the natural tension when firearms are involved, everyone was a little impatient, but even Annie had to admit that a pensioner in a Zimmer frame could have got there by the time Superintendent Trethowan recalled the local officers, sent two armed men around the back and two up the front path. Annie glanced at Gervaise, whose expression was set, teeth clenched, Cupid's-bow mouth almost a single straight red line.

Getting no response to their shouts, the AFOs used a battering ram on the door, which splintered open, and the two officers rushed inside, making as much noise as they could. Within seconds, they had disappeared from view, and after a brief silence, Annie heard a muffled shout and then a clicking sound, like some distant cicada chattering in the trees, followed by a scream and a lot of shouting and banging about.

She and Gervaise jumped out of the car and dashed for the garden, but Superintendent Trethowan, outside the house, raised his hand to warn them to stay back, then he went inside. Annie could hear the other two officers breaking in at the back, then more shouting, the sound of a chair or a table crashing over, and finally another loud scream, a different voice this time.

Annie felt her heart beating so hard and fast that she thought it would explode inside her chest. She was shaking all over. For what seemed like ages, nothing happened. The house fell silent again, apart from the sounds of the team walking about inside, doors opening and closing. Finally, Trethowan came out with two officers, and the three of them walked towards the van.

'What happened?' Gervaise asked as they passed by.

But Trethowan simply shook his head. Annie couldn't see his expression because of the protective headgear.

About thirty seconds later, someone shouted the all-clear, and another officer came out carrying a small item wrapped in a tea cloth. So that was what it was all about, Annie thought. So tiny. So deadly. And from what she could see as the man passed right by her, the tea cloth had a map of the Yorkshire Dales printed on it. A moment later, the final two armed response officers came out, dragging between them a struggling and screaming young woman in rigid handcuffs: Erin Doyle. Then came the sound of an ambulance speeding towards them down Market Street.

'Oh, shit,' said Gervaise. 'Here we go.'

2

'Right,' said ACC Ron McLaughlin, when everyone was seated in the boardroom of Western Area Headquarters. 'We've got the house on Laburnum Way locked down. Erin Doyle is in custody, and Juliet Doyle is at the hospital by her husband's bedside. I hardly need to tell you, ladies and gentlemen, that we appear to be looking at a cock-up of gigantic proportions.'

McLaughlin had called the meeting to make some sense out of what had just happened and to determine what should be done next, and by whom. The room was crowded and the atmosphere tense. Though no media had arrived at the station yet, Annie could sense the vibrations thrumming through the ether, hear the tom-toms beating in the distance and see the smoke signals curling into the sky.

In plain grey T-shirts and combats, the AFOs looked as if they had just come from the nearest fitness centre. Annie saw that she was right about one of the team being female. She had seen the woman around County HQ at Newby Wiske on the few occasions she had been there, and they had exchanged brief and polite greetings, but she hadn't known the woman was a trained AFO. Luckily, Western Area hadn't had much use for their services lately. There were few enough women in the force, and Annie reckoned that this one must be very good if she was a member of the AFO team. Training was tough and standards were high. The female officer had closely cropped spiky dark hair over a heart-shaped face, with large eyes, a small mouth and an olive complexion. She was short, with a barrel-shaped, muscular upper body, as if she lifted a lot of weights. Annie caught her eye and gave her a smile of solidarity. She gave Annie a grim, shy smile of understanding back, then turned away.

One of the team members, a youngish-looking fellow whom Annie didn't recognise, seemed paler than the rest and was chewing on the end of a biro. The hand in which he held it was shaking, and it didn't take a genius to work out that he was the shooter, the one who had dashed out of the house and thrown up in the herbaceous border. He didn't look any older than eighteen, but Annie knew that he had to be in his mid to late twenties to have completed the training and psychological testing necessary to be an AFO.

'I think you all know the drill,' McLaughlin went on, once everybody had a coffee in front of them. 'I'm going to hand over to Superintendent Chambers from Professional Standards now, to get the ball rolling. Once we've got the general picture, we'll try to make some decisions on how best to proceed. Reg?'

Chambers cleared his throat, leaned back in his chair and put his pen down on his notepad. The buttons on his waist-coat stretched tight across his chest and belly. Annie thought he had the faintly ridiculous air of a Dickensian character. She had once worked with Chambers for a few weeks and had quickly come to understand why the Internal Affairs Department was always referred to as the 'Rat Squad' on American television programmes.

'Thank you, sir,' said Chambers. 'Let's just get a few facts straight, first of all, shall we? Who called in the FSU?' He had a Home Counties accent, which he seemed to think made him sound posh.

'I did,' said Gervaise. 'We had information that an illegal firearm had been discovered in Erin Doyle's bedroom at her parents' house on Laburnum Way. Miss Doyle had remained there in the custody of her father while her mother reported the weapon to us.'

'Admirable.' Chambers jotted something down, then asked Gervaise, 'Was there any reason to suspect that anyone in the house was in danger?'

'None,' said Gervaise.

'Or that the firearm was a threat to anyone at all?'

'A loaded firearm is always a threat. But there was no reason for us to assume that either Erin or Patrick Doyle intended to use the weapon, either on each other or on anybody else. They were both aware that the mother, Juliet Doyle, had gone to the police station to report finding it. They were expecting us.'

Chambers scratched the edge of his nose and coughed. 'I understand that the daughter was quite upset and angry when the gun was discovered in her room?'

'Naturally,' said Gervaise.

'But you didn't think she was afraid of the consequences, was likely to use the weapon to effect an escape?'

Gervaise took her time before answering. 'I don't think she was even aware of the consequences,' she said finally. 'Most people in her position aren't. They don't really think they've done anything wrong in simply giving house-room to a gun, no matter how they came by it. After all, they haven't used it. I doubt that she even realised she was committing a serious crime. She probably expected to be thanked for keeping it off the streets. If she even knew about it.'

'What do you mean?' Chambers demanded.

'I'm just pointing out that at this stage in our enquiries, we have absolutely no evidence whatsoever that Erin Doyle had any connection with the gun found by her mother on top of her wardrobe.'

'Are you suggesting that someone else put it there?'

'I am simply saying that we don't know,' said Gervaise. Annie could tell she was holding back her irritation.

'I understand from Sergeant Haggerty on the reception desk that Mrs Doyle asked to see Detective Chief Inspector Banks?' said Chambers, shooting Annie a sly glance. Annie knew that Chambers and Banks didn't get on, had crossed swords on more than one occasion since the reorganisation, in which Chambers's department had been relocated to County HQ.

'DCI Banks is one of my best officers,' said Gervaise. 'As it happens, he's on holiday.'

'Gardening leave, is it?' Chambers asked with a smirk. 'We all know he's been off his medication lately.'

'A well-deserved holiday,' said Gervaise, tight-lipped. She looked over at Annie. 'According to DI Cabbot, Mrs Doyle did first ask for DCI Banks, yes. Your point is?'

Chambers turned to Annie. His eyes narrowed. 'So it's true?'

'Yes,' said Annie.

'Any idea why this was?'

'Apparently they used to be neighbours and have remained friends since DCI Banks left the neighbourhood.'

'Why do you think she asked for him by name?'

'Because she knew him. I think she expected that he

would accompany her back to the house, pick up the gun and bring it in to the station.'

'Rather than follow correct procedure?'

Annie shifted uncomfortably in her seat. 'I think that DCI Banks's first priority would have been to defuse the situation,' she said, 'and to make sure that no harm came to anyone.'

'And our priority – the correct procedure – wasn't likely to achieve that?'

'With all due respect, it's not my place to comment on procedure, but I'm certain that whatever DCI Banks *would* have done would have been well within acceptable bounds.'

'I wish I could share your confidence,' said Chambers, his upper lip curling.

'Well, we'll never know, will we?' said Annie. 'Because he wasn't here, and it's all mere speculation.'

'That will do, DI Cabbot,' said Chambers.

Annie gave him a contemptuous look.

'So, in fact, what Erin and Patrick Doyle were expecting,' Chambers went on, 'was for an old family friend to come knocking at their door, give their daughter a stern talking-to, then disappear from their lives for ever with the gun? Problem solved.'

'I wouldn't necessarily say that,' Annie argued. 'I don't know what they were expecting. There are no grounds whatsoever for assuming that DCI Banks would in any way subvert the law, or try to protect Erin Doyle from prosecution for any offence she *might have* committed.'

Chambers sneered. 'Well, we'll never know now, will we, DI Cabbot? He wasn't here.' He had the kind of face that seemed to be wearing a perpetual expression of distaste, Annie had noticed, as if he had just smelled or swallowed something unpleasant. She also felt his eyes undress her every time he looked in her direction. His complexion was like the shiny pink plastic of a child's doll, and his lips were fleshy, wet and red. Annie felt like sticking her tongue out at him, but she managed to restrain herself. That would be childish. Instead, she gave him a sweet smile and sipped some bitter, tepid coffee.

'This isn't getting us anywhere, Reg,' cut in McLaughlin, who, Annie suspected, was well aware of Chambers's shortcomings. 'What might have happened under different circumstances isn't our concern here. Certainly not at this point.'

'No, sir,' said Chambers, with a quick glare at Annie. 'Forgive me. I was simply trying to get a general sense of events. Did anyone telephone the Doyle house, try to talk to the father and assess the situation?'

Gervaise paused. 'We felt that a telephone call might cause too much consternation, given that Erin's mother had already told us that her daughter was distraught, and that Erin and her father were expecting DCI Banks to be in touch.'

Chambers raised his eyebrows. 'Though that *is* standard procedure before sending in the cavalry, isn't it?'

'Let's move on to the incident itself, Reg,' McLaughlin said.

'By all means.' Chambers turned to the young AFO. 'Constable Warburton, would you care to tell us briefly, in your own words, what transpired at Laburnum Way? Just stick to the facts and keep it simple. Don't embellish.'

'Yes, sir,' said Warburton, sitting to attention, if such a thing were possible. He went on to describe how the team had waited while the local police knocked on the door and announced themselves.

'But no one answered, is that correct?'

'Yes, sir.'

'How long would you say transpired between the first officers announcing themselves and your forced entry?'

'It's hard to say, sir,' said Warburton. 'Time can behave very strangely in circumstances like that.'

'I acknowledge that one's perception of time can be affected by stress,' said Chambers, 'but surely you can give me a rough estimate? Seconds? Minutes? Hours?'

'A few minutes at most, sir.'

'Minutes? Very well. A minute can be a long time.'

'Yes, sir.'

'And during that time did you hear anything?'

'Hear anything?'

'Yes, from inside. Any sounds? An argument or anything like that.'

'I thought I heard voices at one point, sir. People talking.'

'Arguing?'

'Impossible to say, sir. They were muffled.'

'But could they have been raised?'

'I suppose they could. I couldn't tell.'

'Very well. What happened next?'

'When it seemed apparent that no one was going to answer the door, we thought it necessary to force entry. That is, WPC Powell and I did. Anything could have happened since the first reports. The girl could have been holding her father at gunpoint. She could even have shot him.'

'Nobody's arguing with your judgement, son,' said Chambers. 'Though the press might take a slightly more jaundiced view of things.'

'I feel that I acted in accordance with the law, sir, and with my training. I'd do the same—'

'Yes, yes. All right. Spare us the self-justification, PC Warburton. What happened when you entered the house? You entered from the front with Constable Nerys Powell, am I correct?' Chambers glanced at PC Powell, and it was clear to Annie, even from such a short look, that he disapproved of the presence of a woman on the team. They both worked at County HQ. Perhaps they had clashed before.

'Yes, sir,' said Warburton. 'We entered the building as instructed, WPC Powell and me.'

Nerys Powell gave him a sad smile of encouragement.

'What happened next?'

'The hallway was very long and dark. It was daytime, but there was no direct source of light.'

'Did you have a torch?' McLaughlin asked.

'Yes, sir, on my belt.'

'Did you switch it on?'

Warburton paused before answering. 'No, sir,' he said. 'There was just no time. It all happened so quickly. I did flick a light switch on the wall as we entered, but the bulb blew.'

'Tell me what happened next.'

Warburton drank some water and rubbed his face with both hands. 'Just as we entered the hall, by the bottom of the stairs, a door at the far end opened, to the right. I knew from my briefing that this was the door to the kitchen, and the kitchen was where the . . . where Mr Doyle and his daughter were said to be waiting. And the loaded firearm. I heard a creaking noise. Then there was a figure in the corridor, just a silhouette really, and I could swear he was waving a sword or some such weapon at me, about to rush us. Like I said, it was still dark in there. Our eyes hadn't had a chance to adjust, and we didn't have time to get out our torches. But we knew there was a loaded weapon on the premises, and I . . . I just reacted as fast as I could, sir, the way any officer would.'

'So you fired?'

'I discharged my taser, sir, yes. As we are instructed to do when faced with someone brandishing a sword or a knife.'

'Yet as far as you were concerned, the weapon you were there to recover was a firearm, and it had been found in the possession of Erin Doyle, not her father?'

'That's correct, sir. But he could have taken possession of it.'

'And just decided to shoot a policeman for the hell of it? Stick to the facts, Constable. You mentioned a sword, not a gun. And this sword was actually a walking stick.'

Warburton swallowed. 'Well, yes, sir. Strictly speaking. But I—'

'"Strictly speaking?" I'd be interested to know how else you would put it? Were you aware of any reason Mr Doyle might have had for attacking you with a sword? Or even a walking stick, for that matter?'

'No, sir. We – I – simply reacted to the circumstances, did the right thing, as per training. There was no time to speculate. Perhaps he had decided to try to defend his daughter? Perhaps he'd realised since the mother went off to see the police that the girl would be sent to jail? Perhaps he felt under threat because things hadn't turned out the way he had expected? I don't know, sir. I just reacted.'

'Are those the thoughts that passed through your mind at the time, or are they explanations you have thought up since?'

'I can't say I really had time to *think* of anything like that, sir. Not at the time. In action, you just sort of fall back on your training. It's not like thinking, finding reasons. That's for later.'

'Where did you aim for?'

'For the chest area, sir. The largest body mass. It's not as if you'd expect a taser to kill someone.'

'I know that, but it *has* happened. Don't you know it's now recommended that firearms officers aim tasers for the arms or legs, not the chest?'

'Sir, it was dark, I felt threatened, and I didn't want to risk missing.'

Chambers cleared his throat. 'Do you have any idea why there was such a long delay inside the house that you were forced to break down the door?'

'No, sir.'

'Were you aware at that time that Mr Doyle was expecting DCI Banks, an old friend, to turn up and sort things out?'

'No, sir, I wasn't.'

'Did you know that he was walking with a stick after a recent knee operation?'

'I did not, sir.' Warburton turned to his immediate boss, Firearms Cadre Superintendent Mike Trethowan, who gave him an encouraging nod. Trethowan was an experienced superintendent of about fifty, with a compact military bearing and a red complexion that Annie associated with high blood pressure. He always seemed cool enough, though, so she doubted that was the reason. Maybe he just burned easily in the sun. 'That information was not in our briefing,' said Warburton.

Chambers turned to Gervaise. 'I take it you didn't know about this, either, Catherine?'

'No,' said Gervaise. 'Juliet Doyle neglected to mention

that her husband was walking with the aid of a stick. I think she was far too het up about her daughter.'

'Her reasons are irrelevant. This should have been an essential part of the briefing. *Essential.* You can't send men into battle on dodgy intelligence. It can mean the difference between life and death.'

Gervaise crossed her arms. Annie was about to make a remark about Tony Blair not being worried about dodgy dossiers when it came to going to war with Iraq, but she decided it wouldn't go down well at this point. She must be growing up, she thought, not sticking her tongue out, keeping her lips buttoned.

Chambers put his pen on his pad. It was covered in a looping, spider-like scrawl, Annie noticed, quite a lot of which appeared to be doodles. 'I think we should wrap this up now,' he said. 'There are a lot of loose ends, a lot more questions to be asked. This is only the beginning.'

'There is one more thing,' said Gervaise.

Chambers raised an eyebrow. 'Oh?'

Gervaise ignored him and looked directly at ACC McLaughlin. 'If we might have your permission to interview Erin Doyle, sir? Before the ground gets muddied.'

Chambers spluttered. 'I don't think that's— '

McLaughlin cut Chambers off, then glanced from him to Gervaise and back. 'I do see the problem,' he said. 'Clearly the discharge of the taser is an incident that needs to be investigated by you and your department, Reg. The Independent Police Complaints Commission will no doubt insist on that.'

Chambers nodded in agreement.

'But on the other hand,' McLaughlin went on, 'we still have the matter of the firearm itself, the reason the AFO team were at the Doyle house to begin with. I think you'll agree, Reg, that we're dealing with a separate investigation here. We need to find out as much as we can about this weapon and where it came from as soon as possible, and I don't think another force would be any better equipped to deal with that than our own. Do you?'

'But it's protocol.'

'It's protocol that someone else investigates the actions of Constables Warburton and Powell and the rest of the AFO team, true, but that same protocol hardly requires an outside force to investigate the firearm we were called to recover in the first place. We have yet to establish any irrefutable link with Erin Doyle.'

'But they're connected, sir.'

'Of course they're connected,' said McLaughlin. He turned to Gervaise. 'Where is the firearm now?'

'On its way to forensic services in Birmingham, sir.'

McLaughlin nodded.

'I insist on being present at all interviews connected with this business, and with any members of the AFO team or anyone else connected with the weapon discharge,' demanded Chambers.

'There you are, you see, Reg,' McLaughlin said, allowing himself a flicker of a smile. 'You're already calling it "this business". To me that simply confuses the issue. We have the matter of the discharge of a taser by a police officer in the course of his duty, yes, but we also have the discovery of a loaded firearm in a young woman's bedroom. I would like to know where that weapon came from, what its history is, whether it has ever been used in the commission of a crime, for example, and how it got into Erin Doyle's bedroom in the first place. Now, I'm aware there's a connection – the officers were there to pick up the firearm, after all – but as far as I know, the handgun wasn't used in "this business", was it? Nobody got a gunshot wound at Laburnum Way, did they? As far as I can gather, the weapon we're interested in remained wrapped in a tea cloth from the moment it was picked up by Constable Powell to the moment we shipped it off to Birmingham. The chain of evidence is quite clear on this.'

'Let's face it,' Gervaise said, 'as soon as the media get hold of this, they'll have a field day. We're all going to be under the microscope – not just for the taser discharge, but for the loaded gun, too – and things are likely to get even more twisted than they are right now. There'll be questions in the house, a Home Office inquiry, a government report—'

'Yes, yes,' said McLaughlin, rubbing his forehead. 'I'm aware of all that, Catherine. I don't need reminding, thank you very much. I'm also aware that my opinion cuts very little ice with Superintendent Chambers here. But I'm still in charge, and I can't see any objection at all to your interviewing Erin Doyle as long as you stick to the matter of the firearm, and she has legal representation present. The sooner, the better.'

'And my request to be present?' cut in Chambers, salvaging as much dignity as he could from the situation.

Before McLaughlin could answer, there came a soft tap at the door. Annie knew that the ACC had specifically asked that they not be interrupted, so she wasn't surprised when he barked out a gruff, 'What is it?'

A grim-faced Harry Potter opened the door a crack and stuck his head through. 'Sorry to disturb the meeting, ma'am,' he said, addressing Gervaise, 'but the hospital thought you ought to know. Mr Doyle. Patrick Doyle. He died ten minutes ago. Sorry, ma'am.'

When Tracy Banks got home from work at about half past five that evening, she was hot, tired and grumpy. The traffic on Otley Road had been jammed up almost as far back as the Original Oak, and it had taken her bus nearly an hour to crawl the short distance from town. It had been a difficult day at the bookshop, too. They had a big-name crime author coming to do an event that evening, and she had spent most of the day on the phone chasing down his backlist from a variety of recalcitrant publishers, books that had been promised for weeks but still hadn't arrived. Still, that wasn't her problem any more. Bugger it, she thought. Let Shauna, the evening shift manager, deal with it. After all, she would also get to go out with the writer and his entourage afterwards for a slap-up meal and a bunch of free drinks at Maxi's. All Tracy wanted now was a joint and a bit of peace and quiet. She hoped Erin was still at her parents' place. Life had been a lot more relaxed without her over the weekend, and the last thing Tracy wanted was another row.

Despite its overgrown garden, the house appeared more impressive than it was, Tracy always thought as she walked up the path toward its solid sandstone façade and mullioned windows. Three bedrooms, one each, a shared bathroom and toilet, large high-ceilinged living room with a draughty bay window, expensive to heat in winter, no double glazing. The kitchen was large enough to double as a communal dining area, though it was rare that the three of them actually ate together.

Luckily, Tracy, Rose and Erin got along well most of the time, though three more different personalities in one place you'd be hard pushed to find. Erin was sloppy and untidy, left a mess behind her everywhere she went. Rose was a bit of a bookworm, and though she kept her things generally tidy, she didn't always seem to notice the general mess and was quite content living in her own world. And Tracy, well, she didn't really know how to describe herself, except she felt angry a lot of the time these days, at nothing in particular, and a little dissatisfied with what life had to offer. No, if truth be told, more than just a little, a *lot* dissatisfied. It wasn't supposed to be like this at all, whatever *this* was. And her name wasn't Tracy any more; most people called her Francesca now.

Despite their differences, the three of them had fun, and somehow it worked, though Tracy found it was always her who ended up cleaning and tidying the mess simply because it got her down, not because tidiness was necessarily in her nature. They had talked about it more than once, and the others had promised to do better, but it remained a problem. At least Rose tried, when she noticed.

Rose was the newcomer, replacing Jasmine, who had left to get married four months ago. Tracy had known Erin since she first came to live in Eastvale, since they were little kids, neighbours from across the street. They were the same age, and had gone through comprehensive school and university together, both ending up living in Leeds, neither in exactly the sort of job they, or their parents, had envisioned.

Rose jumped up and stubbed out a cigarette when Tracy entered the living room. There was a no-smoking rule in the house, and Rose usually went outside into the back garden, so Tracy could tell immediately that something was wrong. An emotional crisis was the last thing she needed.

'What is it?' she asked.

Rose started pacing the carpet, something she'd never done before. 'The police were here today, that's what.'

'Police? What did they want?'

Rose stopped pacing for a moment and glanced at her. 'Only to search the place, that's all.'

'Search? They didn't—'

'No. Relax. They were mostly interested in Erin's room, and they seemed to be in a hurry.'

'But why? What were they looking for?'

'They wouldn't say.'

Tracy ran her hand over her hair. 'Christ,' she said, getting up and heading for the door to the kitchen. 'I need a joint.'

'You can't,' Rose called after her.

'What are you talking about?'

'You can't. I . . . I flushed it.'

'You flushed it! Rose, there was half an ounce of ace weed left, at least. What do you—'

'Well, they could've come back, couldn't they, and gone through all the jars? You weren't here. You don't know what it's like having the police crawling all over the house, asking questions. That way they have of looking at you like they don't believe a word you're saying.'

Oh, don't I? thought Tracy. I lived with one for about twenty years. But Rose didn't know that. Rose was part of the new scene. She had told Rose that her name was Francesca Banks because she thought Tracy was a chav name, and she said her father was a retired civil servant, an ex-pen-pusher, an old geezer, and her mother lived in London, half of which was true. And like the heiress who keeps her fortune a secret to make sure no one falls in love with her for the wrong reason, Tracy also never mentioned that her brother was Brian Banks of the Blue Lamps, whose latest CD was riding high in the charts, and who were hotly tipped for a Mercury Prize. Erin knew, of course, having been a childhood friend of the family, and she had agreed to keep Tracy's secrets, to go along with the deception, because she thought it was cool and fun.

'Christ,' said Tracy, sitting down again. 'Half an ounce of grass.' She put her head in her hands. 'Do you have any idea how much that cost me?'

'Have a drink,' Rose offered cheerfully. 'We've still got some gin left.'

'I don't want any fucking gin.' If truth be told, Tracy didn't much like alcohol or its effects at all. She drank merely because her friends did, and sometimes she overdid it, tottered around the city centre in her high heels and puked in ginnels and snickets, ended up in the wrong bed, any bed. They all drank some sort of alcopop, coloured liquids with a kick. But Tracy preferred a nice joint every now and then, and sometimes E. They seemed harmless enough diversions.

'Look,' said Rose, 'I'm really sorry, but I was scared. I mean, I was shaking like a leaf in case they found it while they were searching the place. You would have been, too. I was sure they noticed how nervous I was, thought I was hiding something. Soon as they left, I flushed it. I am sorry. But they could have come back. They could still come back.'

'OK,' said Tracy, tired of the subject. 'OK, just forget it. Did they ask you any questions?'

'They were only interested in Erin, but it was just vague, general stuff, like about if she had any boyfriends, what she did, who else lived here.'

'Were they looking for her? Did they ask if you knew where she was?'

'No.'

'Did you mention me?'

'I had to, didn't I? They could find out you live here easily enough.'

'What about Jaff?'

'Well, he is her boyfriend, isn't he? I had to tell them who he was. Why wouldn't I?'

'Christ. Did you give them his address?'

'I don't know it, do I? All I know is he lives by the canal. Do you think it's something to do with him?'

'Why would it be anything to do with him?'

'I don't know,' said Rose. 'I know you like him, but I've always thought he was a bit dodgy. The flash clothes and car, the jewellery, that fancy Rolex watch. Where does he get all his money from? There's just something about him that makes me think the police might be interested in him, that's all, something not quite right. Drugs, I'll bet.'

'Maybe,' said Tracy. She knew what Rose meant. She had had the same suspicions about Jaff, but she also fancied him, and she didn't care if he was a bit dodgy. He certainly always seemed to have some weed or coke with him. And the dodginess was part of his appeal for Tracy, that cheeky, devil-may-care bad-boy attitude he exuded. It turned her on. That was part of the problem. He was good-looking, bright, a real charmer, and *maybe* crooked. And he was *Erin*'s boyfriend.

Perhaps the police visit *was* something to do with Jaff. If so, she needed to warn him, let him know what had happened. There was a good chance that she could get to him before the police did. What the hell had the silly bitch Erin gone and *done*? Whatever it was, it must have been in Eastvale, at her parents' house, which was where Rose had said she had gone. Tracy just hoped that none of this would get through to her father, then she remembered that he was away somewhere in the world licking his wounds over a broken love affair, and she didn't know exactly where, only that he wouldn't be back until next week.

'Did they say anything else?' she asked.

Rose frowned. 'Only that they had a warrant to search the house. They showed it to me, but I didn't have a chance to read it. It could have said anything. One of them poked about in here while the others were gone, just in the drawers and under cushions and so on, but his heart didn't seem in it. Like I said, they were mostly interested in Erin. They wouldn't let me go up with them. They didn't examine all the herb jars and stuff, thank God. I was terrified they'd take samples or sniff the basil.'

'I wonder why they didn't,' Tracy said. 'If they were looking for drugs, you'd think they'd have a good look at stuff like that, wouldn't you? I mean, it's hardly the most brilliant hiding place, a jar labelled "basil", is it?'

Rose shrugged. 'They just didn't. Maybe it was something else? I mean, this didn't seem like a drugs raid. Not that I'd know what one was like, of course, but they didn't have sniffer dogs, and they seemed to be in a bit of a hurry. It's like they were looking for something in particular, in Erin's room mostly. Why don't you ring her at home? You've got her number, haven't you?'

Tracy nodded. She knew the number by heart. She also knew that the phone at the Doyles' house had caller display and recorded the numbers of anyone who rang. Then she realised that didn't matter. The police had already been here. They knew this was where Erin had a flat in Leeds. They would also know Tracy's name, her real name, and that she lived here, too. It would hardly set off any alarms if someone from here phoned to ask about Erin. And maybe Mr or Mrs Doyle would be able to tell her *something*.

'You were here on Friday morning when she dropped by to pick up her things,' Tracy said. 'What was she like? Is there anything she said that you've forgotten to tell me?'

'No. She was just pissed off, that's all. Sulky. She didn't say anything except when I asked her where she was going, then she just said she was going home for a few days and stormed out.'

That sounded like Erin in a snit, Tracy thought. She went into the hall, picked up the handset and dialled Erin's home number. The phone rang, then someone answered it, and a man's voice came on the line.

'Hello,' said Tracy. 'Is that Mr Doyle?'

'Who's speaking?'

'Are you Mr Doyle, Erin's dad?'

'I'd like to know to whom I'm speaking. Please identify yourself.'

Tracy hung up. It wasn't Patrick Doyle. She knew a cop's tone when she heard it. But why would a cop be answering the Doyles' telephone? Where were Erin's mother and father? A deep feeling of unease stirred inside her and started to seep like the damp chill of winter through her flesh. Something was wrong, perhaps seriously wrong, and it wasn't only Erin who was involved. She grabbed her black denim jacket and shoulder bag from the stand in the hall and popped her head back around the living-room door. 'I'm going out for a while, Rose. Don't worry. Just keep cool, right?'

'But Francesca, you can't just leave me in the lurch like this. I'm frightened. What if—'

Tracy shut the door and cut off Rose's protests. In a

funny way, she could almost pretend that Rose wasn't talking to *her*. After all, her name wasn't really Francesca, was it?

Erin Doyle made a pathetic figure sitting in Superintendent Gervaise's office late that afternoon, her ash-blonde hair, clearly cut professionally, falling over her shoulders in casual disarray, her cheeks tear-streaked, bags under eyes red from crying, a pale, sickly complexion. Her expression was sullen, and her fingernails were bitten to the quicks. Juliet Doyle had said that Erin's style and appearance had improved considerably over the past six months, but that was hardly apparent right now.

Juliet Doyle had gone to stay with Harriet Weaver, a friend and neighbour across Laburnum Way. Relations were so strained between mother and daughter that Erin would have to stay elsewhere. Patricia Yu, the Family Liaison Officer, was looking into local accommodation, and she would later liaise between the Doyles and the police. Erin would almost certainly get police bail after the interview. They could hardly keep her in custody after what had just happened to her father. The media would go crazy, for a start, and Annie recognised that it would be callous in the extreme to keep the poor girl locked up in a cell overnight after the death of her father, even if they got real evidence against her during the forthcoming interview.

Both Detective Superintendent Gervaise and ACC McLaughlin had agreed that the interview should be conducted in the relative comfort of Gervaise's office. Only a couple of hours ago, Erin had been told that her father was dead, and a grungy interview room hardly seemed appropriate.

There were only four people in the spacious office.

Gervaise was stuck in meetings with McLaughlin and the Deputy Chief Constable at County HQ, so Annie sat in her chair opposite Erin, who was on the other side of the desk. Chairs had also been brought in for Erin's solicitor, Irene Lightholm, and for Superintendent Chambers, who had been granted his request to be present. Annie just hoped the fat bastard wouldn't keep interrupting. The same went for Irene Lightholm, who sat perched on the edge of her seat like a bird of prey, with a nose to match. Her pristine notepad rested on the pleated grey material of her skirt, which itself lay across her skinny thighs.

It had been agreed that Annie, as Gervaise's deputy investigating officer, should do the questioning, and she was, as agreed, required to stick to the issue of the loaded gun, and avoid anything relating to the death of Erin Doyle's father, or the actions of the AFOs. It was something of a balancing act, and she didn't think it would be easy. As McLaughlin had said, the two issues were closely related. Annie felt she had everything working against her: the poor girl's state of mind, the hyper-vigilant lawyer, piggy-eyed Chambers. Best just to ignore them all. Focus on Erin. Keep calm and carry on. She got the formalities out of the way as quickly and painlessly as possible, then began.

'I'm sorry about your father, Erin,' she said.

Erin said nothing. She just stared down at the desk and chewed on a fingernail.

'Erin? I really need you to talk to me. I know you're upset, and you want to be with your mother, but can you please just answer a few questions first? Then you can go.'

Erin muttered something. She was still chewing on her nail, so it was hard to tell what she said.

'What was that?' Annie asked her.

'I said I *don't* want to be with my mother.'

'Well, I know I'd want to be with mine,' said Annie. *If I had one*, she thought.

'She turned me in,' Erin said, her hands clasped in her lap now, twisting. She was still staring at the desk, and her voice was muffled, her words hard to make out. 'How would *you* feel?'

'She did what she thought she had to do,' Annie said.

Erin gave her a withering glance. 'You *would* say that.'

'Erin, that's not what I'm here to talk to you about, however much it hurts, however bad it feels. I want you to tell me about the gun.'

Erin shook her head.

'Where did you get it from?'

'I don't know anything about it.'

'Why did you bring it home with you and hide it on top of your wardrobe?'

Erin shrugged and picked at her fingernail.

'Who gave you the gun, Erin?'

'Nobody.'

'Somebody must have given it to you? Or did you buy it yourself?'

Erin didn't answer.

'Are you hiding it for someone?'

'No. Why do you think that?'

Annie knew that she was getting nowhere, and she didn't feel that things were likely to change in the next while. It was all too raw and confusing. She was tempted to call it a day and pack Erin off to whatever hotel or B&B Patricia Yu had found, but she was nothing if not persistent. 'Was it someone in Leeds?' she asked.

No answer.

'Your boyfriend, perhaps?'

'I don't have a boyfriend.'

'Oh, come on,' cut in Chambers, trying to sound avuncular. 'A pretty young girl like you? Surely you must have a boyfriend?' He ended up sounding like a dirty old man, Annie thought.

Erin treated the question with the silent contempt it deserved. Annie could tell from her general appearance and body language that her self-esteem was low right now, and that she certainly didn't see herself as a 'pretty young girl'.

Annie gave Chambers a disapproving look and carried on. 'Of course you do. Geoff, isn't it? Don't you want him to know where you are?' Annie didn't understand the look Erin gave her. She carried on. 'Was it Geoff who gave you the gun? Is that why you don't want to talk about him?'

Still Erin said nothing.

'Are you afraid of him? Is that it? I'd be afraid of someone who kept a loaded gun around the house.'

'You don't understand anything.'

'Then help me. I *want* to understand.'

Annie got no reaction.

'Oh, this is getting us precisely bloody nowhere,' Chambers burst out.

'I did it,' Erin said. Her voice was little more than a whisper, and she still wouldn't look up at them.

'Did what, Erin? Brought the gun home?' Annie asked, leaning forward to hear her clearly. But she didn't need to. Erin sat bolt upright and looked directly at her, speaking in a clear, though trembling, voice.

'Not that. But I killed him,' she said. 'My father. It was my fault. I—'

'Now, wait a minute,' Chambers blustered, looking over

at Irene Lightholm, who remained perched on the edge of her chair, enthralled, instead of telling her client to shut up.

Erin ignored Chambers and the solicitor. Annie could tell she was trying to get out what she had to say before she completely lost control. It didn't matter who she was talking to; she just had to have her say. 'It was my fault. What happened to Dad.' She glanced at Chambers, then at her solicitor. 'We heard the banging at the door, the calls for us to open up. Dad asked me to answer because his knee hurt, and he was starting to have chest pains from all the stress. Angina. I . . . I told him to fuck off. I said he could bloody well turn me in if he wanted to, I couldn't stop him doing that, but I was fucked if I was going to answer the door to the Gestapo myself.' She put her hands to her face and started to cry. 'I did it,' she said, between her fingers. 'Oh, God forgive me. I killed him. I killed my dad. It was all my fault.'

Finally, Irene Lightholm found her voice. 'I think you can see,' she said, 'that my client is upset over the death of her father. I take it that she hasn't been charged with anything yet, and as far as I can tell, you don't have enough evidence to charge her. In that case, I think we should bring this interview to a close right now, and you should release my client on police bail.'

'I agree,' said Chambers. 'This interview is terminated. Now.'

Annie wondered whether he realised he was agreeing with a defence solicitor. She ignored them both, walked around the desk, then bent over and put her arm around Erin's shoulders. She expected resistance, a violent reaction, but she didn't get it. Instead, Erin turned her face into Annie's shoulder, grasped hold of her and sobbed her heart out.

3

Jaff had a one-bedroom flat with a balcony on Granary Wharf, down by the River Aire and the Leeds–Liverpool Canal. Tracy had never been inside before, but Erin had pointed out the converted warehouse with the restaurant on the ground floor as they had passed by one night. Very chic. People sat at tables on the quayside outside the cafés under umbrellas advertising Campari or Stella Artois, sipping wine and chatting in the softening evening light. Tracy pressed the intercom button next to his name.

Jaff answered and sounded pleased to hear that it was her. He buzzed her in and she took the lift to the third floor. Jaff welcomed her at the door and led her into the modest but open space of the living, dining and kitchen area, where light flooded through a window that led to the small balcony. The place was messy, with newspaper sections, magazines, CDs and empty cups and glasses scattered here and there, dirty dishes piled in the sink, and a few old wine or coffee stains on the fitted carpet. The colour scheme, shades of blue and green, was a bit too dark and cold for Tracy's taste. A number of framed photographs stood on a shelf above the television set, which was tuned to the BBC news at six. A couple of the photos were of Jaff, clearly in exotic places, but there was one of a beautiful woman in a colourful sari. She had golden skin, long glossy black hair, high cheekbones, large eyes, a perfect, straight nose. To Tracy she looked like a model. One of Jaff's old girlfriends, perhaps?

'Sorry about the mess,' Jaff said. 'The cleaning lady doesn't come till Thursday.'

Tracy smiled. 'No need to apologise to me. It's not as if I'm exactly the tidiest person in the world. Who's that beautiful woman in the photograph over there?' she asked.

Jaff looked towards the shelf. 'That's my mother,' he said.

'Don't be . . . It can't possibly be,' said Tracy.

'It is,' he said. 'Honest. She was thirty-six when that was taken. Four years before she died.'

'Oh, Jaff. I'm sorry.'

'It was a long time ago. She was an amazing woman. Grew up in the slums of Dhaka and ended up one of the biggest Bollywood stars of her day.' As he spoke, staring at the photograph, he seemed choked with emotion. 'Sorry,' he said, with a wan smile. 'I still don't find it easy to talk about her. Let's go outside.'

'OK,' said Tracy, following him. 'I understand.'

It was clear from the cigarette smouldering in the ashtray and the half-full glass of lager that Jaff had been sitting on his balcony. Tracy sat in the opposite chair.

'Good to see you, babe,' Jaff said, touching her shoulder lightly. 'I was going to ring you as soon as the dust settled. Thing is, I had to go away for the weekend. Bit of business. Amsterdam and London. Just got back an hour or so ago. Drink?'

Tracy accepted, more out of politeness than anything else. Jaff went back inside to pour her a gin and tonic. Tracy gazed out over the city beyond the railway tracks. So much had changed since she had first arrived there at university more years ago now than she cared to remember. She could see several distant building sites where the giant cranes had remained stationary for months, since their funds had dried up, the ambitious towers only half finished. The closer view only confirmed what she had felt before about the canal-side development being claustrophobic and ugly. It was too near to the railway lines, for a start, just at the back of City Station, and below the balcony was the canal, a ribbon of murky, stagnant water on which floated plastic bottles, fast-food wrappers and other things she would rather not think about. There was still plenty of activity. At the moment, the area seemed to be one enormous building site. Everything was crammed together cheek by jowl. God only knew what the mish-mash would look like when the builders had finished, if they ever did finish. Tracy doubted that the planners had ever thought of sketching out the whole picture.

It was a warm evening, but she kept her denim jacket on against the chill that always crept in at this time of year when darkness fell. Jaff came back outside with her drink and sat down. Tracy hadn't stayed at the Headingley house long enough to get changed after work and, as usual, she felt quite scruffy compared to Jaff, who was wearing designer jeans and a loose white shirt hanging out at the waist. It stood in sharp contrast to his golden skin. Not for the first time, Tracy found herself admiring his long dark eyelashes, gelled black hair, smooth complexion, lean body, loam-brown eyes and the lithe way he moved. He was beautiful, she thought, like some exotic cat, but there was nothing at all effeminate about him. She also sensed that he could be a dangerous enemy, and there was a hardness in his eyes at odds with the humour and intelligence that also dwelled there. But that combination and contrast excited her, too.

He picked up his glass. 'Cheers.'

'Cheers,' said Tracy. They clinked glasses.

'Ever been to Amsterdam?'

'No. I've been to London, though. Used to live there.'

'Amsterdam's a great city. All those canals. And the clubs. Melkweg. Paradiso. Mind-blowing. Enlightened, too. You can get hash brownies in the cafés, and there are places you can sit and smoke dope and listen to music.'

'Cool,' said Tracy. 'Maybe some day.'

'For sure. So what brings you here? Is it just a social visit, or what?'

Tracy leaned forward and frowned. 'I'm not certain,' she said. 'But I think something's wrong. The police came around to our house today and searched the place, Erin's room in particular.'

Jaff sat up. 'Erin's room? Police? Why?'

'I don't know. I was at work. Rose was there, and she told me about it, but you know what she's like. I'm not sure she got all the details right. Apparently, they also asked questions about who her friends were, including boyfriends.'

'Did Rose say anything?'

'She says she mentioned your first name, but she doesn't know the address, only that you live by the canal. She's scared stiff, Jaff. There's something else.'

'What?'

'I rang Erin at home and a strange voice answered. I thought it was a cop.'

'Why did you think that?'

Tracy couldn't tell him why, that she had grown up listening to cops and recognised the tone, the thrust of the questions. As far as Jaff was concerned, she was called Francesca, and he knew nothing about her father. 'It just sounded like a cop, that's all. Trust me,' she said. 'What's it all about?'

Jaff looked at his watch and stood up. 'Let's see if there's anything on the local news. It should have started by now.' Tracy followed him inside. He cleared away a pile of magazines, and they sat next to one another on the sofa. There was nothing of interest on until the headline recap at the end, before the weather, and then all they got was a little grainy, jerky video footage taken with a hand-held camera, or a mobile, and a voice-over that didn't really explain what was going on, except that an armed police raid had taken place on a quiet leafy street in Eastvale. Laburnum Way. Tracy felt her jaw dropping in shock at the familiarity of it all as she watched. She recognised all the houses, knew almost everyone who lived on the street.

When it was over, they were not much the wiser. Erin's name hadn't been mentioned, nor any possible reason for a police search of the house in Leeds.

'What's going on?' Tracy asked again.

Jaff turned off the TV and stood up. 'I don't know,' he said. 'But I don't like the look of it. An armed police raid? Why? It seems serious. What was Erin doing at home, anyway?'

'After last Thursday,' Tracy said, 'she didn't come back to the house that night. I thought she'd . . . you know . . . just stopped the night with you. On Friday, she came by to pick up a few things to go home for a while, so she said. Rose was there.'

Jaff paced. 'She did stop with me on Thursday night. Well, she stopped here, at any rate. Crashed. Passed out on the sofa. Whatever you care to call it. We weren't on speaking terms by then. It was late. We had a row.'

'Because of what happened earlier?'

'Partly. But it's been brewing longer than that. She's been getting too possessive. Too clingy. I hate that.'

'So what happened?'

'I had to leave early, drive down to London. She was asleep. I left her here.' He paused. Something seemed to dawn on him. 'I left her here *alone*. Stay here a minute, please, would you?'

Tracy did as he asked while Jaff hurried into the bedroom. He came back moments later and seemed even more agitated than before.

'Shit! The stupid bitch.'

'What is it?' Tracy asked, picking up on his sense of alarm.

'I've got to get out of here. They could turn up any moment. The stupid, stupid woman. She doesn't know what she's done.'

'Why? What were they looking for at the house?'

Jaff turned and touched Tracy's hair so gently that she felt a little shiver run up her spine. 'You ask too many questions,' he said. 'You sound like a policewoman yourself. You're not, are you? I wouldn't put it past them to plant such a pretty girl on me.'

'Don't be silly.'

He smiled at her, flashing those so-white teeth. 'Of course not.' Then he went back into the bedroom.

'Will you please tell me what's going on?' Tracy called after him.

'I would,' he answered, popping his head around the door, 'but I don't know. I haven't seen or heard anything of Erin since last Friday morning. And you know quite well what happened on Thursday night.'

Tracy felt herself blush with shame at the memory. 'I'm sorry. It was all my fault.'

'Like I said, it had been building up for a while. That was just the last straw. It doesn't matter. I should never have left her here alone. Now look what she's gone and done. The stupid bitch. She took something of mine. Something . . . really important. Now I have to go and lie low for a while until I know what's what. I just need to put a few things in a bag first. Will you wait here? Please?'

'Of course. If there's anything I can do . . .'

Tracy walked back out to the balcony, leaned on the railings, sipped her gin and tonic and stared down into the oily canal. Laughter rose from a group of people under one of the umbrellas. The drink tasted good, better than she remembered. Why had Jaff asked her to wait? Did he want her to go with him, wherever he was going? To London? An adventure. The idea both excited and scared her. She couldn't just take off with him, surely? But why not? What had she got to hang around in Leeds for? What prospects? What future? Her lousy job in the bookshop? An absentee mother and a father who seemed incapable of growing up? Besides, she was beginning to feel at least partly responsible for whatever it was that had happened between Erin and Jaff, even though she had no idea what was upsetting him at the moment, what she had taken.

It didn't take Jaff long to pack a holdall. In less than five minutes he was back in the living room again. Tracy joined him. They checked that everything was switched off, that his cigarette was properly extinguished, and that the French doors leading to the balcony were securely locked.

'Where are you thinking of going?' Tracy asked.

'I honestly don't know,' he said. 'But I have to get away from here till things cool down. It's not safe. If I were you, I'd just go home. It's really nothing to do with you.'

'Look,' Tracy said hesitantly. 'I wish I knew a bit more about what was going on, but I know somewhere we can go. I mean, if you want to.'

'You do? Where?'

'My dad's place. I've got a key. He's away on holiday till next Monday. That's a whole week. We can at least stay for a few days until you figure out your next move. We'll be safe there. Nobody will think to look for us.'

Jaff considered this for a moment, then said, 'All right. If you're sure. But I have to stop at Vic's on the way to pick up a few things I need from him. We'll borrow his car, too. He won't mind. He can keep mine in his garage. That way nobody will be after us. Vic's number won't mean anything to the police. This sounds great. Where does your dad live?'

'Gratly.'

'Huh?'

'It's in the Dales, a little cottage, very isolated.'

'Perfect,' Jaff said, then he patted her between the shoulder blades. 'What are we waiting for, babe? Let's go.'

The shadows were lengthening when Annie approached Laburnum Way. She knew that she shouldn't be visiting Juliet Doyle on her own like this, that she was risking Chambers's wrath, not to mention Gervaise's and McLaughlin's, but she had a few more questions for Juliet before Chambers cut off access entirely.

She should have gone home hours ago, or called at Banks's cottage to water the plants and take in the post, but she had sat instead in the Half Moon, on Market Street not far from Laburnum Way, sipping a pint of Daleside bitter and picking at a vegetarian pasta after mustering up the willpower to order it instead of fish and chips. Anyway, she consoled herself, pub fish and chips were never anywhere near as good as those from the chippie. When she had finished, she decided that, being so close to Laburnum Way, she would drop in and see how things were. Erin was staying at a guest house near the castle. She hadn't wanted to be anywhere near her mother. Banks's potted plants could wait another day or two, and if he got any parcels they'd only be CDs or DVDs from Amazon, and they would wait safely in the wheelie-bin storage area, where the postman usually left them.

There was still a strong police presence on Laburnum Way: patrol cars, unmarked vehicles, SOCO vans, uniformed officers on guard, mostly keeping the media at bay. A couple of local reporters, one from the paper and one from TV, recognised Annie and asked for comments, but she said nothing.

Harriet Weaver answered the door just moments after Annie had rung the bell. 'Annie, isn't it?' she said. 'Alan's friend. Please come in.' She closed the door for a moment and Annie heard the chain slide off. 'You can't be too careful with all those reporters creeping around the place,' Harriet said. 'We've already had to take the phone off the hook.'

Annie followed her into the house and waited while Harriet put the chain back on and locked the deadbolt. They had met before a few times through Banks, but they didn't know one another well. Harriet, Annie knew, was somewhere in her fifties and had recently retired from driving a mobile library in the Dales. Her husband, David, had something to do with computers, she remembered, and Banks thought him a crashing bore. Annie had never met him. They were also Sophia's aunt and uncle, and Banks had met Sophia through them, at a dinner party at their house. He had told

Annie that he and Sandra and the kids used to live next door, and Harriet had been one of the first to welcome them to the neighbourhood over twenty years ago. Sophia had had been visiting her aunt for years, probably since back when she was a student, or even still a schoolgirl. Annie found herself wondering whether Banks had fancied her that long ago, too. He would only have been in his thirties. It wasn't beyond the realms of possibility. When she'd been seventeen she had gone out briefly with a man in his early thirties, until her father had found out. Anyway, there was no time for such speculation, she told herself, nor any point in it. She wondered how Harriet and her husband felt about the whole Banks and Sophia affair. Uncomfortable, probably. No need to bring it up.

'Let's go inside,' Harriet said, leading Annie into a cosy living room with an upholstered three-piece suite and a large-screen TV. 'I was just doing the dishes,' she went on. 'David's out on a rush job and Juliet's upstairs lying down. As you can imagine, she's exhausted, poor thing. It's been a terrible day. A wretched ordeal.'

'So you know what's happened?' Annie said.

'More or less. Most of it, anyway. Juliet hasn't said much. I think she must still be in shock. But what can I do for you?'

'First of all, I'm not supposed to be here,' Annie said. 'The Independent Police Complaints Commission will be working with our Professional Standards Department on setting up a separate inquiry into Patrick Doyle's death.'

'That makes sense. I've heard about that sort of thing. Anyway, don't worry, your secret's safe with me.'

'Oh, it's all right. Plenty of my colleagues probably saw me come here, though I doubt they'd think anything of it. I just wanted you to know that I'm here unofficially. Really, I just wanted to see how things are, how Juliet's doing. And you, of course. I feel partly responsible, you see. I was the first one to see Juliet this morning, and I was out in the street, in front of the house, when it happened.'

'That hardly makes it your fault, dear,' said Harriet. 'I'm sure you did your best for her. Anyway, as I told you, she's exhausted. It's been a long confusing day for them. With Patrick gone and Erin not talking to her, poor Juliet doesn't know whether she's coming or going. The doctor's given her a mild sedative.' She shook her head slowly. 'It's going to take them a long time to come to terms with this. Juliet blames Erin for Patrick's death, and I'm sure Erin must blame herself, too, to some extent, but she must also feel betrayed by Juliet. I mean, her own mother informing on her . . .'

'Quite a conundrum,' said Annie. 'It's good of you to put Juliet up.'

'Where else could she go tonight? She's got a sister in Durham, so perhaps she'll go and stay with her later. But for now . . . Do you have any idea how long all this will take? How long they'll be shut out of their home?'

'I'm sorry,' said Annie, 'I don't.'

'Days? Weeks? Months?'

'I've known houses to be locked down for weeks,' Annie said, 'but I doubt that will happen in this case. It looks fairly straightforward. Legally, I mean, as far as an investigation is concerned. I understand that it has far more of an impact emotionally.'

'But you'd say a few days, at least?'

'Yes.'

'Oh, look at me. I'm so sorry. I've been sitting here picking your brains, and I haven't even offered you anything to drink. Cup of tea? Coffee? Something stronger?'

'A cup of tea would go down a treat,' said Annie. 'I have to drive back to Harkside.'

'Just give me a minute. Make yourself at home.'

Annie relaxed on the sofa while Harriet went into the kitchen to make tea. The kettle must have boiled very quickly because she came back with a teapot and two cups and saucers on a tray in no time. She had no sooner put the tray down on the low table than Juliet Doyle drifted in behind her wearing a long green dressing gown that trailed around her black slippers. Her eyes were puffy from sleeping pills or crying, or both, and her skin was pale and dry.

'Who is . . .' Then she saw Annie. 'You.'

Annie stood up. 'Yes,' she said. 'I wanted to come and see how you were.'

'How do you think I am? Besides, if anyone should know, it's you. It was supposed to be quite simple.'

'Look, I'm sorry about what happened,' Annie said, 'but we have our procedures.' She knew it sounded lame the moment it came out and deserved the contempt it got.

'Your procedures got my husband killed.'

It wasn't true, of course; Annie knew there were many contributing factors to Patrick Doyle's death, the 'perfect storm', but there was no point in saying that here and now to his bereaved wife. As the day had progressed, Annie had found herself feeling more and more guilty, first as she had faced Erin Doyle, and now as she faced Erin's mother. She had begun to resent Warburton and the entire AFO team for what they had done and for putting her in such an awkward position. An injured man with a bloody walking stick and a dicky heart, for crying out loud. How could anyone mistake that stick for a sword, even if the hall light had decided to burn out at the very moment they switched it on? But she bottled up her feelings and her guilt and carried on as best she could.

'I'm sorry,' she said again, then sat down and accepted her cup and saucer from Harriet.

'Sugar?'

'No. No, thanks.'

Harriet turned to Juliet. 'Can I get you anything, love? Some tea?'

Juliet managed a flicker of a smile. 'Maybe some hot chocolate, if you've got any.'

'Coming up.' She glanced anxiously at Annie, who nodded, then left for the kitchen again.

Juliet Doyle sat down and wrapped her robe around her. 'What do you want?' she asked.

'Nothing,' said Annie.

'I can't believe it was just this morning,' Juliet said. 'It seems so distant, so long ago.'

'Grief can do that.'

Juliet looked at her sharply. 'How would *you* know? Besides, I don't think I can even *feel* grief yet. I don't know what I feel. Those drugs . . .' She laughed harshly. 'My husband's dead and I don't even feel anything.'

'It'll come,' Annie said. *And when it does, you'll wish it hadn't*, she thought.

'I suppose you've got more questions?'

'One or two. But I honestly did just want to see how you were doing, and how Harriet was coping. But as far as Erin's future is concerned, you can help. She hasn't been charged with anything yet.'

'What do you mean? How can I help?'

'The gun. Right now it's a mystery. We know nothing about it, how it got on top of her wardrobe, how it fell into her possession, if it did. It's something we're going to be looking into very closely, and if you could help, that would go a long way towards influencing the CPS and any charges they might bring.'

'But I don't know how it got there or where it came from,' Juliet protested. 'Besides, why should I want to help Erin? She was partly responsible for . . . for what happened.'

'But she's still your daughter.' Harriet came back with the steaming mug of hot chocolate and handed it to Juliet, then glanced at Annie again, who gave her the OK to stay with them. 'You said you thought there was a boyfriend involved,' Annie went on. 'Geoff. Do you know anything more about him?'

'No,' said Juliet. 'Only what I told you. You can't think he's involved in this, too?'

'Well, it's one explanation. I find it hard to believe that the gun was Erin's.'

'But Geoff? He's got a good job, a proper job. He sounds like a nice lad. He's certainly been a positive influence on our Erin.'

'So you said before. Did she usually have problems?'

'Oh, Erin always has a boyfriend. The boys flock to her. Moths to a flame. But she always seems to be having boyfriend trouble, too. She certainly knows how to pick them.'

'I've been there myself,' Annie said, smiling. 'So perhaps an ex-boyfriend is involved? Can you help me there? Any names?'

Juliet put her hand to her brow. 'I can't really think now,' she said. 'My brain feels too soft. But I'll try later. All right?'

'That's all I'm asking,' said Annie. 'It could really help

Erin.' She put her empty cup down on the tray, stood up and smoothed the front of her skirt. 'Thank you for the tea, Mrs Weaver, and for your time, Mrs Doyle. I really must go.'

'Harriet, please. You're very welcome. I'll see you out.'

Juliet Doyle sat gazing into space with the mug of hot chocolate at her lips. She didn't say goodbye.

Harriet saw Annie to the door. 'I'm sorry,' she said. 'She's very upset, as you can see.'

'I understand,' said Annie. 'I honestly didn't come to grill her.' She opened the door. The light was almost gone, and a chill breeze ruffled the evening air.

'You know, you could do a lot worse than ask Tracy Banks,' Harriet said.

Annie paused on the doorstep. 'Tracy Banks?'

'Yes. Alan and Sandra's young lass. They share a house in Leeds. Her, Erin and another girl. I don't know her name. They did, anyway. Have done for ages. Didn't you know that?'

'DCI Banks doesn't tell me a lot about his family life,' Annie mumbled. 'I wonder why Juliet didn't mention it when she came to the station.'

'Too upset, too agitated, I should imagine. Juliet's quite highly strung under that capable and efficient surface. If I found a gun in my daughter's bedroom, I have no idea how I'd react, what I'd do or say. I doubt that I'd be thinking very clearly.'

'True,' said Annie. 'It's a tough one.'

'Anyway, I've known both the families for years. Erin and Tracy have been friends since they were knee high to a grasshopper. Used to be inseparable.'

'Have they really?' Annie had to think very carefully how

to play this one. She smiled. 'Thanks very much. Maybe I'll have a word with Tracy.'

She checked her watch as she headed down the path. It was too late to go to Leeds tonight, she thought, but she would go tomorrow after work, in her own time. Just a social call to see how Tracy was doing, make sure she wasn't in any trouble, too, and if she was, see whether there was any way of sorting it before Banks got back.

'Park at the other side of the garage, there,' Tracy said, pointing ahead. 'It's by the woods and nobody will see the car there. Not that anyone passes by here.' It was almost dark, and the headlights showed an impenetrable tangle of branches and tree trunks ahead, just beyond the cottage and its small garage.

'Fuck me, this *is* isolated,' said Jaff, coming to a halt. 'Downright bloody creepy, if you ask me. How does your old man stand it out here? It'd drive me insane.'

'He likes being alone,' said Tracy. 'Sad, isn't it?' They got out of the car, and she stood for a moment, listening. All she could hear was the sound of Gratly Beck trickling over the terraced falls, the occasional rustling of an animal in the woods and the distant call of a night bird. The waterfall was a sound she liked, and she remembered sitting out there on the wall chatting with her dad on summer evenings when she visited during term time, muted music playing in the distance, Billie Holiday or Miles Davis. She saw a couple of bats fly across the moon in the cloud-streaked sky. She didn't mention them to Jaff because you never knew; some people were scared of bats, and he might be one of them. They had never bothered her.

Jaff trod out his cigarette end and heaved his holdall out

of the back of the car. Tracy wondered what was in it. It
certainly looked heavy. 'Shall we go in, then?' she said.

Jaff nodded.

Tracy felt in her pocket for her keys. She knew that her
dad had installed a new security system over the summer,
but he had told her the code in case of emergencies. As soon
as she opened the front door, she tapped in the numbers
she had memorised, the beeping stopped and the green light
came on. She shut the door behind them and switched on
the lamp on the small table to her left. Tracy had always
thought it odd that the front door opened immediately into
her father's small home office, where he worked at the
computer or sat quietly to read over files and reports. It
used to be the living room, she remembered, until the recon-
struction after the fire, when he had the entertainment room
added on at the side and a conservatory built at the back.
He probably spent more time in those rooms now, reading
and listening to music. The builder had cut a doorway in
the wall beside the fireplace, over to their left, which led to
the entertainment room. Another door, to their right, led to
the narrow wooden stairs up to the bedrooms, and the door
straight ahead led into the kitchen, which was where Tracy
first took Jaff. She knew there would be no food around the
place, so they had picked up an Indian takeaway on the road
out of Leeds. It would be cold by now, but Tracy could
reheat it in the microwave.

Jaff took out his mobile and checked for a signal, then he
turned to Tracy. 'Have you got a mobile?' he asked.

''Course.'

He held out his hand. 'Let me see it.'

'Why?'

'Just let me have a look at it. Please.'

Puzzled, Tracy searched through her bag till she found the mobile. She handed it to Jaff.

'Got an account with the provider?'

'Yes.'

'Thought so. Don't you know they can trace you through this?'

Tracy crossed her arms. 'I can't say I do. It's not something I've ever really had to worry about.'

Jaff gave her an amused glance. 'Well, you do now. We're both fugitives.' He switched her phone off, then put it in his holdall.

'Hey!' said Tracy, reaching her hand out. 'Just a minute. I need that.'

Jaff held the bag behind his back. 'No you don't. Radio silence. Any emergencies, we'll use this one I picked up at Vic's. It's a burner. OK?'

'A what?'

'Don't you watch *The Wire*?'

'Well, actually, no. I tried it once, but I don't like any of the characters. There's no use watching something if you don't have someone to cheer for.'

Jaff laughed. 'I suppose that's one way of looking at it, though I can't say I care, myself. Anyway, it's disposable, a throwaway, pay as you go. No contract, nothing in my name, or in Vic's, for that matter.'

Tracy felt annoyed about being separated from her mobile – her lifeline, as Erin had always teasingly called it – but there was something rather exciting in Jaff talking about radio silence and burners, and the fact that they were on the run, 'fugitives', as he had said, trying to avoid detection. She had never done anything like that before, had always been Little Miss Goody Two Shoes, more or less. 'I didn't think it mattered,' she said. 'There didn't even use to be any coverage out here.'

'Trust me. There is now.' Jaff stretched out his arm and traced the line of her cheek down to her chin, which he cupped briefly between his thumb and forefinger and gave her a quick kiss on the lips. 'Your old man got any decent music?'

'Just old stuff, mostly,' Tracy said, experiencing a delicious little shudder at his kiss. 'You know. Sixties pop. And jazz. Lots of opera, too.'

'Nothing wrong with a bit of Miles Davis or Puccini. Where does he keep it?'

Tracy led him into the entertainment room, with its large flat-screen TV at the far end, surround sound and shelves of CDs and DVDs. 'He's got the whole place wired for sound,' she said. 'Bit of an anorak, really.'

'I think it's cool,' said Jaff. As he flipped through the CDs and took them off the shelves in handfuls, he would glance quickly at the title, then make some comment about it being naff and toss it on the floor. Finally, he seemed to find something he liked and slipped the disc in the player. Tracy recognised the music: My Morning Jacket, *Evil Urges*. Erin had played it constantly back in Headingley. What on earth was her father doing with that? It must be something to do with his last girlfriend, Sophia, Tracy thought. Sophia had more modern tastes in music than her father, who seemed stuck in the sixties time warp when he wasn't playing jazz or bloody opera.

'Anything to drink?' Jaff asked when they went back into the kitchen.

'Well, there's some wine.' Tracy checked the fridge for beer, but it was empty, then she opened Banks's drinks cabinet and gave a little curtsy. 'And this. Tra-la!'

'Jesus,' said Jaff. 'Likes his booze, doesn't he, your old man? Good taste, too.' He picked up a bottle of Highland Park. 'We'll save that for later.' Then he went over to the wine rack on the floor by the door to the conservatory and knelt down. 'Stonewell Shiraz, St Emilion, Côtes de Nuits, Vacqueras, Amarone, Barolo, Ripasso, Châteauneuf-du-Pape. Not bad. Not bad at all. None of your cheap Asda specials here. We can have a real party. I think I'm starting to like your old man. What does he do for a living?'

'Retired civil servant. He goes on cruises. I think some of the wine belonged to my uncle Roy,' Tracy said. 'He was rich, but he died. Dad got the wine and some of his money.' She found Jaff a corkscrew in the drawer, and he opened a bottle of Châteauneuf-du-Pape while she put the takeaway in the oven to heat up. Tracy wasn't sure the wine would go well with vegetable samosas, chicken tikka masala and naans, but she was willing to try it. She noticed that Jaff had poured them both a large glass and was busy sitting at the pine breakfast nook rolling a joint. When he had finished, he licked it, put it in his mouth and lit it. Tracy smiled to herself. To think they were doing this in her father's house! She went over to join him, and he offered the joint to her. She took a hit. It was strong stuff. It made her head spin, but in a nice way. She drank a mouthful of wine and nearly choked on it, but she got it down. 'The curry won't be long,' she said. 'Want to go in the conservatory to eat? It's nice out there and the music pipes through.'

'Sure,' said Jaff, sucking on the joint and passing it back to her. He edged off the bench, then he turned on the small television set that sat on one of the bookcases above the nook. 'Let's see if we can find some more news first.'

They caught the brief local broadcast after *News at Ten*,

and the day's events in Eastvale were the lead item. This time, the reporter seemed to know a little more about what was going on. Jaff turned up the volume so they could hear what was being said over the music. First came the now-familiar image of Laburnum Way crowded with vans and police cars. Apparently, an armed police unit had entered No. 12, Erin's parents' house, at 10.45 that morning, and there had been an incident within the house involving the discharge of a weapon. One man, believed to be the owner of the house, had been taken on a stretcher to Eastvale General Infirmary. There was no further word yet on the weapon, on the condition of the wounded man, or on how or why it had happened, but the police said they would hold a press conference in the morning. Neither Erin nor Jaff was mentioned. One of the neighbours reported that she had seen an armed officer carrying what appeared to be a gun-shaped object wrapped in a tea cloth out of the house. Tracy thought she could see Detective Inspector Annie Cabbot on camera, in the background, talking to someone in uniform. Of all her father's girlfriends since he had split up with her mum, she had liked Annie the best.

Jaff turned off the TV. 'Damn,' he said, stubbing out the roach. 'It's exactly as I thought. They've found the gun.'

'Gun?' echoed Tracy. But Jaff ignored her. 'What gun?'

The microwave beeped. They took their cartons of food and glasses of wine through to the conservatory, where 'Librarian' played through extension speakers Banks had set up, and settled into the cushioned wicker chairs.

'Nice,' said Jaff, scooping up a mouthful of chicken tikka with his naan. 'I'm starving.' Tracy noticed that he had found a serviette in the kitchen and had tucked it into the neck of his shirt to catch any sauce that might drip while he ate. He

might not care much about a clean and tidy flat, Tracy
thought, but a dazzling white shirt was obviously important
to him. And he looked good in it. He finished his wine in
one long swig. 'Go get the bottle, will you, babe?' he said
to her. 'Might as well polish it off.'

Tracy laughed and shook her head at him – it was a long
time since a man had given her orders like that – but she
went to get the wine.

'Well, it's a fine mess you've gotten us into,' said Jaff when
she came back.

'What do you mean?' Tracy asked. 'What mess? I haven't
done anything. What's Erin been up to? What gun are they
talking about? What's going on?'

'You know, technically, one could argue that this is all
your fault.'

Tracy pointed her thumb at her own chest and laughed.
'*Moi*? How do you work that out?'

'What happened last week. Thursday night. That's when
it all started.'

It was true that last week was when the trouble had begun,
when Erin had left for home. She had always been insanely
jealous about Jaff, and she had always suspected that Tracy
had her sights set on him, which she hadn't, really, though
she did think he was fit.

They'd been at a club in the city centre that Thursday
night, wasted on E and hash, and it was really late, nearly
time to go home. Erin had gone to the loo, and Tracy was
dancing a slow dance with Jaff, feeling his warmth, feeling
the sexy, sensual edge of the drugs work on her, the hardness under his trousers pressing against her. She hadn't even
been thinking about it; it had just happened. All of a sudden,
it seemed, they were kissing on the dance floor under the

disco light, so romantic, tongue and everything, then someone grabbed Tracy's arm and pulled her away. It was Erin, of course, and she was furious. She yelled at Tracy, hit her across the face, called her a slut and a slag, a slapper and a whore, then ran off.

Jaff dashed after Erin, leaving Tracy alone on the dance floor, people staring at her. She started to feel nervous and paranoid then, her cheek burning, the good rush and the sexy glow all gone. She grabbed her bag and went after them, but they were nowhere in sight. They had disappeared down one of the alleys off Vicar Lane. Tired and disoriented, she had walked to the station and taken a taxi home, then crawled into bed, where she had slept only fitfully. Erin hadn't been there when she got back, and she wasn't there in the morning when Tracy got up to go to work, either, but Tracy thought nothing of that at the time. She assumed Erin must have made up with Jaff and stopped the night at his place. But she still wanted to talk to her, wanted to apologise and explain that it had just been the mood, the E, the music, blame it on the bossa nova, on Rio, or whatever.

It was only when Tracy got back from work that Friday evening that Rose told her that Erin had been by to pick up some things and had said she was going to stay at her parents' house for a while. Tracy had rung Erin at home, but she wouldn't talk to her except to say that she had split up with Jaff, and it was all Tracy's fault.

'It was only a kiss,' Tracy said to Jaff. 'Don't you think Erin overreacted a bit?'

'Sure, but that doesn't help me now, does it? Look what's happened.'

'What's wrong?' Tracy asked. 'Nobody mentioned you.'

'Well, they wouldn't, would they? They'd hardly want to tip me off.'

'But what's wrong? What are you so worried about? What was Erin doing with a gun? Or was it her father's? It sounds as if he's been hurt.'

'Pour me some more wine and I'll tell you all about it.'

Tracy poured.

'The gun was mine,' Jaff said. 'And now, thanks to dear Erin, the police have got it.'

'What?'

Jaff paused, then said, 'The gun was mine. All right? That woman the reporter talked to was right. It was a gun wrapped in an old tea cloth.'

'Was it registered?'

'Of course it wasn't. You can't register a handgun in this country these days.'

'But why did Erin take it?'

Jaff ran his hand over his hair and sighed. 'I don't know. To spite me. To hurt me. She must have taken it after that night we had the row, the morning after, when I left her alone in the flat.'

'And you didn't notice it was gone?'

'It's not exactly something I look at every day. Besides, I told you, I was away on business all weekend. I only noticed when I checked after that piece we saw on the news back at the flat.'

'But where did you get it from? What do you need a gun for?'

Jaff put his hands to his ears. 'Will you stop it with the third degree? Please? Too many questions. That doesn't matter. You don't need to know. I was doing a favour for a friend, that's all. The point is that the police have got it now, and if I know Erin, she'll be blabbing away to them in no time, if she hasn't already. Hell hath no fury and all that. Do you think they'd know to look here for you?'

'Nobody's looking for me, and no, they wouldn't think to look here even if they were. We're safe. Don't worry. Besides, Erin would never tell them your name.'

'How do you know?'

'She just wouldn't, that's all.'

'Well, I appreciate your loyalty to her, especially after what happened, but they give out stiff enough penalties just for *thinking* about a gun these days. What would you do if PC Plod says he can make a nice deal with you if you tell him what you know?'

'She won't tell. What are you going to do now?'

'I need time to think. I've got some contacts down south. Useful contacts, but these things take time. Right now, I'm going to roll another joint. Bring in the Highland Park, will you? The wine's finished. And a fresh glass. This one's got lees in it.'

Tracy went into the kitchen. She leaned against the fridge and put her head in her hands. The weed was misting up her brain. She needed to pull herself together. What was going on? What did she think she was doing? Here was good little Tracy, the apple of her daddy's eye, practically breaking into his house, drinking his best booze, making a mess with a man she barely knew, who had just told her that her best friend had stolen his gun and run away with it. How had she got mixed up in all this? It was all so confusing.

But she hadn't been the apple of her daddy's eye for quite a while, she realised. For a few years now, ever since she had graduated with a less than desirable 2:2 degree, it had all been about Brian. *Brian. Brian. Brian.* The Blue Lamps.

My son the rock star. And Tracy, with her lousy degree and her dead-end job, could rot in hell as far as he was concerned. That was the truth of it. They exchanged texts occasionally, even phone calls, but she didn't think he had visited her once since June.

She wouldn't mind so much, but all the time they had been growing up, she had been the one who worked hard at school, who stayed in night after night to do her home-work, who was called a swot by the other kids, who came top of the class, always got great exam results, was expected to go places. Brian was a lazy sod who did everything at the last minute, or copied it from one of his mates, and then dropped out to start a rock band. She had done everything right, so why did her father love Brian more? Well, screw him. She was having her own adventure now, and she was damn well going to see it through. She'd show him. She'd show them all.

Tracy thumped the fridge and picked up the Highland Park from the table, where Jaff had left it. She took a long swig from the bottle, and it burned all the way down, then she grabbed two crystal glasses from the cupboard and tottered back into the conservatory.

4

The woman at the wine-tasting was definitely smiling at Banks. He had seen her there yesterday, too, and had thought she was by herself. Right now she was talking to an elderly couple from Lansing, Michigan – he knew because he'd chatted with them yesterday – but she was definitely looking his way. Perhaps she needed rescuing.

Banks smiled back and walked over.

The man from Lansing, Michigan – Bob, Banks remembered, who worked in farm machinery – saw him coming. 'Well, if it isn't my old buddy, Al. What a pleasure to see you again.'

Banks said hello to Bob and his wife Betsy, waiting for them to introduce the mystery woman, who stood by rather shyly, he thought, eyes cast down, looking into her almost empty wine glass. She had appeared tall from a distance, but when he got closer Banks saw she was probably only about five foot three or four. She was oriental, but Banks had no idea where exactly she might come from, or what age she was. There was no grey in her glossy black hair, which hung down over her shoulders, and no lines around her almond eyes.

'This here's Teresa,' said Bob. 'All the way from Boston.'

Teresa looked up at Banks and held out her delicate hand. He shook it. Her skin was soft and silky, but her grip was firm and dry. She wore a couple of rings on her fingers and a silver bracelet that matched her hoop earrings.

'Pleased to meet you,' said Banks.

'Likewise,' said Teresa.

'Can I get anyone another drink? I need one myself.'

Bob and Betsy declined, but Teresa handed him her glass and said, 'Yes, I'll have a Sauvignon Blanc, please.' The glass was warm from her palm, and Banks noticed a little semi-circle of pink lipstick on the rim.

The hotel called it a wine-tasting, but Banks thought of it more as an excuse to get a couple of glasses of alcohol under his belt before dinner, a bit of a social mixer, and a cheap promotion for the winemaker. It wasn't that you actually had to discuss the wine's forward leathery nose, or fill out a tasting card. It was definitely a nice gesture on the part of the hotel, as was the tarot reader, who sat poring over an arrangement of cards with a portly, bearded, anxious-looking man in baggy shorts sitting opposite her.

On the whole, Banks had decided, he liked America. Having spent plenty of time back in the pubs in England listening to his mates slag off the USA and its people, he found that while Americans were easy to ridicule and could often appear obnoxious abroad – which is something you could just as easily say about the British and the Germans – at home they were mostly a delight, from the family diners and roadside honky-tonks with local country bands, to the city wine bars, hotels and fancy restaurants. And they understood the concept of a service industry. Like now. The woman at the bar collected his glasses, asked him what he wanted and handed him full fresh ones, smiling as she did so, saying she hoped he was enjoying the wine. Maybe she didn't mean it, but Banks said he was. Sometimes a smile and a little politeness go a long way. Try that in your average English pub, he thought, where the concept of wine runs about as far as red or white and sweet or dry, and a grunt is the most likely response to a hello. He carried a Pinot Noir and the Sauvignon Blanc carefully back through the throng.

'Look,' said Bob, glancing at his watch. 'I'm afraid we have to skip out now. The show starts in half an hour. You folks have a good time.'

And with that, they were gone. Banks handed Teresa her glass, and the two of them stood in rather awkward silence as the conversations buzzed around them. She was wearing a sleeveless flower-print dress which curved in to accentuate her narrow waist and ended just above her knees, cut low enough to show a tantalising glimpse of smooth cleavage. Around her neck she wore a string of coloured glass beads and had fixed some sort of coral pink flower in her hair just above her right ear. Her complexion was flawless and smooth, her nose small and straight, her lips full, curved slightly upwards at the edges.

Banks would hazard a guess that she had her origins in Thailand, or perhaps Vietnam, but he didn't know enough about the differences in the physiognomy of the Far Eastern countries to be certain. She looked as if she smiled a lot, but Banks sensed there was also a seriousness and sadness about her. He probably had an instinct for such things, he thought, given the way his life had been going lately. But it was definitely getting better.

'It's a nice hotel, isn't it?' said Teresa after a sip of wine.

'Yes,' Banks agreed, looking around at the Mediterranean-themed decor, with its warm terracotta glow, shaded table lamps, ornate ceiling and cornices, paintings and gilt-framed mirrors. They were standing near a painting of Earth resting amid a cornucopia of fruit and foliage in what appeared to be a desert landscape. The Monaco *was* a nice hotel, Banks thought, and it also had the advantage of being in one of the most interesting cities he had visited so far on his two-and-a-half-week odyssey: San Francisco. Banks especially liked cities he could walk around, and San Francisco was one of the best, once you got used to the hills. He had already taken the cable car and strolled along the waterfront to the Golden Gate Bridge and halfway across it, all on his first day, finishing the evening with a very expensive martini at the Top of the Mark, looking out on the Bay Area lights way in the distance. Tomorrow he planned to walk along Fisherman's Wharf, and then perhaps go up Coit Tower for another view.

'How long are you staying?' he asked Teresa.

'Just until Wednesday.'

'Me, too,' said Banks.

'You're English, aren't you?'

'Yes,' Banks said. 'Thank you for not guessing Australia or New Zealand. Not that I have anything against those places, mind you, but I get it a lot.'

'Oh, I wasn't guessing. My grandfather was English. From Hull.'

'Really? I know it. In fact, I don't live all that far away from Hull. If you don't mind my asking, how on earth did you . . . you know?'

Teresa laughed. 'How does a girl who looks like me have relatives from Hull? Easy. Don't laugh. They owned a Chinese restaurant.'

Banks couldn't think of anything to say.

'You should see your face,' she said, laughing at him. 'I'm joking, of course. I'm not Chinese. My grandfather was a sailor, and somehow or other he found himself on a French merchant ship. He made many visits to the Far East and ended up settling in Vietnam. So, you see, I, too, have English blood in me. Hull blood.'

Banks lowered his voice and leaned closer to her. 'It's not something I'd boast about in public,' he said. 'You know what they say about Hell, Hull and Halifax?' He caught a whiff of her perfume, delicate but a little sweet and heady, cut with a hint of jasmine.

'No. Tell me.'

'It was the thieves' litany. "From Hell, Hull and Halifax may the Good Lord deliver us." Sixteenth century. There was a particularly nasty jail in Hull and the gallows at Halifax. I think Hell rather speaks for itself.'

Teresa laughed again. 'You English people are so strange,' she said. 'I've never been there, but I'd like to go some time, just to see it.'

Banks couldn't imagine why anyone would want to go to see Hull – it wasn't exactly a major tourist destination – though he enjoyed its rough charm, the docks and its down-to-earth people. Hull also had a Premier League football team, a big plus in the north-east these days. 'Maybe one day you will,' he said. 'Look, I know this probably sounds a bit forward, but are you here by yourself?'

He thought Teresa blushed before she averted her eyes. 'Yes,' she said. 'I . . . I . . .' Then she made a dismissive gesture with her free hand. 'I'm sorry. It's a long story.'

'Maybe you'd like to have dinner with me tonight and tell me? I don't have any plans, and I'm a good listener.'

Teresa put her hand to her chest. 'Oh, I'm sorry,' she said. 'I mean, I would, you know, really, but I can't. I've already got . . . I have to be somewhere.'

'Of course,' said Banks, embarrassed that he had asked. 'I understand.'

She rested her hand on his arm. 'No, it's nothing like that,' she said. 'Really. I'm going to have dinner with my son and daughter-in-law and their kids. It's one of the reasons I'm here. In fact, I must hurry. I just felt I needed another drink before facing the little terrors. My grandchildren, that is.'

Banks didn't think she was old enough to have grandchildren, but he thought it would sound like a terrible come-on line if he told her that. 'I see,' he said.

She widened her eyes. 'Tomorrow? I mean, that's if you're not, you know, you don't . . .'

'Tomorrow would be perfect,' said Banks. 'My last night here.'

'Mine, too.' Teresa knocked back the rest of her drink, set the glass on a nearby table and took a packet of breath mints from her handbag, or purse, as they called them in America, Banks had learned. She caught Banks looking at her. 'It's all right. I'm not an alcoholic. I'm not in the habit of doing this. It's just with the kids, you know, and my daughter-in-law is so disapproving. Religious. Her father's a Baptist minister. Shall we meet here?'

'Fine,' said Banks. 'Same time? Seven? Shall I make a reservation somewhere?'

'Let me do it,' said Teresa. 'I know the city.'

'OK,' said Banks. 'See you tomorrow.'

Then Teresa hurried off and Banks was left alone. The tarot reader glanced over at him with a conspiratorial smile, and for a moment he considered having his fortune told. He quickly dismissed the idea. It would either depress him or give him false hope. He smiled back, finished his drink and headed out to see what the evening had to offer.

The first thing he saw, around the corner on Taylor, was an old street lady being sick in the gutter. After she had staggered away, three pigeons swooped down and started pecking at the chunks. Sadly, it wasn't such an unusual sight in this area of the city. As Banks walked along Geary, a homeless black man in rags followed him for about half a block, raging about how mean people were. It could have been London, Banks thought, until he got to Union Square and saw the cable car go by with people hanging off the sides, laughing and whooping, heard the bell clanging, the underground cables thrumming. With no particular destination in mind, he crossed the square and started wandering the downtown streets. Sooner or later, he knew, he would find a friendly looking bar or restaurant, where he could while away the evening.

The room on the ground floor of the Western Area Headquarters that the officers always used for their press conferences had a small elevated area that passed for a stage and contained all the wooden chairs they could rustle up. Annie and Superintendent Gervaise had gone over the developments with ACC McLaughlin with regard to what should be mentioned and what they should keep to themselves for the moment. The best they could hope for, Annie thought, was to dispel a few rumours and douse the flames before they roared out of control. Already, she felt, it was getting a bit late for that.

Patrick Doyle's death had thrown a spanner in the works, not only because it had occurred during a sanctioned police operation, but because a taser was involved. One piece of information that had come to light at the hospital was that Patrick Doyle had suffered a heart attack two years ago.

Though he had been responding well to medication, and his recent ECGs and echoes had all been good, there remained some minor damage to the heart that would never repair itself. They should have known that before sending Warburton and Powell in with tasers. That's what the media would say, too, when they got hold of the story. The taser debate sold a lot of newspapers.

In addition to the local press and TV, there were reporters from the major national dailies – *Mail, Sun, Guardian, Telegraph, Express, Times, Independent, Mirror* – and one or two feature writers looking for something a bit more in-depth – gun crime, today's youth, or police-related deaths.

The small room was buzzing with speculation and excitement when Annie and Gervaise entered that Tuesday morning and stood by the door to observe ACC McLaughlin in action. The space wasn't so large that anyone needed a microphone, but the conference had been set up so that the proceedings could be recorded on digital video, and there were also a couple of TV cameras discreetly positioned in the back corners.

Annie surveyed the room and noticed the backs of a few familiar heads, including some she had seen at Laburnum Way yesterday. She leaned against the back wall by the door and sipped coffee from the mug she had brought with her as the reporters settled down and McLaughlin began his prepared statement.

'Yesterday morning at ten forty-five a.m.,' he began, 'police were called to an address on Laburnum Way, where a loaded firearm had been reported. Unable to gain permission to enter from the occupants of the house, the Authorised Firearms Officers effected entry, and during the ensuing operation a man was injured by taser fire. He later died of complications in Eastvale General Infirmary. A loaded gun was recovered from the scene. Now, I'm sure you have many questions, and I'm sure you also understand that my replies have to be necessarily restricted at this point in the investigation.'

Hands went up all over the room, and the man from the *Daily Mail* got the first question. 'I understand that a Mr Patrick Doyle was the registered owner of the house in question. Was he present at the time of the police assault? Was he the one who died? If so, how did it happen?'

'I must object to your use of the word "assault" as unnecessarily inflammatory,' McLaughlin said. 'The officers were dealing with a potentially very dangerous situation. But let me do my best to give you a clear and succinct answer, seeing as you know most of it already. Mr Patrick Doyle was indeed the registered owner of 12 Laburnum Way. He was on the premises at the time the AFOs entered. He was injured by the discharge of a taser and has sadly since died of unrelated injuries in Eastvale General Infirmary.'

Reactions buzzed about the room and more hands went up. McLaughlin picked a local reporter next, Annie noticed. 'Yes, Ted.'

Ted Whitelaw from the *Eastvale Gazette* stood up. 'You said "unrelated injuries". Was Mr Doyle's death directly *caused* by the taser discharge, or wasn't it?'

'That we can't say at the moment,' said McLaughlin.

'Can't or won't?' someone shouted.

McLaughlin ignored the lone voice. 'Mr Doyle's body is awaiting a post-mortem examination,' he went on calmly, 'and until that has been carried out, we won't be able to say with any degree of certainty exactly what caused his death.'

'But isn't it likely?' Whitelaw persisted. 'We all know that tasers can kill.'

'This is neither the time nor the place to enter into a

debate on tasers,' said McLaughlin. 'We'll have to await the post-mortem results before we know any more.'

'I understand that taser deaths are often related to drug use or pre-existing heart conditions,' Whitelaw went on. 'Did Mr Doyle have a heart condition? Did he use drugs?'

'Patrick Doyle had a heart attack two years ago,' said McLaughlin, 'but according to his doctor, he was in excellent shape.'

'Were the armed officers who entered his house aware of this heart attack?'

'They had not been advised of his condition, no,' said McLaughlin.

'Why was that?'

'It's not for me to speculate. That remains to be determined.'

'Was it because you didn't know about it?'

McLaughlin said nothing.

'So would you say the taser *could* have been responsible for his death?' Whitelaw pressed on.

'This was a very unfortunate incident, and it will be investigated thoroughly. Now, you've had more than your fair share of questions, Ted. It's time to sit down.'

Whitelaw sat, smirked and began scribbling on his pad.

'You said the incident would be investigated thoroughly,' said the *Daily Mirror* man. 'Can you tell us who by?'

'The actions of the officers involved will be investigated by Superintendent Chambers, from the Professional Standards Department, who will be working with an outside team brought in by the Independent Police Complaints Commission, according to protocol.'

'But it will be a *police* investigation, won't it?' asked the woman from the *Guardian*.

'The last time I checked, Maureen,' said McLaughlin, 'the police were the best-qualified organisation in the country to carry out such an investigation. Whom do you suggest we bring in? The librarian? A local antiques dealer? The little old lady down the street who takes in all the stray cats?' His Scottish accent grew more pronounced with his sarcasm.

The woman smiled. 'I was merely pointing out that it's simply another case of the police investigating their own,' she said, then sat down.

McLaughlin searched around for another raised hand. He didn't have far to look. 'Yes. You, Len.'

It was Len Jepson from the *Yorkshire Post*. 'My question is a simple one,' he began. 'Why was a team of Authorised Firearm Officers breaking down the door of a pebble-dashed semi in a nice middle-class street in Eastvale on a quiet Monday morning?'

A ripple of laughter went around the room.

'As I said in my statement, we had reliable reports that there was a loaded firearm on the premises,' said McLaughlin, 'and when our duty officers got no response to their requests for peaceful entry, the AFOs were called in. It's standard procedure, Len. You should know that.'

'How many AFOs were involved?' asked a reporter from the *Independent*.

'Four. Two at the front and two at the back, as per usual. SOP.'

Another hand. 'Yes, Carol.'

'You mentioned in your statement earlier that a loaded gun was recovered from the house. Had it been used?'

'The weapon had not been recently discharged.'

'Who does it belong to?'

'That we don't know.'

'Where is it now?' asked another voice.

'It's been sent to the Forensic Science Services in Birmingham for further examination.'

'Any idea how it came to be in the house?'

'That matter is under investigation.'

'Was it anything to do with Erin Doyle?'

'I'm sorry, but I can't make any further comment at present.'

More hands. McLaughlin picked the woman from the *Darlington & Stockton Times*. 'Jessica?'

'You've been singled out before for your rather, shall we say, left-wing views on some subjects of public concern, such as racial profiling, overcrowded prisons and the use of police force. Can you tell our readers what your personal thoughts on this matter are?'

McLaughlin managed a tight smile. Some people, Annie knew, called him 'Red' Ron, and he pretended not to like it, though she thought he was secretly rather proud. His father, who had worked in the Glasgow shipyards after the war, had been a strong trade unionist, and some of the old socialist ideals had rubbed off on his son. 'My personal opinions on the matter in hand are hardly relevant,' McLaughlin said. 'The point at issue here is that a life has been tragically lost, and a family is in mourning. I ask you all to respect their grief.'

'Do you respect it?' someone called out. 'Isn't it true that you've been interrogating and harassing the Doyle family since yesterday morning?'

'I can't discuss the details of the ongoing investigation at this stage, but I can assure you that there has been no harassment on our part.'

More grumbles and shuffling, then another voice spoke

out. This time it was Luke Stafford of the *Sun*. 'What part did Erin Doyle play in all this?' he asked. 'Patrick Doyle's daughter. Was the gun hers?'

'I'm not at liberty to discuss such details of an ongoing investigation.'

'So you think it was? She was seen by a neighbour being led out of the house in handcuffs,' Stafford went on. 'And isn't it true that she was mixing with some pretty bad company in Leeds? Drug dealers and such scum?'

Annie could see that this was the first McLaughlin had heard of it. It was the first she had heard of it, too. They must have sent a reporter to dig around. 'I can't comment on that, Mr Stafford,' said McLaughlin, 'but if you have any information pertinent to our investigation, I hope you'll do your duty as a citizen and come forward with it.' Then he stood up. 'I'm afraid that's all for now, ladies and gentlemen. This conference is over.'

Annie could tell that the crowd wasn't happy with the way things had gone. They had wanted blood and had got merely the scent of it. God only knew what they would write now.

McLaughlin was also clearly not happy. On his way out of the door, he leaned towards Annie and Gervaise and said between gritted teeth, 'Just what the hell was all that about? What do we know about Erin Doyle's life in Leeds?'

'Nothing yet, sir,' said Gervaise. 'We've hardly started our investigation.'

'The newspapers obviously have. I suggest you get a move on. Let's bloody well find out what's going on before the red-tops get there, shall we? I want results, and I want them fast. I also want them *first*.'

'Yes, sir,' said Gervaise. When McLaughlin had gone, she turned to Annie and said, 'In my office in an hour.'

This could be interesting, Annie thought. She had planned on going down to Leeds on her own after work to talk to Tracy Banks, anyway, but now the Leeds connection was an official part of the investigation. She should tell Gervaise that Erin Doyle and Tracy Banks shared a house; there was no doubt that she would find out soon enough, anyway. But Annie also thought that she owed it to Banks to keep his daughter out of trouble, if she was in any trouble, if that was at all possible. She decided to tread cautiously and keep her own counsel for the moment, at least until she had a better grasp of exactly what it was they were investigating.

Of course, the inevitable had happened. Tracy and Jaff had stayed up most of the night, first drinking Banks's Highland Park and smoking joints in the conservatory, laughing and playing Animal Collective, Fleet Foxes and My Morning Jacket, then ransacking the DVD collection for something to watch. They had settled on one of the Jason Bourne films, basically just a long chase punctuated by close-combat fights and shoot-outs. Again, Jaff had chucked the DVDs he didn't like on the floor, which was getting quite littered by then. Tracy remembered the cases crunching and splintering under their feet as they stumbled towards the stairs. After that, things had got very blurry.

When she awoke at about half past ten in the morning, she was lying naked under the duvet in the guest bedroom, and Jaff was nowhere in sight. Her head ached, but if she tried, she could piece together most of what had transpired.

They had taken the bottle of whisky upstairs to her father's bedroom, and there she had tumbled on to the bed with Jaff. Soon he was kissing her and his hands were groping all over her body. She had struggled a bit and thought at one point she might have told him to stop because she didn't feel well. She remembered that she felt weird about doing it in her father's bed, and her stomach didn't feel too good after all the whisky and wine. But Jaff was urgent. Soon he'd got her blouse off, and his hand wandered down the front of her jeans. Then they were coming off, too, and . . . well, that was when she was sick.

She had managed to turn away just in time and do it over the edge of the bed. She had thought that would stop him, put him off, especially when she had to go and rinse her mouth and brush her teeth. But when she had come back, jeans all zipped up, blouse straight and buttoned, he had been lying there on his back stark naked, smiling and huge, and he had started all over again. Her head had still been spinning, and she hadn't been able to find the will or the strength to stop him. Not that she had really wanted to. She didn't want to be thought a tease, and she was quite flattered by his attentions. She had also felt a little bit better by then, and she had quite liked it; after all, she *had* fantasised about sex with Jaff often enough, had even kissed him on the dance floor. A lot of girls, Tracy knew, would have swapped places with her in the blink of an eye. And she was doing it in her father's bedroom.

She couldn't really remember what it had been like, but she recalled that Jaff hadn't taken long, despite the amount he'd had to drink. It had all been over in a matter of moments. Jaff had then fallen fast asleep, or passed out. When Tracy had been sure that he wasn't going to wake up for a while, she had crept out of her father's room and gone to the other bedroom, the one she used to sleep in when she visited. And that was where she woke up to bright sunshine and bird-song. She had forgotten to close the curtains. For a moment, she panicked, not knowing where she was, then she realised. She also remembered what she had done and where her clothes were.

She wandered back into Banks's bedroom and got dressed. Jaff was nowhere to be seen, and the house was silent. After using the bathroom and taking some of Banks's paracetamol, she went downstairs, calling Jaff's name softly. She found him in the conservatory curled up in one of the wicker chairs, a half-full glass of whisky and an overflowing ashtray on the table by his side. He looked almost angelic, she thought, long eyelashes, moist lips slightly parted, making breathy, snuffling sounds. She felt like kissing him, but she didn't want to disturb him.

Tracy made some tea and toast in the kitchen as quietly as she could, then she decided to set about tidying up. First, she took a bowl of water and a cloth upstairs to clean the sick off the bedroom floor – thank God it was wood and not a carpet – feeling herself flush with embarrassment – how *could* she? – then she moved down to the entertainment room. Not sure where to begin there, she wandered back into the kitchen to refill her cup with tea.

That was when she thought of her mobile, and she realised that while Jaff was asleep, she could probably get it back. It could be ages before he found out what she had done. Jaff had put it in his holdall, she remembered. He was probably right about it being dangerous to use. She had heard about people being traced through their mobile signals – her dad had mentioned it more than once – and Jaff seemed to know what he was talking about. It would be nice just to have it with her, though. It would be a great comfort. And she would keep it switched off. Surely that could do no harm? Surely Jaff couldn't possibly object to that, even if he did find out?

Tracy was just about to go over and open Jaff's holdall on the breakfast table when he emerged in the conservatory doorway, stretching, yawning and rubbing his eyes. Ah, well, Tracy thought, maybe later.

'Morning,' she said. 'Cup of tea?'

Jaff grunted. Clearly not a morning person. Tracy made tea anyway. He drank it with milk and two sugars, pulled a face and told her he preferred coffee. She made coffee.

When he had poured his first cup, he said, 'I'm starving. Is there anything left to eat?'

Tracy had checked both the fridge and freezer, not to mention the cupboards. There were a couple of tins of baked beans and some soup, but that was it. They ate cold baked beans from the cans.

'After this, we've got to go shopping if we plan on staying here,' Tracy said. 'There's absolutely nothing left to eat. We have to go to Eastvale.'

'How long did you say your old man's going to be away?'

'Until next Monday. We're all right for a bit. Have you had a chance to think things out yet?'

'Sort of.'

'And?'

'I reckon we should stay here as long as it's safe,' Jaff said. 'Say till the end of the week. We'll let things quieten down a bit. It's nice and isolated here, nobody to come around asking awkward questions. And nobody will think to look for me here. Even if someone does come, you can talk to them, tell them everything's OK and send them packing. After all, it's your dad's house. You've got every right to be here, haven't you? There's even some decent music and movies. Not to mention the booze. I reckon we've lucked out.'

'But we can't stay here for ever,' Tracy argued, vague images in her mind of the further damage Jaff might do to her father's home. She'd enjoyed last night's careless abandon and wild freedom, but it couldn't go on indefinitely.

'I know that, babe.' Jaff ambled over and ran his hand over her hair, her cheek, her breast. 'I just need to put a few plans into operation, that's all. I know people. I've got an old college mate down in Clapham who can get us fixed up with new passports, no questions asked, but I need a few days to make some calls and set things up. These things don't come cheap. I'm just saying we've got a good hide-away for now, and that's all we need. Soon as I'm organ-ised, we can go down to London, then get out of the country. Once we're over the Channel, we're home free.'

'Not these days,' said Tracy. 'There's Interpol and Europol and God knows what other pols. I've seen programmes on telly.'

'You worry too much. Don't be a drag, babe. All I'm saying is that if you know how to disappear, you can do it over there.'

'And you know?'

Jaff kissed her. 'Trust me. And maybe you should get a different lipstick while we're in Eastvale. Pink, maybe. I don't like that dark red colour. Same goes for the nail varnish. It looks slutty. Get something lighter. Is there anything you can do about your hair? I liked it better without the coloured streaks.'

'They'll wash out easily enough,' Tracy said. She touched her hair and licked her lips self-consciously, then examined her scarlet nails. Still she felt uneasy. She wasn't sure that she wanted to change her appearance and go into forced exile over the Channel with Jaff, much as she fancied him.

After all, she didn't know him very well and *she* hadn't done anything illegal. *She* wasn't on the run. In fact, she wasn't even sure what she *was* doing, or why. All she'd done wrong so far was help make a bit of a mess of her dad's place and drink some of his booze. But she decided to concentrate on the moment, on the now. She could deal with the rest later.

Not so far away, in his eighteenth-century manor house on the north-western fringes of Ripon, 'Farmer' George Fanthorpe stood at his picture window and surveyed his domain as he mulled over what he had just been told. He could see his own flushed, craggy face, round shoulders and thick curls of greying hair reflected in the glass. Beyond his reflection lay the garden, his pride and joy, with its beautifully trimmed lawn, swings, slide and a seesaw for the kids, topiary hedges, cinder paths, fountains, flower beds and vegetable patches where Zenovia liked to spend her time, though today she was on a shopping trip in York.

The high walls that enclosed the garden were mostly covered by climbing vines and partially hidden by trees, though where the garden sloped down, there were enough gaps in the foliage to make the view of the Wensleydale hills beyond Masham a magnificent one. Today, the frozen waves of hills had become grey, muted humps, each higher than the one before it, undulating into the far distance. Fanthorpe loved that view, could watch it for hours. It was even more spectacular from the bedroom window, without any obstruction in the way at all. But the walls were necessary. They were also topped with broken glass. 'Farmer' Fanthorpe had enemies.

The greyness of the weather reflected his mood that afternoon. There were things happening in the far-flung reaches of his empire that he didn't like, didn't like at all. He prided himself on running a slick operation, and the snippets of news that Darren had just given him were disturbing his equilibrium, to say the least.

'You're certain it's Jaff's girlfriend?' he asked, half turning.

'Certain,' said Darren, who had been standing behind him in silence, arms folded.

Fanthorpe knew that Darren wasn't an alarmist, not one to exaggerate or get in a tizzy over nothing. Cool, Darren was, even in a scrape. Especially in a scrape. And he understood the value of intelligence. 'And they found the shooter in her house?'

'Parents' house. It was on the news.'

'Just a shooter? I mean, they didn't mention . . .?'

'Just a shooter. The cops shot her old man with a taser. He died.'

Fanthorpe turned his back on the view and moved closer to Darren. 'Tough titty. You know this is the last thing we need right now, don't you? The last thing. What with negotiations with the Russians going so well. The Lithuanians falling into line. And the Albanian deal. What does that stupid bastard think he's up to, giving his shooter to his fucking girlfriend? And where is he? He was supposed to be here with the stuff last night. Last fucking night.'

'I don't know,' said Darren. 'Maybe he didn't give the gun to her. Maybe she took it *and* the stuff. The cops aren't saying. What do you want us to do?'

'Is Ciaran with you?'

'In the car.'

Fanthorpe paced the room, thinking furiously. He didn't want to do anything that would draw further unwanted attention to himself – and pretty much all attention was unwanted in his line of work, which involved criminal business of astonishing breadth and variety, from the merely grey to the out-and-out black: moving things around, matching demand with supply, whether drugs, dirty money, luxury cars or unwilling sex-trade workers. His daughters went to the best school in the county, and his beautiful young Serbian wife didn't have to get dishpan hands. Fanthorpe wanted to keep it that way. And the manor house, too; that was a given.

It often amazed him how utterly still Darren could stand. He didn't even blink while he waited for the answer.

'And this was all on the news this morning?'

'Yes.'

'Has Jaff's name been mentioned?'

'Not yet. We think the girl must be keeping shtum.'

'It won't last,' said Fanthorpe. 'It never does.'

'She's on bail. We might still be able to get to her. We could—'

Fanthorpe held his hand up, palm out. 'No,' he said. 'No. I appreciate the sentiment, Darren, I really do. And if anyone can do it, you and Ciaran can. But it's too risky. I know we've done similar things before with witnesses and other problems, but the risks far outweigh the advantages this time. If she doesn't name him, someone else will. You can't tell me they don't hang around with other people like themselves. Don't like to show off a bit, flash the cash around. You know kids today. Clubs. Pubs. Loose tongues. A social circle. No. If she doesn't tell them, someone else will.'

'Then what?'

'First, I want you to pay a visit to Jaff's flat. You know where it is. That posh place by the wharf in Leeds. Here's the key. He's still got something of mine, and I want it back. Maybe he heard what happened to his girlfriend and took off somewhere, took it with him, even though he must know what that means, but . . . well, have a butcher's, anyway.'

Darren pocketed the key. He didn't ask where Fanthorpe had got it from. It didn't matter. 'No sweat, boss. And then?'

'Jaff. He's not as tough as he thinks he is. Once the coppers get to him, and they will, it's only a matter of time before he talks, if he hasn't already. Maybe they'll offer him a deal, too. And he knows too much about us. Way too much.' Fanthorpe shook his head. 'I can hardly believe what I'm hearing. Jaff. You know, he's practically my partner? I've treated that boy like the son I never had. Groomed him. And this is how he repays me.'

'We don't know that he's done anything yet.'

Fanthorpe turned red. 'He's given me fucking indigestion, for a start. And he's let a gun fall into police hands, all because of some stupid tart. If that's not enough, I don't know what is. He's a liability.'

'So what do we do?' Darren asked again.

'Whatever damage is done, we make sure it stops with Jaff. Is there anything concrete to link him to us?'

'Tenuous, at best,' said Darren. 'Rumours. Innuendo. Nothing we can't deal with. No loose ends we can't tie up.'

Fanthorpe nodded. 'As I thought. Well, rumours and innuendo are about as much use as a fart in a force-nine gale, but they can cause a lot of peripheral damage. So it stops with Jaff. See to it.'

'Right, boss.'

'Find him. Pay him a visit. Don't bring him back here. Take him somewhere nice and quiet. Find out exactly what's going on. Let Ciaran loose on him if you have to. He must be getting thirsty for blood again by now. It's been a long while. Get what you can out of him. Get my stuff back for me. Give me a bell when you've done it, and I'll give you further instructions then. Think you can you handle it?'

Darren gave him a look of wonder that he should ask such a question.

''Course you can,' said Fanthorpe, patting Darren's shoulder. ''Course you can, my lad. You haven't let me down yet. Remember. It stops with Jaff. First get my stuff back, then . . . then . . .' He paused and drew the edge of his hand across his throat. 'It stops.'

5

Detective Superintendent Gervaise occupied her predecessor Gristhorpe's old office, as befitted her rank, but it was far less cluttered than it had been when the old man was in residence, Annie thought, far more spick and span, light and airy. A fresh coat of pale blue paint had worked wonders. The bookcases held works mostly relevant to the job, rather than the rows of leather-bound classics Gristhorpe had kept there, and the volumes were interspersed with the occasional cup or mounted award for dressage and fencing, along with silver-framed family photographs. A white MacBook sat open on her orderly desk, pushed slightly to one side. Street sounds drifted in through the open window – a car starting, school-children calling out to each other across the market square, the sliding door of a large delivery van – along with the occasional breath of fresh air and the aroma of warm bread wafting up from Pete's Bakery.

'Sit down, Annie,' said Gervaise. 'I've already sent for tea. Earl Grey all right with you?'

'Fine,' said Annie. She crossed her legs and leaned back in the chair.

Gervaise toyed with a paper clip, unbending it slowly, her Cupid's-bow lips pursed. 'I like the blonde highlights,' she said finally, turning her blue eyes on Annie. 'What made you do that?'

'I don't know. Blondes have more fun?' Annie was far from certain that she'd done the right thing. Having her hair cut short in the first place was one step towards a new look, but the highlights were quite another, and she was still feeling self-conscious about them.

'And are you? Having more fun?'

'Not at the moment, I must admit.'

'Me neither.' Gervaise paused and put the paper clip down. Annie noticed a bubble of blood on the tip of her index finger. 'Look, we've had our ups and downs, you and me, but I like you, Annie. I want you to know that. Despite your often misguided loyalty to DCI Banks taking precedence over correct procedure, and even simple common sense at times, I like you. And I want to build on that. How are things?'

'What do you mean?'

'It's a simple question. How are things? Your life? In general. How are you doing?'

'I'm fine, ma'am.'

'And would you tell me if you weren't?'

'Probably not.'

'So I haven't earned your trust yet?'

'It's not a matter of . . .' Annie began. Then she stopped.

'Of what? Go on.'

Annie shook her head.

'I suppose what I meant,' Gervaise went on, 'was you and Alan. DCI Banks. In the short time I've been here, it could hardly have escaped my attention that the two of you have a somewhat special relationship, and—'

'There's nothing untoward about it, if that's what you're getting at,' Annie said. 'No romantic involvement. No impropriety whatsoever.'

'Whoa there.' Gervaise held her hand up, palm out. 'Methinks the lady doth protest too much. But that's by the by. I wasn't referring to your sex life. Ah, here's the tea. Come in, Sharon. Put the tray down here, please. Thank you.' The WPC who had brought the tea smiled, nodded and left the room.

'We'll just let that mash a while, shall we?' Gervaise said. 'Then I'll play mother. No, what I meant before was that you actually complement one another quite well in your work. I know things have a tendency to go awry once in a while, especially when DCI Banks is around, and some things don't always look too good on paper, but your cases get solved, you get results. Both of you.'

'Thank you, ma'am.'

Gervaise leaned forward and linked her hands on the desk. The tiny bubble of blood smeared the knuckles on her left hand. Her diamond engagement ring sparkled as it caught the sunlight. 'Let me tell you, quite frankly, that I'm worried about Alan. I've been worried about him ever since that business with MI5 last spring. There's something . . . different about him. And one hears . . . rumours. I understand he split up with his girlfriend, too?'

'Yes. Sophia.' Annie had never really taken to Sophia, had always believed she could see right through her, see her for what she was – vain and shallow, used to being desired and celebrated as a muse by men. Sophia needed their adoration, she fed on it, and the attentions of an older, attractive man of Banks's stature had flattered her ego. For a while. Until a better offer came along, someone who would write poems or songs for her, perhaps. But she couldn't say that to Gervaise. It would sound like sour grapes, as it if it were born out of envy and jealousy. Which it partly was. Since

Banks had split up with Sophia and become uncommunicative, Annie had found herself frequently thinking of their short time together. He had been hers once. Could she have hung on to him? Should she have tried? Even taken a transfer to some other county force not too far away so that they wouldn't have to work together? Because that had been the problem, she had discovered; she hadn't been able to work alongside him *and* be romantically involved.

'Is there more to it than that?'

Annie snapped herself back to the present. 'I'm sorry?'

'I asked if there was anything else that was worrying him. I'm not asking you to betray any sort of trust, you understand. I ask entirely out of concern for his welfare. And for yours, too, of course. For the team.'

'No, I don't think so,' said Annie. 'Not that I can think of. At least, there's nothing he's said anything to me about. It's just . . .'

Gervaise leaned forward a fraction more. 'What?'

'Oh, nothing. I had the same feeling, too, that's all. That something else was going on. That he was haunted by something. Or that he'd reached the end of something. But he doesn't confide in me. Maybe he's gone away looking for new beginnings?'

'Then let's hope he finds some. When exactly is he due back at work? It's in my files somewhere. Monday, isn't it?'

'That's right.'

As Gervaise shuffled some papers on her desk, she noticed the blood, picked up a tissue and wiped it off. She pressed a couple of keys on her MacBook. 'I'm just a bit concerned about him walking right into the middle of all this, especially as he knows the Doyles.'

'He'll deal with it,' said Annie, with more conviction than

she felt. 'And he's resilient. Whatever happens, he'll come through. We shouldn't worry about him too much.'

'I suppose we have enough to worry about as it is.'

'What are we going to do?'

'Do? As we're told, of course. Which is to work in conjunction with Superintendent Chambers and his team, and not to step on his toes. I understand he's bringing in a couple of PSD officers from Greater Manchester to conduct the investigation for him. Firearms Cadre Superintendent Trethowan will continue to manage the scene, the Doyle house.'

'And us?'

'Our job remains the gun found in the possession of Erin Doyle. Or should I say, found in her bedroom. As yet we have no proof who put it there.' Gervaise looked at her watch. 'I think the preliminary report on the firearm from Birmingham should be with us before today's over. I'll be SIO on this and you will be my deputy. Which means that you and Winsome and Harry Potter will be doing most of the work, as you can imagine, things being what they are around here. You can have DC Masterson, too. She needs to get her feet wet. I'm guessing, but I think much of my time will be taken up by meetings and discussions of various kinds. Not to mention bloody paperwork. I don't want any complaints about you from the family or from Superintendent Chambers. Do I make myself clear?'

'Yes.'

'I trust you have appointed a Family Liaison Officer?'

'Patricia Yu. She'd done the requisite courses and has over a year's experience.'

'Very well. I'd like you to proceed very carefully with the investigation, and keep me posted. Regular reports.' She tapped her desk. 'Here. In my office.'

'Yes,' said Annie. She stood up to leave.

'And Annie?'

Annie turned at the door and raised her eyebrows.

'Watch your back. I don't trust Chambers any more than you do.' She paused. 'And about DCI Banks. If anything . . . Well, you know what I mean.'

'Yes, I know,' said Annie.

It was after lunchtime before Tracy got Jaff on the road to Eastvale. He had dragged his feet so much that she had offered to go and do the shopping alone, which would have suited her far better, but he wouldn't have any of it. She wasn't leaving his sight, he told her. Such devotion, she replied. He missed the sarcasm.

The roads and the Swainsdale villages were busy with tourist traffic, and nobody paid Vic's silver-grey Ford Focus any special attention as they passed through Gratly, Helmthorpe or Fortford. Jaff drove cautiously, hovering just above the speed limit the whole way, like most of the other cars, except when he got stuck behind a tractor and slowed to a crawl, cursing so much that Tracy cracked up laughing. 'It's amazing,' she said. 'Like you've never been in the country before.'

Jaff laughed with her. 'I've been on worse roads than this, babe. But you're right. Tractors and caravans. I'm with Jeremy Clarkson on that.'

When they got to Eastvale, the sky had clouded over. They parked in the pay-and-display under the Swainsdale Centre and took the escalator up to the shops. The centre itself was bustling with people. For a moment, Tracy worried that she might bump into someone who recognised her, then she realised it didn't matter if she did. Nobody knew what was going on with her and Jaff. Nobody knew they were lying low until a spot of bother passed over.

Sometimes, Tracy wondered whether anybody actually went out to work any more. She knew the economy was bad, but it seemed strange to her that if people were unemployed, or simply hadn't any money, they were in the shopping centre all the time. Unless they just came there to sigh through the windows at things they couldn't afford, which seemed stupid. Most of the people she saw were young enough to have jobs, if there were any. Some were mothers pushing their kids in prams, of course, or trailing them around by the hand, but others didn't look much more than school-leaving age, and very few of the shoppers seemed old enough to be pensioners.

The two of them blended in easily with the crowd. They bought newspapers at WH Smith's and picked up a couple of CDs and DVDs at HMV. Jaff bought three white shirts, a Boss sports jacket and a new pair of designer jeans. He eyed Tracy up and down. 'You know, you could do with some new clothes, too, babe,' he said. 'I can't say that charity-shop look really does a lot for you.'

Tracy felt hurt. It was true that most of the clothes she was wearing came from charity shops, but no one had told her before that they didn't look good on her. It wasn't as if she bought granny's cast-offs or anything like that. But Jaff led her around the shops and she ended up with some Levi's, a blue silk blouse, a burgundy pencil skirt with a matching top, and several expensive T-shirts of various colours. He also bought her a fitted kid leather jacket to replace the ripped denim one she was wearing. Jaff said he hated it, so she threw it in a rubbish bin.

When Tracy tried the clothes on, she felt sophisticated,

more like a *Francesca* than ever, and when she examined herself in the changing-room mirror she realised that she would probably look even better when she had washed the streaks out of her hair. She would do that when they got back to her dad's cottage. She had her mother's colouring – natural blonde hair and dark eyebrows – and now that she had her hair cut short, in a sort of pixie-ish, spiky style, and was wearing good clothes, she resembled a professional young woman more than a student. The pencil skirt emphasised her slim waist and hips, and the top made the best of her small breasts. She liked what she saw, and it amazed her that Jaff had such immaculate taste, even regarding the clothes *she* should wear. He even bought her some sexy underwear, and a nice leather Gucci shoulder bag to carry everything in, instead of the fraying canvas book bag she'd been using for ages. That followed the denim jacket into the rubbish bin.

Tracy needed to buy shampoo and conditioner, pink lipstick, the shade Jaff had said he liked, some nail-varnish remover, and a toothbrush and toothpaste. She had none of these things in her shoulder bag, which was all she had brought with her from Leeds, and had had to use her father's toiletries that morning.

They went to Superdrug, where Tracy found what she needed. When she reached for her debit card, ready to pay, Jaff took hold of her hand 'What do you think you're doing?' he whispered. 'Are you crazy or something?'

'I've got no cash left, Jaff,' Tracy protested. 'I *need* these things. I've got to pay somehow.'

'Well, you can't use your debit or credit cards,' he whispered, glancing around. 'They can be traced. It's like the first thing they do. Didn't you know that? Aren't you taking this seriously?'

'But you used yours. I saw you.'

'It's corporate, and it can't be traced to me.'

'But why . . .? Never mind.' Tracy realised that she hadn't got used to thinking like a fugitive. Perhaps she wasn't taking it seriously, regarding it more as a fun game, as make-believe. She wasn't sure that she wanted to grasp the full reality of the situation, either, but for the moment she knew that she had to go along with Jaff. Soon, she was certain, everything would be settled, and they could all go back to the way things were, whatever that was, but for now she had to be up to the adventure. 'Nobody's looking for me,' she said.

'Doesn't matter. They might be. They will be. It's best to be cautious. OK, babe? Here, it's not very much. Take this.' Jaff gave her a lopsided grin and pulled a wad of cash from his pocket. He discreetly peeled off a couple of twenty-pound notes and handed them to her. 'This should cover it. Keep the change in case you see anything else you fancy. Don't even *think* of using your plastic. If you need anything, come to me.'

Tracy took the money. She knew better than to ask where it had come from, just as she had known not to ask him why he was carrying an untraceable credit card. This whole shopping expedition was making her head spin, making her feel a bit scared and, perhaps, a bit excited.

Last of all, they went to Tesco's and bought lots of ready-to-cook meals, things they could just nuke in the microwave, like pizza, quiches, chicken Kievs and curries, mostly, along with eggs, bread, bacon, milk, chocolate bars and biscuits for when they got the munchies, more tins of baked beans, cheese and packaged meats for sandwiches. That would see them through until the end of the week, Tracy thought. They didn't need to buy wine, Jaff said, because her father had more than enough quality stuff for them to be going on with.

Back at the car, they loaded their purchases in the boot. 'That was fun,' Tracy said. 'What do you want to do next?'

'I'm hungry,' said Jaff. 'Want to go for a pub lunch or something?'

'Sure,' said Tracy. 'We'll stop somewhere on the way back.' She was standing by the car looking down over the terraced gardens and the river, which rushed along over rocks in little waterfalls below the steep castle walls to her right. She remembered walking there with her father when she was younger, holding his hand tight as they passed near the edge of the sheer drop, afraid of falling, asking him how the little flowers could grow out of the crumbling stone. He told her they were called rosebay willowherb and they could also grow after forest fires. She thought what a lovely name that was for something so strong and durable. Sometimes the wind was so wild that she thought it would blow them both away like autumn leaves, but he had said he wouldn't ever let her go, and he never had. Not until now. When she turned to Jaff, she had tears in her eyes.

'What is it?' he asked.

'Just the wind. And the sun. I should have bought some sunglasses back at Superdrug. Look, there's still an hour left on the meter. Would you like to go and have a look at where Erin lives? You know, the street on the news last night. We can see if there's still anything going on there.'

'Is it near here?'

'Not far.'

'OK. Sure,' said Jaff. 'But let's be careful.'

They left the shopping centre by the York Road exit and crossed the cobbled market square, past the Queen's Arms and left along Market Street. Tracy was wearing her new tight-fit Levi's and a crisp white T-shirt that felt soft and sexy against her skin. She felt good. Jaff took hold of her hand. They passed the police station where her dad worked but, of course, she couldn't say anything to Jaff. She had a sudden image of the bed and the mess they had made back at the cottage. Whisky stains and worse on her father's sheets.

They hadn't gone far when Jaff started to complain about the distance and how hungry he was, but Tracy just laughed at him again. 'You're a real city boy,' she said. 'I'll bet you don't walk anywhere.'

'That's what cars are for,' he said. 'Is it much farther?'

'Just past that next zebra crossing.'

Even before they got to Laburnum Way, careful to stay on the other side of Market Street, Tracy could tell that the police hadn't finished there yet. The cul-de-sac wasn't blocked off – the people who lived there could come and go as they pleased – but police cars and vans parked at awkward angles would make it difficult for anyone driving in and out, and would certainly discourage sightseers.

Erin's house had police tape on the gate and over the door – Tracy could just see the blue-and-white pattern – and two uniformed officers stood on guard. As Tracy and Jaff gazed surreptitiously, just two young lovers passing by, some men came out of the front door wearing white coveralls and elastic covers for their hair and shoes. The SOCOs. Tracy realised she had met some of them, and she hoped that no one recognised her. But how could they, the way she looked now? Besides, she reminded herself, she wasn't wanted for anything, and there was no way they'd know who Jaff was, even if they were looking for him. Nobody seemed to pay any attention to them. It was one thing to watch it on TV, Tracy thought, but quite another to see it like this, at close quarters, as it was happening.

'Jesus Christ,' said Jaff, picking up the pace a bit when he saw the SOCOs. 'Is that where she lives? This looks serious.'

'They *did* find a gun,' Tracy reminded him. 'They take that very seriously. And you don't often get that sort of thing in a nice middle-class street like Laburnum Way.'

'I don't suppose you do,' said Jaff. 'It is a bit bay-window. But even so . . . Does it really take that many of them?'

Tracy could have told him that it did, and why, what each one of them did and how long they might be there, but she held her tongue. 'How would I know? We can go back another way, if you like,' she said, leading him down a street to the left that linked up with York Road, near the college. 'It's a bit longer, but we don't have to walk past the police again. Anyway,' she said, 'we don't even know that anyone's looking for you yet, do we?'

'They will be,' Jaff said. 'If not now, then soon. Even if Erin keeps quiet, someone's bound to talk. They'll track down her other friends, people from the clubs, the restaurant where she works. We have to be careful.' He looked around and gave a little shudder. 'Come on,' he said. 'Let's get back to the car and find somewhere to eat outside town. I'll feel safer away from here.'

Banks walked along Fisherman's Wharf in the morning sunshine eating fresh crab cakes in a piquant red sauce from a paper carton, the Golden Gate Bridge at his back. He watched the tour boat sailing over to Alcatraz and wondered whether he should go. Maybe not, he decided, after all. Historic or not, it would be too much like a busman's holiday.

Touring a prison and being shut in a cell, even if Al Capone had once been there, held no real appeal for him. Not even for a minute. And he was supposed to be getting away from all that. Or so he had thought. He knew he couldn't run away from his problems; that he would take them with him wherever he went. But a change of scene and time to think, at least, had seemed essential. A trip would give him new sensations, new experiences and, at best, it would inspire him. At worst, it would be just another collection of holiday snaps he would download to his computer and probably never look at again.

The horror of the bomb blast he had witnessed in London and the sense of guilt that he had been responsible for an innocent man's death still kept him awake at nights. He could smell the smoke, see the blood and hear the screams every time he laid his head down. And his car crashed in slow motion time after time. He stared at the body sprawled bleeding on the bonnet of his Porsche, while government agents told him it was probably the best thing that could have happened for all concerned. He remembered the rain, blood and tears that streaked down his face on his long walk home in the dark. Could he have handled things differently? Should he have? Probably. But he hadn't. What was done was done, and he couldn't run away from it simply by taking a flight to America.

Then there was Sophia's betrayal. The image of her sitting across the table from another man in the wine bar, and later on, at her front door, of the man's hand resting proprietorially on the small of her back as she put her key in the lock, glanced quickly up and down the street and invited him into her house, still lingered. Her subsequent silence had hurt even more. He had left phone messages, written letters, but he had heard nothing. It was like dropping a stone into a deep dark chasm and waiting for a splash or echo that never came. No cry in the dark. Nothing. She had said she needed time, space, and she was certainly sticking to that.

After nearly two months of silence, Banks received a banal, chatty email from Sophia, which ended, 'I've moved on. You should do the same. Have a good life.' It was sent from her BlackBerry, for God's sake, or so it informed him at the bottom. Definitely not with a bang; much more of a whimper. At least that quickly put paid to any lingering hopes of romantic reconciliation he might have been harbouring. After that, he felt mainly contempt for Sophia. He didn't like feeling that way about someone he had once loved, so he was working on indifference. It was the closest he could come to forgiveness.

Banks leaned against the wooden railing of a pier and stared across the bay at Mt Tamalpais, the sleeping maiden. He could make out her shape easily enough, the long, flowing hair, the soft curve of her breasts, the flat belly and thighs. She had drowned while swimming to meet her lover, or she had lain down there in dejection after being spurned, and had wept her tears into the bay, depending on which version you believed. Bank glanced down into the ruffled blue water then back towards the majestic bridge, more orange than gold, to his eye. He felt a sense of inner peace that he hadn't had before he came away, and he thought of that night in the desert.

It was the third or fourth day of his trip, and he was in Arizona. He had visited the Grand Canyon and Sedona, and he now planned on driving across the desert from Phoenix to Los Angeles, then up the coast to San Francisco. As he drove, he played desert music on the car stereo through his iPod adapter, or what he thought of as desert music: Captain Beefheart, Lucinda Williams's *Car Wheels on a Gravel Road* and Dylan's soundtrack from *Pat Garrett and Billy the Kid*. He also played a lot of Handel oratorios very loud. Somehow, they seemed to chime with the sense of the place for him.

He had driven a meandering course on and off Interstate 10, stopping occasionally to visit various attractions. Here he had experienced the desert landscape the way he had always imagined it. Mile after mile of nothing but sagebrush, tumbleweed, clumps of prickly pear and and tall, gangly saguaro cacti; unrelenting dry heat. In the evening, the long range of jagged peaks that never seemed to get any nearer caught the fading light, all earthy shades of terracotta, red and brown.

That night he had found a motel off the beaten track. It wasn't quite the Bates Motel, but it had a similar creepy, run-down atmosphere about it, fortunately without the big eerie house on the hill behind. The desk clerk was sixty if he was a day, a bald Mexican with a paunch, a Pancho Villa moustache and a case of five o'clock shadow so advanced it was probably six or seven o'clock on his face, though it still stopped short of a beard. When the clerk smiled, Banks noticed that he was missing his two upper front teeth. At least he didn't resemble Norman Bates in the slightest, and there wasn't a stuffed animal in sight. The room Banks took was clean and quiet, and the small, friendly diner next door served a good steak, though he would probably have had to travel a long way for a decent bottle of wine to accompany it. Instead, he settled for a jug of cheap Californian burgundy.

Around two in the morning, unable to sleep, Banks got up and walked outside. The desert nights were cool, but in

August that meant the temperature went down from about anywhere between 85 and 100 to 75 or so, still T-shirt weather for a British tourist. Even so, Banks found he needed his light windcheater that night as he struck out from the motel across the road into open desert. The stars shone bright and clear, more than he had ever seen before, so close he felt he could reach out and grab a handful, along with a yellow sickle moon. Not for the first time, Banks wished he could recognise more constellations than Orion and the Big Dipper. He could see the Milky Way and trails of distant nebulae between the stars. Was that the Crab Nebula overhead? In front of him, he could just make out the saw-toothed silhouette of a mountain range in the far distance.

He hadn't really known what to expect from his journey, but that night he realised there *was* something he wanted, something ineffable, inchoate, and suddenly it didn't seem so unbelievable that he might get it from a place such as this. He felt an odd tingle of anticipation, as if he were on the verge of what he had been waiting for, his revelation, his epiphany.

Someone had once told him that there were places you could go that would change you, which was probably why so many kids in the sixties set off for India or Kathmandu. It might be a country, a culture, religion, or perhaps a certain kind of landscape – the ocean, mountains, a desert. It might be a place associated with a powerful childhood experience, or with a dream. Sometimes, perhaps, you just didn't know. But it changed you.

Banks had been having a dream from time to time since his childhood, and it stayed with him. He was swimming underwater through waving fronds that tried to grab him and pull him down. The dark rocks below terrified him with their shifting shapes, and with the thought of what lurked in the depths between them, through underwater tunnels that led to other tunnels, narrower, deeper and darker. He was running out of air, his lungs straining, his strength failing, when he finally broke the water's surface and found himself on the edge of paradise. The damnable thing was that he couldn't remember anything about it. It was a special place, he knew that much, one that had the power to change him and heal him, but all he remembered was the journey, the darkness, the fear and agony of his bursting lungs, and that blissful moment when water ceased to be water and became air, when darkness became light and the white sand led . . . somewhere green and pure.

For so long he seemed to have been struggling in the dark, and in that desert night, when the motel's blinking red neon was nothing but a dot on the horizon, he found an epiphany of a kind. But it was nothing momentous. No road to Damascus, no lightning strike of revelation or enlightenment, as he had hoped for. First, he was aware only of the silence when he stopped, a silence unlike any he had ever known – nothing rustling, no animal sounds, no birdsong, no distant cars or lorries. Nothing. Just the smell of dry earth and the tall, still silhouettes of the saguaro cacti, arms reaching out and up, all around him.

The epiphany, when it came, was nothing more than a simple, fleeting ripple of happiness that went through him as a light, cool breeze might brush one's skin on a hot day. He felt as if something had clicked into place, like the final number of a combination lock, the tumblers finding their positions. That was all. He wasn't even sure whether it was something opening or closing, but he knew that he would be OK, that he *was* OK, that he could deal with things. His problems didn't matter in the midst of the desert night – the myriad stars above and grains of sand under his feet. He would still hurt. He would still carry the burden of his past mistakes. He would still feel the deep ache of loss and betrayal and guilt and horror. Paradise would always remain just beyond his reach. But he would go on somehow. Perhaps not in the same way he had been, doing the job he did, but somehow. Future uncertain. Prospects unclear. End always near. He remembered thinking that he was a long, long way from home, but, oddly enough, he didn't feel so far away at that moment.

Banks took one more look at the dark range of peaks on the horizon, then he turned and walked back to the blinking pinpoint of light. He slept like a baby until the blinding sunlight found him through a chink in the curtains at nine o'clock the following morning. After a huge breakfast of eggs and ham and hash browns at the diner, he checked out and headed for the interstate to Los Angeles with Vieux Farke Touré's 'Slow Jam' playing loudly through the car stereo.

The satnav got Annie to Leeds easily enough after work on Tuesday, but once off Otley Road it had a difficult time negotiating the twists and turns of Headingley, and she found herself getting more and more frustrated. That it was the tail-end of rush hour didn't help, either, but she wanted to time her arrival for roughly that period between when people get home from work and before they go out again for the evening. She knew that Tracy Banks worked at Waterstone's on Albion Street in the city centre, and that her hours were probably irregular, but she didn't think the shop stayed open particularly late.

The preliminary gun report hadn't told them much except

that they were dealing with a 9mm Smith & Wesson automatic, over twenty years old, and the serial number had been filed down. There were ways of recovering it, of course, but they would take time. As yet, too, there was no record of a registered owner. It would also take some time to run the weapon through the National Firearms Forensic Intelligence Database and check it for fingerprints to run through IDENT1.

If they wanted to know whether the gun had been used in the commission of a crime – which, of course, they did – it would have to be fired under controlled circumstances, and the bullet compared with the information in the Integrated Ballistics Identification System. If the result was positive, to be absolutely certain, the bullet would then have to be compared with the *actual* bullet and/or cartridge casing fired during the crime. Rush or not, this would all take time. There was no explanation yet of how the gun had come into Erin Doyle's possession, and Erin still wasn't talking. A boyfriend was everyone's natural assumption. Juliet Doyle had mentioned someone called 'Geoff', but Rose Preston had told the Leeds police that Erin's boyfriend was called 'Jaff'. An easy mistake to make if you didn't see it written down. Whoever he was, they hadn't got a line on him yet.

When the satnav told Annie that she had reached her destination, she was still two streets away, but she managed to find her way easily enough with the aid of a simple *A to Z*.

The house was the kind of property that had probably belonged to a moderately wealthy family between the wars, Annie guessed, as she took in the weathered sandstone, gables and slate roof. The lawn, surrounded by a low wall, was overgrown, weeds poking between the flagstones of the path. When Annie got out of the car, she noticed that it had just begun to rain, more of a fine drizzle really. So much for the late summer sunshine. She knocked at the door and a young woman she didn't recognise opened it. She was wearing oval glasses with black rims, a short skirt, black tights and a black T-shirt emblazoned with the logo 'Scars on 45', a rock band, Annie guessed. Her light brown hair was tied in a ponytail.

Annie introduced herself and showed her warrant card. The girl said her name was Rose Preston and asked her in as if a visit from the police were the most natural thing in the world.

'I was just having my dinner, if that's all right,' Rose said.

'Fine,' said Annie, following her into the living room, where Rose picked up a fork and a bowl of pasta – probably microwaved – from the coffee table, and sat with her legs folded under her on the armchair opposite the TV, where *Emmerdale* had just begun.

'Sorry to interrupt your programme,' Annie said.

'Oh, that. It's nothing. Just company while I eat.' Rose picked up the remote from the arm of the sofa, pointed it at the TV set and pressed. Chastity Dingle disappeared in the midst of an angry tirade directed towards Paddy.

'I'd have thought you had more than enough company, sharing with two other girls,' Annie said, remembering her own student days.

'If they were ever here.'

'Anyway, that's what I've come to see you about. I'm looking for Tracy Banks. Is she home yet?'

Rose seemed confused. 'Tracy Banks, did you say? There's no one with that name lives here.'

Annie confirmed the address with Rose again. She was certain it was the same one that Harriet Weaver had given her the previous evening, though she could have transposed a number. The area was full of student housing. 'Are you sure?' she asked.

'There's Francesca Banks,' said Rose. 'Maybe it's her sister or something?'

'Or her middle name?' Annie suggested. She didn't think Tracy had a middle name, but it was possible. 'She's about five foot five, twenty-four, blonde hair to her shoulders, dark eyebrows. Has a degree in history from the University of Leeds, comes from Eastvale, works at Waterstone's. She grew up with Erin Doyle, the other girl who lives here.'

'That sounds like Francesca,' Rose said.

'Must be her middle name, then.'

'But it must be a while since you've seen her,' Rose added.

'What do you mean?'

'She got her hair cut short a few weeks ago and put a few coloured streaks in it. Pink. Purple. You know. Nothing permanent, but she looks different. She got a tattoo and a couple of piercings as well.'

'Piercings?'

'Yeah. Nothing drastic. Eyebrow and just below the lower lip.' Rose paused and smiled. 'I mean, there may be others she hasn't told me about, more intimate ones, but I don't think so.'

That didn't sound like the Tracy Banks Annie knew, a bright, sensible, hard-working young woman with good prospects, working at a temporary job in a bookshop until something more like a career came along. Banks was always so proud of her. Still, people change, and fashions, especially among the young, don't necessarily mean that much. Annie had worn some pretty weird clothes in her time, including torn jeans and a safety pin through her ear. Some of the nicest, most creative, intelligent people she had ever met had green mohawks, ragged T-shirts and rings though their noses. Even so, it was a bit of a shock to hear about Tracy's makeover. The new name, too. *Francesca*. What was all that about? Had she joined a cult or something?

'Is she here?' Annie asked.

'No, she's gone.'

'Gone? Where?'

'I don't know. I don't know anything. Nobody ever tells me anything.'

'Hold on a minute, Rose. What are you talking about?'

Rose put her bowl down on the table. 'I'm the new girl. Erin and Francesca have been friends for years. They grew up together. Jasmine left to get married, and I'm the new girl. I've only been here since just before Francesca had her hair done and all. I don't think I fit in.'

'Do you know where Tra . . . where Francesca is?'

'No.'

'When did she go out?'

'Last night.'

'Did she come home?'

'No. I haven't seen her since teatime yesterday, and I've been here all the time. I don't have a job yet.'

'So you're saying she went out yesterday evening and hasn't been back?'

'Yes. She came home from work, as usual. I told her the police had been to search the place, then she got all panicky and dashed off.'

'Is that unusual, or does she often stay out all night?'

'Well, it wouldn't be the first time, if you know what I mean.'

'Did she take anything with her? An overnight bag, or

something? You know, as if she were going away for a few days?'

'No. Just her ripped denim jacket and her tatty shoulder bag. She didn't even take a toothbrush. Mind you, the shoulder bag's probably big enough to get the kitchen sink in if you wanted to. I don't know what all she keeps in it.'

'And you're sure you've no idea where she went?'

'What's happening with Erin? Where is she?'

'Erin's fine. She's being cared for. You heard about her father?'

Rose nodded. 'On the news tonight. It's terrible. You shouldn't use those things on people, you know. They're for animals. Even that's cruelty.'

'I'm worried about Francesca,' said Annie. 'Are you sure you have no idea where she went, where she might be?'

'I think she might have gone to see Jaff.'

'Jaff?'

'Yes. Erin's boyfriend. To be honest, I think there was something going on there, if you know what I mean. I don't like to tell tales out of school, but I think maybe Francesca fancied him, too. You can tell about these things. There's been a bit of friction between them lately.'

'Erin and Francesca? This past week?'

'Yes. Before Erin went home.'

'So you think Erin might have been jealous of Francesca and this Jaff getting too close?'

'I think so. I can't be sure, but I think so. He's very handsome. I know I'd be jealous all the time if he was my boyfriend. Some hope of that.'

Annie leaned forward and clasped her hands on her knees. 'This is very important, Rose. At what point did Tracy, or Francesca, start to panic and decide to go out?'

'It was after she'd rung Erin's house in Eastvale.'

'Who did she talk to?'

'I don't know. She didn't talk to anyone, really. I just heard her ask if she was speaking to Mr Doyle, then she hung up in a hurry and dashed off.'

If Tracy had made the call to Erin's house at around seven o'clock yesterday evening, Annie thought, then almost certainly a police officer would have answered the phone, as the Doyle house was already under lock-down. Patrick Doyle was dead, Juliet was at Harriet Weaver's, and Erin herself was on police bail in a B&B near the castle. The officer who answered would have asked who was calling, and why. Something about that phone call had scared Tracy off. But why? What was she hiding? 'Had you already talked to her about Jaff?' Annie asked.

'Yes. She asked if I had mentioned him, or her, to the police.'

'And had you?'

'Why wouldn't I? I've got nothing to hide.'

But maybe Jaff and Tracy had, Annie thought. 'Is Jaff Erin's boyfriend's real name?' she asked.

'It's short for Jaffar. I don't know his last name.'

'Is he Asian?'

'Half Indian, or something.'

'Do you know where he lives?'

'Granary Wharf. But I don't know the address. It's an old converted warehouse with a restaurant on the ground floor. The three of us were walking past once, just when I'd decided to take the room. We'd been out celebrating with a drink somewhere near by. Anyway, Erin pointed it out, like she was really proud, you know. Showing off that her boyfriend had money.'

'And does he?'

'Seems to have.'

Granary Wharf was certainly a posh address. Even Annie had heard of it. Now was the time she should ring the station, she realised, and report her findings to Superintendent Gervaise. But if she did that, it would be out of her hands, beyond her control. If Banks's daughter was in trouble, Annie wanted to see what she could do to nip it in the bud, if it wasn't already too late, and she couldn't do that with Gervaise holding her back. 'Do you mind if I have a quick look at Francesca's room while I'm here?' she asked.

'No skin off my nose. It's the second door on the left at the top of the landing.'

Annie climbed the stairs and opened the door. It was a spacious enough room, painted mauve and furnished like the usual student bedsit, with a desk and chair, bookcases, chest of drawers full of underwear and T-shirts, and a closet built into the wall, where Tracy hung her dresses, skirts, tops and jeans.

There was a compact CD player and a small stack of CDs – Florence and the Machine, Adele, Emmy the Great, Kaiser Chiefs, Arctic Monkeys, the Killers. Beside them stood a few books, mostly history, which had been Tracy's subject at university, and a few modern novels: *The Kite Runner*, *The Time Traveller's Wife*, *The Thirteenth Tale*. There was no sign of a computer or a mobile. If Tracy had a phone, as Annie was certain she must have, then she had taken it with her.

Annie opened the drawer on the bedside table and found some personal items: tampons, condoms, an old prescription for a yeast infection and some cheap jewellery. When she went back downstairs Rose was on the living-room couch, and the TV was on again. *EastEnders*. 'Do you happen to know Francesca's mobile number?' Annie asked.

'Sure.' Rose picked up her own mobile from the low coffee table and read out a number. Annie called. No response. She thanked Rose, then said goodnight and set off home for Harkside.

6

Banks sat in Vesuvio's tavern, at the table beside the door, with his back to the window, sipping his pint of Anchor Steam and examining the copy of *The Maltese Falcon* that he had just bought at City Lights next door. It was one of his favourite films, but he had never read the book. Hammett had written about San Francisco in the thirties, and apparently there were still places associated with him. Maybe Banks would offer to take Teresa to John's Bar & Grill, where Sam Spade had enjoyed his chops. Banks had read about it in the guidebook and knew the restaurant was still in business, and not too far from their hotel.

For now, though, he was visiting an old beatnik haunt on Columbus, and the man at the bar in the beret, talking to the frizzy-haired barmaid, looked as if he might have been there since Jack Kerouac's time. The bar had a high ceiling and an upper balcony, empty at that time of day. A screen behind the bar flashed random surreal images, and the walls were covered with old framed newspaper articles about San Francisco's history. Banks had walked all the way from Fisherman's Wharf, through North Beach, with its Italian cafés and wedding-cake houses, and the cold beer was going down nicely.

Los Angeles and his two-day drive up the Pacific Coast Highway were just memories now that he was in San

Francisco, near the end of his trip. His thoughts drifted from the book he was reading to that night in the desert, as they often had, to that strange fleeting kiss of happiness. At first it had surprised him that he was a stranger to it, that it was something he barely remembered feeling before, except perhaps once or twice as a child. He had always possessed too restless a nature, and restlessness precludes lasting happiness. He had never stopped to smell the flowers or listen to the ocean. And if he wasn't restless, he usually felt a kind of vague, mellow sadness punctuated by the occasional eruption of anger or irritation. There had been moments of bliss, of course, but they were infrequent and ephemeral, and he often wondered whether such a moment could ever be sustainable. Was that the nature of happiness? That it came and went like a breath of desert air? That it was something only definable by its absence? Or was it just *his* nature? He would probably never know. And what did it really matter, anyway?

Everything changes. Nothing changes. His revelation was that there was no revelation. To change his life in any significant way, he would have to make a leap of faith and accept such new tenets, new versions of the truth, cultivate new patterns of behaviour, bow to some authority, even. He would have to *believe*, and he didn't think he could do that. He didn't even think he wanted to.

So he would go on uncomfortably inhabiting his own skin, taking happiness (like that all so brief desert breeze) where he could find it, beauty where it revealed itself to him, and try not to dwell too much on his failures and losses. The count was way too high – Kay, Linda, Sandra, Annie, Michelle, Sophia. And if he did get a little maudlin and sentimental once in a while, so be it. He could revel in the

lovelorn wisdom of Dylan, Billie Holiday, Nick Cave and
Leonard Cohen with the best of them, and drink fine wine
or whisky till he fell asleep on the sofa with finely wrought
phrases about life's sadness and irony, love lost or unre-
quited, ringing in his ears. The rest of the time there was
Beethoven, Schubert, Bill Evans, Miles and Trane. And that
was about as much revelation and enlightenment as he was
likely to get in this lifetime, he decided.

Banks stretched like a cat in the sunlight coming through
the window and drank some Anchor Steam. A cigarette
would have gone down nicely, too, but they were a thing of
the past now, not just for him, but even for bars like this.
Kerouac and Ginsberg would be turning in their graves.
Eastvale seemed light years away, though Banks realised that
he was actually starting to look forward to going home. He
didn't miss the job, but he missed Annie, Winsome,
Gristhorpe, Hatchley, even Gervaise and Harry Potter. They
were the closest he had to friends outside his parents and
Brian and Tracy, whom he also missed. He missed his cottage
by the beck and woods, his CDs and DVDs. To hell with
Sophia, *la belle dame sans merci*. Let her grapple with her
own demons. He had had enough. Everything comes around.

But before he left for home tomorrow, he had a date with
a beautiful, interesting woman called Teresa. He finished his
pint and headed out on to Columbus, noticing the sign on
the corner: Jack Kerouac Alley. He plugged in his iPod,
which played a jaunty live version of the Grateful Dead's
'Scarlet Begonias' from Winterland, 1974, perfect for a beautiful day in San Francisco, then he walked down the hill and
bore right, through the lower end of Chinatown, across Union
Square towards his hotel.

★

'Christ, what on earth do you lot want this time?' Rose
Preston said when she opened the door to let the two men
in about an hour after Annie had left. She was just in the
middle of watching *Holby City*, which she did like, and she
really didn't want to be disturbed.

The two men exchanged puzzled glances.

'Sorry,' Rose said. 'It's all right. Come in. I just hope it
won't take long, that's all.'

'Ah, watching *Holby City*, I see,' said the taller of the two.
He had big shoulders and a tanned, shiny bald head, whereas
his colleague was slight and round shouldered, with wispy
ginger hair and a pale, almost albino, complexion. 'I don't
mind that myself, though it's a little gruesome for my taste
sometimes. Still, I wish I got to see it more often. But with
the hours on this job . . . Anyway, I'm DS Sandalwood, and
this here's my colleague, DC Watkins. Just pretend he's not
here.'

Sandalwood flashed a warrant card. Rose didn't even
bother to look. She'd seen enough of them over the past two
days to last her a lifetime. 'What is it this time?' she asked.
'Honest, there's nothing more I can tell you. I'm new here.
I don't really know the other girls.'

'What do you mean, "this time"?'

'Well, you can hardly fail to be aware that this isn't the
first visit I've had from the police lately, can you? Or don't
you even talk to each other?'

'The lines of communication do get jammed up once in
a while, I must admit,' said Sandalwood. As he spoke, Watkins
was busy poking around the room, looking under cushions
and in the sideboard drawers.

'What's he doing?' Rose asked.

'Like I said. Don't mind him. He can't help himself.

Habitual nosy parker. Stands him in good stead in this job
sometimes, though, I can tell you. Like a bloodhound. Any
chance of a cuppa, love?'

'I'd hoped you wouldn't be staying long enough.'

Watkins glanced towards Sandalwood from over by the
bookcase. 'She's got quite a gob on her, don't she?' he said.
He had a thin, squeaky voice, which reminded Rose of fingernails grating on a blackboard.

'Now, now,' said Sandalwood. 'There's no need to fall
out. Why don't you go and have a good shufti around the
rest of the house while the young lady here and I have a
little chinwag?'

Watkins grunted and left the room. Rose could hear him
climbing the stairs. 'What's he doing?' she said. 'He can't
just poke around wherever he wants like that. Where's your
warrant?' Rose made to go after Watkins, but she felt a grip
like a circus strongman's around her upper arm. First it hurt,
then her whole arm went numb. 'Ow!' she yelled, trying to
yank her arm away. 'Gerroff!'

But Sandalwood held on and dragged her down into a
chair none too gently. 'Sit down, young lady,' he said between
gritted teeth. 'And speak when you're spoken to.'

It was remarkable how still he remained through all this,
Rose thought, not moving a muscle that didn't need to be
moved. She straightened her glasses. 'Who are you?' she
said. 'You're not police. You're—'

The blow wasn't hard, but it was enough to stop Rose in
her tracks, and she hadn't seen it coming. 'Shut up,' said
Sandalwood, pointing a stubby finger at her. 'Just shut the
fuck up, or I'll get DC Watkins back down here and you'll
know what real pain is. He enjoys hurting people, Watkins
does. For me it's just a part of the job.'

Rose didn't need telling twice. Her arm was beginning to ache, and her cheek stung. She started to cry.

'And you can shut off the waterworks, too,' Sandalwood said. 'They won't get you anywhere with me.'

'What do you want?' Rose instinctively crossed her legs, aware that her skirt had ridden up and she was probably showing far too much thigh.

Sandalwood caught her gesture and laughed. 'It's all right, love,' he said. 'Don't worry. That's not what we're after, tempting as it looks.'

Rose flushed and curled her fists tight on her lap. She felt powerless and scared. If she'd had a gun, she would have shot Sandalwood right there and then. She could hear the other one, Watkins, moving about upstairs. He was in her room now, going through her things, and the thought made her flesh crawl.

'A couple of simple questions. Straight answers from you and we're gone,' said Sandalwood. 'Deal?'

Rose said nothing, just stared down at her fists, watching her knuckles turning white.

'Deal?' Sandalwood said again.

Rose nodded. All she wanted was for them to be gone. The doctors were working desperately over a bloody patient in *Holby City*. Suddenly it didn't seem as exciting as it once had.

'Where's Erin Doyle?'

'You must know,' said Rose. 'It's been on telly and in all the papers. She's in Eastvale. Probably in jail now.'

Sandalwood nodded encouragingly, as if the question had been a test and Rose had managed to pass. 'Do you know a bloke called Jaff? Paki bastard?'

'I've met him a few times.'

'He's been shagging this Erin bint, right?'

'They've been going out together, yes. You don't need to be so crude.'

'Now we're getting somewhere. Where is he? Where's Jaff?'

'I don't know.'

'You'd better not be lying.'

'Why would I lie? I hardly know him. Like I said, I've met him once or twice. He's Erin's boyfriend.'

'You ever been to his place?'

'Never.'

'Well, we've just dropped by, and he's not there. The bloke down the hall says he scarpered with some woman last night. Seemed in a bit of a hurry. Any idea who that is or why he'd do a moonlight?'

'No.'

Watkins came back and stood in the doorway, shaking his head, then he held up three fingers. Sandalwood gave him a nod then turned back to Rose. 'DC Watkins tells me there are three of you living here. Who's the third?'

'Francesca. Francesca Banks. But I think her real name's Tracy.'

'Francesca but her real name's Tracy? What the fuck are you talking about?'

'I don't know.' Rose put her hands to her face and started crying again. 'You're scaring me.'

'Tell me about this Francesca.'

'She knew Jaff, too. I think she fancied him. She disappeared. She went out last night and she hasn't come back. Please go away. Please leave me alone. I don't know anything.'

'Is she the woman Jaff scarpered with? Don't lie to me this time.'

'She might be. She's got short blonde hair with a few coloured streaks. She was wearing jeans and a denim jacket.'

'Stud under her lower lip and a ring through her eyebrow?'

'That's right.'

Sandalwood looked at Watkins. 'That's the one that was with Jaff. Where are they?'

'I don't know!' said Rose, in exasperation. 'Don't you understand? She's gone. Probably with Jaff. That's what the policewoman kept asking me. But I told her the same. I don't know. I don't know.'

'What policewoman?'

'The one that was here just before you.'

'We don't know nothing about any policewoman.'

'Look, I don't know what's going on. Honest. It's none of my business. I think Erin's in jail, and I don't know where Francesca is. Or Jaff. I don't understand any of this. All I wanted was a room I could afford. This is all so *not* my problem.'

'Seems like it's very much your problem at the moment, young lady,' said Sandalwood, looking around the room. 'Seeing as you're the only one here, apart from us.'

'Don't! Please, don't,' said Rose, holding her hands over her face again and sobbing. But instead of the blow she was expecting, or the sound of a gun cocking, the next thing she heard was the front door slamming. She put her hands down and opened her eyes. Were they really gone? Could it be true? She turned off *Holby City*, no longer interested in doctors and bleeding patients, and checked every room. They'd left a bit of a mess upstairs, but they were definitely gone.

Well, that was the bloody limit, Rose decided. She went to her room and threw what few clothes and books she had into a suitcase, packed her toiletries and make-up into her holdall, then paused for a moment to look around and check that she hadn't forgotten anything. She hadn't. She had obviously had the misfortune to end up in a house full of bloody lunatics, and her nerves couldn't stand it any more. She would post the rent she owed later. Right now, if she hurried, she might just be able to catch a train or a bus back to Oldham and her mum and dad. At worst, she could phone home and her dad would drive over and pick her up. He'd complain, and he'd lay on the I-told-you-so guilt trip long and thick, but he'd do it. Anything had to be better than stopping a moment longer in this madhouse, she thought. Then she slammed the door behind her and pushed her key through the letterbox.

Annie was sitting cross-legged on her living-room floor, focusing on her breathing, letting the thoughts come and go like bubbles, holding on to none of them, her mind fixed on her breathing. *In, out. In, out.*

A knock at the door broke her concentration. Irritated, she glanced at her watch. After ten. Who would come calling at this time? The spell was broken anyway, so she got up slowly, aware of her knees cracking from lack of practice, and answered. It was Nerys Powell, the female AFO.

'What are you doing here?' Annie asked. 'You shouldn't be here. Chambers will go spare.'

Nerys held up her hands. 'I know. I know,' she said. 'And I'm sorry. But can I talk to you? Please? Just for a minute or two. There's no reason Mr Chambers has to know about it, is there?'

'How did you find out where I live?'

'I've got a friend in Human Resources.'

'Who?'

'Just a friend.'

'I could find out easily enough, you know.'

'Why do you say that? What do you mean?'

Annie sighed. 'Nothing,' she said. 'Just that you shouldn't be here. It's inappropriate.'

'What are you so afraid of? Being seen with me? If that's the case, the quicker you let me in the better. Besides, we're miles from Eastvale. I know it's late, and I'm sorry. I did come earlier but there was nobody home. I've been wandering around getting lost, trying to pluck up the courage to come back. I stopped for a couple of drinks. I just want to talk to you, that's all. Nobody has to know.'

'I don't know. I shouldn't.' Annie chewed on her lip and thought for a moment, still disoriented from being snapped out of her meditation. Nerys certainly didn't appear drunk. Then she made a snap decision and stood aside. 'OK, you can come in. But just for a couple of minutes.'

Nerys entered the room. 'Cosy,' she said, looking around.

'Just another word for cramped.'

'Bijou.'

'Another word for too small.'

Nerys laughed. 'No, I like it. Seriously.'

'Sit down. Can I get you a cup of tea or something. Coffee?'

'Nothing, thanks.'

'You sure?'

'My body is a temple.'

'Well, I'm having a glass of wine.'

'In that case . . .' said Nerys.

Annie went into the kitchen and took a bottle of Pinot Grigio from the fridge. She felt uncomfortable with Nerys's visit and knew she shouldn't be talking to her, or even listening, but she was feeling rebellious after today's excitement. She was also frustrated by her visit to Tracy's house in Leeds, and her later one to Jaff's flat in Granary Wharf. It had been easy enough to locate. There had been nobody home there, of course, and one of the neighbours had informed her, before slamming his door in her face, that the police had already been around asking questions, that he had told them all he knew, and that he was damned if he was going to repeat it all again to her.

So she decided she might as well lend her ear to Nerys for a while. *You never know,* she told herself, *you might even learn something.* She opened the wine and took it through to the living room along with two glasses. Nerys was on her knees by the small selection of CDs on the lower shelves of the bookcase. She was wearing blue jeans that showed a bit too much arse-crack and a light windcheater over a black T-shirt, none of which did much to disguise the muscles or hide the bulge at her waist when she stood up. Probably pure muscle, too, Annie guessed. 'See anything you like?' she asked.

Nerys glanced over at her. 'Nope,' she said. 'But then I'm not much of a one for music. Not like your boss, I hear.'

'Alan? Yes, he does have a bit of a reputation. I can't say I've got a clue what he's listening to half the time. Some of it sounds pretty good, but some of it, well, to put it frankly, it just sounds like a bull with a pain in its testicles to me.'

Nerys laughed and accepted her wine before sitting down. She was a good three inches shorter than Annie, though much stockier, and her hair was so short and spiky that it resembled a military crew cut. Her eyes were green. 'Cheers,' she said, holding out her glass.

Annie clinked hers against it. 'Cheers.'

'He's got quite a reputation in other areas, too, around County HQ, your DCI,' said Nerys.

'Oh? What do you mean?'

'Bit of a cowboy. Likes to do things his own way.'

'I suppose so. But don't we all, if we think ours is the right way?'

'True enough. It's so hard to be certain, though, isn't it? I'm more used to following orders. The Firearms Cadre is very discipline oriented.'

'I suppose it has to be,' said Annie. 'But that wouldn't suit Alan, you're right. Still, I don't suppose it was Alan Banks you came to talk about?'

'In a way, it is,' said Nerys. 'Mmm, this is nice.'

Annie shrugged. 'Just cheap Italian plonk.'

Nerys stood up again and walked over to a framed watercolour of Eastvale Castle in the evening light. 'That's good,' she said. 'Whoever painted it really caught the light at that time of a winter evening.'

'Thank you,' said Annie.

Nerys's jaw dropped. 'You mean . . .? You? I never dreamed.' She smiled. 'Honest?'

'Honest,' said Annie, feeling herself blush. 'Why would I lie? It's all right. Why should you know, anyway? It's just a hobby, that's all.'

'But you're so *good*. So talented. Have you ever thought—'

'Look, Nerys, I appreciate the compliment and all, but can you just get to the point. I'm sorry, I don't mean to appear rude, but . . .'

Nerys sat down again. 'No. No. Of course. You're right. I suppose I'm just nervous, that's all. I tend to blether on a bit when I'm nervous.'

'Why should you be nervous?'

'Well, you're a DI and I'm just a lowly PC.'

'You're hardly lowly. Besides, you're the one with the gun.'

'I'm not carrying. Honest.' She held her arms out. 'Want to check?'

'The point?' said Annie.

Nerys finally let her arms drop, sat back down in the chair and seemed to relax a little. She ran her finger around the rim of her glass. 'That stuff at the meeting yesterday, about Mrs Doyle asking for DCI Banks. Is it true?'

'Yes, it's true,' said Annie. 'They're old friends. Neighbours.'

'Would he have gone?'

'I think so. Probably. But he's not here.'

'Where is he?'

'America. A long way away.'

Nerys took a sip of wine. 'Pity he wasn't here. It would have saved us all a hell of a lot of trouble.'

'Not what Chambers thinks.'

'Chambers is an arsehole.' Nerys put her hand to her mouth. 'Sorry. I shouldn't have said that in front of you.'

Annie couldn't help but laugh. 'No, you shouldn't,' she said. 'But you hit the nail right on the head.'

'I understand you worked for him once?'

'For my sins. You know a lot.'

'When the shit hits the fan like this, I make it my business to know as much as I can.'

Annie raised an eyebrow. 'Your friend in Human Resources again?'

Nerys grinned. 'Another one, this time. Records.'

'My, my, but you must have a lot of friends.'

'No. That's the problem. I don't. I've never felt so alone. So isolated.'

'But that's ridiculous,' said Annie. 'You AFO teams have a reputation for being close and tight knit. Your lives depend on one another.'

'It's true enough on the job,' said Nerys. 'It's our training. But it doesn't always work that way off duty.' She leaned forward in her chair and looked Annie in the eye. The direct-ness and intensity of her gaze were disconcerting. 'Look, I'm a woman in a man's world. More than that. I'm a gay woman in a man's shooting club. You might think they treat me like one of the lads, but they look at me more as a freak.'

'I'm sure that's not the case.'

Nerys's upper lip curled in a sneer. 'What do you know?'

'Nothing, I suppose,' said Annie. 'What got you into it in the first place, then? I mean the Firearms Cadre?'

'I didn't really know what I wanted to do. I mean, in the force. I did all the courses, surveillance, vehicle pursuit, worked undercover, even traffic. I was all over the map.'

'And?'

'I suppose it was my dad, really. He was a Para. Real *macho*. Got killed in Iraq two and a half years ago. Another sniper. Dad was really a perfectionist, a technician. I grew up around guns, the smell of them, the mechanics. Christ, I could dismantle and reassemble a Heckler and Koch or a Parker-Hale in the dark, going by sound and touch alone.'

'That sounds like a useful skill,' said Annie.

'Well, you never know.'

'But you never thought of this before, when you first joined?'

'Not really. It wasn't as if I wanted to follow in my dad's footsteps. Not until he got killed. Then it all seemed to make sense. And I'm good at it. They fast-tracked me. I'm the youngest on the unit apart from Warby.' They let the silence stretch for a while, as Nerys no doubt thought about her dead father and Annie thought about Banks. Where was he? Los Angeles? Reno? Tucson? She knew he was somewhere in the American south-west. She wished she were there with him. 'I don't want to be on Firearms Cadre for ever, though,' Nerys said.

'Ambitious?'

'A bit, I suppose. I'd like to work in counter-terrorism eventually.'

'Sounds challenging.'

'I like a challenge. That's also why I'm worried about . . . you know . . . all this . . .'

'A big blot on your copybook?'

'Yes.'

'There's probably not an officer in the service who hasn't made a mistake. I mean, there's some people would say DCI Banks is a walking disaster area. Our friend Chambers, for a start.'

'What's he really like?'

'Chambers?'

'Yes. He reminds me of that fat comedian with the bowler hat, the one in those old black-and-white films.'

'Oliver Hardy?'

'That's the one. But seriously. Do you think he supports gay rights? Has a soft spot for cuddly lesbians?'

Anne couldn't help but laugh. She topped up their wine glasses. The level in Nerys's was much lower than hers, she noticed. 'No, I shouldn't think so. He's more the kind who thinks every woman he meets can't wait to drop her knickers for him. And he probably believes that all a lesbian needs to cure her is a good stiff twelve inches of Reginald Chambers. Though my guess is it's closer to three or four inches.'

Nerys laughed. 'But what do you really think about him?'

Annie swirled the wine in her glass, then drank some more. She didn't like remembering her time with Chambers; the memories weren't good ones. 'Let's just say we didn't get along too well and leave it at that, shall we?'

'So what can I expect? He's going to try to crucify us, me and Warby, isn't he?'

'Oh, for crying out loud,' said Annie. 'Don't be so bloody melodramatic. He's not that bad. There are plenty worse than him around. I said we didn't get along. That's all. It was probably as much my fault as his. It wasn't exactly my dream posting. I don't get on with very many people, if you must know.'

'So I've heard.'

'Why doesn't that surprise me?' Annie checked her watch. 'Look, I hate to rush you, but if you've finished . . .' There was no way she would be able to get back to her meditation now, not after this disruption, not to mention the wine, but at least she could watch TV or something and veg out. Almost anything would be better than this.

'I'm sorry,' said Nerys, her lower lip quivering. 'I didn't mean to spoil your evening . . . I mean, I just wanted to know if I could count on you, if you're on my side. I'm sorry to waste your time. I'm just worried, that's all.'

Then Annie saw tears in her eyes and softened. She hated herself for it, but she was a sucker for tears. Worse than any man she'd ever met. 'Come on,' she said, pouring more wine. It was going down quickly; the bottle was almost empty. 'Pull yourself together, Nerys. Look, Chambers isn't going to crucify you. After all, it wasn't you who fired the taser. He's an arsehole, yes, and a bully and a male chauvinist pig, but as far as I know he plays straight. At worst, he'll play up to the media and give them what they want. He's a PR man at heart, not a copper. But he's not going to fit you up, for crying out loud. He'll discover the facts and play it by the book, obnoxious bastard as he is.'

'But that's just it, isn't it? That's the problem. The facts. What are they? And doesn't it all depend on how someone else interprets them? What version will the media want? There could be as many different stories of what happened on Monday morning as there were people present.'

Annie knew that was true. She had once seen a film called *Rashomon*, one of her father's favourites, which told the same story from several different viewpoints. Same facts. Different stories. 'Perhaps,' she admitted. 'But there's nothing you can do about that. And he's got his team from Greater Manchester to keep him on the straight and narrow. He's not a law unto himself, much as he might like to think so.'

'I just need to know what to expect, so I can be prepared. What did he do to you when you worked with him?'

'Didn't your friend in Human Resources tell you?'

'Nobody really knows but you.'

Annie took a deep breath and followed it with a draught of wine. 'It was a long time ago,' she said. 'Seven, eight years or thereabouts.' *And why does it keep coming back to haunt me?* she wondered. She thought she had finally seen the end of Janet Taylor, Lucy Payne and the Chameleon case over a year ago, when it had come into her life again with a vengeance. Now Chambers was back. 'Chambers himself didn't do anything to me,' she went on. 'Back then he was simply a lazy, lecherous, time-serving arsewipe who got others to do his dirty work for him while he got all the glory. Whatever glory there is in a job like that. Mostly he got his jollies from what he saw as his vindication in the gutter press. He always swayed with the wind of public opinion.'

'Why didn't he retire when he'd put in his twenty-five? I heard he was practically living on the golf course.'

'The reorganisation gave him a new lease on life, a renewed purpose. More power. Now he just seems to want to put as many coppers away as he can before he retires. But it's not as if some of them don't deserve it, and like I said, he's not bent. He plays by the book.'

'But he has an agenda?'

'Oh, yes. With Chambers, you're always guilty until you're proved guilty. Especially if the newspapers say so.'

'So I'm right to be worried?'

'The two cases are very different,' said Annie. 'PC Janet Taylor, the one I was working on, killed a notorious serial killer who had just hacked her partner to pieces in front of her eyes and was about to do the same to her. Unfortunately, a civilian called John Hadleigh, who had shot a burglar in his home about three hundred miles away, was convicted of murder around the same time. It would have appeared bad if a police officer had simply walked away scot free after killing someone. End of story.'

'Even a serial killer? The Chameleon? I know about that case. I've studied it.'

'Then you'll know what I'm talking about,' said Annie. 'But you had to be there to understand the political climate and the media circus. Anyway, I convinced the CPS to lower the charge against Janet Taylor to manslaughter. You know the rest.'

'So it was politics? This woman, Janet Taylor, was a sacrificial lamb?'

'Hardly a lamb, but yes. Partly. It always is politics where the Chambers of the world are concerned. You should know that. The higher you climb up the greasy pole, the more desperate you are to keep your grip.'

Nerys swallowed and sat for a moment, apparently contemplating what Annie had told her. 'Can I count on your support?' she asked finally, in a small voice.

Annie spluttered on a mouthful of wine and patted her chest as she coughed. 'Christ, what on earth do you mean by that?' she said when she could talk again.

'I told you. I feel so alone. So isolated. I've got nobody to talk to.'

'You're not alone. You've got your team beside you, your boss behind you. Besides, it's not you Chambers is after, is it? It's PC Warburton. He fired the taser.'

'Don't kid yourself. It's all of us. If Warby hadn't tasered the bastard, I'd have shot him. Or one of the lads coming through the back would have.'

'Was it that bad?'

'Uh-huh. It was dark. The hall light bulb blew when Warby turned it on. You don't expect something like that. We knew there was a loaded gun in the house. We were already on high-tension alert.'

'Nobody even thought you'd have to go in that way,' said Annie. 'And nobody could have known the light bulb would choose that particular moment to blow.'

'We have to be prepared for eventualities like that. Act as if we *are* going in.' Annie topped up their wine. The bottle was empty now. 'It was dark,' Nerys went on. 'You could cut the tension with a knife. Like Warby said at the meeting, we didn't know what might have happened since we were called in. They weren't talking to us. The girl could have lost it, grabbed the gun. Anything. When he came out of the kitchen, Patrick Doyle, he was just a silhouette with what could've been a raised sword or baseball bat in his hand, even a shotgun. Warby just reacted first, that's all. I might be the best marksman, but Warby's got the fastest reaction time of us all.' She smiled to herself. 'Would've made a great gunslinger in the old west. Fastest draw in the Wiske, we call him.'

'Why was the walking stick raised?'

'He was angry. Doyle. I think he'd already been having a row with his daughter. They'd been absorbed in their own little drama – and when we broke his door down and he heard that bloody almighty racket, well, people don't take kindly to things like that, do they? He was just mad at us, that's all, waving his stick about. Understandable. I don't suppose he knew we were armed. He was just expecting an old mate to drop by – DCI Banks – not armed officers in full protective gear. He couldn't see us, either. The light was on in the kitchen, so his eyes wouldn't have adjusted that quickly. We probably looked like Martians in the darkness of the hall. It's not something you expect, is it?'

'It certainly isn't,' said Annie.

'So you know whose side public opinion is going to be on?'

'I can take a guess.'

Nerys shook her head slowly, then finished her wine. 'It's not fair. You can do all the training scenarios you want,' she said. 'Just like Dirty Harry walking through a movie set shooting at cardboard cutouts. But when it's real, it's different. In training you *know* you can't get shot or cut. But when it's real . . . You don't aim for an arm or a leg. Warby did the right thing. I'll stick by him. I just want it to go down that way. I want them to see it for what it really was, mistakes and all, not set out to crucify one of us or sacrifice us to the press or public opinion. We do a necessary job and a damn good one, but it's messy sometimes, and for better or for worse, people need us. But that doesn't mean they want to acknowledge us or give us medals. They certainly don't have to like us. Mostly they want to forget we exist, or to bury us.'

'I can't control that,' Annie said. 'But there are enough checks and balances. I'm still sure they'll do a good job, remain impartial.'

'I wish I had your faith. I'd better go.'

Annie stood up, but not so fast that she seemed as eager to get rid of Nerys as she really was. The thought crossed her mind that Nerys had drunk the lion's share of the wine. Was she going to drive? Perhaps Annie should offer her a bed for the night? But she didn't want to do that. Best just leave the subject alone entirely and not even ask about driving. Maybe it was irresponsible of her, but the alternative was a minefield of complications. 'OK,' she said. 'I hardly need see you to the door. It's not far. But I will.'

Nerys smiled. 'Thanks.'

'You OK?'

'I'm fine.' Nerys opened the door. 'For what it's worth,' she said, pausing and resting her hand lightly on Annie's arm, 'I've heard good things about you, and I've seen you around County HQ a few times. I always rated you. I thought you were all right. I liked you from the start.' She leaned forward and quickly pecked Annie on the cheek then glanced down shyly at the doormat.

Annie thought Nerys was looking at her legs, and she shifted awkwardly on her feet. Suddenly, she felt self-conscious that she was wearing only the black leggings and baggy white T-shirt she had put on for meditation and yoga. The T-shirt came down only as far as her hips, and she felt exposed. 'Look, Nerys,' she said. 'I'm flattered and all. I don't know . . . you know . . . what ideas you've got about me or anything, what you might have heard, but I'm not . . . you know . . .'

'Oh, no. I know you're not gay. It's OK. Don't worry. I wasn't making a pass. Honest. Anyway, you're not really my type. I just said I think you're all right, that's all.'

'Appearances can be deceptive.'

'I take my chances where I find them.'

When she had gone, Annie closed the door and leaned back against it. *Not my type.* What had Nerys meant by that? Should she feel insulted? What was wrong with her? Was it even true? Nerys's actions had seemed to belie her words; she had definitely been flirting at times.

Annie was also struck by the troublesome thought that if Nerys Powell, Warburton and the rest of the AFO team were going to be sacrificed on the bloody altar of public opinion, then the detectives who were supposed to have briefed them thoroughly would be lucky if they got to walk away. The walking stick. The dicky heart. Should Annie or Gervaise somehow have been able to find out about those and warn the team that went in? And whether they could have or not, would they be expected to have done so? Because that was ultimately all that mattered: what Chambers and public opinion thought they *should* have done, not what had actually happened, or why. These were not comforting thoughts.

Annie locked the door, opened another bottle of wine and settled down to a nature documentary about elephants on BBC2.

★

Banks offered to pay the bill, but Teresa would have none of it.

'My country, my treat,' she said.

In the end, there was nothing he could do but capitulate. They had enjoyed a marvellous dinner at an intimate Italian restaurant she had chosen in North Beach, and the last thing he wanted to do now was spoil the mood with an argument over the bill. 'Thank you,' he said. 'It was a great choice. Wonderful.'

'Somehow, I think the company helps, don't you,' she said, giving the maître d' a quick smile as he discreetly whisked away the tray.

Banks shared the last of the wine between them and set the bottle down on the red tablecloth. 'Yes,' he said. 'Yes, it certainly does.'

'What's wrong?' Teresa said. 'You suddenly sound sad.'

'Do I?' Banks shrugged. 'Maybe because it's my last night here.'

'You mustn't think that way.'

'I mustn't?'

'No, of course not.' The waiter returned with the credit card receipt. Teresa added a tip and signed it with a flourish. Then she picked up her purse. 'Let me just visit the powder room,' she said, 'then I want to show you something.'

Banks nodded. While she was away, he sipped his wine and glanced at the slightly garish, commercial painting of Lake Como on the wall opposite him. Annie wouldn't like it, he thought, finding it odd that he should suddenly think of Annie when she was thousands of miles away. Maybe it *was* time to go home. But he was certainly enjoying his evening with Teresa. She was recently divorced, she had told him over dinner, with grown-up kids and grandchildren, and she worked as a child psychologist back in Boston. This trip was a present to herself on her decree absolute coming through, and an excuse to visit her family. She was also, she told him, thinking of moving permanently to California and had been making a few exploratory calls regarding jobs and accommodation.

The little restaurant bar was to the right of Banks, and he could see out of the corner of his eye the rows of bottles gleaming. Should he suggest a cognac? Perhaps it would be best to wait until they got to the hotel bar. After all, Teresa had already paid the bill here. And there was something she wanted to show him.

Teresa took his arm as they walked out on the quiet side street and made their way towards Columbus, busy and brightly lit, past the Condor on the intersection with Broadway. Instead of taking Grant, with its arches, pagodas, restaurants and cheap souvenir shops, they walked down Stockton, a street of small grocery stores with piles of exotic vegetables and dried goods out front. Even at ten o'clock it was still crowded with shoppers haggling over their purchases and testing the quality, spilling from the sidewalk on to the road. Banks remembered his old sergeant in London, Ozzy Albright, telling him that San Francisco had the biggest Chinatown outside of China itself. They had been in the London Chinatown at the time, much smaller, during his last case down there in 1985. It was a case that had come back to haunt him just before he came away, as such things often did, which was why he thought of it now. You might have to wait a lifetime for justice, but sometimes you got it in the end. Like karma.

Teresa was chatting away at his side, and Banks realised he hadn't been listening, had been drifting into times past. 'Where did you say we were going?' he asked.

She gave him a sharp glance. 'I didn't,' she said. 'It's a surprise. I told you.'

'Right.'

Soon they left the crowds behind. There were fewer shops and the street became darker. 'This is the Stockton Tunnel we're walking on,' Teresa said. 'And what we want is . . .' She looked around her, as if verifying something with her memory. 'Over here.' She pointed to a small alley over to their right atop the tunnel off Bush Street, running parallel to Stockton. It was called Burritt Street, Banks noticed as they approached. 'Sorry,' Teresa said. 'It's been a long time.'

'What is it?' Banks asked. 'Are you leading me down a dark alley?'

Teresa laughed. 'Not very far down,' she said. 'It's here. Look.'

And she pointed to a plaque on the wall. Banks could just about read it in the ambient street light. ON APPROXI-MATELY THIS SPOT MILES ARCHER, PARTNER OF SAM SPADE, WAS DONE IN BY BRIGID O'SHAUGHNESSY.

Banks stopped and stared. So this was the place where it happened. He turned to face Teresa and grinned.

'Well, you did say you were a detective,' she said. 'I just thought you might find it interesting.'

'I do. I've just started reading the book, too. I'd never realised. I mean, I know the story isn't true, but the city is so vivid in the book, almost a character in its own right. I never thought I'd . . . I'm stuck for words.' He read the plaque again. 'But it gives away the ending.'

'Yes, it does, rather, doesn't it? But is that so important?'

'I've never thought so,' said Banks. 'Besides, I've already seen the movie, and so far the book is following pretty closely.'

'I think you'll find it was the other way around. Here,'

Teresa said, fumbling in her purse. 'Stand right next to it. I'm going to take your picture.'

Banks stood. First came the flickering of the anti-red-eye, then the flash itself. While Banks was still blinded by the light, a voice came from the end of the alley.

'Would you like me to take one of the two of you together?'

By the time Banks could see again, Teresa had handed her camera to the man, whose wife, or girlfriend, stood looking on, smiling, and she took her place next to Banks, resting her head on his shoulder by the plaque. The camera flashed again. The man checked the display to see that it had come out all right and handed the camera back to Teresa, who thanked him.

'How did you know he wouldn't just run off with your camera?' Banks asked, as they went down the steps beside the tunnel.

'Oh, don't be such a cynic. You have to have a bit of trust in people sometimes or it's hardly worth living.'

'I suppose so,' said Banks.

'Besides, they were walking along hand in hand. People like that aren't usually petty thieves.'

Banks laughed. 'Maybe you'd make a good cop after all,' he said.

Teresa smiled. 'Surely it's just common sense.'

They continued down Stockton Street, crossed Union Square and walked along Geary back to the hotel. A cable-car bell dinged up Powell towards the Mark Hopkins, where Banks had drunk his martini on his first night in the city, and a crowd was coming out of the Geary Street theatre as they passed. They were staging Noël Coward's *Brief Encounter*, Banks noticed. There were a few of the regular street people around – Banks recognised the black man in rags and the old woman – but nobody bothered them.

When they got to the Monaco, Banks asked, 'How about a quick nightcap in the bar?'

Teresa paused, still holding on to his arm. 'No, I don't think so,' she said. 'Too many people. They would spoil the mood. Too noisy. I've got a bottle of good Napa Valley Cabernet Sauvignon in my room. Why don't you come up with me and we'll have that nightcap?'

There was no mistaking the promise in her eyes. Banks swallowed. 'Well,' he said, 'that would just about make the perfect end to the perfect last day of a perfect holiday.'

7

'Jaff?'

'Yeah, babe, what is it?'

'What exactly is going on?' Tracy asked. 'I mean, why are we doing this? Why are we on the run? Why do you want to go to London and get across the Channel so badly?'

'It's better you don't know too much,' Jaff said. 'Like I said, it's my problem, not yours. I'm only grateful you've found me a place to lie low for a few days while I get things in motion down there.'

'But it's my problem, too, now,' said Tracy. 'Besides, I won't say anything to anyone. I won't talk. We're in it together now, aren't we? I've helped you so far, but I'm still in the dark. Sometimes you make me feel like a prisoner. Maybe I can do more to help.'

'You're not a prisoner. We just have to be extra careful, that's all, and I know how to do it. It's better if you listen to me. You've already been a great help, Fran. Don't think I'm not grateful. That's why I don't want to burden you with too much knowledge. You know what curiosity did, don't you? Just believe me. It's safer this way. OK? Now come on, babe . . .'

'Oh, Jaff, no, not now, Jaff. Not again. We just . . .'

But before Tracy could say another word, Jaff had pulled her towards him and clamped his lips firmly on hers. She offered only token resistance. He was a good kisser; she had to admit that. And the rest of their lovemaking was pretty spectacular, too.

When they had finished, Jaff seemed to drift off to sleep again, and Tracy found herself returning to her growing concerns. This was the start of their second day in her father's house, and she was beginning to feel a little uneasy about being there. She was hoping that Jaff would get bored with being in the country and decide they should leave for London soon. He had already made a number of long phone calls and seemed to sound pleased with the way things were going down there. Whatever those 'things' were.

It had been OK at first, just a bit of harmless fun and a chance to vent her spleen against her absentee father, but now every moment longer they stayed, the more uncomfortable she began to feel. What had yesterday seemed like a mildly exciting lark was now turning out to be something more serious, and Tracy wasn't sure if she could get out of it. Jaff needed her to get rid of any unwelcome callers, for one thing, though he said she wasn't a prisoner. She could just walk away, she supposed, and leave Jaff to his fate, but for some reason she didn't want to do that. It wasn't only the thought of leaving him in her father's house alone, she really *wanted* to be with him, wanted the adventure, so see it through, whatever it was. She did care about him. She just hated being kept in the dark. She wanted a bigger part in his plans. And she felt cut off from the world without her mobile. It scared her.

The cottage was also a total mess already, with empty wine bottles all over the place, stains on the carpets and furniture, and those CDs and DVDs scattered all over the entertainment room floor. Tracy wasn't by nature a vandal, or even a messy person, and this chaos disturbed her. She had tried to clean up a bit last night, but had been too stoned to make much of a dint.

She was probably a fugitive, too, now. Or at least people might start to think so. Rose, for example. The police knew all about Erin and the gun, certainly, though there had been nothing on the news yet to indicate that they had found out it belonged to Jaff, or that they were even aware of his existence. But Tracy knew from her dad's work that they often kept things back from the public. It doesn't always do to put your sirens on at full volume when you want to sneak up on someone and catch them unawares.

They could be closing the net at this very moment, Tracy thought; the cottage might already be surrounded. Then she admonished herself for being paranoid. Most likely, Erin had gone into one of her long silences, and the police couldn't be too hard on her because they'd just killed her father, which had been on the news late yesterday.

That had knocked Tracy for a six. Mr Doyle was a nice man, she remembered. He always gave her and Erin money for ice cream when they were kids playing in the street and the Mr Whippy van came around. He'd taken them both to the Easter fair in Helmthorpe once, Tracy remembered, when her dad had to work, as usual, and Mr Doyle had let Tracy and Erin go on rides like the waltzers, the dodgems and the speedway. Her dad would never have let her go on them at her age then, just the boring swings or the merry-go-round with all the little kids.

Jaff stirred, threw the sheets back and got out of bed. It was almost midday, but then it had been another late night of wine, joints and movies. And sex. 'I'm hungry,' he announced. 'Why don't you go down and make us some breakfast while I have a shower?'

'What did your last servant die of?' Tracy muttered as she dragged herself out of bed.

'What?' said Jaff. 'What was that you said?'

'Nothing,' Tracy replied.

'Yes it was.' Jaff held her chin. 'You made some remark about servants. You think I should be a servant or something? Is that what you mean? Because my mother's from Bangladesh? Because of the colour of my skin?'

Tracy shook herself free. 'Jaff, that wasn't what I meant at all, and you know it wasn't! It's just a saying we have here, when people ask you to do things they could easily do for themselves. For crying out loud, get a grip.'

'I know what fucking sayings you have here,' said Jaff, pointing his thumb at his own chest. 'Where the fuck do you think I come from? Straight off the boat? I fucking grew up here.'

'All right, Jaff! I didn't mean—'

'People never do. They just assume. All my life people have assumed things about me.' He pointed at her. 'Don't assume.'

Tracy held her hands up in mock surrender. 'Yes, sir,' she said. 'Sorr-ee.'

'And don't take the piss.' Jaff glared at her. Tracy could hardly believe at that moment that she had once thought his eyes gentle and beautiful. They were cold and hard now, his mouth sulky. 'You'd better mean it, Francesca,' he said at last, his voice a little softer but still not without a trace of menace. 'I hate people who make assumptions about me. You don't know what I am. Who I am. You know nothing about me.'

'Fine,' said Tracy, beginning to wish she'd never brought Jaff to her father's house, wishing she'd never met him, never fancied him, never kissed him on the dance floor, never made love with him all night. She felt like crying. 'I'll just go and make some breakfast, shall I? Bacon and eggs do you OK?'

Jaff smiled. 'Fantastic. And a big pot of coffee, too, babe. Good and strong. I'm off for that shower.' Then he simply turned and walked away, whistling, as if nothing had just happened between them.

Tracy stood there slowly shaking her head. She would have liked to have used the bathroom to clean herself up a bit first, but it was a small cottage, and there was only one. Instead, she went downstairs and washed her hands and face in the kitchen sink. She realised she was still trembling a little. Jaff could be cruel without knowing it.

She could hear the shower running upstairs as she gathered together the food for breakfast. A fry-up was the easiest option, she thought, if not the healthiest, so she dug out a couple of frying pans and put them on the rings, adding liberal dollops of cooking oil. Cooking wasn't exactly one of her fortes, but she did know how to fry eggs and bacon, and you needed plenty of hot oil to splash over the eggs to get the tops done properly. First she put the coffee on, then she got the bacon crackling and turned her attention to the eggs. But before she put them in the pan, she fed two slices of toast into the toaster, then glanced towards the breakfast nook.

She bit her lower lip as she thought about what to do. Jaff's holdall was on the bench behind the breakfast table. If she wanted her mobile back, which she did, now was probably the best chance she was going to get. In all likelihood he wouldn't even notice it was missing. The bacon was spitting and sizzling and the coffee pot making its usual gurgling sounds as it turned water into black gold. Tracy hoisted the holdall on to the table and unzipped it.

What she saw inside took her breath away, but not so much that she didn't first reach in and rescue her mobile, slipping it into a zipped pocket of her new shoulder bag. Then she went back to make sure that her eyes weren't deceiving her. But no. There it all was, laid out for her to see. Wad after wad of twenty- and ten-pound notes, fastened with rubber bands. And mixed in with them, several brick-sized packages of white powder wrapped in plastic. She counted four altogether. Cocaine, Tracy thought. Or heroin. Four kilos, probably. She delved deeper, thrusting her hand between the wads of cash until, underneath everything, it touched something cool, hard and metallic.

It was only when she had her hand around the handle of the gun, still deep inside the holdall, that she noticed Jaff leaning against the door jamb, a white towel wrapped around his waist and a sheet of paper in his hand, head cocked to one side, watching her, a curious smile on his lips, but not in his eyes, she noticed, not by a long chalk. Christ, she thought, I should have trusted my instincts and run while I had the chance.

As Annie had expected, Western Area Headquarters was starting to feel like the main concourse at King's Cross by early afternoon on Wednesday. Chambers was skulking around with his imported Mancunian sidekicks, whom Annie had christened Dumb and Dumber, and several AFOs were wandering around the corridors aimlessly, or cluttering up the small canteen, including Nerys Powell, who gave Annie a conspiratorial smile, then blushed and lowered her gaze as they passed one another on the stairs. Just what she needed.

Banks had once told Annie that Chambers reminded him of the Vincent Price character in *Witchfinder General*, and when Annie had watched the film with him later, she had seen what he meant. There was no great physical resemblance, of course, but he had that same air about him, the barely controlled pious zeal that hinted he was satisfying unsavoury personal appetites through his work, as well as serving public morality.

Annie would catch him staring at her now and then with a strange hungry look in his eyes that was only partly sexual, and occasionally he would go into a whispered conference with Dumb and Dumber, who would scribble notes, all calculated to cause maximum anxiety and paranoia, which it did. She and Chambers had parted on bad terms after she had told him exactly what she thought of his handling of the Janet Taylor case, and now she was beginning to think that he was the sort who bore a grudge. More than that, he was the type of person in whom slights and grudges fester for years, ultimately bursting out into vengeance.

Superintendent Gervaise had sent around a memo announcing a meeting of all the senior Serious Crimes staff at three o'clock in the boardroom, when they could expect a visit from the ballistics expert who had been working on the gun. Before that, Annie thought, she would take the opportunity to slip away for a quiet lunch and a pint – knowing that it might be her last chance for some time – and she would take Winsome with her. They had a lot to talk about. Winsome had been concluding the paperwork on her investigation into the hit-and-run, and she needed to be brought up to speed.

The Queen's Arms was out of the question, as was the Hare and Hounds. Superintendent Gervaise had proved to be rather adept at tracking down the various watering holes Annie and Banks had started using. But with Winsome driving – she refused to drink a drop on duty, and hardly drank much at any other time – the whole of Swainsdale was their oyster. Well, within reason, Annie thought. But at least they could get out of the town centre and find a little village pub with tables outside and a nice view. So many had closed down recently, after the smoking ban, the floundering economy, cheap booze shops and easy trips to fill up the boot in Calais. Some of the best pubs in Swainsdale opened for lunch only on weekends, but there were still a few good ones left.

They found a suitable place halfway up a hillside in a tiny village off the Fortford road. It faced a small, triangular green of well-kept grass with a couple of park benches under an old elm tree. The pub had picnic tables out front, where Annie sipped her pint of Dalesman bitter and Winsome her Diet Pepsi as they waited for their food. If any of the other lunchtime customers were astonished at the sight of a six-foot black woman, long legs stretched out, encased in blue denim, they were much too polite to show it, which indicated to Annie that they must be tourists. Locals usually gawped at Winsome.

It was a fine enough day, warm and sunny again, though a few dark clouds were gathering in the west, and the only nuisances were the flies and the occasional persistent wasp. The swallows were still gathering.

Annie admired the pattern of drystone walls that straggled up the hillside to the sere reaches where the limestone outcrops began. To her right, she could see the lush green valley bottom, and the village of Fortford itself a couple of miles away, near the meandering tree-lined river. She could also see the flagstone roofs and the whitewashed façade of the Rose and Crown beside the mound of the old Roman settlement. The Roman road cut diagonally up the daleside and disappeared in the far distance. The air smelled of fresh-mown hay tinged with a hint of manure and smoke from a gardener's fire. Despite the activity at the police station and the harbingers it brought, Annie nevertheless felt this was a good day to be alive as she breathed the late summer air. All mists and mellow fruitfulness. The kind of day that sticks in your memory. It made her think of the final lines of the Keats poem she had had to memorise at school: 'Hedge-crickets sing; and now with treble soft / The red-breast whistles from a garden-croft; / And gathering swallows twitter in the skies.'

'Zoo time back at the station, I see,' said Winsome.

'That's why I wanted to get away for a while,' Annie said. 'That and . . .'

Winsome raised a finely plucked eyebrow. 'Come on. Give. I was thinking things have been dull around the place for a while now,' she said.

'Ever since you drop-kicked that drug dealer over a fourth-floor balcony?'

'It wasn't a drop-kick. And it was only the third floor.'

Annie took a sip of beer. Winsome had got quite a bit of press out of that escapade, which was probably the main reason why the locals knew who she was, and gawped at her. 'There's actually been quite a lot going on,' Annie said.

'Only I haven't been in the loop. Doug and I have been investigating that hit-and-run on the Lyndgarth Road.'

'And?'

'Case closed. Witness got a partial number plate and it was easy sailing from there. 'Course, it didn't help that our two victims weren't talking.'

'Oh? Why not?'

'Up to no good. Off their faces on drugs, weren't they?' Winsome said with a smile.

'Well, it's time to get you in the loop now. How's Harry, I mean Doug, coming on?'

'All right,' said Winsome. 'Yeah, he's all right. Maybe he lacks the killer instinct and that extra edge you need if you want to be a good detective.' She shrugged and grinned. 'In some ways he's like a little brother. I try to keep him out of trouble.'

'I never took you for the maternal type, Winsome. Anyway, you can't play nursemaid for ever.'

'I know. I know. He's a good detail man, though, memory like a steel trap. And let's face it, how often does the job get physical around here?'

'We can't all be fearless warriors, I suppose,' said Annie.

'It's my heritage. My ancestors were fearless warriors. It's in my genes. I'm thinking of investing in a spear.'

Annie laughed. 'You're scary enough without.' She drank some more beer. 'Besides, I'd love to see Madame Gervaise's face if you did walk in carrying a spear.'

'It would certainly give her something to think about.'

A pale, skinny young girl who looked as if she ought to be in school came with their food: burger and chips for Winsome and cheese and tomato sandwich for Annie.

'So what should I know?' Winsome asked after the first bite.

'It's hard to know where to begin,' Annie said.

'What does the boss think?'

'Madame Gervaise? She's being cagey. Wants to see which way the wind's blowing. I can't say I blame her with Matthew Hopkins running around like a man on a divine mission.'

'Matthew who?'

'Hopkins. The witchfinder general. Chambers. It's a pet name.'

'I wouldn't have him as a pet. Or even name one after him.'

'Anyway,' Annie went on, 'Chambers may very well be the least of our problems. Things are complicated, and it's going to be difficult to keep everything in its proper compartment. First off, and high priority as far as I'm concerned, is that we found a gun on our patch, as you probably know already. Rather, the parents found it and shopped their daughter.'

'I do know about that. Wouldn't you?'

'If I had a kid and I found a gun in her room?'

'Yes.'

'Probably,' said Annie. 'I don't know. Somehow it goes against the grain. Tough one, though.'

'Not for me,' said Winsome. 'I'd do it in a shot. No pun intended.'

'Your dad's a cop, mine's an artist.'

'What difference does that make?'

'I don't know,' said Annie.

'But we're both cops.'

'I just meant that I might try and deal with the situation on my own. You know, talk to her, try to understand. The way things are between mother and daughter now, any chance of anyone understanding anything has gone right out the window.'

'Sometimes it's not the most important thing.'

'What is, then?'

'That no one gets shot.'

Annie gave a little shudder. 'Fair enough. Maybe I'm

overplaying the liberal mum. Maybe I'd just shop the little bastard and have done with it. That's probably why I'm lucky I don't have any children.'

'Yeah, I could just see you turning in your own kid. Softie.'

'Anyway,' Annie went on, 'the house is still in lock-down and we're waiting on ballistics. Should know more by this afternoon. The girl's on bail – bed-and-breakfast arrest – and the mother's stopping with a friend. And you know what happened to Patrick Doyle.'

'Yeah,' said Winsome. 'It's terrible.'

'Plus I had a visit last night from one of the AFOs involved. Wanted to know if I was on their side.'

'Are you?'

'I'd like to say I was on the side of truth and justice, but somehow with Chambers around, words like that turn to ashes in my mouth.'

'But you're not going to lie for anyone, are you? You don't even know them.'

Annie put her hand on Winsome's forearm. 'No, Winsome, I'm not going to lie for anybody. Christ knows, I wasn't in the house, I don't know much to start with, but when Chambers gets around to me, I'll answer all his questions honestly to the best of my ability, and if I don't know the answers, I'll say so.'

'Can't say fairer than that.'

'Who said fair had anything to do with it?'

'Cynic.'

'Yes, well . . . Don't forget, I worked with Chambers once.'

Winsome gobbled up her burger and started picking at her chips. 'Where do I start?' she asked, glancing up at Annie from her plate.

'You know DCI Banks's daughter?'

'Tracy? Is that her name?'

'That's right. Though she seems to have taken to calling herself Francesca these days.'

'That's nothing. Kids often go through periods of dissatisfaction with the names their parents gave them,' said Winsome. 'I know I did. I called myself Joan for years in school.'

'Tracy's twenty-four. She's not a kid.' Annie shot Winsome a glance. 'You did, though? Really? Joan?'

'Yeah. I wanted an ordinary name. I hated Winsome. Didn't you ever change your name?'

'No. Somehow or other, I've always been just Annie. So you know Tracy, then?'

'I've spoken with her at the station once or twice. Nice girl, or so she seemed. I can't say I *know* her. Is there a problem?'

'Maybe. Not only has she changed her name,' Annie said, 'but she's changed her appearance, too.'

'So? People do. Look at you. You got your hair cut and highlighted. You used to dress like a hippie and—'

'All right. I get your point.' Annie touched her head self-consciously. 'True enough. I'm not trying to make anything out of it in itself. You're right. Sometimes people just like a change. It's just that she also seems to have disappeared.'

'Seems to have?'

'Yes, well, this is where we enter the realm of total conjecture, or fantasy, as Madame Gervaise would say. Which is why I'm talking to you here and not to her at the station.'

'Because I'm more gullible?'

'No. Because I can't think of anyone more level headed. Hear me out, Winsome. You can tell me if you think I'm talking rubbish.' Annie pushed her empty plate away and drank some more beer. Her glass was close to empty, and she fancied another. Given what chaos the afternoon might bring, though, she decided to abstain and ordered a coffee and some sticky toffee pudding and custard instead. 'Erin shares a house in Headingley with two other girls,' she began. 'Rose Preston and Tracy Banks. The Leeds police searched the place on the afternoon of Erin's arrest. Rose was present. Apparently, when Tracy got home from work that evening and Rose told her what happened, she went ballistic. She seemed most concerned about some bloke called Jaff, Erin's boyfriend. Erin's not talking, so we can't get anything about him from her. Tracy took off almost immediately Rose gave her the news, and she hasn't been seen or heard from since.'

'How do you know all this?'

'I paid a visit to the house yesterday evening and talked to Rose. I also called at this Jaff's flat – nice place, down by the canal – but it was all locked up and there was nobody home. One of the neighbours told me the police had already been around asking questions. He seemed in a bit of a huff, kept his door on the chain, said he didn't have to answer any more questions. He was right. There wasn't a lot I could do, so I went home.'

'Some people are like that,' said Winsome.

'I rang DI Ken Blackstone in Leeds this morning, and guess what? He checked and told me they hadn't sent anybody to Granary Wharf yesterday.'

Winsome frowned. 'So what do you think's going on?'

'I don't know. This is where it becomes pure conjecture on my part. Rose got the impression that there was something between Jaff and Tracy, or so she told me. Tracy certainly seemed unduly concerned about this Jaff, at any rate. Whether she knew about the gun or not, I have no idea.

I know this is all mere speculation, but given that both Tracy and Jaff seem to have disappeared from view, it's my bet that they've gone off somewhere together, probably headed south. If the gun does belong to Jaff, then he's obviously scared that Erin's going to tell on him, or that the police are going to track him down through it, so it's easy to see why he might want to make himself scarce.'

'So he's on the run. Makes sense. You really think he's used this gun?'

'Not recently, according to the preliminary ballistics report. The point right now is that he was probably the one who owned it, whatever the reason.'

'And Tracy's part in all of this?'

Annie ate some more pudding, then washed it down with coffee. 'Don't know,' she said. 'Either she is involved, and she's gone with him, or she's not involved but she's gone with him.'

'Or she's gone somewhere else. On her own.'

'Maybe,' said Annie. 'But unlikely, don't you think? The timing is just too coincidental.'

'Circumstantial is what it all is,' said Winsome. 'But you've got a point. The thing is, I can't believe Tracy's mixed up in anything bad. Not the DCI's daughter.'

'I agree she always seemed like a decent kid, but people change, Winsome, fall in with the wrong company, develop a chip on their shoulder, start to resent their lives or the way they perceive they're being treated. Rebellion. It comes in many shapes and sizes, and not only when you're a teenager. Twenty-four isn't all that old. If she really fancies this Jaff bloke . . . Christ . . .'

'What?'

'Nothing. Just remembering my own bad-boy phase.'

'Bad boy?'

'Yes. Don't you know what bad boys are, Winsome?'

'I don't think I've ever really had much experience of them.'

'A bad boy is unreliable, and sometimes he doesn't show up at all, or if he does, he's late and moody, he acts mean to you, and he leaves early. He always seems to have another iron in the fire, somewhere else to be. But always while you're waiting for him you can't really concentrate on anything else, and you have at least one eye on the door in case he's the next one to walk in the room, even though you think he might be seeing someone else, and when you're with him your heart starts to beat a little faster and your breath catches in your chest. You might be angry, but it won't last, and you're happy for a while when he gives all his attention to you, and then it starts all over again.'

'Sounds awful,' said Winsome.

'But it's exquisite agony,' Annie said. 'Sometimes he doesn't turn up for days on end, and your heart aches for him. He goes to bed with your best friend, and still you forgive him, still you want him.'

'*You* had a bad-boy phase?'

'Of course. Paul Burroughs. But I was only sixteen. I got over it early.' Annie didn't want to talk about the later bad boy who turned out to be a psychopath. She certainly didn't have a great track record when it came to choosing the men in her life. Winsome knew about the psycho anyway, and would be far too diplomatic to say anything. It was much easier to talk about Paul Burroughs.

'Was he unfaithful?'

'Of course he was. Bad boys are always unfaithful. That's the first rule.'

'What else did he do that was so bad?'

Annie smiled fondly as she remembered. 'Paul? Oh, nothing serious, really, not at first. Just minor stuff, fun stuff, run of the mill. But he was a daredevil. He couldn't care less.'

'Like what?'

'Well, one night, after midnight, for example, we broke into the local marina and borrowed a speedboat.' Annie couldn't help but laugh at Winsome's expression of horror. 'If the harbour police hadn't caught us, we'd have ended up in France, or more likely we'd have crashed on the rocks or something and drowned. He knew how to get it started – he could start anything with a motor – but he hadn't a clue how to handle the wheel.'

'What did the police do?'

'Obviously not very much, or I wouldn't be here with you today.' Annie shrugged. 'A slap on the wrist, that was all, really. Or it would have been except . . .'

'What?'

'Well, Paul had a lot of problems with his family. His dad had gone off with another woman, and his mother was a bit of a zombie. She drank a lot and took tons of Valium. He was so mixed up and angry, you just wanted to hold him and make it all go away.'

'Did you?'

'No. Me? I'm not the type. Besides, you can't cuddle bad boys. The problem was that he picked a fight with the biggest harbour cop when we got back on land, and he ended up in a cell for the night. That was only the beginning. After that, I didn't see him any more, but I heard later that he had a lot of problems with the law, stealing cars, joyriding, then muggings, assault, burglaries, stuff like that.'

'And now?'

'No idea. Prison, perhaps.'

'So he was a bad boy in the making?'

'Yeah. But bad boys aren't always criminals. It's more a state of mind. It never happened to you?'

'Sugar, the bad boys where I grew up were *really* baaad. Not just some sissy skinny-ass white boy stealing a motorboat. They carried machetes and AK47s.'

Annie laughed. 'Anyway, who knows? Maybe it all goes along with this change in Tracy's appearance, the piercings, the name. Like I said, rebellion can happen any time, take many forms. All I know is that I'd like to find her and get things sorted, and I'd like to do it before she's got the combined police forces of the whole bloody country on her trail. Either she's thumbing her nose at us all, or she's scared, but she maybe needs help, whether she knows it yet or not.'

'And Alan?'

Annie shook her head. 'He won't be back until next Monday, though I've got his mobile number for emergencies only. I *could* call him, wherever he is, as long it's not some remote far-flung desert outpost. And that reminds me. I should drop by his cottage after work today. It's been a while. Those poor plants of his will be fair gagging for a drink of water by now.'

'But you aren't going to ring him?'

'I'm not sure it's that kind of emergency yet. It's my gut feeling that if I can get Tracy out of all this before he gets back and finds out about it, the better all around.'

'So what do you want me to do?'

'Walk softly and carry a big stick. Keep under the radar. Even though we're only doing our jobs. You're not tarnished by the firearms business, so you're still in something of a privileged position.'

'So keep my head down and my eyes and ears open?'

'That's about it. Once this business gets into top gear, they'll probably be scrutinising me as closely as a bug under a microscope. Soon I won't be able to go to the toilet without filling in a form. First off, if you could find a way to uncover as much as you can about this Jaff, it would be a great help. You might start with Rose Preston in Headingley. She doesn't know a lot, but I'm convinced she knows more than she was telling me.'

'I take it you've got their addresses?'

Annie gave her them. 'As for Jaff, I'm afraid I don't have anything *except* the address right now. And I don't think there's much point in going there again. His first name's Jaffar, by the way. And the name next to his bell says J. McCready. We'll need to know a lot more than that.'

'I can always use my natural charm.'

Annie smiled. 'Yeah, there's that.' She wagged her finger at Winsome. 'But absolutely no drop-kicking.'

'It wasn't a drop-kick!'

'I don't understand,' said Tracy, holding up the gun by its long barrel. 'I thought Erin had taken your gun.'

'Put that away.' Jaff took the gun from her and put it back in the holdall. 'She did,' he said, sitting down at the breakfast table and placing the sheet of paper face down beside him. 'This is a different one. Another one. I got it from Vic. Those eggs will be like rubber if you don't get a move on. I like my eggs runny.'

As if she were in a trance, Tracy served up the bacon and eggs and poured two mugs of coffee. 'But why do you need another gun?' she asked.

'Ta. Dunno. Protection. I just feel safer that way.'

Tracy regarded him through narrowed eyes. She had felt scared at first, seeing him standing there in the doorway, knowing how unpredictable he was becoming, but somehow now he seemed just like a little boy, naked from the waist up, tucking into his bacon and eggs – because clearly no matter what Tracy felt, it wasn't going to stop him from eating his breakfast, or from doing exactly what he wanted. Tracy wasn't hungry. Her stomach was too full of butterflies, so she just munched on a slice of dry toast and sipped black coffee. She had expected an explosion of rage when he caught her going through his holdall, maybe even that he'd hit her or something, but nothing had happened except this. Definitely an anticlimax.

'Have you ever used it?' she asked.

'Of course. Not this one, but one like it. You have to get the feel of it.'

'To shoot someone?'

'Don't be silly. Just out in a field, like, tin cans. Target practice.'

'I don't like guns.'

'You don't have to. Nobody in their right mind does, but sometimes they're useful.'

'For what?'

'I told you. Protection.'

'From who?'

'It's better you don't know.'

'The person that stuff belongs to?' Tracy gestured towards the holdall. 'The heroin or coke or whatever it is? Did you steal it?'

'It's coke,' said Jaff. He paused with a forkful of bacon and egg halfway to his mouth, the yolk dripping, wiggled his eyebrows and looked her in the eye. 'Wanna try some?'

Tracy couldn't help but laugh. 'Not right now, thank you very much. I'm serious, Jaff.' She had tried coke a few times, first at university to stay awake during her exams, then later at clubs and bars. She liked it well enough, and it usually made her randy, but it soon wore off and left her feeling shitty for hours. She certainly didn't want to feel randy again right now, and she was feeling shitty enough already.

'Look, I told you before,' Jaff went on. 'You've no idea what's going on. You've—'

'Do you think I'm stupid, Jaff? Is that what you really think? The only reason I don't know what's going on is that you won't tell me. I've asked you. But you won't. If we're going to keep on being in this together I need to know more. You'd be surprised. Perhaps I can help. Just how deep are you into all this?'

'All what?'

'You know what I'm talking about. The drugs. The money. The guns. What are you? Some kind of wannabe gangster? A gun-running coke dealer? Like you just walked out of a Guy Ritchie movie or something? A rock'n'rolla? Is that it?'

'I don't—'

'Because I'm not stupid, Jaff. Maybe all I know is that I'm on the run from the police in my dad's house with a lad I hardly know, who just happens to have a few kilos of cocaine, several thousand quid and a loaded gun – I assume it *is* loaded? – in his holdall. It certainly *sounds* like a movie to me.'

Jaff smiled at her. It was supposed to be his charming aren't-I-a-naughty-little-boy-but-you-can't-help-but-love-me-anyway-can-you? smile, but it didn't work this time. 'I suppose you think I owe you an explanation?'

'Well, yeah. That would do for a start.'

'Look, I didn't ask you to come with me, did I? It wasn't my—'

'Don't give me that load of bollocks, Jaff. You know damn well that if it wasn't for me you wouldn't be sitting here at my dad's breakfast table, eating bloody bacon and eggs.'

'You're beginning to sound a bit like a fishwife, you know,' Jaff said. 'Why don't you just shut it, chill out and go with the flow?'

Tracy snorted and gave him as disgusted a look as she could dredge up, then she took a deep breath. There was one thing she had to be grateful for. Jaff had been so concerned about her finding the money, the coke and the gun that the mobile seemed to have completely slipped his mind when he checked the holdall. 'You're right,' she said. 'So how do you suggest I go about doing it? Chilling? And, I mean, what exactly *is* the flow? What should I do to go with it?'

'Nothing, babe. That's the beauty of it. You don't have to do anything.'

'Because I'd just like to know what our plans are, for a start, that's all.'

'*Our* plans?'

'Well, not so long ago you were going to make a few phone calls, get things organised, then we were going to hook up with some mate of yours in London who does dodgy passports and disappear over the Channel, right? Or did I get that bit wrong, too?'

'No. That's still the general idea.'

'Then I hope you weren't planning on carrying that holdall with you.'

'Give me a break! I'm going to get rid of all that stuff in London. Except the money, of course.'

'Including the gun?'

'Including the gun. That's why this takes time to organise, why we're still here. Do you think I'd be crazy enough to try and carry a gun and four kilos of coke across the border?'

'I don't know, Jaff. I really don't know just how crazy you are. Right now I think maybe I don't know you.'

'Just trust me, that's all.' Jaff reached out his hand but Tracy didn't take it.

'You keep on saying that,' she said, 'but you don't give me much reason to trust you, holding things back from me.'

Jaff waved his fork in the air. 'It was for your own good.'

'What was? I don't see how.'

'Let's not fight, babe,' Jaff said, polishing off the rest of his breakfast. He tapped the sheet of paper beside him with the tip of his fork. 'Besides, I was about to say something to *you* before I was so rudely interrupted.'

Suddenly, Tracy felt more nervous than angry. She fingered her necklace. 'Oh? What was that?'

'This here piece of paper. I found it in a desk drawer in the front room. It—'

'You shouldn't go rummaging through people's drawers. It's not—'

Jaff slammed his knife and fork down so hard he broke the plate and the cutlery clattered to the floor. 'Will you just fucking shut up with your what's right and what's not right bullshit!'

He yelled so loudly and his eyes turned so cold and hard that Tracy felt herself on the verge of crying again. She was sure that her lips were quivering, and she struggled to hold back the tears. She wasn't going to let him see her cry, even if he could sense her fear. She wouldn't give him that satisfaction.

'Is it clear now?' Jaff went on. 'Are we on the same page?'

Tracy nodded, chewing the edge of her thumb.

'Right,' he went on, as calmly as anything. 'As I was saying. I found this letter in one of the drawers, and it turns out to be interesting, very interesting indeed.'

'What is it?' Tracy asked in a small voice.

'Your name is Banks, right? Francesca Banks?'

'That's right.'

'And your father is DCI Alan Banks of the North Yorkshire Police?'

'Yes. I mean—'

Jaff let the sheet of paper drop. 'Your father's a fucking cop, and you didn't see fit to tell me?'

'It didn't seem important. He's not here, is he? What does it matter who he is, what he does?'

'*What does it matter?*' Jaff tapped the side of his head. 'You *lied* to me, babe. Are you certain you're not stupid? Because that's not what I'm hearing from where I'm sitting.'

'There's no need to be insulting. So, he's a policeman. So what?'

'Not just a policeman. A DCI. That's Detective Chief Inspector.' He laughed. 'I've been shagging a DCI's daughter. I can't believe it.'

'You don't have to be so crude about it.'

'Make up your mind, babe. Are you an angel or a whore? On first impressions between the sheets, I'd definitely go for the latter, but you seem to talk a whole lot of rubbish about morals and duty, and me being insulting and crude. So just what exactly are you?'

'How would you notice what I do or don't do between the sheets, as you so crudely put it? All you're interested in is your own pleasure. I might as well be an inflatable doll for all you care.'

'You've got about as much enthusiasm as an inflatable doll. Isn't that what it's all about? Fucking? You take your pleasure where and when you can.'

'Oh, you're a marvel, Jaff, you are. A philosopher, too.'

Jaff pointed at her. 'Shut up, bitch. I'm warning you. I don't like sarcasm.'

Tracy glared at him. 'Anyway, what does it matter if my dad's a DCI?' she repeated.

'It matters because when a copper's involved they pull out all the stops, that's why. They stick together. It matters because it makes everything ten times harder. You're a copper's daughter. There's nothing he won't do to get you back. Nothing. This is personal for him, and he's got the whole bloody country's police force on his side. Get it? We're seriously outnumbered.'

'What do you mean, get me back? From where? From who? I can just walk out of here any time I want, can't I?'

'Get real. Things have changed. As you said, we're in this together, and nobody's going off anywhere without the other until it all gets sorted.'

Tracy felt a chill and a tightening in her chest. So it was true; in his eyes, she was a prisoner now, a hostage. Or a burden. 'I told you. He's on holiday. He won't be back till Monday. How could he come looking for us? He's got no idea what's going on.'

'But he soon will have when he gets back. Or he'll hear about what's happened from his mates and come back early. He could be on his way now.'

'No, he won't be. He doesn't care about me that much.'

'Just shut up and let me think.'

'Look,' said Tracy, as calmly as she could manage. 'Why don't I just go? Really? I'll go back to Leeds right now, as if none of this ever happened. I can get a bus to Eastvale from the village. You can drive on down to London in Vic's car, get your passport and finances sorted and disappear. It'll be all over and done with before my dad gets back from holiday. He needn't know a thing.' The words sounded hollow and desperate to her even as she spoke them.

'Now it's you who must think *I'm* stupid,' said Jaff.

'Why?'

'Do you think I'm going to let you just walk out of here and tell the cops everything you know?'

'I won't tell them anything. I don't even know anything. Remember? You haven't told me anything.'

'You know about the coke, the money and the gun. That's enough.'

'But you'll be even worse off with me as a travelling companion. You can hardly take me with you, can you? I'll only slow you down. Just let me walk away now, Jaff. Please.'

Then Tracy saw the look on his face and froze.

'Well,' Jaff said, 'it seems to me that gives me just two options. Either I don't let you out of my sight for a second from now on, or . . .'

And Tracy went cold to the marrow of her bones when she realised exactly what the second option was.

8

'This is Naomi Worthing,' said Detective Superintendent Gervaise to the Serious Crimes team assembled in the board-room late that afternoon. 'She's come up from Birmingham to tell us all about the gun we sent down. Many thanks for the quick work, Naomi.'

Naomi smiled at Gervaise. 'Not a problem,' she said. 'We got a lucky break.' She was a plump middle-aged woman with greying hair and a benevolent manner, hardly what Annie would have expected in a ballistics expert. She seemed more like Miss Marple than a member of the *CSI* cast. Her audience was small – only Gervaise, Annie, Winsome, Harry Potter and Geraldine Masterson, who was new to Major Crimes and dead keen to make a good impression.

'I'm not going to bore you with all the technical details,' Naomi began, 'but basically we're dealing with a nine-millimetre Smith & Wesson automatic, or, more correctly, semi-automatic. This particular model dates from the mid-eighties. It has a four-inch barrel, a sixteen-round capacity, and it weighs just under two pounds unloaded. Any questions so far?'

'Isn't Smith & Wesson an American company?' asked Annie.

'Yes. The pistol in question was manufactured in the USA,' replied Naomi. 'Which perhaps makes it a little rarer around these parts than a Czech or a Russian model. I mean, you wouldn't find one for sale in the local pub. And, of course, a Smith & Wesson would cost you a lot more money.'

'Are they readily available over here?'

'On and off. Though they're certainly not as common at street level as the eastern European models I mentioned. Look, if I can perhaps make a guess at where you're going with this, Detective . . .?'

'Cabbot. DI Annie Cabbot.'

'Yes, well, I wouldn't let the fact that this pistol is American in origin influence your search for its owner and user. The odds are that it has been floating around the UK since the nineties, if not before. It's a very popular, simple and practical piece of equipment, and ammunition for it isn't hard to come by.'

'Did you say "user", Naomi?' Gervaise asked.

Naomi turned to her. 'Yes. That's what I was about to get to. The reason I came up here, rather than simply filing a written report. Not that a trip to Eastvale isn't always a pleasant prospect.'

'Do tell,' said Gervaise.

Naomi helped herself to coffee, added milk and sugar and opened her file folder. 'There were two rounds missing from the magazine. Bullets *and* casings. That's often the case with automatics, as you probably know. They eject the casing after firing. A clever criminal picks up his spent casings and disposes of them, but sometimes people are careless, or in a hurry, and leave them lying around.'

'Any idea when the shots were fired?' Annie asked.

Naomi shook her head. 'We can't ascertain *when* they were fired by examining the pistol,' she said. 'Only that they were fired *from that magazine*.'

'But perhaps even from a different gun?'

'It's possible, I suppose, but unlikely. Unfortunately, as I said, we don't have the spent casings, so we can't check them against the firing pin to make sure. Unless someone's trying to pull a very elaborate trick, though, I would say there's no reason to doubt that the bullets were fired from this pistol.'

'I see. Sorry, please go on.'

'Naturally, we then consulted the National Firearms Forensic Intelligence Database, which is a bit of a mouthful, so I'll refer to it as the NFFID in future. There we discovered that a pistol of this description had been used to commit an unsolved murder in November 2004. This information, of course, is not conclusive. It merely refers to a case number and the general model and kind of ammunition consistent with that we found in the magazine, but it piqued our curiosity. The next step involved shooting the gun under controlled circumstances in order to obtain a sample of a used bullet we could then run through IBIS – that's the Integrated Ballistics Identification System – don't we just love acronyms? The result is that we found a definite link between this pistol and the 2004 crime. The next step we need to carry out, for absolute certainty, is to get hold of one of the actual bullets retrieved from the victim and do a physical examination, side by side, though a comparison microscope. This is the kind of thing you see on TV crime programmes, lands and grooves. Looks very sexy on screen.'

'And where would you get hold of one of these bullets?' Annie asked.

'West Yorkshire. I'm not sure exactly where they are, but they *should* still be locked in an evidence room somewhere.'

'Where did the shooting take place?'

'Woodhouse Moor. Leeds.'

'I'm not sure where they keep their cold-case exhibits,' said Gervaise, 'but that'll probably be Weetwood, on Otley Road. On the other hand, you might be better off talking to the Homicide and Major Enquiries Team first. We may be the largest single county force in the country, but West Yorkshire's got a much bigger urban population than we have, and they've got all the specialists. We've got Wildlife Crime Officers, and they have a homicide squad. They'd probably be the ones to handle a case like that.'

'Thanks,' said Naomi. 'I've dealt with them before. That'll be my next stop.'

'So what can you tell us pending a physical comparison?'

Naomi sipped her milky coffee. 'Not much more, I'm afraid. You'll have to get the rest of the details from the investigating team. All I know is that on November fifth 2004, a suspected drug dealer called Marlon Kincaid was shot to death near a bonfire site on Woodhouse Moor.'

'Any witnesses?' Annie asked.

'Not according to what little information I've got. As I say, though, the NFFID and IBIS files are skimpy on details. I'm sure the detectives involved will be able to tell you a lot more.'

'Bonfire Night, though,' said Annie. 'Fireworks might be useful to cover up the noise of gunshots.'

'Indeed,' said Naomi. 'Oh, there is one more thing. It may be important. We examined the pistol for fingerprints, of course, and we found only Patrick Doyle's, the ones you sent us, on the grip and barrel, which is consistent with his checking to see if it was loaded. We did, however, find two clear sets of prints on the magazine itself, only one of them belonging to Patrick Doyle. People often forget that. They have to load it by hand, you see, and they hardly ever think of wearing gloves. The magazine remains protected inside the handle, and the prints are preserved. There are also several partials on the cartridges, and they also appear to match the mystery prints on the magazine.'

'Anything there?'

'We ran them through IDENT1, of course, but I'm afraid they're not on file.'

'So no name and address?' said Gervaise. 'No easy arrest?'

Naomi smiled. 'Is there ever? No. I'm afraid you'll have to sweat this one through. When you do come up with a suspect, of course . . . well, the prints are there for comparison. Even then, I'm afraid, all it means is that the person handled the magazine and the cartridges, not that he or she committed the murder.'

Gervaise looked at Annie. 'I suppose we'd better start with Erin Doyle,' she said. 'Can you get in touch with Vic Manson and deal with it, Annie?'

'Of course.'

Gervaise checked the time. 'It's getting a bit late now, but if you and Winsome could head down to Leeds first thing tomorrow and see what you can find out from the case files and the investigating officers, we might start getting somewhere.'

It was almost seven o'clock by the time Annie got out of the station and into her car. The little purple Astra had finally given up the ghost earlier that summer, but she was quite pleased with the Megane she had bought as a replacement. Especially with the price.

Since the meeting, she had tracked down a sulky and passive Erin Doyle at her bed-and-breakfast by the castle, and, accompanied by the Family Liaison Officer, Patricia Yu, had brought her back to the station, where her fingerprints had been taken. After all the paperwork and running back and forth, Annie felt like nothing more than a large glass of wine and a nice long bath when she got home. So numb was her mind that she had driven almost a mile in the wrong direction – towards her own cottage in Harkside – before remembering that she was supposed to go to Banks's cottage to water his plants and pick up the pile of post from the floor.

For a moment, Annie wavered, weighing the wine and the bath against a lengthy detour. Surely she could postpone the visit until tomorrow? The plants would survive, and the post would be mostly bills and special offers on magazine subscriptions and cases of wine. But she felt guilty enough about her neglect already. He would be back soon, and if it seemed that she hadn't discharged her duties, she would feel even worse, no matter how forgiving he might be. She drove as far as the next roundabout and turned back the way she had come.

As she passed the police station, she thought of Chambers, who had been strutting around all afternoon with Dumb and Dumber in tow, giving everyone the evil eye. Annie was down for her official interview the following morning, and she wasn't looking forward to that at all. She knew how it would go. Chambers would get Dumb or Dumber, or both of them, to conduct the interview, because they were supposedly unbiased, while he would sit there ogling her as she squirmed, loving every minute of it, thinking he was setting the world to rights. She would have to remember to wear trousers or a long skirt and a loose top that came all the way up to her chin, maybe even her polo-neck jumper – the loose one, not the tight one.

She turned on to the main Helmthorpe road and left the town behind. She would drive home over the moors, she decided. She loved the purity of the bleak landscape in the soft evening light, the unfenced roads where sheep wandered, the broad sky and magnificent vistas. The heather would be in bloom, too, which was always a bonus, and sometimes you could just make out the pale moon in the milky-blue evening sky. When she got home, she would have the wine and the bath.

Cheered by the prospect of an evening drive over the moors, and by her decision not to take the line of least resistance and go straight home, Annie turned left in Helmthorpe, by the school, and drove up the hill to Gratly. A hundred yards or so past the little stone bridge over the beck, she turned right into Banks's drive, a narrow dirt track with a few patches of gravel here and there. It led under a canopy of lime trees and came to a halt in front of the cottage. Beyond were the woods, and to Annie's right, behind the low drystone wall, Gratly Beck ran over its terraced waterfalls, then on through the village and down into the centre of Helmthorpe, on the valley bottom. It was a beautiful spot, and she had often envied Banks.

Annie parked outside the small cottage. When she turned off the engine and got out of the car, she could hear birds singing in the woods and down the valley, over the beck. She could also hear music. It was some sort of modern rock, distorted guitar, thrashing drums and pounding bass. What was odd was that it seemed to be coming from the cottage. Just next to the garage, she spotted a car she didn't recognise. A Ford Focus, maybe a little the worse for wear and certainly in need of a good wash. There was a dent in the rear wing and rust around the wheel arches. She knew that

Banks had been talking about trying to sell the Porsche all summer, but as far as she knew he hadn't been able to get the right price. The Ford certainly hadn't been there the last time she had called to water the plants.

Banks had complained to her that when you're trying to sell a Porsche, people either assume that you're loaded already, or that you really need the money. Consequently, they think they can get away with a quick deal at a low price. He wasn't loaded, but neither did he need the money. He just wanted to sell the car. Annie suspected it might be because it still reminded him too much of his brother, whom it had belonged to, even though Roy Banks had been dead for some time now. Banks had never really got used to it. But even if he had sold it, he wouldn't have bought a banged-up Ford Focus. He'd probably have gone for a Volvo, or even an Audi, she thought. He wasn't exactly a *Top Gear* kind of bloke – he had driven an old Cortina until it practically fell apart, for crying out loud – but he wouldn't be seen dead driving a car like this. She had a quick peek in the garage and, indeed, the Porsche was still there.

Which raised a question: whom did the Focus belong to? Annie made a note of the number, then she dug in her bag for Banks's front-door key and put it in the lock. Maybe Tracy or Brian had come to stay and Banks hadn't thought to let her know. Or some kids could have broken in. When the door was open, she stood on the threshold and shouted, 'Hello! Hello! Who's there?'

Nothing happened at first, then the music got quieter and the door to the entertainment room on her left opened. Out walked Tracy, carefully shutting the door behind her.

'Tracy,' said Annie. 'I didn't know you had a Ford Focus.'

'I don't,' said Tracy. 'I just borrowed it from a friend.'

'I see.'

Tracy did look different, but not that much, Annie thought. It was the haircut, mostly, a little punkish. She wore little or no make-up, perhaps a trace of pink lipstick, and was dressed in a simple outfit of blue jeans and a light blue sleeveless V-neck top, leaving an inch or two of bare midriff. The piercings weren't extreme, just a ring at the edge of one eyebrow and a stud under her lower lip, like thousands of other young women. She did look older than Annie remembered, though, and there was a certain sophistication about her she hadn't noticed before. Tracy also seemed nervous.

'Is something wrong?' Annie asked.

'No. What could possibly be wrong? What do you want? Nothing's happened to Dad, has it?'

'No,' said Annie, shutting the door behind her. 'Nothing like that. I said I'd water his plants and pick up the post while he was away, that's all. How about a cup of tea or coffee or something?'

'Cup of tea?'

Annie gestured towards the kitchen. 'Yes. You know, the little bag you put in a pot and add water to. In there.'

'Oh, right. Sure.'

Annie followed Tracy to the kitchen, noticing how she wasn't entirely steady on her feet. Her voice had seemed a little slurred, too, her eyes unfocused, and her concentration didn't seem what it normally was. Annie suspected drugs, or perhaps it was just booze. 'Anyway,' she said, 'it's a stroke of good fortune finding you here. I was getting a bit worried about you.'

'Worried? Why?'

'Surely you must know about Erin, your housemate?'

'There's still some coffee left in the pot. I don't know how long it's been there. Will that be OK?'

'It'll be fine,' said Annie. 'Plenty of milk and sugar, please.'

Even the milk and sugar didn't disguise the bitterness of the burned coffee oils, but Annie sipped politely and leaned against the kitchen door jamb. 'It's a nice evening,' she said. 'Shall we go into the conservatory? That's where the plants are, too. I still have to water them, unless you've done it?'

'Plants?'

'Yes, the ones I came to water. Green things in pots.'

'Oh. Right. Yeah.'

Annie filled an empty jug by the sink and walked through to the conservatory. Tracy followed her. The room was a mess. Unwashed plates and cups sat on the low table along with half-full wine glasses, one on its side, sticky red wine drying on the glass surface. 'Been having a party?' Annie asked.

'That. Oh, no. Just an accident. I was meaning to clean it up. Just haven't got around to it yet.'

'Want some help?'

'No, it's OK. I'll do it later. Do you want to sit down?'

'I think I will, if that's OK.' Annie set her water jug on the table and sat. 'I was saying, about Erin . . .'

'That's nothing to do with me,' Tracy said quickly, biting on a fingernail. 'I saw it on the news.'

'But you already knew what had happened before that, didn't you?'

'How? What do you mean?'

'Rose told you when you got home from work the other evening.'

'Oh, yeah. That's right. She said the police had been round, or something like that. She didn't seem to know much.'

'You don't seem very clear about it yourself.'

'Like I said, it's nothing to do with me, is it?'

'What are you doing here?'

'I just came to get a bit of peace and quiet, that's all. What's wrong with that? I'm entitled. It's my dad's house.'

Annie held her hand up. 'All right. Hold your horses, Tracy. Nobody's saying you're not. Did you come straight here after you left the house in Headingley?'

'Of course I did. Where else would I go?'

'It's just that I got the impression you were rather concerned about Erin's boyfriend. Jaff.'

'Jaff? But how do you . . .?' Tracy let her sentence trail off. 'I should have known. You've been spying on me for Dad, haven't you?'

'I had no idea you were here,' said Annie. 'As I told you, I came to bring in the post and water the plants.' She cast her eyes over the various pots and hanging baskets. 'It looks as if they could do with it, too.'

'I'm not very good with plants. They all seem to shrivel up and die if I go near them.'

'So I see.' Annie paused, and Tracy showed no interest in prolonging the conversation. Annie stood, picked up the jug and began to water the plants. 'Where is he, Tracy?' she asked casually, over her shoulder.

'Who?'

'You know who. Jaff. Is he here?'

'Here? Why would he be here? I told you, I came for a bit of peace and quiet.'

'Maybe you fancy him? Maybe you thought you'd help him hide out for a while, until the spot of bother he's in passes over.'

'Bother? What bother? I don't understand.'

'It was his gun Erin had, wasn't it?'

'I know nothing about any gun.'

'It was used in a murder six years ago, Tracy. A young lad by the name of Marlon Kincaid. Ring any bells? We need some answers here.'

'I don't know what you're on about.'

'Erin's father's *dead*. Did you know that?'

'Well, Jaff didn't kill him. It was you lot who did that. The police.'

'Fair enough,' said Annie.

'Anyway, I liked him,' Tracy said in a soft voice. Annie thought she could see tears in her eyes. 'He was always good to me, Mr Doyle. I'm sorry he's dead.'

'Look, I'm not here to throw blame about,' Annie said, 'but I don't think this is the answer, do you?'

'I haven't done anything. You'd better go.'

'I know you haven't done anything, but don't you think it's time you went back home? Maybe your friend needs you, Erin. Have you thought about her?'

Tracy bit her lower lip.

'OK, Tracy,' Annie said. 'No more messing about. I know Jaff is here with you, and he's wanted for questioning in the murder of Marlon Kincaid.'

'I've never heard of any Marlon Kincaid.'

'That's probably a good thing. I'll bet Jaff's heard of him, though. Look, the only issue is, are you both going to come with me, peacefully, or do I have to send for a patrol car?'

'No! You can't do that. You don't understand. You have to go now. He's got . . . he won't . . .'

'He won't what, Tracy? He doesn't have a choice.'

'He won't like that. Can't you just let us go? Please. We'll leave here. I'll tidy up, honest. Then we'll just go. But please leave now.'

'I can't do that, Tracy. You know I can't.' Annie thought she saw a shadow flit beyond the frosted glass of the conservatory door. Quickly she moved forward and opened it. 'Are you Jaff?' she said, as she glimpsed the dark figure reaching into a large holdall on the breakfast table.

'Be careful,' shouted Tracy. 'He's got—'

But Annie wasn't listening. 'Because if you are I think it's time—'

Before she could finish the sentence she heard two dull pops and felt as if someone had punched her hard in the chest and shoulder, then her body started to turn cold and numb. Her legs wobbled and gave under her, then she became aware of falling backwards, like floating through space, on to the table, which smashed beneath her weight. Shards of glass stuck in her back. Pottery crashed on the terracotta tiles. Glasses broke. Someone screamed, far away. Annie tried to call out and reached up her arms to cling on to some sort of imaginary lifeline, but she couldn't grasp it. Exhausted and fighting for breath, a great weight on her chest, she fell back on the broken glass and pottery and everything swirled from her mind like water down the drain. Her chest and throat felt wet and bubbly when she tried to breathe. Then the lights went out.

When Winsome got to Leeds, the house in Headingley was locked up tight, with no sign of Rose Preston or anybody else. A neighbour said she had seen Rose walking towards the bus stop with a suitcase the previous evening. After a few calls on her mobile, Winsome was able to track down Rose's parents' address in Oldham. It wasn't far, but the traffic on the M62 was dreadful at that time of the evening, and it was going on for half past eight when she arrived at the small terraced house, just around the corner from Gallery Oldham, the shiny new arts centre and library.

Rose answered the door herself, and on seeing Winsome's warrant card she rolled her eyes and said, 'What now?'

'I'd just like to talk to you for a few minutes, that's all,' Winsome said.

Rose grabbed a light jacket from a hook by the door. 'OK,' she said. 'I don't suppose I've got much choice. But I've already told you lot everything I know. My parents are out, and I certainly don't intend being alone with you, so let's go to the pub round the corner.'

When they turned the corner, all Winsome could see was another hill with red-brick, slate-roofed terraced houses on either side. But one of these had a sign outside, and it turned out to be the local pub. Winsome felt as if she were walking into someone's living room when they stepped inside, but the interior was done out like a proper pub, complete with customers, bar, video machines, pool table, plush banquettes and iron-legged tables. It was on a split level and either took up two houses or had the same powers over dimension as Doctor Who's TARDIS. Winsome was a secret *Doctor Who* fan. She would never tell her colleagues at work because they were sure to make fun of her – they all thought her so straight and logical – but she had always dreamed of being the Doctor's companion, of travelling the universe through space and time, meeting Shakespeare, battling monsters and egomaniacal madmen, arriving back on Earth before she had even left.

She bought an orange juice for herself and a pint of lager and lime for Rose, and they sat down on one of the banquettes.

'Why were you so upset when I turned up?' Winsome asked. 'And why would you be so afraid of being alone with me? Am I that scary looking?'

'No, it's not you. I'm just being more careful, that's all. I mean, it's not because you're . . . you know. It's nothing to do with that.'

'Well, I'm glad to know it's not because I'm tall,' said Winsome.

Rose managed a weak smile. 'I meant because you're black. You know I did. You're teasing. Anyway, it's nothing to do with that. I've just had it up to here with the police, if that's what they really were.'

Winsome frowned. 'What do you mean? Surely nobody's given you a hard time during all this? What reason would they have?'

'Maybe not at first,' Rose said, sweeping back a stray tress and tucking it behind her ear. 'I mean, it was a bit of a shock the police coming around and searching the place and all that, right? But they were OK.'

'And DI Annie Cabbot? Didn't she come by to see you?'

'Yeah. She was all right, too. Just wanted to chat about Erin and Francesca, you know.'

'So what's the problem?'

Rose turned away. 'The other two.'

'What other two?' Winsome had no idea that the Leeds police had sent anyone to interview Rose after the search of the house. Annie certainly hadn't mentioned it. She *had* mentioned that two men had turned up at Jaff's flat passing themselves off as police officers when nobody had, in fact, been sent out there. She could check with DI Ken Blackstone when she went to Leeds with Annie in the morning, of course, and she would. But for the moment it seemed a promising place to start her chat with Rose.

'Don't you know?' Rose said. 'Don't you ever talk to each other?'

Winsome smiled. 'Not very often, no. Especially if they're from another county force. I mean, they'd be West Yorkshire, while Annie and I are North Yorkshire.'

'That's what they said, more or less. But it still seems weird to me. All wrong. I had a feeling they weren't real policemen right from the start. Anyway, they said their names were Sandalwood and Watkins, but I suppose they were lying about that, too. I don't remember what they said their ranks were.'

'But they wore plain clothes?'

'Yes.'

'Did you get a good look at their warrant cards? Did you see if they said West or North Yorkshire?'

'No. They sort of pushed their way in. It all happened so quickly I didn't really catch what was written on them. I don't think they looked liked yours, though.'

'How were they dressed? Suits? Casual?'

'Casual. Jeans. Button-down shirts. One of them wore a tan windcheater and the other had a sort of linen sports jacket on, light blue.'

'That's good, Rose,' said Winsome, making notes. 'You've got a good eye for detail.'

'I like to draw. You have to really look at things if you want to draw them.'

Winsome glanced up from her notebook. 'Do you think you could draw them for me? Now. Could you do that? Head and shoulders.'

Rose nodded. Winsome went to the bar and asked the bartender for a few sheets of unlined paper. He managed to find some in the office and handed them to her without question. When she got back, she put them on the table and handed Rose a pencil from her briefcase. Rose's hand moved deftly and confidently over the paper, sketching an outline, filling out the details. Finally, she slid the pages over to Winsome. 'That's the best I can do from memory.'

Winsome didn't recognise either of the men Rose had drawn, but that didn't necessarily mean much, especially if they were from West Yorkshire. But somehow, she doubted that they were. She didn't think they were police officers at all. One of them was burly and overbearing, with hardly any neck and a shaved head perched atop his broad shoulders.

'He was the biggest,' Rose said. 'And he had a tattoo on the back of his neck. It looked like a dagger or a cross, or something like that. I'm not sure exactly what it was. Some sort of symbol, anyway. It was small, but you could see it above his shirt collar.'

Winsome studied the other sketch. This man was slighter, thinner, more ferret-like in his features, perhaps more intelligent, too, in a feral sort of way, with fine, unruly hair – ginger, Rose told her – a very pale complexion and cold eyes.

'He was the scariest,' Rose said, as if reading her thoughts. 'Watkins. I mean, the other one looks big and mean, and he wasn't very nice, but this one . . .' She tapped the sketch. 'I'm glad he was out of the room most of the time. He gave me the creeps. He didn't say much, but he's the one I was really afraid of. And the other one told me he really likes hurting people.'

'Did they hurt you? Threaten you?'

'The big one, Sandalwood, shoved me down in the chair once and gave me a slap across the face. That hurt.'

'We wouldn't do that, Rose. Not real police. I know people

say things about us sometimes, and it's easy to be cynical, but really . . .' She thought of her famous 'drop-kick' and went on, 'I mean, if we're dealing with hard cases who want to hurt us, maybe we'd get a bit physical, but not in a situation like this. Not with someone like you.'

'I told you I didn't think they were real policemen. But there wasn't much I could do, though, was there? I felt threatened by them. It was much safer just to go along with them and do what they said. I thought they were going to beat me up or kill me. Or . . .'

'What?'

'Well, he leered at me once, the big one, and, I was scared he might be going to rape me or something.'

'Did he try anything like that?'

'No. He just laughed at me when he saw what I was thinking, like, and said not to worry about that, tempting as it was. I felt dirty.' She hugged herself. 'Totally powerless. They could have done anything.'

Winsome noticed that her glass was almost empty. 'Another?' she offered.

'I shouldn't, but yes, please. Talking about it brings all the feelings back. Can I have a Bacardi Breezer this time?'

'Sure.' Winsome brought her the drink and another orange juice for herself. 'What did they want to know?' she asked, sitting down again. 'Did they ask about the gun Erin had?'

'No. They never mentioned it.'

'Did you know anything about it?'

'Not until I saw it on the news.'

'Did they ever mention someone called Marlon Kincaid?'

'No.'

'Did Erin or Francesca ever mention him?'

'No.'

'You're certain?'

'Marlon Kincaid? It's a funny name. I'd remember.'

'What other sorts of questions *did* they ask you?'

'One of them had a good look round the place. Watkins. Upstairs and everything. The other one asked me the questions. He wanted to know if I knew where Jaff had gone – that's Erin's boyfriend. I told him I didn't. Then he wanted to know about Francesca. He said someone had seen Jaff and her leaving the flat by the wharf together. I said I didn't know where they were, which is true.'

'How did they know about Francesca, that she was with Jaff?'

'They didn't. They were only guessing from what they'd heard at the flats. But they knew there were three of us living in the house, and they must have worked it out. They wanted to know who she was.'

'So you told them?'

'What else could I do?' Rose pleaded. 'You weren't there. You don't know what it was like!'

A couple of the regulars were giving them curious looks. 'OK,' said Winsome. 'Stay calm. It's all right. I'm not blaming you.'

Rose sipped her drink. 'I'm sorry.'

'Was the gun Jaff's?'

'I don't know. How would I know? I never even knew it existed. Erin certainly never mentioned anything like that.'

'What do you think?'

'I wouldn't be surprised. I never did trust him. Too flash for my liking.'

'Why would Erin take it, do you think?'

'I don't know. To make him mad, maybe? She was pissed off at him. Something was going on between the three of them – Erin, Jaff and Francesca. I don't know what it was, they didn't tell me anything, but something wasn't quite right.'

Winsome made a note, then asked, 'What did they do next?'

'I can't remember. Nothing. They wanted to know where Francesca was, where Jaff was, but I kept telling them I didn't know. I was so scared they were going to hurt me anyway, but they just left.'

'You're one lucky young woman,' said Winsome. 'They must have believed that you didn't know anything else and thought there was no percentage in harming you. They also weren't worried about you being able to identify them. They were pros, by the sound of it.'

'Pros?'

'Yes. Professionals. Amateurs often hurt people. They're careless, impulsive. Professionals are more careful. They know that can only bring trouble and attention, and that's not what they want.'

'Yes, but professionals in *what*?'

Winsome paused. 'That I don't know,' she said. 'But I'm going to have a very good crack at finding out. Now tell me more about this Jaff.'

'My God! What have you done?' Tracy could only stand there staring down at Annie's body lying across the broken table among the smashed glass and pottery. Annie's face was ashen, covered in a sheen of sweat. There wasn't much blood, just little smears around the two small holes in her yellow top. But that didn't mean much. There would be internal bleeding. 'You've killed her.'

'What choice did I have?' Jaff said from the doorway, the

gun still in his hand. 'She wasn't going to just go away, you know. She *knew*.'

'But . . .' Tracy continued to stare down at Annie's immobile form. For a moment, she thought she could see her chest heave and make a gurgling sound with the effort of trying to breathe, but it could have been an illusion. 'We have to call an ambulance.'

'Like hell we do. Besides, it's too late. What we've got to do is get out of here fast.'

Jaff grabbed Tracy firmly by her upper arm and dragged her out of the conservatory into the kitchen. He tossed his gun back into the holdall and hefted it on to his shoulder, while still holding her with his free hand. Tracy squirmed and tried to wriggle out of his grasp, but she couldn't. He was wiry but strong. Her arm was starting to go numb. Finally, he put the holdall down and gave her a sharp, stinging slap across the face. 'Stop it,' he said. 'Pull yourself together. We're leaving. Now.' Tracy grabbed her shoulder bag from the bench before he pushed her through the door into the living room. She stumbled and banged the side of her thigh against the sofa. It felt as if someone had kneed her hard right on the muscle. Jaff pushed her again and she tripped into the front door face first. Blood trickled from her nose. She thought it might be broken. He grabbed her jacket and thrust it towards her. 'You might need this. The nights are getting cold.'

Tracy felt dazed as she stumbled outside. She wiped the back of her hand across her face. 'Jaff, please let me call an ambulance. Nobody could have heard those shots. If she's not dead already, she'll die for sure if we just leave her here.'

'That's her lookout.' Jaff fumbled for his car keys, letting go of Tracy for a moment. She walked around to the passenger side. Perhaps if she took off into the woods, made a dash for it? But no. He would give chase and find her, then he would kill her. Besides, if she did that, she would never even get a chance to try to save Annie, if that were even possible.

There was one thing she could do with her moment of freedom, while Jaff was at the driver's side opening the door, and she was at the passenger side. She took out her mobile, keeping it low, hidden by the car and her body, and pressed 999. There was no way she could do it without Jaff hearing, so she had to be really quick. There was an ambulance station in Helmthorpe, she knew, so it shouldn't take them too long. When she heard the answering voice, she put the phone to her mouth and said, 'Ambulance. Newhope Cottage, Beckside Lane, Gratly. Come quickly. Please. Someone's been shot—'

Before she could say any more, Jaff had dashed around the car and snatched the phone from her hand. In his anger, he threw it to the ground and crushed it with his heel again and again until the pieces were scattered over the gravel. That was it, Tracy thought, her heart sinking even lower. Her lifeline. Gone. She was alone now. Alone with a killer. He shoved her into the passenger seat and started the car.

Tracy began to shake. She couldn't get the image of Annie out of her mind: just lying there, pale, still and bleeding on the broken glass table. But at least she had made the 999 call, however dearly it had cost her. If there was any hope at all, that was it. Now she had to turn her mind to her own predicament, which it didn't take a genius to work out was a lot worse than it had been only half an hour ago.

She had thought Jaff was going to kill her after he had discovered that her father was a policeman, but he had come up with another option: to keep her as a hostage until he had got to safety. He had told her he could use her as a bargaining tool in negotiations. Her being a DCI's daughter was a double-edged sword, he went on, and he intended to be the one who was wielding it.

But Annie's shooting changed everything. He'd be far less concerned about killing a second person now, and far more worried about his own escape and safety. She could still be a bargaining tool, but she had just become more expendable than before, especially after making the phone call.

'What are you doing?' she said, snapping out of it when she saw Jaff was about to turn right at the end of the drive.

'Do you think I'm stupid?' Jaff said. 'Since your little act of rebellion with the mobile, that main road down there is going to be full of police cars and ambulances. I'm going the other way.'

Jaff headed for the open moors. The sun was still up, but the shadows were lengthening, and the light was turning softer, streaks of faint pastel colouring the pale blue sky. Soon it would dip below the hills and the sky would darken. Tracy thought she could hear a siren in the distance. God, she hoped she was right, hoped they were in time. 'Don't you realise how what you've done changes everything?' she said. 'One of their own? They'll pull out all the stops on this.'

'What the hell else was I supposed to do?' Jaff snapped. 'Hold out my hands for the cuffs? Anyway, you should know,' he went on, giving her a sidelong glance. 'Copper's daughter. Traitorous bitch. But they don't know what's happening yet. They don't know about me. She'd never have come by herself if she'd known the truth.'

'Maybe she had no reason to suspect you'd got hold of another gun, or that you'd shoot her,' Tracy said. 'Maybe she did come to water the plants. But it didn't take her long to suss out the situation. She knew more than you think. And that means others will probably know, too.'

'You can't be certain of that.'

'I know how they work. Would you rather take the risk?'

Jaff didn't reply.

Tracy contemplated her position. Perhaps it was for the best that he had turned right at the end of her dad's drive. She knew the moors; she had come out here with her father many times after his divorce, walked the hidden paths with him for hours, explored hidden clefts and gullies, the abandoned quarries and old lead-mine workings. There were twelve miles of open moorland between her father's cottage and the next village of any significance. Jaff was like a fish out of water here, dependent on her to show him the way. It gave her an advantage, especially if she could find an excuse to get him to stop after dark.

She was still wondering how the hell she could get out of his clutches for as long as it took to disappear when, just two miles along the narrow, unfenced road, the car gave up the ghost.

Jaff tried to start it up again a few times, then cursed, got out and started kicking the tyres. 'Fucking Vic! Fucking idiot!' He kept repeating it like a mantra.

Though the sun had just set, there was still daylight left, but Tracy took advantage of Jaff's tantrum by edging towards the drystone wall beside Topfleet Woods. Perhaps if she could escape into there, she could keep far enough ahead of him to double back down to Cobbersett, a tiny village on the daleside just to the west of Gratly. From there she could easily make it to Helmthorpe and get help. She doubted that Jaff would pursue her for very long through the woods if he thought the police were after him. He would want to go forward, not back. Nimbly, she hopped over the wall and ran into the trees.

But she underestimated both Jaff's intentions and his speed. He had kept his eye on her. In no time at all, she could hear him behind her, and soon she felt a tight grip around her neck. She jerked to a halt, her head snapping back, and screamed in pain.

'Shut up, or so help me I'll strangle you here and now,' said Jaff between gasps for breath. 'You stupid bitch. You're losing us time. Get back to the road. Get us the fuck out of here, not back where we came from.'

'Let go. I can't breathe. You're breaking my neck.'

'Promise you won't run any more.'

'I promise! I promise! Let go!'

Jaff let go. He caught his breath, hands on knees, while Tracy massaged the back of her neck. It obviously wasn't broken, or she wouldn't still be standing, but it certainly hurt like hell. Finally, Jaff turned and started walking back to the car, cocky and confident enough to simply leave her to follow. She hated him at that moment more than anyone ever in her life, and she was tempted to take off again. But he was faster than she had thought, and this time if he caught her, he would probably kill her. She paused and stooped to look for a stone she could smash his head in with, but there was nothing. He turned and looked at her, shook his head, then carried on walking again. Head hung low, still massaging her neck, she followed like a shameful Eve following Adam out of Paradise. Some paradise.

'We've got to get rid of the car,' Jaff said. 'There's a gate up ahead. You can help me push it there and through, then we'll see if we can't hide it on the other side.'

Tracy felt too defeated to respond. Her nose hurt, her neck hurt and her heart ached. So she followed him.

9

Banks had been on the plane since 4.55 on Wednesday afternoon, and by his watch it was three o'clock in the morning when they finally stopped circling Heathrow and began the slow descent. It was broad daylight outside. He hadn't slept – he never did on planes – but at least he hadn't drunk any alcohol; he had heard that abstinence helped to alleviate jet-lag. The food had been pretty dreadful, and the choice of movies not much better. Mostly he had read *The Maltese Falcon* until his eyes got too tired, then he took out his iPod and listened to Angela Hewitt playing Bach's keyboard concertos. The noise-cancelling headphones he had bought before flying out had been expensive, but they were well worth it. The music came out loud and clear, while everything else was a distant background hum. Somehow, Bach managed to calm and relax him on a flight in a way that most other music didn't.

But soon the instructions came to turn off all electronic devices, along with the information that the time in London was 11.05 a.m. on Thursday morning, and the temperature was eighteen degrees Celsius. Banks packed up his iPod and headphones and took out his book again for the last few minutes. At least they hadn't barred people from reading old-fashioned print on the final descent. Yet.

He could see London spread out below him between the

clouds as they came in to land from the east: the meandering Thames, the green sward of a large park, Tower Bridge,
busy streets and clusters of buildings, all the familiar landmarks gleaming in the bright sunshine. It looked like a fine
day, but all he really wanted to do was crawl into bed. He
had booked a hotel room in the West End and planned on
spending the weekend in London, seeing old friends, before
taking the train back up north on Monday morning. He
hoped the hotel room would be ready for him when he
arrived.

The plane bumped along the runway, and after a lengthy
ground journey came to a halt beside a jetway. In no time
at all, Banks was shuffling along the miles of airport corridors with the rest of the weary passengers to Passport
Control. The EU line wasn't very long, and it was soon
Banks's turn to walk up to the officer and present his passport. She checked the photograph against his face, scanned
it through her computer, checked it again, then turned around,
and two burly men who had been hanging back keeping an
eye on the arrivals walked forward.

'Mr Banks? Can you please come with us, sir,' one of
them said in a voice that made it clear that he wasn't asking
a question.

'What is—'

'Please, sir.' The man took his arm and led him away from
the queue.

Banks had done the same thing to enough people himself
– albeit in slightly different circumstances – to know not to
expect any answers. Maybe they thought he was a terrorist.
Maybe they would waterboard him. They could do what
they wanted, and there was nothing he could do about it.
Most likely, he thought, it was something to do with that

business with MI5 earlier in the summer. He'd made a mess of things then, and he had also made some dangerous enemies. They had long memories; they didn't forget. Was this some kind of payback for what he had done? And how serious were they? Whatever it was, he certainly wouldn't get to say anything until they arrived where they were going. He felt panic rise in his chest; his heart thumped, and he found it difficult to breathe. He also felt faint and light headed from jet-lag and lack of sleep. And fear.

They led him down the corridor towards the baggage reclaim area and through a heavy door to the left marked AUTHORISED PERSONNEL ONLY. After a few more twists and turns along dim and airless passages, they got to an unmarked office door. One of the men opened the door, and with a gentle but firm touch to the small of Banks's back, the other made sure he went inside. Then the door closed behind him.

The office was larger, cleaner and better appointed than he would have expected, but there were no windows, and a little fan sat on the desk slowly churning the stale humid air. It was who sat behind the desk that surprised Banks. Perhaps it shouldn't have. Detective Superintendent Richard Burgess was somehow connected with Special Branch, and he had helped Banks out with a case earlier in the summer, the one that had made him so nervous about all this security business to start with. At the sight of Burgess, he relaxed a bit, and his heart rate slowed closer to normal, but there was still something wrong about this, because DS Winsome Jackman was also in the room. What on earth was she doing there?

'You all right, Alan?' asked Burgess. 'You look a bit peaky.'

'It's not every day I get picked up at Passport Control by airport security. What the hell's going on?' Banks realised that Dirty Dick knew only a part of what had happened earlier that summer, and that Winsome knew nothing, so they couldn't really have any idea of the sort of images that went through his mind, or the level of terror he felt, when two burly plainclothes security officers dragged him off without explanation. After the experiences he had had, he could easily believe that people had been led into those very same corridors and had never been seen again.

'Take a pew,' said Burgess, pushing a bottle of Laphroaig and a plastic cup towards him. 'Sorry about the lack of crystal-ware. This is still your tipple of choice, isn't it?'

'I'm not sitting anywhere or drinking anything till someone tells me what's going on.'

'I'm sorry about the welcoming committee,' Burgess went on. 'Had to be done, though. I can't go out there. And they had no idea why they were doing it. They were just following orders. It's the only way they do things around here. Winsome will explain.'

'What orders? Whose orders? Winsome?'

'Pour yourself a drink first and sit down,' said Burgess. 'Go on. Believe me, it'll help.'

Though he had switched from whisky to red wine a couple of years ago, Banks did as Burgess suggested. Immediately he smelled the acrid peaty malt, he felt his throat constrict and his skin burn, but he managed to take a sip. The warmth flooded his veins. He could get used to this again. 'Just get on with it, then. What's going on?'

Winsome's expression was grave, and now Banks feared that something might have happened to Tracy, Brian, his mother or his father. This was the way they told you about a death in the family. The solicitous tone, a drink, a chair to sit on, the sepulchral expressions.

'I'm sorry, too,' said Winsome. 'But I think it was the best way. Detective Superintendent Gervaise knew what flight you were returning on, and Mr Burgess was kind enough to help out with airport security. Otherwise, I'd be standing out in arrivals holding up a sign with your name on it.'

'I think I'd have spotted you without the sign, Winsome. Come on. Give. What is it?'

'It's Annie,' Winsome said, leaning forward. 'There's no easy way to break this. She's . . .'

'Annie? She's what? Get it out.'

'Annie's been shot.'

Banks fell back in his chair and put his hands to his burning cheeks. 'Shot?'

'Last night. I didn't want to risk you seeing it in the paper, sir. It even made some headlines. That's why . . . I mean, if you'd gone wandering in the concourse . . . you might have . . .'

Banks instinctively reached for the Laphroaig, tipped the plastic cup towards his mouth and took a large mouthful. It burned as it went down, but it helped bring his mind into sharper focus. 'How serious is it?'

'It's very serious,' Winsome said. 'They've sent for her father.'

'But she's still alive?'

'Yes. But it's touch and go. One of the bullets nicked her right lung. It collapsed. The lung and chest cavity filled with fluid. She almost didn't make it to the hospital.'

'One bullet?'

'She was shot twice. Once in the chest and once in the shoulder. The second bullet shattered the clavicle and fragmented. It'll cause mobility problems, but they say it'll heal in time. The surgeons were operating most of the night. They may have to go in again.'

'Good God,' whispered Banks. 'Have you caught whoever did it?'

'Not yet. Our information's a bit sketchy.'

'Where is she now?'

'Cook University Hospital. Middlesbrough. They don't have the facilities at Eastvale General to deal with that kind of trauma.'

'Not many people get shot in Eastvale,' Banks pointed out.

There was a pause. Burgess reached for the Laphroaig bottle, and Banks saw him exchange a glance with Winsome.

'What?' Banks said. 'Is there something else?'

'It didn't happen in Eastvale,' said Winsome. She glanced at her watch. 'Look, do you want to head up to Middlesbrough and see her now? We can pick up your suitcases at the baggage reclaim on the way out, and I'll fill you in on everything I know. There's a helicopter—'

'A helicopter?'

Burgess cleared his throat. 'Least I could do, mate. I put in for a Learjet, but budgets being what they are these days . . .' He managed a weak grin.

Banks stared at him and swirled the remaining whisky in his cup before finishing it off. 'Thanks,' he said. Then he held up the empty cup before he set it down on the desk. 'And for this, too.'

Burgess just nodded, then he got up and opened the door to have a brief word with the two security guards, who were still waiting outside. 'They'll escort the both of you out of here,' he said.

Winsome got to her feet.

'Right, then,' said Banks. 'Let's go.' He paused in the doorway. 'Just one thing. If Annie wasn't shot in Eastvale, where exactly did it happen?'

'In Gratly, sir,' Winsome said. 'In your conservatory.'

Tracy didn't know exactly what time it was when she awoke from a terrifying dream that skittered off back into her subconscious the moment she opened her eyes, leaving her wide awake and afraid. She must have dozed off for a while, she realised. Going by the height and position of the sun through the bare roof beams and gaps in the stone walls, she guessed it was mid-morning. Her face and arm hurt, she felt dirty and wanted a shower, but most of all she needed desperately to go to the toilet.

They were in a ruined barn. Though most of the roof was gone, and large sections of the stone walls had collapsed, it had provided some shelter for the night and, more importantly, a place to hide and remain unseen in the early daylight hours. But they had no food, and Tracy realised now that she was also desperately hungry.

Jaff slept on, snoring and snuffling occasionally, tossing and turning on the hard floor. How could he? Tracy wondered. Her hands and feet felt numb from the rope he had found in the boot of Vic's car and used to tie her up. She couldn't even move enough to dislodge the fat black spider that was crawling over her bare midriff. She hated spiders. It tickled and seemed, to her, to be deriving some pleasure from the discomfort it was causing her, though she knew that was ridiculous. Maybe it would bite her. It just wouldn't go away.

All night she had fought off panic attacks by deep-breathing, but she still felt on the verge of some sort of breakdown as she watched the spider's progress. And she knew that if she caused any trouble now, Jaff would certainly kill her. She was here under sufferance because she might be useful. He now felt he had nothing to lose. He had already shot Annie, probably killed her, and who knew who else he had shot with the gun Erin took? Annie had mentioned someone called Marlon Kincaid, so maybe Jaff had shot him, too. Her only chance was to take to the open moorland the first chance she got, and she couldn't do that while her hands were tied behind a post and her ankles bound.

As she sat there waiting for Jaff to wake up, Tracy cried and longed for her father. Perhaps he *had* ignored her, neglected her in favour of Brian, perhaps he *hadn't* really understood her and failed to sympathise with her failure, to realise how much it had meant to her, especially in the light of her brother's success, but she couldn't really blame him for all that. At least, she didn't want to any more. He had his own life, and she knew it had been difficult enough since her mother had left. Not that she blamed her mother, either. But the baby had been a bit hard to take. Growing kid, now. A half-sister. But she should have been kinder, more under-standing. She *would* be, if ever she got out of this.

The birds had started early, and the cacophony of their different voices continued through the morning. Tracy's bladder hurt more and more with every second that passed, but she wasn't going to sink to the indignity of peeing her pants. She had been hoping for hours to hear the sound of a tractor or some other vehicle approaching before Jaff awoke, but there had been nothing so far but the birds. Nor had she heard any human voices. They were too far from the road. Besides, she realised, what chance would a poor farmer or a couple of ramblers have against Jaff and his gun?

Anyone who approached them would most likely be walking to their death. About an hour ago, she thought she had heard a helicopter overhead, but it hadn't swept close enough to see them through the bare roof. Maybe it would come back. And if there was a helicopter, there were others searching, on foot and in cars.

It had been hard work, but they had managed to hide the car. The wall was just high enough to obscure it from the road, and they had covered the top with branches and scrub. It wouldn't stay hidden for long, though. Someone would enter through the gate and see it soon enough. With any luck, Tracy hoped, that would be sooner rather than later, and the police would realise they were out on the moors somewhere.

Only a few miles from where they had dumped the car, they had come across the barn and, as the sun was already rising, Jaff had said they should hole up there for a while. Tracy had known by then that he was stumped, that he hadn't come up with a plan to get out of this situation. He was lost without wheels. What did he hope to do? Hide in the barn all day and then tramp off through the heather again when darkness fell? He had almost broken his ankle twice last night tripping over heather roots or clumps of springy grass, so he wouldn't want to try that again in a hurry. It would take them days at this rate, and the net would surely be tightening. The whole country would be alerted to the search by now, Tracy hoped. But it was best to keep her mouth shut about that, she realised. If Jaff hadn't thought of these things, of the full extent of what he had done, she wasn't going to tell him. The longer they were out here in the wilds, the more chance she had of escape, or of being found.

Tracy struggled against the ropes once more, but they didn't give; they just tightened and caused her more pain. The spider fell off her stomach and scuttled away. She felt the hot tears trail down her cheeks. Jaff must have sensed something, because suddenly his eyes were open, and he was dragging himself up into a sitting position, clearly stunned, Tracy thought, probably not sure where he was. At that moment, he had the little-boy-lost air about him, the kind of look that had once made her want to hold him and smooth his hair. Now she just wanted to smash his head in with a lump of stone and run away as far and as fast as she could. If she got the opportunity, she would do it, too. She checked the ground for a loose rock. Perhaps when he untied her, she would get her chance.

'I need to go to the toilet,' Tracy said.

Jaff rubbed his eyes. 'Then go.'

Tracy squirmed. 'I can't. You tied me up. It hurts.'

He seemed to think about that for a moment. Then he got to his feet and walked over to her. 'You'd better not try anything.'

'I won't.'

Slowly, he untied her feet first, then, kneeling behind her, her hands, carefully winding up the rope and putting it back in his holdall. He clearly intended to use it again, Tracy thought, which probably meant that he wasn't going to shoot her just yet. Unfortunately, there were no handy stones to smash into his head, and she wouldn't have been able to manage a surprise attack, anyway.

Finally, Tracy was able to get haltingly to her feet. She jogged up and down and rubbed her wrists to get the circulation moving. The movement made her bladder hurt even more. She turned to walk outside.

'Where do you think you're going?' Jaff said.

'Outside.'

Jaff shook his head. 'I'm not letting you out of my sight for one second. Not after the stupid stunts you pulled last night.'

'But I want some privacy.'

'And I want a plate of bacon and eggs and a pot of hot coffee, but neither of us is going to get what we want. If you want to go, you go here.'

'At least turn away,' Tracy begged.

Jaff folded his arms. 'No.'

She tried to stare him down, to hold back her need, but the pressure was too much. In the end, she turned her eyes away from his stare, and, face burning with shame, turned her back to him, let down her jeans and squatted.

George Fanthorpe didn't like being seen in public with Darren and Ciaran, but he didn't like them coming to the house too often, either, especially if Zenovia and the kids were home. He tried to balance things as best he could, family and business, and when they did go out in public, as they were doing now, having lunch at the Wheelwright's Inn just outside the village, he insisted that Darren wear a polo-neck jumper to cover the tattoo on the back of his neck, and that Ciaran wear a suit and comb his hair. That way, they gave an almost credible appearance of business colleagues.

Luckily, the Wheelwright's Inn had a tiny private snug, and the landlord was always happy to accommodate Mr Fanthorpe if he rang ahead. After all, Fanthorpe was the local squire in all but title, the lord of the manor, and the locals were deferential to him, practically doffed their caps when he walked by. It was a role he loved, and he didn't intend to jeopardise it by taking the risk of anyone finding out how and where he got the money to run his legitimate businesses, such as the dairy he owned, which helped support a good number of the area's cattle farmers. Not to mention a great deal of the land thereabouts, which he leased to farmers at reasonable prices.

With their food on order and three pints of Sam Smith's Old Brewery Bitter before them, they got down to business. Fanthorpe wanted a cigarette, but you couldn't smoke in pubs any more, not even in the snug. Couldn't smoke bloody anywhere. Zenovia wouldn't even let him smoke in his own house. The one *he'*d paid for, with *his* money. All he had left was the garden shed, a shabby, musty, dim and dusty domain for a multimillionaire to escape to for a smoke and a quick gander at *The Economist* three or four times a day.

'Right, lads, so what do we have so far?' Fanthorpe asked after wetting his whistle and wiping the moustache of foam from his upper lip.

Darren gave him the details of their visits to Jaff's flat and the girlfriend's house, where they had had their little chat with Rose Preston. Ciaran, as usual, said nothing, merely nodded occasionally.

'So he's definitely done a runner, then?' Fanthorpe concluded.

'Looks like it.'

'With one of his girlfriend's housemates?'

'That's right.'

'The dirty, cheating bastard. Still, it shouldn't be too hard to find out who she is.'

Darren cleared his throat. 'Er, we already know that, boss.'

'Good work. I won't ask you how. You didn't hurt anyone, did you, Ciaran?'

Ciaran gave a twisted smile. 'Not yet.'

'Good lad.'

'She calls herself Francesca,' said Darren, 'but young Rose told us that her real name is Tracy. Tracy Banks.'

'Tracy Banks?' said Fanthorpe, suddenly alert. 'Did you say Tracy Banks?'

'Right, boss. Why?'

'Fuck. I suppose it could be a common enough name, but if it's the one I'm thinking of, she's a copper's daughter. Alan Banks. DCI Alan Banks.'

'The one up Eastvale way?'

'That's the one. Remember him?'

'I remember him now,' said Darren. 'Ciaran and I did a bit of research into his family a few years ago. I just couldn't place the name.'

'Mr Banks and I have crossed swords on a couple of occasions, as you know. I make a point of finding out everything I can about my enemies. Nothing proven, mind you. He never got anything on me, but a few years ago, when he was local CID, he was sniffing a bit too close for my liking. You'll both remember that. He's second-in-command of Western Area Major Crimes now, under that new woman superintendent. Gervaise. Quite a reputation, he has. Bit of a maverick, too, by all accounts, which is why they say *he'll* never make superintendent. Doesn't always play by the rules, or go by the book.'

'All the more fun for us, then,' said Darren. 'Would you like us to have a word?'

'With Banks? Are you fucking insane? That'd be a red rag to a bull. No, no, we leave him well out of it. The last thing we need is the police knowing any more than they do already. Right now they've no reason to come talking to us.

I'm just saying be careful. If his daughter's involved, it could mean more trouble than we expected. He'll be mental. Things could escalate.'

'What about the girl we talked to? Rose. She'll remember us. Should we deal with her permanently?'

'I don't want you dealing with anyone right now. Keep a low profile. Either they've already talked to her, or she's too scared to say anything. Either way, it doesn't matter. Let's stay focused here.'

Jelena, the Czech serving girl, brought their meals. It took her two trips, and Fanthorpe flirted with her, as usual, and ogled her arse as she wiggled away. Darren and Ciaran didn't seem interested. But they never did. Sometimes Fanthorpe wondered about those two. If truth be told, he wouldn't have minded half an hour in a haystack with the lovely Jelena, even a full hour, but he knew how far to push it. He had plenty of opportunities to play away from home on his 'business' trips. No point doing it on his own doorstep. Around these parts he was a well-respected family man, and it was in his best interests to keep it that way. So he stuck to flirting and drew the line at anything further. Though he wondered whether she might be interested in a quick trip to London next week, dinner at the Ivy, take in a West End show.

'The problem is,' said Darren, bringing Fanthorpe back to the matter at hand, 'that if it *is* her, this Tracy Banks, then she's gone over to the dark side, hasn't she?'

'The dark side? Jaff? Is that meant to be some sort of a fucking joke?'

'No.' Darren seemed genuinely nonplussed.

'Because if it is, it's not very funny.'

'No, boss. What I mean is, Jaff's hardly the sort of bloke you associate with *nice* girls, is he?'

'I don't suppose he is, now you come to mention to it,' said Fanthorpe. 'He's a bad 'un through and through. But these young lasses. Some of them like that sort of thing. Got minds of their own these days, they have.'

'Between their legs, more like,' said Darren.

'You watch your tongue. I've got daughters of my own.'

'I didn't mean—'

'Just watch your tongue, that's all.'

'Sorry, boss. Have you seen the news today?'

'Haven't had time,' said Fanthorpe, who found most news, except the economic kind, boring. All they could talk about was sport, sex and politics, anyway. Or crime.

'There was a copper shot in Swainsdale last night. They're not saying much, except it was a woman, a DI, no less, and she wasn't even on active duty at the time. There's rumours she might not survive.'

'Jaff?'

'Well, he'd have had to get hold of another gun if his girl-friend took the one he had.'

'Easy enough for him,' said Fanthorpe. 'He's got a mate imports them by the crate-load from Lithuania. Baikals with silencers. Right pieces of shite, if you ask me. Converted from firing tear-gas pellets. I ask you. But they're deadly enough in the right hands. No, the shooter's no problem. Not for Jaff.' Fanthorpe rubbed his stubbly chin. 'I always thought there was something not quite kosher about our Jaff, much as I loved him like my own. A bit too independent minded. I wouldn't be at all surprised if he had a few of his own little enterprises going on the side, a few irons in the fire we don't know about.'

'Then it's not our problem, is it?'

'It is now. He's made it our problem. He's taken something

of mine, and he's got himself in trouble with the law. I don't take kindly to any of that. He's opened us up to the kind of exposure and attention we don't want. Sooner or later, when the police come knocking, someone talks. Right now, I wouldn't trust Jaff as far as I could throw him. He's capable of anything. Look how bloody moody and unpredictable he is. And that temper of his. Like a barrel of dodgy dynamite, ready to go off at any moment. No, I don't want Jaff on the loose. But this Tracy Banks business adds a whole new dimension. You sure the copper getting shot is connected?'

'Has to be, doesn't it?' Darren said. 'I mean, that part of the world, Swainsdale, bit of a backwoods, really, innit? Nothing much happens there. Now all this. It'd be too much of a coincidence if they weren't connected, wouldn't it?'

'Jaff?'

'I wouldn't be surprised,' said Darren. 'You said it yourself. He's a loose cannon.'

'And you think the Banks girl is on the run with him?'

'Along for the ride, by the sound of it. I'll bet he's giving her plenty, too. Bit of a randy goat, our Jaff. Maybe she just likes a bit of rough?'

'What a fucking idiot.'

'He's on the run. Like an animal. He's not thinking clearly. Not acting rational. Desperate.'

'Well, that gives us an edge, doesn't it?' said Fanthorpe, detaching some flakes of crispy batter from his fish. The soggy white meat tasted oily. There was something not quite right about it, and his stomach was already making grumbling sounds. Maybe he should follow his doctor's advice and lay off booze and fatty foods. 'An edge. Because we're going to remain cool, calm and collected about this. Aren't we, gentlemen?'

Both men nodded.

'Right. Where was this policewoman shot?'

'I don't know, boss. They only said her wounds were life—'

'I don't mean that, you idiot. Where in Swainsdale? Eastvale? Helmthorpe? Lyndgarth?'

'They didn't say.'

'Boxing clever, eh?' Fanthorpe sipped some more beer and finished his fish and chips, which tasted better now, then he said, 'Right, this is the situation as I see it. The way I put the pieces together, our Jaff was on the run or hiding out somewhere in Swainsdale with Tracy Banks. Running from a gun charge his girlfriend was no doubt helping to bring against him, which, as we know, not only means a five-year stretch, which is bad enough, but the kind of police scrutiny a lad in Jaff's business couldn't survive. And he's running with something of mine, something of great value. Not to mention the fifty grand he was supposed to deliver. As Alan Banks works out of Western Area Headquarters in Eastvale, I think we can safely assume it's the same Tracy Banks. Somehow or other, one of the local plods caught up with them, and Jaff, silly, lovable, impulsive bugger that he is, pulled a gun and shot her. That means Tracy Banks is either with him all the way, or she's suddenly become a distinct liability. I'd guess the latter. Either way, she'll slow him down.'

'Unless he just shoots her and dumps her?'

'Possibly,' said Fanthorpe. 'But he'll know she might be useful to him. Jaff's not stupid. We need to find them before the police do, or we've seen the last of our little commodities.'

'And the money,' Darren added. 'Let's not forget the money. It'll end up under some copper's mattress. But where are we supposed to start? Swainsdale's a bloody big place, and it's mostly full of nothing.'

'If I know Jaff,' Fanthorpe said, 'he'll be heading for the city. He's a city boy at heart. He's got contacts in London, the old boys' network. You'd be surprised how many of them are crooked. He's got people who can get him anything he needs, for a price, no questions asked. That's the class he comes from, remember. He always thought he was a cut above you and me. But he's got to get there first. I assume he's got a car. You can't get around in that part of the world without wheels. But he wouldn't use his own car. He wouldn't want every patrol car in the area looking out for his number plate, would he?'

'He might have stolen one,' Darren suggested.

'Only if he could be certain the owner was well out of the way for a few days so he couldn't report it stolen. But point taken. Now, I happen to know he's got an old mate in Leeds called Victor Mallory. The Baikal boy, as it happens. I've used him myself for freelance jobs once or twice. Just small stuff. Nothing important. They went to school together down south. One of those posh bum-boy places. Eton or Harrow, or whatever. Anyway, they're close. This Mallory lives just north of the Leeds ring road, near Harrogate Road, where all those golf clubs are. Alwoodley, something like that. According to my sources, he's as dodgy as Jaff, and not only with the guns. Clever with a test tube, they say.'

'Alwoodley's not so far from the airport, is it?' said Darren. 'Maybe Jaff got on a flight to Benidorm or somewhere?'

'Don't be a fucking idiot, Darren. He couldn't get on a plane to anywhere. Not with what he's carrying. Everyone has to go through them security scanners now. They can see what you had for breakfast.'

'Sorry, boss. Forgot.'

'No. Wherever he's going, he's got to drive, and he's got to unload the stuff in this country, unless he's a lot more bloody organised than I think he is and has his own network of couriers and mules, which I very much doubt. He might risk a bus or a train, but he'd be worried they're already keeping an eye on the stations. So my guess is he's driving a car nobody knows he's got. So here's what you do. You go pay this Victor Mallory a visit. I'll give you his address. Be discreet. Find out all you can from him and give me a buzz on the throwaway. The throwaway, mind you. Not the landline. And see if you can find out exactly where that copper was shot. If Jaff's behind it, it'll give us at least some idea of what route he might be taking. But it's my guess he's headed for the bright lights.'

'He could be there by now,' said Darren.

Fanthorpe clapped his hands. 'Well, all the more reason to get moving right away, isn't it? And ask Jelena to bring me another pint and a plate of them profiteroles on your way out, would you?' *Maybe now would be a good time to ask her if she fancies a couple of days away, no strings,* he thought.

10

Banks felt queasy after the helicopter ride as he followed Winsome along the hospital corridors towards intensive care, across the hall from the large, modern operating suite. During the flight, Winsome had tried to fill him in on the general outline of what had been happening in his absence, but the helicopter had been noisy, they had had to wear earmuffs and conversation had been all but impossible.

Banks felt numb, too, partly from lack of sleep and jet-lag, but also because of the news he had been given about Annie. He needed to get back into gear fast, but he somehow couldn't quite persuade his body or his brain to make the shift. As a result, everything seemed slightly out of phase, movements in his peripheral vision distracted him, sharp sounds jarred him, and he started to develop a throbbing headache. If he was going to collapse, he thought, he was in the best place for it.

A short, muscular woman with spiky hair came up to them as they neared Annie's room. 'DCI Banks? DS Jackman?'

Banks stopped. He thought he recognised her from somewhere, but he couldn't put a name to the face. Was she a bearer of bad news?

'You won't remember me,' she went on. 'I'm PC Nerys Powell, with the AFO team? I was with the unit that went to the Doyle house.'

Banks didn't understand what she meant, but Winsome seemed to be following all right. 'I know you,' she said. 'I've seen you around HQ, and you were at the meeting on Monday.'

'We're spending a lot of time there these days,' Nerys said. She turned to Banks. 'Look, sir,' she said, 'the officer on the door won't let me in to see Annie. She spoke very highly of you. Will you let me know how she's doing?'

'Why do you want to know?' Banks asked. He knew he sounded brusque, but he was anxious to get past her, to Annie's bedside.

'We were working on the case together. She was kind to me. That's all. It's been . . . things have been . . . very difficult. I sort of feel responsible.'

'Things are difficult for *me* right now,' said Banks, brushing past her. Then he half turned. 'I'll keep you informed, PC Powell. I promise. Go home now. Get some rest.'

Intensive care had facilities for about sixteen patients, but an arrangement of curtains and screens allowed for a certain amount of privacy. Banks's knees felt weak when he approached Annie's bedside. She seemed so small, frail and lifeless, lying there against the white sheets amidst the machines and tubes. But the monitors were beeping steadily, and the LCD lights were all on. He thought he could see her blood pressure at 139/81 and her heart rate at 72, which wasn't so bad, as far as he knew. Probably lower than his, at any rate. A nurse stood by the bedside adjusting one of the tubes, and Banks asked whether he might hold Annie's hand.

'Just for a few moments,' she said.

So Banks sat there holding the limp hand, Winsome standing behind him. The other hand was bandaged up and held fast in the brace along with her injured shoulder. The IV needle was taped to the back of her good hand and several tubes were attached. Banks could see that she was getting blood and some sort of clear fluid, probably saline, with whatever medication she was being given. There was a yellow clip on her finger, also attached to a machine, to measure the oxygen levels in her blood. The lower half of her face was covered by the tube in her mouth and the tape that held it in place. Her eyes were closed. Her pale hand was warm to his touch, but there was no grip, no life in it. For a moment his universe shrank to that small space, defined by the steady in and out of the pump that was giving her breath. If he looked closely, he could see her chest gently rising and falling with its rhythm.

Banks felt a stir of air behind him and turned to see a slight Asian man. He hardly seemed old enough to be out of medical school, but he was wearing a charcoal-grey suit, white shirt and tie, not the bright turquoise scrubs that are the sign of a medical student. Banks had seen plenty of them on his walk down the corridors to intensive care.

'That's enough, now,' said the nurse, putting her hand on Banks's shoulder. 'This is Mr Sandhar. He's the star surgeon on our trauma team, and he operated on the patient. Perhaps you'd like to talk to him?'

Banks thanked her, kissed Annie on the forehead and left her side. Mr Sandhar led Banks and Winsome through another maze of corridors into a small consultation room. There was only one chair, so Banks and Winsome sat side by side on the examination table. Its tissue-paper cover made a crinkling sound as they sat. A chart on the wall depicted the circulation of the blood. Sandhar's chair was next to a weighing machine.

'Can you give it to us in plain English?' Banks asked.

Sandhar smiled. 'Of course. Believe it or not, we usually do try to translate medical jargon into layman's terms wherever possible for friends and family. Obfuscation is not our business.'

'Glad to hear it.'

'Perhaps it would be easier if you were to ask me questions? I should imagine you are quite used to being in that position.'

'Well, I'm hardly going to interrogate you,' said Banks, 'but I can certainly ask the questions if you prefer. First of all, can you tell me what happened?'

'Ms Cabbot has been shot twice. One bullet entered her chest, passing through the middle lobe of her right lung, and the other hit her left clavicle and fragmented, causing a fracture. She was perhaps fortunate in that neither bullet exited, though that very fact alone caused an entirely different set of problems.'

'Those being?'

Sandhar crossed his legs and rested his hands on his lap. 'From my information,' he said, 'the response time of the ambulance was within ten minutes, which is excellent for a rural area, and for a "Category A" emergency, which this most certainly was. Whoever made that 999 call probably saved the patient's life. As I understand it, that person has not been found, but I think that's your domain rather than mine. To continue, the patient had already lost a significant amount of blood by the time the paramedic arrived, but had the weapon been more powerful, and had the bullets exited, there's no telling how much more blood she *would* have lost. With an entrance wound only, you see, the skin has a certain elasticity, and it closes around the point of entry.' He used his thumb and forefinger to mimic the puncture hole closing. 'Not so much blood is spilled.'

'So Annie was lucky the bullets didn't go all the way through,' Banks repeated. 'I see. That's probably the good news. What about the other problems?'

'Most of Ms Cabbot's bleeding was internal, and the leaking fluid put pressure on her lungs, not allowing them to expand.' Again, he used his hands as he talked, moving his open palms close together, as if about to applaud, or mimic the action of bellows. 'One of her lungs collapsed and, as you can imagine, she experienced serious breathing difficulties as a result. If the other lung had stopped functioning, she would have died before the ambulance arrived. Luckily, it didn't. The paramedics acted quickly and had the knowledge and equipment to deal with the situation en route. They managed to stabilise her in Eastvale General Infirmary and then airlifted her here.'

'But she's going to be all right?' said Banks. 'You fixed it? I mean, you operated?'

Sandhar paused. 'We operated. But I must stress that the patient is far from out of danger yet. It could go either way.'

'What do you mean?'

'Right now there's a struggle going on. If she's strong enough, she'll win it. At the moment, no one can predict the outcome.'

'She's strong,' Banks said.

The doctor nodded. 'Good. She will need to be.'

'When will you know more?'

'The next twenty-four hours are crucial. We'll be monitoring her constantly, looking for any signs of decline or improvement. There's nothing else we can do right now but wait. I'm sorry.'

'Is there anything *we* can do?'

'If you're religious you can pray.'

'And if not?'

'You can hope.'

Victor Mallory was pleasantly stoned after a few drinks at lunchtime and a nice spliff when he got home. He had just put Toru Takemitsu's *I Hear the Water Dreaming* on the CD player, and was about to lie down and drift off for a while when he heard the doorbell ring. If he had already been lying down, he thought, he might not have bothered answering. But it could be important. Maybe Jaff had brought his car back, or maybe the nubile Marianna from the golf club had taken him up on his offer, after all. So he answered it.

Immediately he opened the door, he knew he had made a mistake and desperately wished he could close it again. Stoned or straight, he wouldn't have liked the look of the two men who stood there. They could mean nothing but trouble. Panicking, he did try to shut the door, but his reactions were too slow, and they easily pushed their way into his hallway. They would probably have broken the door down, anyway, he realised. In his business, he met some nasty types from time to time, and he generally found that he could talk his way out of most situations, but this time he wasn't sure. They didn't look like good listeners.

The smaller one with the ginger hair resembled a speed freak, bad teeth and all, and Victor didn't like speed or speed freaks. They were wild and unpredictable. That was why he stuck to making E and the good old psychedelics like acid, mescaline and psilocybin. Not a huge market these days, it was true, but in his eyes, they beat crystal meth and crack cocaine, and the kind of people you had to deal with in that world. People like this. It could only be to do with Jaff, who wasn't anywhere near as fussy about what he took, or what he sold to make a living.

'Come in, gentlemen,' he said. 'Make yourselves at home.'

They didn't appear to have a sense of humour. They pushed him into the living room and sized the place up. The smaller one checked out the rest of the house to see whether anyone else was there, while the big bald one sat silently eyeing the modern art on the walls: prints by Dalí, Hockney, Magritte, Rothko. The smaller one returned and, satisfied that they were quite alone with their quarry, they first closed the heavy curtains and turned on the standard lamp, then they got down to business.

'First,' said the big bald man, 'will you turn that fucking racket off? It makes me feel like I need a shit.'

Confused, Victor turned off the CD player. 'I like it,' he said. 'It's really quite soothing if you let—'

'I'd also ask you to turn those bloody paintings around if you could,' the man went on, ignoring him. 'They have about the same effect on my bowels. But we don't have time to mess about. Ciaran.'

The ginger-haired man came forward, gestured for Victor to sit on one of the hardbacked chairs from the dining table and proceeded to use heavy grey duct tape to fasten his legs securely to it with his arms around his back. To finish off, he ran the tape around Victor's upper body and fastened him tightly to the chair-back.

Victor sat passive and silent through all this. He didn't want them to think he was going to cause trouble. There was a chance that this was all a dream, and he could close his eyes and make it go away. He tried, but it didn't. They hadn't taped his mouth shut, so he assumed they wanted to ask him questions, which was a good sign. The paranoia was building, though, getting its hooks into him, but as long as he could talk, there was hope. Gift of the gab, that's what everyone said about Victor. He could charm the birds out of the trees. This need not come to a bad end.

'Right,' said the bald one, once Victor was trussed up to the other's satisfaction. 'You may not know this, but one thing I've learned over the years is that the secret of fear isn't the inflicting of pain. Not at all. It's to do with the *anticipation* of pain. So what we're going to do is this.' He took an object from the small grip he had put down on the sofa beside him and set it on the low glass coffee table. 'Know what this is?'

'An egg timer?'

'More properly known as an hourglass or a sand clock. See how it's shaped? That's why they sometimes talk about women having hourglass figures. Did you know that?'

Victor did, but he wasn't keen to appear too clever in front of these men. He had dealt with similar types before and found that at the first sign of intellectual superiority they became more resentful and, therefore, more aggressive. A public school education followed by an Oxbridge degree was definitely not an advantage in these circumstances. 'No,' he said. 'I didn't. I thought it was an egg timer.'

'You turn it over, and the sand falls through the tiny hole from one glass bulb to the other. Very clever, really. Sometimes I could watch it for hours. Of course, it doesn't take hours. It doesn't even take anywhere near an hour, so why they call it an hourglass I don't fucking know, except it looks like a woman's figure, and they talk about hourglass figures, don't they? Now, these you might find even more interesting. Ciaran.'

The other man took a large folded pouch from the same grip, set it on the table next to the hourglass and unfurled it.

'This is Ciaran's collection of surgical instruments,' the man went on. 'Not that he's a surgeon or anything. Didn't have the Latin, did you, Ciaran?'

'That's a judge,' said Victor.

'What?' the bald man asked, fixing Victor with a blank stare.

'He could have been a judge, but he didn't have the Latin.' Victor regretted the words immediately they were out. They smacked of superiority. What the hell did he think he was doing, correcting this yahoo's quotation?

'What the fuck are you talking about?'

'Sorry. The sketch. It's Peter Cook and Dudley Moore.'

The two men looked at one another and shook their heads. 'Whatever,' the bald one said. 'Anyway, like I said before I was so rudely interrupted, our Ciaran's no surgeon. Bit of an amateur, really. But he likes the tools, and he likes to dabble. The collection's a bit of ragbag, no rhyme nor reason to it, except Ciaran's personal tastes.' The bald man picked up the sharp gleaming instruments one by one. 'Now, I don't know what all these are, but I do know that some of them are used in dermatology. Know what that is? A clever boy like you should do, university education, Latin and all. No? It means they're sharp enough to peel an eyeball. Gives a whole new meaning to keeping your eyes skinned, doesn't it? Others are meant for making deeper cuts through layers of fat or muscle. And then there are things that keep the edges of the wounds open or hold back the underlying organs and tissue while the doctors do their business and put their hands inside, or rip things out.' He held up a hooked instrument. 'Retractors of various sizes and designs. Clamps, too, to slow down the bleeding. And most of these other blades are so sharp that they probably don't hurt very much at first, like when you cut yourself shaving, you don't really feel it. But eventually the pain comes. Delayed reaction. The blood's already there, of course. All over the place by then, I should imagine.'

As the bald man talked, Victor felt his spirits sinking and his heart rate rising. He knew the kind of damage and pain these instruments could inflict. Even the dental probe terrified him. His mouth was dry and his skin clammy. 'Why are you doing this?' he croaked. 'What do you want? I haven't done anything. You don't have to do this.'

Ciaran busied himself with the instruments, lovingly and carefully polishing each one with a white cloth.

The bald man looked on, smiling. 'What a perfectionist. I tell him not to bother, they'll only get bloody again, but every time, without fail, he has to polish his instruments. Maybe he's just an optimist? Maybe he thinks he won't have to use them this time?'

'He doesn't,' said Victor, licking his lips. 'He doesn't have to use them. What do you want? I'll tell you. If it's money, take it.'

'We don't want your money, and I'm sure you'll tell us plenty,' said the bald one. 'But I'm also sure you can understand that we have to be *certain* you're telling us what we need to hear, not just what we want to hear. There's a subtle difference.'

'I'll tell the truth.'

The man laughed. 'Hear that, Ciaran? He'll tell the truth. That's a good one. Where have you heard that one before?'

'What do you mean?' Victor's mind was clear enough now

for him to worry because the bald man had no hesitation about calling Ciaran by name, if that was his real name. And that couldn't be good, could it? 'I won't talk. I won't tell anyone,' he added, for good measure.

'No, that you won't,' said the bald man. 'See those tongs and that blade there? Very good for loose tongues, those are.'

Victor swallowed. His tongue felt too big for his mouth.

The bald man clapped his hands. 'But that's all farther down the road. After we've reached what I call the point of no return. First off, let's just have a go, shall we? See how we start off. Starter for ten, eh? An educated lad like you ought to know *University Challenge*. Let's see how far we can get without resorting to any serious unpleasantness.'

'That's fine with me,' said Victor.

'Good. The way it works is like this.' The man turned the hourglass until the sand started slowly sifting through the tiny hole into the other glass bowl. 'I'm not sure exactly how long this takes,' he said. 'To be honest, I've never actually timed it. But while the sand is still running, Ciaran here will hold back with his instruments. That's the amount of time you've got to give me the answers I need. Understand?'

'Yes. Yes. Please. Go on. Ask me anything. Hurry.' Victor glanced at the sand. It was moving far faster than the laws of physics allowed, he was certain, rushing through at an alarming rate.

'Calm down, Victor. There's no hurry. Plenty of time.'

'Please. Ask me what you want to know. Start now.'

'*Need* to know.'

'All right. *Need*.' Victor wanted to yell, 'Just bloody get on with it!' as he eyed first the cascading sand, then the shiny, curved retractor that Ciaran was polishing. He felt his bowels loosening. He said nothing.

'We'll start with questions we think we know the answers to already. That way we'll know if you're lying. A kind of litmus test. You're a friend of Jaff McCready's, yes or no?'

'Yes.'

'Right. Good start. Did he come to see you recently?'

'The other day. Yes. Monday, I think.'

'Well done. What did he want?'

'To swap cars for a few days.'

'Did you swap?'

'Yes. He's a mate. He was in a jam. You help out a mate in a jam, don't you?'

'Highly commendable. Tell me the make, colour and number of your car.'

Victor told him.

'What else?'

'I don't understand.'

'What else did he want?'

'Nothing.'

'Tut tut, Victor.' The bald man tapped the hourglass. It seemed to make the sand move even faster. 'Time's running out.'

'All right, all right! He wanted a shooter.'

'And you just happened to have one lying around?'

'I have a source. I help people out sometimes. Jaff knew that.'

'So you gave him a gun?'

'Sold him one. A Baikal. With a silencer.'

'I'm not interested in the make. You're wasting time. Is that all?'

'Yes, I swear.'

'Where is he?'

'I don't know. He just drove off. I didn't even see which way he went.'

'Where was he going?'

'I told you. I don't—'

'Victor, you don't have long left. Better stick to the truth.'

'I . . . he . . . he said he had a girl waiting outside in his car.'

'Tracy Banks?'

'I don't know. I didn't see her, and he didn't mention her name. I thought his girlfriend was called Erin, but you never know with Jaff.'

'Quite the ladies' man, eh?'

'Yes.'

'Where were they going?'

'All he said was that they were going to chill out at her dad's place in the country for a couple of days while he got things organised, then he was heading down to London.'

'Where in London?'

'I don't know. Honest, I don't. He didn't say.'

'Victor . . .'

'Why would I lie?'

'I don't know. Your time's running out. *I* certainly wouldn't lie in your position. But you *are* lying, aren't you?'

Victor licked his lips. 'Look, he's got a mate in Highgate. Bloke called Justin. I've only met him once. He's involved in people-smuggling and all kinds of nasty shit. It's not my scene at all. I don't know his last name. Jaff said Justin would help him out if it came to it. Fake passport and all that. That's all I know. Honest.'

'Highgate's a big place.'

'I'm sorry. That's all I know.'

'Maybe Ciaran will be able to get a bit more out of you?'

Victor struggled at his bonds, but it did no good. 'I don't *know* any more.'

The bald man watched the sand contemplatively for a few moments, then he said, 'What do you think, Ciaran?'

Ciaran stared at Victor for what seemed like an age. The sand flowed through the tiny hole. It was almost all gone now. Victor's mouth was so dry that it hurt his throat when he tried to swallow. He felt that if this went on much longer he was going to start crying and begging for mercy.

'Nah,' said Ciaran, and rolled up his instruments. 'Not worth it. He doesn't know any more.' Victor's mouth dropped.

The bald man picked up the hourglass and put it back in his grip. 'Close call, Victor,' he said, going over and ruffling Victor's hair. 'Very close call. We'll let you get back to your shitty music again. But remember – we know where you live. I suppose I don't need to tell you what'll happen if there's any comeback on us for this, do I?'

Victor shook his head.

'Good lad.' The bald man slapped Victor's cheek playfully, but still hard enough to hurt, two or three times, then said, 'Ciaran.'

They turned off the light and walked towards the door.

'Aren't you going to cut me free?' Victor asked in a small voice.

The bald man paused in the doorway. 'I don't think that would be a good idea,' he said. 'Ciaran's hand might slip with the blade. Like another layer of skin, that duct tape. I tell you what, though.' He took the tape out of the grip and walked over, cutting off a short strip with a pocket knife. 'This'll help save you from yourself. Don't worry. Someone will turn up eventually. They always do.'

'But how will I explain—'

The man slapped the tape over Victor's mouth before he could finish the sentence. 'Use your imagination, Victor. Use your imagination.' Then they left, pausing only to turn on the CD player on their way out.

Hospitals always depressed Banks, and sitting in the coffee shop watching the people taking a short break from dealing with sick children, relatives dying of cancer or lying there senile in geriatric wards didn't help at all. The couple at the next table were talking about the side effects of prostate surgery. Banks tried to shut it out and concentrate on what Winsome was telling him. At least the coffee was good, and he got a chocolate rush from the KitKat. It was well after lunchtime, but he wasn't really hungry. Sleep seemed a long way off, too, after seeing Annie lying there like that and hearing what Winsome and Mr Sandhar had told him. A nurse had informed them that Annie's father, Ray, was on his way up from St Ives by train.

'So, as far as I can gather from what you've told me so far,' Banks summarised, 'Annie was shot when she went to my cottage to water the plants. Didn't it also cross her mind that Tracy might be there with her boyfriend?'

'Probably not. I'm sure she didn't really think that would be the case, or she would have brought in back-up.'

'Not if she thought she was protecting me or Tracy,' said Banks gloomily. 'Not if she didn't want anyone else to know, thought she could nip any problems in the bud. Go on.'

'He's not really Tracy's boyfriend. He was Erin Doyle's.'

'But Erin's been arrested for possession of a handgun?'

'Yes. She's out on police bail.'

'This boyfriend . . .?'

'Jaff. His name's Jaffar McCready, but everyone calls him Jaff.'

'He's most likely the one who shot Annie?'

'So we think.'

'And Tracy made the 999 call?'

'Yes,' said Winsome. 'It was a female voice, and it was her mobile number. I've also heard the recording at the dispatch centre. It sounds like Tracy, as well as I can remember. She sounds scared.'

'As well she might,' said Banks.

'We found her mobile phone at the scene, close to where we think their car was parked. It had been smashed to pieces. The SIM card was still intact, and it showed the phone hadn't been used since Monday.'

'Isn't that when this whole business started?'

'It's when Juliet Doyle turned up at the station to report finding a firearm in her daughter's bedroom, yes. According to Annie, she asked for you.'

'Me?'

'Yes. I should think she hoped you would deal with it without making too much of a fuss, that things would go better for Erin.'

'I see,' said Banks. 'But I wasn't there, and things went haywire. Erin got arrested and Tracy went to tell the boyfriend.'

'Looks that way,' said Winsome.

'And Juliet Doyle?'

'She's stopping with Harriet Weaver. No charges against her, naturally.'

'Naturally. I don't suppose this Jaff would want Tracy using the phone if he thought we might link the two of them and track her down through her mobile use. But she loved that mobile. She was never off it. He must have taken it from her on Monday, kept it switched off. Was she there with him willingly? She can't have been. What do you think?'

'We honestly don't know,' Winsome said. 'She might have been. In the first place. I mean, according to Rose, she went over to his place of her own free will. After that we don't know how events unfolded, but she must have been the one who took him to your cottage. Maybe he forced her to take him. It's possible. All we know is what Tracy's housemate told us. But we don't know what happened after they got there – the place is a bit of a shambles – but, like you, I can't believe Tracy would willingly have anything to do with Annie's shooting.'

'Of course not,' said Banks. 'It's absurd. However this all started, I think we have to assume that Tracy's under duress right now. She's a hostage of this Jaff McCready. That's an odd name, by the way. Know anything about him?'

'I've been doing a bit of digging. His mother's from Bangladesh. Was. She died of breast cancer nearly twenty years ago. She was only forty. Anyway, she was a model. Very lovely, by all accounts. She married Jack McCready. He came from East Kilbride originally, but he built up an empire of bookmakers down south and did a bit of investing in the movie business. That's how they met. He liked to hang about with the stars and directors and such.'

'Don't we all?' said Banks. 'I've heard the name, seen his photo in the papers and his name in the gossip columns from time to time, starlet on each arm sort of thing. Can't say as I've ever met a bookie I could trust. Dead, though, isn't he?'

'Heart attack,' said Winsome. 'Eight years ago. There were rumours about him. Money-laundering, nobbled horses, fixed races, what have you. Nothing proven, and the death was all above board. Anyway, the parents split up when Jaffar was eight. He went with his mother to India. She became quite a famous Bollywood star there. I think Jaffar himself got used to a certain amount of fame and celebrity rubbing off on him. Then his mother died tragically, and he was sent back here. He was thirteen then. His father put him straight into boarding school, no love lost there, I imagine, then he went to Cambridge. Read philosophy.'

'Bright?'

'Average. He got through. They said that he could have applied himself more.'

'They said that about me, too. "Could have tried harder." Troublemaker?'

Winsome smiled. 'I think McCready was more of a misfit, really. He's got no form. Definitely not your run-of-the-mill disaffected youth.'

'No,' said Banks. 'Perhaps a bit more deeply psychologically scarred. How old is he?'

'Thirty-one.'

'Jobs?'

'Never had one, as far as we can determine.'

'Was he on our radar at all?'

'No. But I had a chat with Ken Blackstone, and West Yorkshire are aware of him. That's all. Nothing concrete, just a lot of suspicions. Drugs, mostly. They suspect he's linked with an illegal laboratory, among other things. Something to do with an old mate from Cambridge, a chemistry student. It's an ongoing investigation. A slow one, Ken says. They haven't found anything yet.' She took the two sketches that Rose Preston had made from her briefcase. 'And these two charmers are also looking for Jaff and Tracy. They pretended to be police officers, gave Tracy and Erin's housemate a hard time.'

Banks examined the sketches. They were good quality,

bold, confident lines and subtle shading. He was no expert, but he thought Rose showed talent as an artist.

'She said their names were Sandalwood and Watkins.'

'That's a lie,' said Banks. They're Darren Brody and Ciaran French.'

Winsome's jaw dropped. 'You know them?'

'I made it my business to know them. We've met in passing. They work for George Fanthorpe, better known as the Farmer.'

'I know that name.'

'You should. One of the best-kept secrets in the county. Thinks of himself as lord of the manor, gentleman farmer, owns a dairy and acres of farmland, stables and horse-training, too. Lives near Ripon. His crooked reach stretches as far as Middleham. Beyond, too, probably.'

'They were asking about Jaff, and his dad was a bookie,' Winsome said. 'Think there might be a connection?'

'I doubt it,' said Banks. 'Perhaps at one time. But Jack McCready is long dead, and Fanthorpe's main source of income is drugs. Cocaine and heroin, mostly. Bulk. Never sees or touches the stuff himself, of course. Mr Big. Mostly deals with the student population. The farming businesses are a nice façade, handy for laundering the money. He's probably the only dairyman making a healthy profit these days, or any kind of profit. The racehorses are a hobby – the sort of thing a country squire might be expected to take an interest in. The stables might actually be profitable.'

'How do you know about him?'

Banks finished his coffee. 'Just one of those things. I talked to a minor drug dealer called Ian Jenkinson at Eastvale College about six years ago, just a follow-up for a West Yorkshire case, and he let the Farmer's name slip in connection with a murder on Woodhouse Moor. Another low-level dealer called Marlon Kincaid, who catered mostly to the Leeds student population. Apparently Jenkinson got some of his supplies from this Kincaid, who in turn, we think, got them from Fanthorpe's organisation. Or should have done. As it turned out, he was freelancing, and this annoyed the Farmer. I paid the Farmer himself a visit. Smooth bastard, played the part well, but you know how you get a feeling sometimes, develop an instinct?'

'I'm getting one now,' Winsome said. 'It can't be a coincidence.'

'What can't?'

'That name you just mentioned: Marlon Kincaid. I hadn't got around to telling you yet, but we're almost certain that the gun we found at the Doyle house was used in his murder on November fifth 2004.'

'That's about the right time,' said Banks. 'Very interesting.'

Winsome nodded. 'Indeed. Maybe we should have another chat with this Ian Jenkinson, if we can find him. What happened?'

'Well, it was like I said, a hunch. I did a bit of digging, but I couldn't get below the surface. All the snitches clammed up. Scared. Next time I went to see the Farmer, Ciaran and Darren here were with him, lurking in the shadows. Business associates, he introduced them as. I noticed them on a couple of occasions after that, following me, parked over the street, shopping in the same supermarket. Always said hello and smiled, asked after the family. That sort of thing. Mild intimidation.'

'And were you intimidated?'

'A bit. Those two have a nasty reputation. Darren's just

a thug, not without brains entirely, but a thug nonetheless. Ciaran takes a genuine pleasure in hurting and humiliating people. Rumour has it they've killed more than once, and the killings are linked to Fanthorpe. But you know the way it goes sometimes. No evidence. Perfect alibis. Then something else came up. Marlon Kincaid was well known as a dealer to the student scene, and most people felt the planet was a better place without him. We got no farther on Fanthorpe or on the murder. You know as well as I do that someone in that business can antagonise a lot of people, from rivals to disgruntled parents whose kids have overdosed. West Yorkshire checked all the avenues, but came up with nothing. We were only marginally involved because of the Ian Jenkinson connection. We had nothing on the Farmer to start with. He's never been charged with anything. Maybe the forensic accountants could have made a case if they'd got access to his books, like they did with Al Capone, but we didn't even have enough for a warrant. The CPS said forget it. There were more urgent matters screaming for our attention. Fanthorpe faded into the background with a little flag beside his name. Ciaran and Darren disappeared from my life. I can't say as I ever forgot any of them, but nor did I lose any sleep over them, either.'

Winsome studied the sketches. 'I can see that you wouldn't forget them in a hurry. Ugly customers. I wonder why they aren't more concerned about people giving descriptions of them after a visit?'

'They rely on the implied threat that they'll come back and take their revenge. Most of the people they deal with are the same sort of scum as they are, so they know that. Rose isn't from their world.'

'Will they go after her? Should we offer her protection?'

'I don't think so. She's not important enough for that. She was a means to an end, whether they got what they wanted out of her or not. It's my bet they'd have no further interest. They've moved on. They don't care if we know what they look like or find their prints all over the house. They know that, for one reason or another, it won't go any farther. If the worst comes to the worst, they'll have rock-solid alibis. Do you have any leads beyond what happened at the cottage? I need to find this little gobshite who's abducted my daughter and scrape him off my shoe. If you'll pardon the crude talk.'

'I'll pardon it this once, sir,' Winsome said, 'because I know you're upset.'

'Thank you.'

'One thing I've been meaning to ask.'

'Go ahead.'

'About Tracy being involved. Are you going to call your family and let them know? Sandra? Brian?'

Banks thought for a moment and massaged the bridge of his nose with his forefinger and thumb. The caffeine and sugar rushes hadn't lasted. He felt exhausted again, wanted nothing more than to lie down right here and now and curl up in the fetal position. Conversations hummed around him, but they were all meaningless drivel. 'I don't think so,' he said. 'Not yet, at any rate. The last thing I need right now is Sandra on my back, or even Brian running around trying to help. They'd only get in the way. Besides, as far as I know he's on tour with the band somewhere.'

'But shouldn't they be informed by you before they read about it in papers or see it on the TV news? We can't keep the details of what's happened from the media for ever.'

'I suppose they should. But why worry them at this point?

Worst-case scenario, I'll tell them later. Best case, all goes well, and they'll never need to know.'

'What about your mum and dad. They *are* Tracy's grand-parents.'

'They're on a cruise,' said Banks. 'They're always on a cruise these days.'

Winsome shrugged. 'It's your decision. They'll probably find out when they get back, anyway.'

'Probably. But that's then, and this is now. What's the latest?'

'I'm not up to speed,' said Winsome. 'Remember, I got the airport detail.'

'OK. Thanks for doing that, by the way. Let's head for the station and see what we can find out. What's my role to be in all this? I can hardly sit at home and twiddle my thumbs, but I doubt that Madame Gervaise will want me on the case.'

'She wants to see you about that as soon as possible,' Winsome said. 'I'm sure she'll find you something to do. And as far as sitting around at home is concerned, I think you'd better organise some alternative accommodation to twiddle your thumbs in as soon as possible.'

Banks looked puzzled. 'What? Why?'

'Maybe you've forgotten the protocol, sir, but your cottage is now a crime scene. It's locked down. You can't go home.'

11

Banks made the phone call to arrange for his accommodation on the way to Western Area Headquarters in the patrol car Winsome had arranged. Mrs Haggerty was shocked by the recent shooting in the village. 'In a policeman's house, as well,' she said. 'What are things coming to?' And she proceeded to tell Banks that the last, and only other, shooting they had had there was in 1942, when a local farmer mistakenly fired his shotgun at a tramp, thinking he was a German spy. The tramp suffered only minor injuries, and no charges were brought.

Luckily, the flat that she had let to Banks once before, when Newhope Cottage was being rebuilt after the fire, was vacant. An American couple had booked it, she said, but the husband had lost his savings and his job in the recent financial collapses over there, and they had had to cancel at the last minute. At least, Banks thought, he would be on familiar territory, and he did still have all the clothes and toiletries he had taken on holiday with him. There was a washer-dryer unit in the flat, he remembered, so he could have clean clothes again by tomorrow.

Western Area Headquarters seemed much more crowded than usual, but Annie's shooting had cast a sombre pall over the place. A number of officers nodded grimly to Banks as he walked in, and Winsome helped him carry his suitcase

and hand luggage upstairs before heading for the Major
Crimes squad room to check whether there were any developments.

When Banks opened his office door, he found that the
space was already occupied. By this time, the shock and jet-
lag had eroded his patience to breaking point.

'What the hell are you doing snooping around my office?'
he said, dropping the heavy suitcase and carry-on bag on
the floor. 'Get out.'

Superintendent Reg Chambers remained seated behind
Banks's desk. 'Welcome home,' he said. 'Nobody told me
you were coming in today, but now that you're here we
might as well have a little chat.'

Banks glanced around. Everything seemed as he had left
it, as best he could remember, and he knew that he had
locked his filing cabinets and drawers. There was a master
key, of course, but Detective Superintendent Gervaise had
that. And Chambers would never be able to guess his
computer's password. 'I still want to know what the fuck
you're doing here.'

'My job, DCI Banks. I'm on an active investigation. That
means I have the run of the station.'

'I don't think so.'

Chambers waved his hand and stood up. 'Mere techni-
calities,' he said. 'Anyway, let's not get off on the wrong foot.
It's the only quiet haven in the building. I needed a bit of
peace and quiet, that's all. Don't worry, I haven't touched
anything. You can have it all to yourself again.' He picked
up his folders from the desk. 'I'll go now.' Then he paused
in the doorway. 'Unless . . .'

'Unless what?'

'Well, I *would* like a word with you. We could do it later, of course, but why not do it now, seeing as we're both here? That is, if you're up to it? I understand you've been on holiday?'

Banks walked over to the window and looked out over the cobbled market square. Reassuringly, it hadn't changed. Then he turned and rested the backs of his thighs against the cold radiator. 'Why do you want to talk to me?' he asked. 'I wasn't here. This has nothing to do with me.'

'Your name was mentioned. You know the people involved. You might be able to help.'

'I doubt it.'

'Even so ... Look, I heard what happened to Annie Cabbot,' Chambers went on, a deep frown wrinkling his brow. 'I'm really sorry. How is she?'

'Touch and go,' said Banks. He walked back over and sat in his own chair, which was still unpleasantly warm from Chambers, and offered the superintendent the seat opposite. 'Let's do it now,' he said. He would rather have waited, but there was also a slim chance that he might pick up a useful scrap of information from a chat with Chambers. Besides, he wasn't going to show the man weakness or tiredness; that was just the kind of thing Chambers fed on.

Chambers sat down and scratched his head. 'Right, well, I suppose you must have some idea of what's been going on around here in your absence?'

'Yes,' said Banks.

'Yes, well, it's my job to get to the bottom of it.'

'You're after portioning out blame according to the demands of the media, that's what you're doing. Basic public relations. Let's not try to dignify it. Remember who you're talking to.'

'Well, if you're going to take that attitude I can't see us getting anywhere, can you?'

'Don't get in a huff. It's you who wants to talk to me, after all. Ask your bloody questions. And make it quick. Just remember, you're not talking to some frightened probationary constable who's forgotten to pay his tea money this week.'

Chambers puffed out his considerable chest. 'It's my brief to investigate the conduct of all officers concerned in the lethal discharge of a taser against Patrick Doyle and the events leading up to that tragic occurrence. In case you don't know, that incident happened on Monday morning at the home of the deceased during a routine police operation.'

'Routine? There was nothing routine about it from what I've heard.'

'Then perhaps you've heard wrong? Or you haven't heard enough.'

'Anyway,' said Banks, 'like I said, I'm not involved. I was out of the country.'

'It's my understanding that a woman came to this police station asking for you.'

'Juliet Doyle. Yes. I know her. But as I said, I wasn't here.'

'In what capacity do you know her?'

'We used to be neighbours.'

'Is that all?'

'You're trying my patience, Chambers.'

'So your relationship with the Doyle family was as a family friend?'

'Yes.'

'The daughter, too?'

'*Yes*. And Patrick was a good friend, so knock it off with the innuendos. There's nothing there, and no reason for it.'

'I'm concerned as to why this woman should ask for you in person when she came to report an illegal handgun.'

'It's natural enough to seek out someone you know in a difficult situation, isn't it?'

'Don't you think she did it because she expected special treatment?'

'I don't know. It's not my place to speculate as to motive. Or yours. As I said, a familiar face goes a long way if you're upset.'

'Do you think Mrs Doyle had any idea of the legal penalties involved in possessing a handgun?'

'I have no idea. Probably not. Most people don't.'

'Because this is her daughter we're talking about. And there's no denying prison time would be involved.'

'She did what she thought was best.'

'That's easy enough to say.'

Banks got up and walked over to the window again. The butcher over on Market Street, to his right, was taking all the cuts of meat from his display window, and his assistant was scrubbing the trays. A last-minute shopper dashed in through the door and the butcher looked up with a smile to serve her. Banks turned to face Chambers. 'Why are you asking me these questions? What do you hope to gain? I've already told you, I wasn't here. You should be concentrating on the AFOs involved.'

'Don't tell me my job.' Chambers thumped the table. 'That woman asked for you specifically, and I want to know what you would have done if you'd been here.'

'Oh, that's it,' said Banks. 'We're dealing in would-haves and what-ifs now, are we?'

'A man died.'

'You don't have to remind me. He was my friend.'

'Could you have prevented it?'

'Could I? I don't know. What does it matter? It would have been out of my hands. You want to know what I would have done? It's easy. I would have got as much information as I could from Mrs Doyle and tried to verify, then assess, the circumstances. In all likelihood, I would have logged the incident, and it would have been passed on to our Area Control Room. The ACR would no doubt inform the Divisional Duty Inspector responsible for the area concerned, and she would, in turn, make the Force Duty Supervisor aware of the log. They would discuss the circumstances, and the FSUP would then ask that more information be gathered. Once that had been carried out, the FSUP would request that the DDI deploy a conventional double-crewed response vehicle, ensuring that all officers had full Personal Protective Equipment. The FSUP would then . . . Do you really want me to go on?'

'No. That's quite enough.'

'But that's the procedure. Don't try to teach your grandmother to suck eggs, Chambers.'

'You wouldn't have gone around there by yourself?'

'Well, that would probably have been the best course of action to take, wouldn't it? They would have been expecting me, so they wouldn't have felt threatened. Mrs Doyle would have been accompanying me, and she would have let me in, so I wouldn't have had to break down the door. And I wouldn't have been carrying a taser or a weapon of any kind. But that's not following the rules, is it? What the bloody hell did you expect me to say?'

Chambers looked fit to burst. He made a noise somewhere between a huff and a snort, then lumbered to his feet again. 'You're not being helpful, you know. You're impeding the investigation. I'll be making a note of this.'

'I'm not impeding anything. This is pure fantasy. What happened happened. I was five thousand miles away or more. But you do that,' said Banks calmly. 'You go ahead and make your notes. But before you do, be aware of one thing.'

Chambers paused at the door. 'And what may that be?'

'Things have changed since you started this particular witch-hunt—'

'I obj—'

'A policewoman has been shot. Annie Cabbot. My friend. My partner.' He felt himself choke up and struggled for control. Even as he spoke the word 'partner', it sounded odd to his ear. Blame Dashiell Hammett and three weeks in America. He would normally have referred to Annie as his colleague, or oppo, or even as his DI, but 'partner' sounded good. She was. He would use it from now on. He remembered a line from *The Maltese Falcon* about when a man's partner gets killed he's supposed to do something. Annie hadn't been killed, thank God, but he still knew that he had to do something, and he could start by putting Chambers in his place. Annie would approve.

'A policewoman has been shot,' Banks repeated. 'The media and the politicians won't be all over the AFOs and their tasers from now on. They'll be on our side. The hue and cry will be about how many illegal handguns are floating around out there, and you will have nothing to gain from crucifying anyone inside the department.'

'That's not what I—'

'So why don't you think about that? Circumstances change. If you want to be a poster boy for the media, get with the game. And make sure you're on the right side. Close the door behind—'

Just then there was a tap at the door. Chambers stepped back and Detective Superintendent Gervaise popped her head around. 'Didn't interrupt anything, did I? Ah, Superintendent Chambers, I see you're finding your way around without any difficulty. Alan, welcome back. Fancy a cup of tea and a chat? My office. Now.'

Tracy could tell that Jaff was fed up with walking. He had been quiet and sulky for the past hour, no doubt trying to come up with a new plan, like growing wings.

They had been walking under cover of as many wooded areas as they could find, which were few and far between up on the moors, and as far from even the most minor unfenced roads as they could get. At one point, they had spent over an hour walking along the narrow bottom of a weed-and-nettle-choked gully, getting stung all over. Surely somebody must have found the abandoned car by now and reported it to the police, Tracy reckoned. She wondered how long it would take them to link it with her and Jaff and Annie. Would they have Vic's name on their records? How was Annie doing? Was she still alive? There were too many questions she couldn't answer.

They had managed about eight or nine miles in all since they'd left the cottage, having driven only the first two before the car broke down, and they were now deeper into the moors than she had ever walked with her father. Tracy had lost the advantage of knowing the lie of the land. She hadn't heard the helicopter again, and they were too far away to hear cars on the road. Not that there were any roads. To anybody seeing them from a distance, they would probably have looked like a pair of ramblers, though closer observation would have revealed that they were hardly dressed for the part, and that Jaff's walking skills certainly left a lot to be desired. Most of the time he seemed to walk as if he were striding down a city street, Tracy thought, without paying attention to the land beneath his feet. Which was why he tripped and fell so often.

Tracy had been alert the whole time, but there hadn't been a single opportunity to steal away without the certainty of Jaff's catching her. He wasn't going to let her out of his sight for a moment; her failed escape attempt after the car had broken down, and the embarrassing experience that morning, should have told her as much.

It was mid-afternoon when they came to the crest of a long grassy slope and saw the car park below. There was no village, no houses, only the half-full car park, with its public toilets, stone walls and pay-and-display machines, at the end of a rough track that wound away into the distance and disappeared over the next hill. On the far side, a stile in the drystone wall led to a public footpath, with a wooden sign-post, which stretched for several hundred feet then dipped into a wooded area and disappeared from sight. Tracy recognised where they were now. She *had* been here before.

'What the fuck's that?' Jaff asked.

They lay on their stomachs looking over the brow of the hill. A blade of grass tickled Tracy's nose, and she rubbed it. 'It's popular walking country around here,' she said. 'I think that's the car park for Rawley Force, a local beauty spot. A lot of people do a circular walk from there.'

'How long does it take?'

'About three and a half hours. Why, do you fancy trying it?'

'Don't be fucking clever. But I do have an idea. We could practically be in London in three and a half hours.'

Tracy's heart sank when she realised what he was saying. 'You're going to have to come up with something better than that,' she said. 'Haven't you realised that every copper in the country will be looking for you since you shot Annie Cabbot?'

'Stupid bitch asked for it.'

Tracy sighed. 'I'm hungry,' she said, hoping he would admit to feeling the same way and delay what he obviously had in mind.

'Me, too,' he said. 'But it'll have to wait. Come on, let's get closer.'

They kept behind the brow of the hill and made their way in a sweeping curve towards the car park. When they were directly above it, about two hundred yards away, Jaff commanded her to stop and lie low again. The deep cleft of a dried-up stream-bed ran beside them down the hill-side. Jaff pointed to it. 'If we go that way, no one will be able to see us from the road or the footpath. Can we get to the M1 from here? And don't lie. I'll soon find out, and you'll regret it.'

Tracy pointed to their left. 'We have to take that track. It's the only way out. I think it ends at a B road and we turn left to get to the A1. It joins the M1 farther south, around Leeds.'

'Right. I know that part. That's what we'll do. And you'd better not be lying.'

Tracy started to get up, but Jaff pulled her down beside him again. 'Don't be too hasty. We wait till the next car turns up. That way we know we've probably got three and a half hours before they call the alarm.'

Resignedly, Tracy lay on her stomach again. They didn't have to wait long. It was a beautiful afternoon, just enough of a light breeze to take the edge off the heat you build up on a good long walk. An old white van pulled up, and a young man and woman got out. They wore walking boots and had tucked their trouser legs into their socks. They were also carrying sticks and rucksacks, and the man had some maps in a plastic bag hanging around his neck. 'Perfect,' Jaff said. 'Anoraks.'

'But how are you going to get it started? What about the alarm?'

'An old banger like that? Piece of cake.'

And it was. They scrambled down the stream-bed, Jaff falling and cursing only once, and approached the van. There was no one around. Jaff got the back doors open easily with one of the keys he carried in his pocket, and once inside, it took him no time at all to hot-wire the ignition. The inside of the van smelled of paint thinner and sawdust.

'I can see you've done this before,' Tracy said.

Jaff grinned. 'You could say that. Put it down to a misspent youth. I used to work for a bloke who collected luxury cars for shipment overseas. Know what I mean? Years ago. I was just a kid. Fresh out of uni. Some of the newer models are really tough because of all those computerised keys and alarm systems, but these things are a doddle. And it's perfect. Everyone'll think it's a builder's van. No one takes any notice of crappy white vans.' He drummed his hands on the steering wheel and whooped, 'All right! London, here we come!' Then they set off towards the A1.

'You look terrible, Alan,' said Gervaise, as they sipped tea in her office later that afternoon.

'Nothing that a good night's sleep won't cure,' Banks

said. 'Only somehow I don't think I'll be getting one for a while.'

'I'm sorry about the cottage, but I'm sure you understand. We have no choice. We can arrange for alternative accommodation, if you like?'

'Not a problem,' said Banks. 'It's sorted. I could use a car, though. Mine's in the garage. At least, I assume it's still there?'

'It's there,' said Gervaise. 'Don't worry. You can sign one out from the pool in the meantime. How are you doing, Alan? Seriously. I feel I should welcome you back, but I'm afraid it's not much of a welcome.'

'I feel about as bad as I look,' Banks said. 'You're right about the homecoming. Seeing Annie there in the hospital, I . . .' He shook his head and turned away as his eyes filled with tears. Then he took a deep breath, felt his anger stir, and sipped some tea. 'But I've got to hold it together somehow. It won't do anyone any good if I go to pieces.'

'It's not your responsibility to hold everything together. Perhaps you should go and catch up on sleep.'

'I really don't think I could do that. Not with Annie at death's door and Tracy out there with some homicidal creep. Could you?'

'Perhaps not. How was the holiday?'

'It was great. Really. Just what the doctor ordered. I'm sure it did me the world of good. A bit of a distant memory now, though.' It was hard to believe that only yesterday he had woken up beside Teresa in San Francisco, had breakfasted with her at the Monaco and waved goodbye as she left for the airport in a taxi. He had had time for one last walk around Union Square and a quick lunch at Scala's Bistro, beside the Sir Francis Drake Hotel, before packing, checking out and heading for the airport himself. It had been a beautiful, fresh day. The blue skies, fluffy clouds and sweet, gentle Pacific breeze were no harbingers of what lay ahead.

'I assume you're up to speed with what's been going on?' Gervaise asked.

'Most of it.'

'This is a very delicate situation,' she went on, making a steeple of her hands. 'We're understaffed and overworked and, as you saw, we've got Superintendent Chambers breathing down our necks.'

'Oh, I wouldn't worry too much about him.'

'But I do. It's very important that you don't go charging in like a . . . a . . .'

'Bull in a china shop?'

Gervaise smiled. 'I was trying to think of something less crude than the usual cliché, but that'll do for the moment. Yes.'

'Softly, softly, catchee monkey.'

'Good God, give it a rest. Look, you were out of the country when the shit hit the fan,' Gervaise went on, 'so you might think there's absolutely no reason why you shouldn't work on this. But there are three reasons.'

'Annie and Tracy, for starters?'

'Yes. You're emotionally involved, and that should disqualify you from any active role in these investigations. You also know the Doyles, don't you?'

'Yes. Our kids more or less grew up together. Pat was a good mate, though I hadn't seen him in a while. I'm gutted to hear what happened to him.'

'It's a terrible business. You're also very close to Annie, and we don't know how deeply Tracy's involved yet.'

'Surely the main thing right now is that she's in danger, and that we need to find her?'

'Yes. Yes, of course it is. And we're sparing nothing. Our budget's already gone to hell in a handbasket. The local air search-and-rescue team is involved, and they're sending the helicopter out again as we speak. But what I'm saying is that there might be some surprises ahead, and I don't want you on a short fuse. I also don't want you to give Chambers or anybody else even the slightest impression that you've been in a position to tamper in any way.'

'Tamper with what?'

'You know damn well what I mean. Fix things if it turns out your daughter is in this nasty business up to her eyeballs.'

'I appreciate your plain speaking on this, but I don't think you know either me or my daughter as well as you think you do.'

'Don't go all defensive on me, Alan. I don't need that.'

'What do you expect? You accuse my daughter of being a criminal and me of being corrupt enough to tamper with evidence. Just what the bloody hell do you expect me to say?'

'OK, OK. I'm sorry. Perhaps I went a bit too far. Put it down to pressure. These last few days have got everyone's nerves in a tizzy. I was simply trying to stress that Superintendent Chambers is already dead set against you having any involvement at all in this. I'm going out on a limb here. I know damn well what you're like. If I warned you off, you'd do it, anyway, and that could cause problems for everyone. We can hardly lock you in a cell until it's all over, and if you go off on your own half cocked, God only knows how much damage you could end up doing. Now, I've talked to ACC McLaughlin, he's talked to the Deputy

Chief Constable, and we all agree that there are good reasons you should be brought in, assuming you want to be, but that you have to play down the personal angle. You have to toe the line. You can't let your personal feelings drive you. Objectivity, Alan; that's what we want from you. Your brain, not your brawn. Do you think you can manage that? We'll all be keeping a sharp eye on you. And you have to stay away from the taser business altogether. You must be aware of the risk we're taking in doing this. Superintendent Chambers—'

'Chambers can go back to his kennel and lick his balls as far as I'm concerned.'

'An interesting image, but not one I care to dwell on. Look, I know there's no love lost between the two of you, but he's not without influence with the DCC, or even the Chief Constable.'

'People like him never are.'

'Alan, I'm trying to help you here!'

'I know. I know,' said Banks. 'And I'm grateful. Yes, I want in. Yes, I'll keep my personal feelings under control. I'll behave myself. I'll stay away from the taser business, and I'll try not to throttle the toerag that's got my daughter when I find him. No, I won't tamper with any evidence. And I'll try to keep out of Chambers's way. Good enough?'

'It'll have to be, won't it? Shall we get down to business?'

'Absolutely. Anything more on the gun?'

'Yes. Naomi Worthing from Forensic Science Services rang me from Leeds a short while ago. She got the bullets that killed Marlon Kincaid from West Yorkshire Homicide and Major Enquiries. SIO was a Detective Superintendent Quisling. Retired now. Lives in Shipley. Better still, our killer also left the spent casings at the scene, so she's got them, too. That should provide an exact match of gun and cartridges used in the crime when she gets back to the lab.'

'Prints?'

'Nothing new. No matches on IDENT1, and we checked them against Erin Doyle's *and* her mother's. No matches there, either.'

'We need to check them against Jaff McCready's, too,' said Banks.

'It's in motion. Leeds police are getting a warrant to enter his flat in his absence. They'll get prints from some of his personal effects.'

'Ask them if they can find a photograph of him, too. The media . . .?'

'They're still frothing at the mouth over the taser incident and Annie's shooting. Christ, Alan, it's hard to believe, I know, but it only happened last night. Everything's moving so fast. Anyway, that should distract them for a while, but not for long. They're already watching us like hawks. We're keeping a lid on this manhunt as best we can. Certainly on the fact that a senior police officer's daughter is involved.'

'I appreciate that. But Tracy's not involved; she's been abducted.'

'Alan, there's no concrete evidence of that yet, just the broken mobile.'

'You can't tell me that Tracy would willingly have anything to do with the shooting of Annie Cabbot, or any shooting, for that matter.'

'That's not what I'm saying, and you know it. I'm with you on this. Stop being so bloody minded. We have to play it carefully. As I said, we're still keeping a lid on it. But they have a way . . .'

'I know their ways. It means we need to move even faster than they do. We also need to talk to Ian Jenkinson and—'

'Hang on, hang on, Alan. You're going too quickly for me already.'

'Didn't Winsome explain?'

'Explain what? She hasn't had a chance to explain anything yet.'

Banks told her about the Marlon Kincaid murder, Ian Jenkinson and the connection with Ciaran and Darren, who were now looking for Jaff and Tracy, and who were connected with the Farmer, George Fanthorpe.

Gervaise whistled. 'Curiouser and curiouser. OK,' she said. 'In the light of what you've just told me, you're right. We do need to talk to Ian Jenkinson and to Detective Superintendent Quisling. I'll send Doug Wilson and Geraldine Masterson.'

'What was Erin doing with the gun?' Banks asked. 'I take it you do believe it belonged to McCready from the start, and that she didn't come across it through some other means?'

'We don't have any concrete evidence of that, and we haven't charged her with anything yet. She's on police bail. But that's what we think. Annie thought so, and Winsome agrees. We're still digging into McCready's background. But we're not sure why it was in Erin's possession.'

'Well,' said Banks, 'I'd guess that he either gave it to her for safe keeping, or she took it.'

'Why would he need her to keep it safe for him?'

'Maybe he was expecting trouble from the police?' Banks suggested. 'We can ask Ken Blackstone in Leeds. Maybe he got nervous about having it around the flat in case he got caught doing something else he was planning, and they searched the place.'

'And if she took it?'

'Angry with him. Trying to make him mad, get his attention.'

'There is some evidence that they were involved in a dispute at a Leeds club the day before Erin arrived home with the gun.' Gervaise cleared her throat, then said, 'I'm sorry, but there's also evidence your daughter was involved in that dispute, too.'

'Tracy?' said Banks. 'I hadn't heard about that. How?'

'Jealousy.'

'Tracy and Erin were fighting over McCready?'

'Sounds that way.'

Banks put his head in his hands. Suddenly he felt more weary than he had ever imagined he could. 'I thought she had more sense.'

'I'm sorry,' said Gervaise.

'Not your problem.'

'Well, it is, actually.'

'What do you think happened?'

'From what I've been able to piece together, I think Erin and McCready ended up back at his flat after the fracas at the club. Maybe they made up, but somehow or other they got to fighting again, maybe the next morning.'

'And Tracy, at this point?'

'Home in her own bed. We think McCready was in Amsterdam and London over the weekend. It's likely he left on Friday morning, and if Erin was alone in his flat for a while, she could easily have taken the gun out of spite and decided to go home for a few days to chill out, as they say.'

'That would explain why McCready didn't go looking for her that weekend.'

'Yes. He didn't know she had it,' Gervaise agreed. 'He

wasn't home. And it probably wasn't something he checked on every day, anyway.'

'Why did Tracy go to McCready's flat in the first place?'

'We think she dashed over to warn McCready that the police might soon become interested in him.'

'Why would she do that?'

'Your guess is as good as mine. Better perhaps. Why do you think?'

'The question assumes that Tracy knew he was dodgy, if she felt she needed to warn him.'

'Maybe she did.'

'How?'

'We're pretty sure that McCready supplied a good deal of E to the club scene in Leeds. Maybe other things, too.'

'Are you suggesting that Tracy takes drugs?'

'Who knows? Maybe she does. Who knows what kids get up to, Alan? But my point is only that maybe she knew somehow that McCready was involved in drugs, and she liked him enough to want to warn him. Young people have different priorities.'

'Then she took off with him?'

'It appears that way. I suppose it seemed like a bit of an adventure. Nobody had been killed, or shot, at that point, remember – the news of Patrick Doyle's death hadn't been announced before the time they would have left McCready's flat, and his death was a taser-related accident, anyway.'

'I suppose if he'd chucked Erin and taken up with Tracy, that might explain some of it,' Banks mused. 'Would Tracy have known about the gun? How much had been on the news by then?'

'We hadn't given the media any information by then, but the TV cameras on the evening local news showed the AFO walking out with a gun-shaped object wrapped in a tea cloth. It wouldn't have taken a lot of imagination to figure out what had happened, if they were watching.'

'So McCready would immediately check on his gun and find it was gone.'

'Yes. But he might not have told Tracy what the problem was. We just don't know.'

'I can tell you one thing for certain,' Banks said. 'Tracy might have gone with McCready willingly at the start, but she's not with him of her own free will now, not after what happened to Annie. Tracy may make mistakes, maybe she even takes drugs and has rotten taste in men, but she's a decent girl at heart. I ought to know.'

'I'm not here to argue with you, Alan. As a matter of fact, I agree that she's in serious trouble, and probably in danger, too. I don't say that to alarm you, and I wouldn't mention it if I thought you didn't know it already. We need to find them and bring this to a peaceful conclusion as soon as possible.'

'How's the search going?'

'We need more men. There's a lot of countryside out there.'

'Where?' said Banks.

'Well, you'd know better than I would, but we doubt they took the road to Eastvale from your cottage because they'd have been seen. The patrol cars sent in response to the call kept their eyes open. That leaves the moorland to the south and the wild areas to the north and west. We've had the helicopter out, but they spotted nothing. We'll be doing more aerial sweeps as the day goes on. We've got men on foot, patrol cars, the lot. But as I said, there's a lot of ground to cover, and they could have gone in almost any direction. Is there anything more you can tell me about Erin Doyle? Had you seen much of her lately?'

'Not a lot,' said Banks. 'You don't when they grow up, do you? I'm afraid I've been a bit neglectful of even my own daughter, too. Obviously. It's been a hard summer. Personal problems.'

'So would it surprise you to hear that Erin had a reputation for running a bit wild?'

'No more so than any other attractive girl her age, I shouldn't think. But no, I wasn't aware she had that reputation.'

'Liked bad boys.'

'That's hardly unusual.'

'It explains McCready.'

'You're assuming she knew how bad he was.'

'If she took the gun and knew he dealt drugs, she had to have some inkling.'

'Are you suggesting that whatever he was into, Erin was involved?'

'It's a possibility we need to consider. She was hardly an innocent bystander.'

'Tracy, too?'

'I'm not saying that. If Tracy does have any sort of relationship with McCready, it's a very recent one. Maybe they just fancied each other, and he was tired of Erin Doyle. But he's shown his true colours now. She can't be too happy about it. She must know she's made a very bad error of judgement.'

'I'm sure she does,' said Banks. 'What's going to happen to Erin?'

'No idea. She's still not talking.'

'I remember when she was a little kid,' Banks said. 'Erin.

She used to wear pigtails and she had freckles across her nose and on her arms. Cute. I took her and Tracy to the Blackpool illuminations once. They loved it. Though I think it was more the staying up late after dark than the illuminations themselves. They both fell asleep in the car on the way home. Brian, too.' Banks shook his head to clear the memory. 'Sorry,' he went on. 'You're right. It's a bit close to home.'

'When Juliet Doyle came to report the gun, she asked for you.'

'So Chambers said. Made quite a big deal of it, in fact. But it makes sense to me. She knows me. Turning in her own daughter must have been a terrible decision for her.'

'Do you reckon she thought you'd go easy on Erin?'

'Probably,' said Banks. 'But I'd like to think I could have defused the situation without anyone getting killed.'

'Maybe you could have, but you weren't here, and hindsight's no use to us now.'

The phone rang. Gervaise answered it, listened for a moment, then thanked the caller and hung up. 'That was Winsome,' she said. 'We've just had a bit of a break. We found the car. Or *a* car. Up behind your cottage, on the moors road.'

Banks gripped the arms of his chair. 'Abandoned?'

'Hidden in the woods behind a wall. Local birdwatcher found it, remembered the news about the shooting and reported it. Preliminary examination indicates the gears were stripped.'

'So they're out on the moors on foot. They can't have got far.'

'Don't get too excited. We can't be sure it's *their* car yet. Though there is confirmation of sorts.'

'What?'

'The last entry in Annie's notebook. It was the car's number plate.'

'She must have made a note of it when she dropped by my cottage. Seeing a strange car there would have struck her as odd under any circumstances.'

'Maybe. But that's all there was. A car number. No time, place or date. She could have seen it any time that day, or even before. This wasn't her *official* notebook, you understand.'

'But still . . . it's a bit too much of a coincidence, isn't it?'

'Yes. Now we can narrow our search, concentrate on the moors. But it's pretty wild up there, as you know. It looks as if they may have spent the night in a ruined barn about three miles from the cottage.'

'What do you think?' Banks asked.

'I think a city boy like McCready will be feeling too exposed up there. Twelve miles of bad roads, or no roads at all for the most part. He'll want to find the nearest large village or small town and probably steal a car. Head for the city.'

'Risky.'

'Everything's a risk since he shot Annie. And the stakes are high.'

'I know,' said Banks. 'The nearest village is Baldersghyll. It's not very big, though.'

'The local station there's been alerted. There's more. The car's registered to a Victor Mallory. Lives in Horsforth, Leeds.'

'Stolen?'

Gervaise shook her head. 'I don't think so. Maybe. But according to Winsome, Victor Mallory comes up on West Yorkshire's radar as one of McCready's suspicious cronies.'

'Any connection with the Farmer, or with Ciaran and Darren?'

'Not that we know of.'

'So Jaff borrowed the car from this Mallory?'

'Looks that way. It's the best lead we've got so far.'

'Anyone talked to him yet?'

'The Leeds police are keeping an eye on his house for us. I thought, perhaps, it would be a good place for you to start. And while you're down there, you could have a word with the Farmer, too. But tread softly.'

'I promise,' said Banks. 'And thanks. I mean, for letting me in on this. I won't let you down.'

'Better not,' said Gervaise. 'Or you'll be the one in the kennel licking your balls. They'll hurt so much.'

On his way back to his office, Banks bumped into the female AFO officer he had met in the hospital. She looked as if she had been lurking in the corridor.

'Any news?' she asked as he opened his office door.

'Come in,' Banks said, and she followed him. 'Sit down. PC Newell, isn't it?'

Nerys sat. 'Powell, sir.'

'Right,' said Banks. 'I remember now. You must excuse me. I'm a bit jet-lagged. Usually I have a much better memory for names and faces.'

'That's all right, sir. I wouldn't expect you to remember me. I was just worried about Annie . . . about DI Cabbot, that's all. I wanted to ask if you had any news.'

'No good news, I'm afraid. It's just a matter of waiting, the doctor said. They'll know more if she makes it through the first twenty-four hours.'

'You mean there's a chance she might not?'

'There's always a chance.'

Nerys bit her lip. 'I'm sorry to hear that,' she said. 'I know that you and her were . . . you know. I know she means a lot to you.'

'It was a long time ago,' said Banks.

'Yes, sir. But I'm sure she still means a lot to you. You couldn't just forget someone like her, could you?'

'If I might ask,' Banks went on, 'why all the concern on your part? I mean, other than that for a fellow officer wounded in the line of duty?'

Nerys turned away and began to fidget. 'Like I said at the hospital, sir, I feel a bit responsible. We were working together. And we talked. She gave me some advice. That's all.'

'Responsible? How could you be?'

'I don't mean it's logical, sir. It's just . . . you know . . . the call . . . the taser.'

'You're the officer who—'

'No, sir. It wasn't me. That was Warby. PC Warburton. But I was with him. I'm his partner. He's a mate.'

'Right. I see. And just how does that make you responsible for what happened to Annie?'

'It doesn't. Not directly, sir. I just *feel* partly to blame. If things had gone differently . . .'

Banks leaned back in his chair. 'Look, PC Powell,' he said, 'if we all adopted that attitude we'd never get anywhere. If. If. If. I could just as well blame myself for not being here when Juliet Doyle came to see me. If I had been, things would have been different again, wouldn't they?' *And my daughter probably wouldn't be God knows where in the grips of some psycho, or Annie lying in a hospital bed close to death's door*, he thought. 'You were only doing your job,' he said.

'Don't start assuming the burden of guilt, second-guessing. There's no future in that.'

'Yes, sir. I mean, I'm not complaining. Everyone's been very good. There's lots of support. Lots of choices. It's nowhere near as bad as I thought it would be.'

Banks smiled. He knew she meant Chambers, who liked to pride himself on the fact that his name and reputation went before him and sent a chill up everyone's spine, put the fear of God in them. 'Hang in there.'

'I'd like to help.'

'Help what?'

'The investigation. DI Cabbot's shooting, the—'

'Hold on a minute,' said Banks. 'Aren't you under suspension?'

'No, sir. They offered me a spot of gardening leave, but I don't want it. I don't think we did anything wrong, and I want to keep working. There's no requirement says I have to take leave or should be suspended. It's just that nobody quite knows what to do with me, where to reassign me. And I like to think DI Cabbot is a friend.'

'I understand your position, believe me,' said Banks, 'and I appreciate it. But it's not going to happen.'

'Why not?'

'For a start, you're a PC and an AFO. You're not CID or Major Crimes.'

'It's not as if DC would be a promotion.'

'I know that. But those transfers take time, paperwork, official approval. And we don't have time.'

'There must be something. I can do other things than just shoot guns. Temporary assignment? Surely there's some way I could help?'

She seemed so crestfallen and forlorn that Banks felt

sorry for her. But there was nothing he could do. He knew he was already in a precarious position himself, and if he encouraged young PC Powell in her ambitions, he could get them both dismissed. 'I'm sorry,' he said. 'There's no place for you here right now. Besides, I don't have any power in the matter. It's not my case.'

'But you could put in a good word for me.'

'It wouldn't be any use.'

'I'm a trained firearms officer. I'm good at what I do.'

'I'm sure you are,' said Banks, suppressing a smile, 'but that's another problem right there.'

'What is?'

'That you're a firearms officer. And that you were one of the firearms officers who entered the Doyle house. Whether you agree with it or not, you and your partner are under investigation. Also, we don't need an Authorised Firearms Officer on this case.'

'With all due respect, sir, this man you're after is armed and dangerous.'

'I'm aware of that.'

'There are rumours . . .'

'What rumours?'

'Just stories going around. That your daughter is somehow involved. That makes you emotionally involved in the case.'

So the word was out. Banks wasn't particularly surprised. In many ways, a police station was just like any other workplace. Rumours and gossip abounded. 'I wouldn't believe everything you hear,' he said stiffly.

'I don't, sir. But I've heard that this Jaff McCready is a nasty piece of work. If it was his gun at the Doyle house, and if he was the one who shot DI—'

'I'm sorry, PC Powell. Nerys. I'm really sorry, but we're ending this conversation right now. I can't give you what you want. I promise I'll do my best to keep you informed about DI Cabbot's progress, but that's all. Do you understand?'

Nerys got to her feet and dragged them towards the door. 'Yes, sir,' she said. 'If you change your mind at all . . .'

'I won't,' said Banks, and he stared thoughtfully at the closed door for almost a minute after she had left.

'You're using the throwaway mobile, right?'

'Course, boss.'

'OK. Go on.' The Farmer was walking along his favourite path in his garden. It was a warm evening, but still he wore one of the chunky cable-knit jumpers he loved so much. The neatly trimmed hedges of topiary and crinkling sound the cinders made underfoot always calmed him down. Not that he needed it. He was confident that Ciaran and Darren would do their jobs and the Jaff problem would be dealt with quickly.

The only angle that caused him any worry at all was Banks's daughter. He remembered the policeman's tenacity and realised he'd had a lucky escape the last time they had crossed paths. It wouldn't be so easy this time, especially if anything happened to the girl. Jaff could be a mad bastard – the Farmer had seen him at work – and if the girl became a liability, her chances weren't very good. Banks would certainly connect him to Jaff in time, and had probably already connected him with Ciaran and Darren. They never usually left a trail of bodies behind them, which was usually a good thing, but it also meant that the girl they talked to, Rose, would probably be able to identify them, and that would be enough for Banks. He was a tricky copper, and he wouldn't give up this time. The Farmer had to weigh what the girl might know against the possible comeback on getting rid of her along with McCready before he came to his decision. If Banks got his daughter back alive, and if he knew that the Farmer had a hand in it, then a senior copper's gratitude might not be a bad thing to have in the long run.

'We got a name,' said Darren. 'Bloke by the name of Justin. Lives in Highgate.'

'That's not much to go on, is it?' said Fanthorpe.

'He's bent. Involved in people-smuggling and dodgy passports. An old mate of Jaff's.'

'Well, well,' said Fanthorpe. 'You need a bit of intelligence for fake documents and people-trafficking, don't you? Knowing Jaff, that probably means he's a mate from public school or university. Isn't that where you meet most of your dodgy friends?'

'Wouldn't know,' said Darren. 'Never went to either. Never went to the comprehensive much, either, come to think of it.'

'It was a rhetorical question, shit-for-brains.'

'What's that?'

'You'd know if you'd been to school, wouldn't you?'

'What do you want us to do now, boss?'

'Quiet. I'm thinking.' Fanthorpe reached the fountain where the four cinder paths met and stood for a few moments watching the bare-breasted mermaids around the edge spout water from their O-shaped mouths, and the little boy pissing at the centre. Zenovia's idea. 'If this Justin's bent,' he went on, 'and if he's involved in people-trafficking, the odds are that he traffics in other things, too. Stands to reason, doesn't it? I mean, I do. If you've got the routes secured and the right people paid off, you use them. Am I right?'

'You are, boss.'

'Either way, Gavin Nebthorpe will know. He knows everyone in the business. Justin in Highgate, you say? Leave it with me, lads. I want you two to head down to London fast as you can. Set off now and you'll probably be there before dark.'

'Where in London? It's a big place.'

'I know it's a big place, Darren. That's why it's the capital of the United Kingdom. That's why the Houses of Parliament are there. Big Ben. Buckingham Palace. That's why the Queen of fucking England lives there. I know it's a big place.'

'Well. Where, then?'

'You'll hear from me before you get there. Keep the throwaway turned on. If for any reason you don't hear from me before you arrive, get yourselves a hotel. Something inconspicuous and anonymous. Out of the way. You'd stick out like spare pricks at a wedding in the Dorchester. You might be doing a bit of wet work down there. Know what I mean?'

'Yes, boss. We're on our way.'

Fanthorpe ended the call and stood by the fountain, a frown creasing his brow, then he keyed in another phone number. As he waited for an answer, he looked at the fountain again. Little boy pissing, indeed. Silly cow.

12

Before heading down to Leeds to talk to Victor Mallory, Banks wanted to see whether he could get anything out of Erin Doyle. He also wanted to see how Erin was bearing up under the strain of all that had happened over the last few days. She'd done a stupid thing, certainly, but he'd watched her grow up; she was a close friend of his daughter's; she and Tracy had skipped and played hopscotch and whip'n'top in the street. What Erin had done needn't ruin her whole life. He wasn't going to write her off and abandon her to the likes of Chambers if he could help it. He wanted to talk to Juliet, too, but she would have to wait. He wasn't a Family Liaison Officer or a guidance counsellor. Finding Tracy was his priority right now, and he doubted that Juliet could help with that. Erin and Victor Mallory just might.

Banks strode across the cobbled market square and started to climb the hill that wound up to the Norman castle overlooking the River Swain. It was a fine evening for a walk, and the fresh air and exercise helped clear his foggy mind. On his way, he passed the burgundy façade of the Café de Provence, where he had enjoyed his first date with Sophia. It seemed so long ago now, but it had only been last March. So much had happened in a mere six months. Now this: thrown straight back to work in the thick of a crisis. The only thing to do was to carry on.

He turned off Castle Hill on to Lamplighter's Wynde, just past the café, and looked for number seven. It was a narrow cobbled street which wound back down to York Road in a steep curve, not even wide enough for cars, and the limestone terraced houses there were among the oldest in Eastvale, dating back in their foundations to Norman times, when the castle was built. In later years, they had been wealthy local merchants' houses, and now they were a tourist attraction and a source of accommodation. Like many houses on the street, the one where Erin was staying had originally consisted of two separate dwellings, which had been knocked into one. The doorway was low enough that Banks had to be careful walking through it, but inside he found a greater sense of space, and far more light, than he had expected.

The landlady inspected his warrant card and pointed upstairs to where Erin was staying. Room five. She called after Banks as he walked towards the stairs. 'She hasn't been out once, poor thing,' she said. 'And she won't eat. She just stays up there in her room fretting all day long.'

'Where's Ms Yu?' Banks asked, thinking he should talk to the Family Liaison Officer before he talked to Erin.

'She's out.' The landlady lowered her voice. 'I think she's visiting the poor girl's mother.'

Banks made sympathetic noises and carried on up the narrow, creaking flight of stairs. The landing wasn't quite flat, as in so many of these old houses, one of the floorboards wobbled, and the walls were out of true. Miniature watercolours of local landscapes hung on the flock-patterned walls, and Banks recognised Hindswell Woods, Lyndgarth village green, Eastvale Castle at sunset, and the little stone bridge in his own tiny village of Gratly.

He knocked on the door, heard nothing, then knocked

again. 'Erin?' he called. 'Erin, it's Alan, Alan Banks. Can I come in?'

Nothing happened for a few moments, then the door swung slowly open, as if of its own accord, on squeaky hinges. Erin, who must have got up to open it, had gone back to sitting on the window seat, staring out at the view, her head turned. Banks shut the door behind him and sat on the only chair by the small writing desk. The room was stuffy, the window shut tight.

At first he didn't speak, leaving an opening for Erin to have the first word, but she kept her gaze averted and her mouth closed. 'Erin,' he said finally. 'I'm so sorry about your dad. He was a good mate.'

Erin said nothing for a moment or two, but Banks thought he noticed her head move slightly. Then, in a small voice, she said, 'It was my fault, you know. It was all my fault.'

'I don't think—'

'You weren't here! You don't know!' The sudden fury of her reaction stunned Banks. 'You weren't here,' she said again, more quietly this time, as she stood up to face him, her face streaked with tears, hands curled into tight fists.

'I'm so sorry.'

Her body relaxed and her shoulders slumped. She gave him a sad glance. 'Oh, I'm not blaming you. That's not what I mean. How could you know? But I was there. I was the one who ... I ...'

There seemed only one thing to do. Banks got up, moved forward and took Erin in his arms. She stiffened and resisted, then she went limp and threw her arms around him, holding on for dear life, and started to sob convulsively. When she managed to gain control of herself, she broke away, embarrassed, and took a tissue from the box on the bedside table to wipe her face. 'Look at me,' she said. Then she turned to face Banks again. 'I must be a sight. I *am* glad to see you. Really. It's been awful. Nobody's been to see me except Patricia. She's nice, but it's not the same. Nobody understands. I've got nobody to talk to.'

'What about your mother?'

Erin started to bite her thumbnail. Banks noticed that all her fingernails were chewed into ugly half-moons, raw and bloody around the edges.

'Erin? I know you must be angry with her for what she did, but she *is* your mother.'

'She reported me to the police.' The anger was gone, replaced by disbelief and pain. 'How could she do that? How could my own mother do that when she knew I'd go to jail?' She looked directly at Banks, her blue-grey eyes disconcerting. 'Would you do that? If it was Tracy?'

'I don't know what I'd do,' Banks said. 'The law against handguns is there for a good reason.'

'But she's my *mother.*'

'She was concerned,' Banks said. 'She didn't know what to do. And she wasn't thinking about the consequences. She certainly didn't intend you to go to jail.'

'How do you know?'

'Because she asked for me. She didn't know how to cope with finding a gun in your room. She was scared. So she came to *me.*'

'But you're a policeman. What did you expect you to do?'

'I'm also a friend of the family. What do you think I would have done?'

'I suppose you'd have followed the rules.'

'I might have been able to help her. To help you, too.'

'Have you talked to her?'

'I haven't had chance yet. I will. But you have to promise me you'll try to forgive her. I must at least have something positive to tell her. Something to give her hope. Think how she must be feeling. Her daughter hates her. Her husband's dead. You can't expect her to make all the moves. You've got to try to meet her halfway.'

'She moved quickly enough to turn me in.'

'She was scared, confused. Have you never felt that way?'

'I don't know. I don't know anything any more.' Erin turned away and rubbed the tears from her eyes.

'Look,' said Banks, 'you've been cooped up here for ages. Do you fancy a walk, a bit of fresh air? Maybe get a bite to eat? A drink?'

Erin nodded. 'A walk would be good,' she said. 'Just let me wash my face first. I must look a mess.'

Banks gazed out of the window as Erin went over to the washstand and bent over. The houses opposite were almost close enough to touch, and just beyond their flagstone roofs he could see the jagged top of the castle keep. Every once in a while a cloud would obscure the sun, casting a shadow over the scene.

Erin tied her hair back in a ponytail, grabbed a light jacket and put it on over her T-shirt. She was wearing jeans, torn at the knees, and a battered pair of trainers. Banks guessed that most of her good clothes were either back at Laburnum Way or in Leeds. She hadn't been taking care of herself; that much was obvious. She had purple-black bags under her dull eyes from lack of sleep, and her complexion was pasty. She also seemed listless and tired, no doubt from shock and lack of food.

They left the B&B and walked back up to Castle Road. Just a few yards farther ahead, a flagged pathway led up to the castle itself, and another branched off along the crest of the hill, circling the castle's outer walls, looking out over the woods down the hill to the river. There were plenty of tourists enjoying a day out, and couples and families were picnicking far below on the grassy riverbanks by the terraced falls. Birds twittered in the trees. Some of the leaves were already turning at the edges. Banks remembered his first months in Eastvale, also around this time of year, how he had walked here many times with Sandra, Brian and Tracy, slowly getting used to their new home, watching the leaves change colour day by day until at last they broke free and drifted down into the river.

Neither Banks nor Erin talked at first. Erin kept her head down and her hands in her pockets. She seemed a slight and vulnerable figure to Banks, far more frail than he had expected, even given the circumstances; more like a little girl again. But then he reminded himself of the problems she had to face – not only her father's death and her mother's blame, but the gun charges, the unfaithful boyfriend, her best friend's treachery. It would be more than enough for anyone.

At the end of the path, a chip van stood outside the car park, and Banks asked Erin whether she would like a burger or a hot dog. She chose the hot dog, and he got one for himself, too, piling on the fried onions and hot chilli sauce, along with a couple of cans of cold Coke. Queuing at the van reminded him of buying ice cream for Erin and Tracy when they were kids.

They found an empty bench below the castle walls and sat down to eat, looking out over the treetops. The foliage almost obscured the East Side Estate and the railway lines beyond, but not quite. Even so, it was an idyllic scene, and from that height, far in the distance, on a clear day like this, he could see the long anvil of Sutton Bank rising across the Vale of York.

Banks pulled the tab on his tin and the Coke foamed and fizzed over his hand. He laughed. Erin offered him a tissue from her pocket, and he wiped it off. The tin had felt cold, but the Coke was too warm. Still, the sugar hit was so good it made him feel a bit giddy at first. Tourists wandered by, and a few curious dogs, attracted by the smells, sniffed and strained at their leads.

Food finished, Banks collected the rubbish and dropped it in the bin beside the bench. 'I've got to ask you a few questions,' he said, sitting beside Erin again and crossing his legs.

She gave him a sly sideways smile. 'I should have known there was a price to pay for that hot dog.'

'The hot dog's free, talking's optional.'

Erin sat silent for a moment, lips pursed, looking out over the panorama, her eyes squinting shut against the sun. Finally, she leaned forward and rested her elbows on her knees, propping up her head. 'Why not? It's a nice place for it. I was just thinking. Do you remember that time we went swimming in the river, in the shallows over there by the woods?' She pointed in the general direction of Hindswell Woods, to the west. 'There was me, Tracy, Brian, Mum, Mrs Banks, and you and Dad keeping an eye on us. We had a picnic, too. Potted-meat sandwiches and dandelion-and-burdock. And Blue Riband chocolate biscuits. They tasted so good.'

'Yes,' said Banks. 'But I'm amazed you remember. You can't have been more than six or seven.' He remembered the day well. He and Patrick Doyle were just getting to know one another then, typically enough, through their children. Patrick had said he was happy to have a police detective living in the street. Now he'd know where to go if he ever got a parking ticket or had a problem with the law. They had all walked through magical woods dappled with sunlight filtered between fluttering leaves, and at that riverside picnic Sandra had chilled a bottle of white wine in the water, and they had sipped it from coloured plastic cups with chunks of old Cheddar and soft Brie on baguettes.

The spot was also close to where some schoolchildren had found a man hanging earlier in the summer, and that had marked the start of the case that had almost finished Banks. But it was behind him now, along with the rest of that troubled time. 'Do you remember the Blackpool illuminations?'

'Vaguely,' said Erin. 'It's not quite as clear. I think I fell asleep in the car. Brian was with us then, too, wasn't he?'

'Yes.'

Erin shook her head sadly. 'She won't even mention his name any more. I talk about the Blue Lamps, she doesn't want to know.'

'Who? Why?'

'Tracy. I mean, if I had a rock star like Brian for a brother, I'd be telling, like, *everyone*. I do, anyway. Tell them I grew up with him. The Blue Lamps are so cool. Do you know she likes to call herself Francesca now because she thinks Tracy's too *Corrie*?'

'No, I didn't know that,' said Banks. And somehow, knowing it hurt him to the quick. Her *name*. The name he and Sandra had given her. 'Why won't she mention Brian?' he asked.

'She's jealous, I'd say, but she won't admit it. Because he's successful and she's . . . well, let's face it, she didn't do very well in her exams, did she? I mean, she knew how much was expected of her, and she feels she's let everyone down, especially herself. Ever since then she's been on hold, sort of dithering. She likes working at the bookshop well enough, but she doesn't see it as a career, or as what she thought she'd be doing by now.'

'But she can still take her academic career farther if she wants. She mentioned teaching once. Surely she could still do that?'

'Sure, if she had the will. But she's changed. There's a lot of negative stuff there. Anger. Low self-esteem. I don't know. I just can't seem to talk to her these days. I mean, you know, before . . . Anyway, what do you want to know?'

'It's hard to know where to begin,' said Banks, still trying to digest what he had just heard about Tracy. He had failed her. He should have paid more attention to her when she needed it, spent more time with her, instead of getting bogged down in his own personal and professional problems and feeling sorry for himself. 'I'm not sure myself, yet,' he went on. 'I just arrived back from my holidays this morning, and I'm still jet-lagged. You'll have to help me a bit.'

'Where did you go?'

'America. Arizona, Nevada and California, mostly.'

'LA? San Francisco?'

'Yes.'

'Wicked. I've always wanted to go there.'

Banks smiled. 'Me, too. And it really is "wicked".'

Erin paused for a moment, then began, 'My father—'

'You don't have to talk about him,' said Banks quickly. 'That's not my case. I mean, I'm not saying that I'm not interested, or I don't care, but because armed police officers were involved, we have to have a special investigation, and I'm not allowed to interfere. Do you understand?'

'I understand. That makes sense.'

'But you shouldn't blame yourself. Nobody could have foreseen that combination of circumstances.'

'Yes, I know. I've been trying to convince myself. It's just that whenever I think about it I can't help but feel that upsurge of guilt. It just floods through me like a dam's burst, and I don't have the strength to hold it back.'

'That's probably a good thing,' said Banks. 'My psychologist friend always told me it wasn't a good idea to hold things back.'

'But you have to sometimes, don't you? Anger? Hatred? Disapproval? Otherwise we'd all be at each other's throats half the time.'

'What about love?' said Banks. 'Should we hold that back too?'

'Sometimes,' she said. 'It might not be a bad thing. In some circumstances. When you think about it, love probably causes more trouble than hate.'

She sounded far too wise for one so young, thought Banks, who had been patiently waiting for years now for the wisdom that was supposed to come with age, to no avail, it seemed. 'Anyway,' he said, 'no matter how bad things seem now, your mother's going to need you before long. Do you think you can cope?'

'Dunno,' said Erin, waving away a troublesome wasp. 'Not much I can do from jail, is there?'

'Why did you take the gun, Erin? I trust you did take it from your boyfriend Jaffar McCready, and that you hadn't already got it from somewhere else?'

'Jaff,' Erin said. 'He calls himself Jaff. I was pissed off at him. I knew he had it – he'd shown it off to me once – and I thought if I took it he'd be angry. You know, like it was his favourite toy or something. I *wanted* to hurt him. I wanted to make him notice me, want me back.'

Now, Banks thought, she didn't sound so wise. 'But it's not a toy. Not like an iPod or a mobile or something. Didn't you think he might be so angry he wouldn't want anything to do with you again? Or that maybe he'd hurt you?'

'No. I don't suppose I was thinking all that clearly. I just took it and went back to the house and picked up some clothes and went home. I was going to give it back to him.'

'OK,' said Banks. 'Do you know why he had it in the first place?'

'Not really. Just for show, I think. I don't think he'd ever actually *used* it or anything. He just liked to play at being a tough guy, that's all. I mean, he did hang around with some pretty shifty characters, and I don't know how he had made so much money, but I don't think it was from working nine to five.'

'Did you meet any of these shifty characters?'

'Sometimes.'

Banks took copies of Rose's sketches of Ciaran and Darren from his briefcase. 'Did you ever see either of these two, for example?'

'They came to the flat once. Jaff told me to stay in the bedroom but the door was open a crack. I saw them and heard them. They were arguing.'

'How long ago was this?'

'Couple of months. Something like that.'

'What were they arguing about?'

'I don't know. Money. Some delivery or other. I think

maybe Jaff did a bit of dealing. Nothing serious, but he knew everyone on the scene.'

'The club scene?'

'Yeah. And the student scene.'

'Is that how you met?'

'No. It was after uni. I was working at one of those posh restaurants in the Calls, and he used to eat there regularly.'

'Alone?'

'Sometimes.'

'Ever with the two in the drawings?'

'No. If he did have company it was usually some expensive suit, not thugs like that.' She smiled. 'I'm not sure they'd even get past the door, the place I worked.'

'Business?'

'It seemed that way. And he did come in by himself sometimes. He didn't like to cook, or even to eat at home by himself. We got to chatting. You know. One thing led to another. He seemed fun. Smart, cocky, ambitious. We'd go to clubs sometimes after the restaurant closed. Like I said, everybody knew him. Mr Big around there. Mr Flash. Always carried a thick roll of twenties. It felt good to be seen out with him. Never boring. But it was hard to keep up with him sometimes. He always seemed to have something else going on, you know, somewhere else to be, or someone else to be with.' She shrugged. 'Now I know who it was.'

'Tracy?' Banks said.

'Yes. Or someone else. I doubt that she was the first. Sometimes he was gone for days without explanation. Not that he owed me one. Oh, don't think I blame Tracy. I was mad, yes, who wouldn't be? She kissed him. She stole my boyfriend. It's not as if she's such an angel, anyway. It's not as if she's hasn't been SUI more than once.'

'SUI?'

Erin glanced at him sideways. 'Shagged Under the Influence. Does that shock you?'

It didn't so much shock Banks as hurt him. To think something like that about his own daughter, to imagine the things that had happened to her when she was too far gone to be in control, made him feel sorry for her, protective. Erin was basically talking about date rape. His own daughter. It made him angry. Why the hell couldn't she have come to him with her problems? Was he that distant and uncaring?

'Do you mean drugged and raped?' he asked.

'Not the way you imagine it. I mean, I'm not saying you're always up for it when you're so off your face, but it's no big deal. It's just a shag. SUI. Anyway,' Erin went on, picking at a hangnail, 'like I said, if it hadn't been Tracy, it would have been someone else. I know that. Jaff was just . . .'

'But it's Tracy he's got with him now,' Banks said.

'What do you mean?'

'It hasn't hit the front pages yet, but he's on the run. Armed. And Tracy's with him. We think he shot a policewoman. Annie Cabbot. Maybe you know her?'

'I remember her, yes. You were close at one time, after Mrs Banks left, weren't you? But Jaff . . .? I can't believe it.'

'We need to find them. Annie could die, and Tracy's in danger.'

'But Jaff wouldn't hurt her.'

'Have you ever seen him be violent?'

'Well, no. I mean, yes, but only . . . you know, someone who tried to rip him off, or put him down because of his colour, call him a Paki or something. He really hated that.'

'So he can be violent?'

'He has a quick temper. But he never hurt me. I can't imagine him harming a woman. Not Tracy.'

'We found a car up on the moors. It belongs to someone called Victor Mallory. Have you ever heard that name?'

'Vic? Yes, of course. He's Jaff's best friend. They went to public school together, then Cambridge. Vic's . . .'

'What?'

'Well, he's like a sort of old-fashioned hippy, really, with his long hair and stuff, but he's weird, too, and a bit scary sometimes. He's very clever, he studied chemistry, but I think drugs have fried his brain. Like he's always looking for new chemical compounds, and he'll try everything himself first. He's definitely blown a few connections.'

'Did he have a gun?'

'I don't know if he had one, but he and Jaff used to talk about them sometimes. You know, like computer nerds, or techies. As if they knew what they were talking about.'

'Maybe they did,' said Banks. 'Did Jaff ever say anything about that gun you took? If it was ever used. Anything at all.'

'No, I don't think so. I don't remember anything. I don't suppose I really know him at all, do I, when it comes down to it?'

'Probably not. How long *have* you known him?'

'Six months. Look, I know I've been a fool, but I'm not stupid. And I'm not a bad person. I want to help. I want to make things right.'

'I know, Erin. Right now, things are difficult, and my priority is finding Tracy and making sure she's safe. Can you understand that?'

'Of course. But how can I help?'

'I need to get some idea of what Jaff might do in a

situation like this, where he might go. How intelligent is he?'

'Oh, he's very bright. He went to Cambridge.'

'So I understand.' That didn't mean very much, Banks thought, certainly not when it came to drug-dealing and evading the law. On the other hand, some Cambridge graduates had quite a good reputation in both those areas. 'Where would he go, do you think? Does he have anyone he might turn to, anyone who might help him?'

'I don't know,' said Erin. 'But he'd probably go to London. I mean, that's where he comes from, and he's got friends down there. He's a city boy.'

'Anyone in particular?'

'I'm trying to remember. He took me with him for a weekend once, but we stayed in a nice hotel in Mayfair, not with any of his friends.'

'He knows he's in a lot of trouble,' Banks went on. 'It's my guess that he would probably want to leave the country as soon as possible, maybe even try to head back to Mumbai, if he still has contacts there, but if he's at all bright, as you say he is, he knows we'll be keeping an eye on the ports, stations and airports.'

'There's Justin,' Erin said.

'Justin?'

'Yes, in London. Another old pal from his uni days. We had dinner with him while we there. One of those fancy places where you get one little plate after another. Justin was there with his girlfriend. She was Slovakian or something like that. Beautiful. Very exotic. She didn't speak much English, I remember. Looked like a model or an actress.'

'Do you remember anything about Justin?'

'Just something Jaff said. I think he was showing off, and

he said something to me about Justin being the man to know if you needed a new passport. Justin didn't like it, I remember. He gave Jaff a nasty look. But I thought maybe he was involved in forging stuff and maybe smuggling people into the country.'

'That sounds like the sort of person Jaff might want to contact right now,' Banks said. 'Do you know where he lives?'

'No. We didn't go back to his place. We went on to a couple of clubs in the West End, I don't remember where. I'm afraid I was a bit drunk by then.'

'Did you get his surname?'

'No. We just used first names.'

'What was his girlfriend called?'

'Martina.'

'Did this Justin have any sort of accent, too? How was his English?'

'His English was excellent, sort of posh, like Jaff's. He did have a slight accent, though, but you really had to listen.'

'What accent?'

'I don't know. I'm not good at that sort of thing.'

'Eastern European? Same as his girlfriend?'

'Maybe.' Erin shrugged. 'I don't know.'

'And you've no idea where they live?'

'I do remember we were talking about property values once, back in the restaurant. Jaff was thinking about buying a flat in London, and he was asking this Justin about it. He said something about Highgate, but that's all I remember. I got the impression that was where he lived. But it's big, isn't it, Highgate?'

'Big enough,' said Banks. But he felt a rush of excitement. There was every chance that if this Justin *was* involved in people-smuggling and dodgy documents, one or other of the Met's intelligence units would have a watching brief on him, and even pinpointing him as living in Highgate might help them narrow their search. Banks was hardly in credit with the intelligence services, but he knew that Dirty Dick Burgess would help him out at a pinch, especially if Tracy was in danger.

'Did Jaff ever talk much about his family, his background?' Banks asked. 'I'm just trying to get a better sense of who I'm dealing with.'

'Not a lot. Jaff's a mummy's boy, really, and I don't mean that in a bad way. He's not a nancy boy or a sissy or anything. But I think he really loved his mother, and his father was more distant, tougher, less involved with him emotionally when he was growing up. Jaff didn't talk about his family or his background much when we were together, except sometimes if the mood came on him. You know, the right combination of booze and E or whatever. Then he tended to ramble, and you had to sort of piece it together. I could be wrong. Anyway, he wasn't too happy about ending up back with his dad after his mother died, and when he went off to boarding school and then university, that was his opportunity to make the break, to grab for his independence. He's got a photo of his mother in the flat. You should see it. She was beautiful. There are none of his dad.'

'Thank you,' Banks said. 'You've been a great help.'

Erin shrugged. 'What's going to happen to me now? I don't mean to be selfish or anything, but I couldn't stand going to jail.'

'Nothing's going to happen. Not for a while. When's your court date?'

'Next month.'

'Get a good solicitor,' Banks said. 'It's true that the law comes down hard on possession of firearms, but you've got a better chance than most. You haven't been in trouble before, you're from a good family, you have character witnesses. It could be worse.'

'Hard to imagine,' said Erin, 'but thanks. That helps.'

'I'll help you as best I can. If you don't know a solicitor, I can recommend one. And if this business with Jaff and Tracy comes to a satisfactory conclusion and no one gets hurt, that could go in your favour, too. You've helped us a lot.'

Erin nodded. They both stood up. 'What are you going to do now?' Banks asked.

'I think I'm going to go to the Swainsdale Centre and buy some new clothes and make-up. I can't believe you'd allow yourself to be seen with me looking like this.'

Banks laughed.

'It is all right, isn't it?' she asked.

'What?'

'To go to the Swainsdale Centre. You know. I don't have to go straight back to the B&B and report in, do I? You're not going to put an electronic tag on my ankle, are you?'

'Of course not,' said Banks. 'You're on police bail. You report when you're told to and you'll be fine. I wouldn't advise leaving town, though. Believe me, there will be more questions. A lot more. But you can go anywhere you want in Eastvale.'

'Except home,' said Erin.

'Except home.'

13

Banks leaned back in his seat and closed his eyes as the car slowed to a crawl at the roadworks on the A1 just north of Wetherby. Winsome had offered to drive him to Leeds. Normally, he would have preferred to go alone and drive himself, but this time he had accepted her offer. He didn't trust himself behind the wheel; he was too wired and too anxious. They hadn't spoken much on the way down, but he was glad of her company and that she had tuned the radio to Radio 3. Vaughan Williams's 'Variation on a Theme by Thomas Tallis' was playing at the moment.

Banks had never felt so weary. Lights danced behind his eyelids. He felt as if he could see the electrical pulses jumping around in his brain projected there, flashing, arcing, short-circuiting. There was simply too much to take in, too much to comprehend, and it was getting more and more difficult for him to focus. Every moment spent tracking down nuggets of valuable information meant more time in fear and danger for Tracy.

But it had to be this way. The real problems might begin only once they had located Jaff and Tracy, and he needed to go into that situation with as much information as he could get. It was his only weapon, his only armour. After all, Jaff had a gun and a hostage.

The traffic on the Leeds ring road slowed them down.

Luckily, they didn't have far to go. Victor Mallory's house turned out to be between West Park and Moortown Golf Club. It was seven o'clock when Winsome pulled up outside the rambling detached house with its cream stucco façade, large garden, gables and mullioned bay windows.

'Not bad,' said Winsome. 'Not bad at all for a thirty-something.'

'Maybe we're in the wrong business?' Banks suggested.

'Or maybe his business is *wrong*.'

'More like it,' Banks agreed. 'If he's a mate of McCready's. There's a lot you can do with a Cambridge degree in chemistry, and it doesn't all involve teaching or working for pharmaceutical companies. But that's for the locals to worry about.' Banks gestured to the silver Skoda parked down the street. 'They've been keeping a discreet eye on him.'

'Hard to appear inconspicuous in a Skoda in a neighbourhood like this,' said Winsome.

They got out and walked over to the parked car. The window was open and Banks caught a whiff of fresh cigarette smoke. It wasn't a pleasant sensation, the way it used to be. 'Anything?' he asked, flashing his warrant card as discreetly as possible.

'Not a sausage,' replied the driver. 'Waste of bloody time, if you ask me.'

'Anyone come or go?'

'No.'

'He in there?'

'No idea.'

'Right. You can get off to the pub now.'

'We go when our guv says to go.'

Banks rolled his eyes and looked at Winsome, who shrugged. 'Suit yourself,' he said.

'Anyone would think they enjoyed sitting there doing nothing,' said Winsome as they walked towards the house.

'Don't assume everyone shares your work ethic, Winsome. Besides, they're sitting on their brains, so maybe that cramps their thinking style. I suppose we got what we asked for, though – a watching brief. I mean, we didn't ask for politeness or intelligence, did we?'

Winsome laughed. 'I'll make a note of it next time.' They walked up Victor Mallory's flagstone path and rang the doorbell. No sound came from inside. 'Curtains are closed. Maybe they've been watching an empty house?'

'Wouldn't surprise me,' said Banks. He pressed the doorbell again. Still nothing happened, but he thought he heard a stifled groan or a muffled call from somewhere inside the house. He glanced at Winsome, who frowned and nodded to indicate that she had heard it, too. The door seemed formidable, but when Banks turned the handle and pushed, it opened. He checked the lock, which was a deadbolt, and saw that it hadn't been secured. There was also a strong chain and an alarm system, but the latter wasn't activated. With the door closed behind them, there was only enough light in the hallway to make out the dim shape of a chair and the outline of a broad staircase leading upstairs.

Banks's eyes adjusted, and he saw three doors leading off the hall. When he heard the sound again, he realised it was coming from the first door on his left, the front room. The heavy door was already ajar, and when he pushed, it opened slowly. The room was even darker than the hall, so he walked over and opened the thick velour curtains. Early evening light flooded in and illuminated the floor-to-ceiling bookcases against one wall, framed contemporary prints and expensive Bang & Olufsen stereo system on another, and the figure lying on the floor at the centre of the room, gagged and bound to a hardbacked chair.

'Victor Mallory, I presume?' said Banks.

All he got by way of a reply was muffled growling and cursing.

'Winsome,' he said, 'could you see if you can find some scissors or a sharp kitchen knife?'

Winsome headed back out into the hall. Banks heard doors opening and closing, and moments later she came back with a pair of scissors.

'Excellent,' Banks said. He bent over Mallory. He smelled the sharp animal stink of urine and noticed a wet patch down the front of the man's trousers. 'First of all, Victor,' he said, 'it's important that you know we're police officers and we're not going to hurt you, so when I cut you free and take off that gag, you don't start screaming and try to make a run for it. Got that?'

Mallory nodded and made more grumbling sounds.

'You'd never make it, anyway,' Banks went on. 'Winsome here is our star rugby player. Flying tackles and drop-kicks her speciality.' Banks heard Winsome mutter something under her breath. 'I didn't catch that,' he said.

'Nothing,' said Winsome with a sigh.

Banks then showed Mallory his warrant card and began to cut him free. He left the gag until last, loosening one of the edges and then ripping it fast.

Mallory screamed and put his hands to his mouth. If the police outside heard him, they certainly didn't come rushing in to put an end to the police brutality.

'You've ripped my lips off,' Mallory moaned. There was a small amount of blood on the carpet where he had been lying, and a patch of his hair on the left side was matted.

'Don't be a baby,' said Banks. 'You OK otherwise? Do you need an ambulance? A doctor?'

'No. No, I don't need an ambulance or a doctor. I . . . I just banged my head when the chair tipped over. I don't think I have concussion. I didn't lose consciousness or anything.' Mallory rubbed his wrists and ankles. 'I could do with some water, though.'

Winsome left the room again and came back with a pint glass filled to the brim. Some of it dribbled down Mallory's front as he slurped it greedily, but he didn't seem to mind.

Banks gave him a while to get his circulation flowing again, and to compose himself.

Mallory avoided Winsome's eye. 'Er, look here,' he said to Banks when he had finished the water. 'I . . . er . . . I had a small accident . . . do you think I might possibly have a quick shower and change before we talk?' He spoke with an educated accent, public school, a little too posh and plummy for Banks's liking.

'We don't have time for that,' Banks said.

'But I . . .'

'Look, why don't we compromise? You can dry yourself down and have a quick change but I'll have to stay with you. Best I can offer. OK?'

'It'll have to do, won't it?'

'I'll make some tea while you're gone,' Winsome volunteered.

'Excellent,' said Banks. 'You're lucky,' he said to Mallory. 'She doesn't usually do tea.' He followed Mallory into the hall and up the stairs. 'Nice house you've got here.'

'Thanks.'

'How much did you pay for it?'

'Too much.'

'No, come on. Quarter? Half? A mil?'

'Four hundred K. A bargain at the time.'

Banks whistled. He followed Mallory into a nondescript white bedroom with an en-suite bathroom and walk-in cupboards and waited while he undressed and threw his clothes in a laundry basket, then rubbed himself down with a green fluffy towel, which joined his clothes, and pulled on a navy blue tracksuit. When Mallory was ready, Banks gestured for him to head back downstairs.

Winsome was waiting on the sofa, a pot of tea, milk, sugar and three mugs on the table in front of her. 'I'll play mother, then, shall I?' she said, pouring.

'Victor,' Banks said, settling down opposite Mallory, who sat in the winged armchair by the fireplace, 'tell us what happened.'

'Two men came,' Victor said. 'They . . . they trussed me up, the way you saw, with sticky tape, then they just left me. I could have starved or choked to death if you hadn't come.'

'We'll cheerfully accept the praise for saving your life,' Banks said, 'but I'd say you're exaggerating just a wee bit. How long have you been like that?'

'I don't know. I lost track of time. They came just after lunch.'

'Maybe five or six hours, then,' said Banks, with a glance at Winsome, who had started to take notes.

'Something like that. I tried to struggle free, but all I succeeded in doing was making the tape tighter. Then I rocked the chair so hard trying to pull away, it fell over. I was helpless, like a tortoise flipped on its back.'

'So we saw.'

'Look, do you mind if I get myself a drop of brandy. This tea's very nice and all, but I've really had quite a shock, you know.'

'Not at all.'

'Can I get . . . I mean, would either of you like anything?'

'No, thank you,' said Banks, holding up his mug. 'Tea will do fine for me.'

Winsome nodded in agreement.

'OK.' Mallory went to the drinks cabinet and poured a generous measure of Remy into a crystal glass. 'That's better,' he said after the first sip.

'I suppose you already know that we'll probably want the same information your previous visitors wanted.'

'I'd guessed that already. But you're not going to tie me up and threaten me with surgical instruments, are you?'

'Is that what they did?'

Mallory gave a theatrical shudder. On second thoughts, Banks realised, perhaps it wasn't so theatrical. 'One of them did. A real psychopath.'

'Ciaran. One of his persuasion techniques.'

Mallory almost choked on his Remy. 'You know who they are?'

'I can make a pretty good guess,' said Banks. 'Winsome?'

Winsome took Rose's sketches from her briefcase and passed them to Mallory. 'Good God,' he said. 'Yes. That's them.' He passed them back to Winsome.

'Then you're a lucky man,' said Banks. 'You still have all your organs intact.' He put his mug down on the table, leaned forward and cracked his knuckles. 'The thing is, Victor, we don't have a lot of time to beat about the bush. They've already got five hours' or more start on us, and there's a lot at stake. A lot more than you can imagine.'

'But who are they? Why me? Are you going to arrest them?'

'That's a lot of questions, and I'm the one supposed to

be doing the asking. Did you know that your friend Jaff McCready works for a man called Fanthorpe, better known as the Farmer?'

'Fanthorpe? No. Who's he?'

'All you need to know is that he's also the employer of Ciaran and Darren, the men who just paid you a visit. And they may have supplanted Jaff in Fanthorpe's favour in recent days.'

Mallory swallowed. Banks could see his Adam's apple bobbing up and down. 'They wanted to know where Jaff is. That's all.'

'Do you know where he is?'

'No, I don't. Honest, I don't.'

'But you must have some idea. The Ciaran and Darren I know wouldn't take that at face value. They'd have cut at least a little finger off, or sharpened it like a pencil, just to make sure, and they don't really seem to have harmed a hair on your head. All the damage that was done, you did to yourself.'

'They terrorised me! Tortured me. In my own home.'

'My guess is,' Banks went on, 'that you talked, and that you talked very quickly indeed. So we'd like you to do the same with us. You owe us that courtesy, at least. I mean, they only tied you up and threatened you with mutilation. We set you free, let you change your wet clothes, gave you a cup of tea and a glass of brandy. You owe us something, Victor. You must see that.'

'You sound just like them.'

'Don't be silly. Where's Jaff McCready?'

Victor turned away. 'I don't know.'

'That's better. Now I know for certain you're lying. I like to know where I stand.' Banks read out the number of the car that had been found hidden off the moorland road. 'That mean anything to you?'

'Yeah. It's my car.'

'Good. I'm glad you didn't try to deny that. Now we're getting somewhere. What was it doing on the moors above Gratly?'

'I don't even know where Gratly is.'

'That wasn't my question. How did it get there? And don't try to tell me it was stolen.'

'OK, so I lent it to Jaff. I assume you already know that or you wouldn't be here. So what? He's a mate of mine. I didn't know what sort of trouble he was in.'

'But you must have known he was in *some* trouble?'

'Well, sure. But like I said, he's a mate. You help out a mate in trouble, don't you?'

Banks thought of Juliet Doyle, who had turned her daughter in to the police when she found a handgun in her possession. Who was going to help them out of their trouble? 'Let's not get too philosophical about it, Victor. We don't have time. What else did you "lend" Jaff?'

'Nothing. I don't know what you mean.'

'Was he with anyone?'

'There was a girl. She stayed outside in his car. I only saw her when they swapped cars and got into mine. He said her name was Francesca.'

'She just stayed outside in the car of her own accord?'

Mallory frowned. 'Of course. Why not?'

'She didn't appear under duress or anything?'

'No, not that I could tell.'

Banks could feel Winsome's gaze on him. He had to tread carefully, he knew, show no emotion. If he used Tracy's true identity to browbeat Mallory, it could all backfire on him if it came to court. Gervaise had warned him he was on thin ice, and he was already beginning to feel it splintering under his feet. 'Did Jaff tell you why he needed to borrow your car?'

'Not specifically, no. He just said he was in a spot of bother and he had to get away. It was only later, when I watched the news . . . heard about Erin . . .'

'You know Erin?'

'Met her a couple of times. Crazy bitch. I told him she was trouble.'

'And what did he say to that?'

'Just gave me that knowing smile of his and said he could handle it.'

'Why was she trouble?'

Mallory scratched his temple. 'She was dead jealous. Impulsive, fiery. And obsessive, too possessive. It's a dangerous combination.'

'Sounds like a young woman in love to me,' said Banks.

'But Jaff doesn't like to be tied down. He likes his freedom. Likes to come and go as he pleases, with whom he wants.'

'So I gather. Did he tell you where he was going?'

Mallory sipped some Remy and looked away. 'Not specifically, no.'

'But he gave you a general idea?'

'Well, he said he needed to lie a low for a while, ring a few people and get some business deals organised. He had some bonds he wanted to sell. He said he was going to London, that there was a bloke he knew there in Highgate, name of Justin Peverell. I remember him vaguely from uni, but I wasn't part of their scene. He was a foreign student, I think. Somewhere in eastern Europe. Anyway, this Justin can fix things like fake passports and that. I knew Jaff was in with some pretty shady people, but I wasn't involved in any of that. I didn't want to know about it.'

'What business deal was he talking about?' Banks asked. 'What are these bonds he mentioned? Do you know anything more about this Justin Peverell other than that he lives in Highgate and deals in dodgy passports?'

'No. Honest. That's all I know. I lent Jaff my car, and he said he was going to London to see Justin. He'd get it back to me somehow, he said, and in the meantime I could use his.'

'Where's Jaff's car?'

'In my garage. He asked me to keep it out of sight for a while.'

'Did you tell Ciaran and Darren about Justin?'

'Yes. I *had* to. They were going to cut me to pieces, man. But I didn't tell them his last name. I just remembered it.'

So Fanthorpe had almost the same information and about five hours' start, thought Banks. That didn't bode well. Fanthorpe would also have the resources to find this Justin – the criminal network. In fact, it would probably be a damn sight easier for him than it would be for Banks if Justin hadn't registered on the Met's radar yet. And no doubt Ciaran and Darren were down in Highgate already awaiting instructions. Still, this sounded like the same Justin of whom Erin had spoken, and they not only had his last name, Peverell, but also the name of his girlfriend, Martina. It might just give them the edge they needed. They could check the electoral rolls, the phone book, even. Of course, if Peverell was from eastern Europe, he probably wasn't using his real name, and if he wasn't a British citizen or resident, that might make him difficult to track down.

But where the hell were Jaff and Tracy? Banks wondered.

They could be in London, themselves, by now. They'd certainly had enough time to get there. Victor's car had been found on the moors only two or three miles from Banks's cottage where Annie had been shot, and from there on, they must have been on foot for a while. They could still be up there, wandering in circles. People had been lost for days on the moors, had died there. It didn't even take a bad storm or a major snowfall. On the other hand, Tracy knew something of the lie of the land from their walks up there, and if they had got hold of another vehicle, they could be anywhere. It was one thing to know where they were going, but it would be much better to know where they were. Especially as Tracy's value to McCready declined with every mile they got closer to Justin Peverell. Jaff certainly wasn't going to fork out for *two* passports. Did he even know who she was? Who her father was? And if he did, how would that affect his strategy?

'I want to know about the gun, Victor,' Banks said.

Mallory seemed nervous. 'What gun? All I did was lend my car to a mate in trouble. I don't know anything about any gun.'

'I don't know if your last visitors asked you about it or not. They probably weren't interested once you'd told them about Justin. But I am. Very interested. We don't know if Jaff had a gun with him when he left his flat, but we think it's very unlikely, partly because Erin Doyle had already run off with it, and her mother had found it and handed it over to us. Which is the main reason why Jaff was running away in the first place. He was certain she'd name him and he didn't want the police poring over his dodgy business deals. So if he didn't have two guns at home to start with, and why would he, then he must have got the second one from you. Stands to reason. As far as we know, this is the only place he stopped before he . . .' Banks was about to say 'went to my house' but he pulled himself up in time. 'Before he went on the run. That gun was used to shoot a policewoman, Victor. The gun we think *you* gave him. A Baikal, in all likelihood.' And, he might have added, it is probably now being used to threaten my daughter into doing what he wants. 'That makes you an accessory.'

Mallory turned pale. 'Jaff did that? No. I can't believe it. You can't lay that on me. I never gave him any gun. I've never had a gun.'

'I don't believe you,' said Banks, 'but I don't have the time right now to thrash it out of you. If I find out that you're in any way connected with that gun, or that you've lied or withheld any information from us, I'll be back, and I'll prove it. In the meantime, don't even think of going on your holidays.'

Banks gestured to Winsome, who put away her notebook and stood up. When they left, Mallory was sitting in ashen silence with a glass of his Remy in his slightly trembling hand. Outside, the watchers were still sitting in their Skoda, plumes of smoke drifting out through the open window. Banks walked over to them and leaned on the roof.

'We've finished for now,' he said, gesturing with his thumb back towards Victor's house. 'But if I were you, I'd get your guv to send in a search team and take his house apart brick by brick. You're looking for handguns and possibly an illegal lab of some kind. If you don't find anything there, then try to find out if he's got another place, a business property, perhaps, or a secret lock-up somewhere, maybe under another name. You never know, it might earn you a few Brownie points, and by the looks of you both, you could do with them. 'Bye.'

When Banks got back to the car Winsome was on her mobile, frowning. She said goodbye and folded it shut. 'I've asked Geraldine to check the electoral rolls and telephone directories for a Justin Peverell,' she said. 'And there's good news.'

'Do tell.'

'We've got a report from the local police station at Baldersghyll. A white builder's van has been stolen from the car park near Rawley Force, about three miles away. It's a National Park spot, and apparently people park there and do the circular walk. It takes about three and a half hours.'

'So what happened?'

'Couple came back a bit early, after only about two hours – seems they hadn't a lot of time so they did the short version – and they found their van gone. Madame Gervaise has acted quickly, and all units have the number and description. It makes sense. Too much of a coincidence that someone else would have just come along and nicked it. It was in the vicinity and general direction Jaff and Tracy would have been heading.'

'Good,' said Banks.

'There's more. Seems the van's a bit of an old clunker. According to its owner, it doesn't go more than about forty.'

Banks smiled. 'Not having a lot of luck with his motors, our Jaff, is he?'

If the speedometer of the stolen van crept up towards fifty, the chassis and engine block started shaking so much that Tracy feared it would fall apart, or that the wheels would drop off. This only increased Jaff's frustration, along with the Wetherby roadworks on the A1, and now an accident blocking the southbound lanes to the M1. It was starting to get dark by the time they finally crawled on to the M1 east of Leeds, and already it was close to two and a quarter hours since they had stolen the van. Time was definitely not on Jaff's side.

Tracy noticed that he was getting edgier by the minute. It was partly the frustration and partly the coke he kept stuffing up his nose. The motorway was plagued by more CCTV cameras and police patrol cars than anywhere else, he complained, and an old white builder's van hobbling along in the slow lane couldn't help but attract unwanted attention. These days, too, he told her, many of the motorway cameras used the ANPR system – Automatic Number Plate Recognition – which meant that they automatically informed the police if a car was stolen. Pretty soon, he was certain, they wouldn't stand a chance on the M1. And it would be at least a five- or six-hour drive at the speed they were going now. More likely, the van would clap out before Sheffield, and they'd be stuck on the open road.

'Fuck it,' Jaff finally said, thumping the steering wheel. 'We're not going to make it. At this rate we won't even be south of Wakefield by the time the van's reported stolen. We've got to get rid of this piece of shit before they find us. They're bound to know we took it pretty soon, if they don't know already. Maybe those people were fast walkers, or they didn't do the whole route for some reason. The cops could be on to us at any moment.'

'But where can we go?' Tracy said. 'They'll have the railway and bus stations covered.'

'I need time to think and make some calls,' said Jaff. 'But first we've got to dump this van.' He drove on in silence for a few more minutes, then indicated a turn at the next junction.

'What are you doing?' Tracy asked.

'I've got an idea. We'll go to Leeds.'

'Leeds? Are you insane?'

Jaff shot her a hard glance. 'Think about it. Leeds is one of the last places they'll be looking for us. They'd never expect us to go back there in a million years.'

But Tracy knew they would. The police didn't always think in quite so linear a fashion as Jaff seemed to imagine when he thought he was being clever. Especially her father. 'Fine,' she said, a glimmer of hope now flickering inside her. Leeds. She knew Leeds. It was home turf. 'Your place or mine?'

'Neither. I'm not so stupid as to think they won't be guarding *our* places, or that the neighbours won't be vigilant and report any sounds. Vic's is out of the question, too. They're bound to have traced the other car to him by now.'

'What if he talks?'

'Vic? He won't talk. He's an old mate. We've been through a lot together.'

'Like what? Cross-country running with your backs to the wall, or showers with the games teacher after rugger?'

'You don't know fuck all about it, so just shut the fuck up. Besides, Vic doesn't know anything. He doesn't know where we are.'

'I'll bet he knows where we're going, though, and who we're going to see.'

Jaff just glared at her, which told her she was right and he was worried. The coke paranoia was kicking in. There was a short stretch of road through a desolate industrial estate in Stourton between the M1 and the M621 into Leeds, and Jaff concentrated on making the correct turns at the roundabouts, then he pulled into the entrance of a deserted warehouse yard.

'What are you doing?' Tracy asked. 'Why are you stopping?'

'No need to piss yourself. We're getting out of these filthy clothes and putting some clean ones on. You go first.'

Tracy crawled into the back of the van and opened her bag. It was a relief to change out of her old clothes and put on some of the clean, fresh ones Jaff had bought her at the Swainsdale Centre just the other day. Hard to believe only such a short while ago things had been so good between them. Now he was like another person: Jekyll and Hyde. She changed her underwear, too, and only wished she could have a bath first. The best she could do was get back in the front and use the mirror to put on a little make-up while Jaff changed quickly himself and then climbed back into the driver's seat.

'That's better,' he said, laying out another two lines of coke on a mirror and snorting them through a rolled-up twenty-pound note. 'Sure you don't want any?'

'No, thanks,' said Tracy. 'Where are we going now?'

'First off, we'll dump this piece of shit in Beeston. It won't last five minutes there. Then we'll find a nice hotel in the city centre, and I'll make some phone calls. There's no one else I trust up here, but I'll work out a plan, don't you worry.'

'How are we going to get to London?' Tracy asked.

'So many questions. I think I know where I can get us a clean car first thing in the morning. Bloke I know owns a garage in Harehills. MOT, road tax. No questions asked. Then we'll be down to London in no time.'

Tracy was thinking furiously. Leeds might be her best chance yet if Jaff got a bit too cocky about their safety there. She had been hoping for her break on the moors, but it hadn't come. Now she couldn't see an easy way out at all, no matter where they went or what they did. They would either get to London, in which case she would be at the mercy of Jaff and his friends, who would certainly want to leave no witnesses behind, or they would run into a police roadblock and Jaff would try to shoot his way out, or put the gun to her head and use her as a hostage. Whichever way she looked at it, things were bad, and her only possible hope was her father, if they had got in touch with him. It was Thursday, and as far as she could remember, he was due back in the country today. He was planning on staying the weekend in London, but surely someone must have got news of Annie's shooting to him by now?

'They'll be looking for two of us, you know,' Tracy said. 'An Asian male and a white female. We're making it easy for them.'

'So what do you suggest? I bleach my skin white? You tan yours brown?'

'I suggest we split up. They'll never find you alone in Leeds. You could probably even take a train down south and they wouldn't find you. Not on your own.'

'You don't think they've got my picture out everywhere? And you a copper's daughter.'

'Maybe they have,' Tracy argued. 'But they're still looking for the two of us. Police get blinkered like everyone else. Some of them are pretty thick, too, as a matter of fact.'

'But not your dad. And it's my bet he'll be the numero uno leading the search for you.'

'They won't let him do that. It's too personal. They have strict rules against that.'

'Think they'll be able to stop him?' Jaff paused. 'Anyway, let's say you're right. You're still my insurance policy, and I'd be a fool to leave my insurance behind.'

'If he is leading the search, the way you say, it's because of me. Without me you stand a much better chance.'

Jaff shook his head. 'Maybe it's partly because of you. But it's also because of that bitch I shot back at his house. Think he's going to give up on her? He was probably shagging her. They stick together.'

'It's not like that. You can drop me off right here, or in the city centre. I can make my own way home.'

'I'm sure you can. Right into your father's police station. I'll bet you've got plenty of friends there, and you'd be more than happy to answer all their questions.'

'You'll have a much better chance of getting to London and out of the country without me.'

'Who said I wasn't already planning on getting out of the country without you?'

His words didn't surprise Tracy, but she still felt shocked all the same. 'What?'

'Surely you don't think I'm planning on taking you with me now, after everything that's happened? It's not as if you've exactly proved to be an asset, is it?'

'What are you going to do with me?'

'I haven't decided yet. I'll think of something.' He gave her a crooked sideways smile. 'Justin might have some ideas. Who knows? You might even be worth something. There's still a market for young white female flesh in some places, and Justin's speciality is getting people over borders with the minimum of fuss and the maximum of profit. Or maybe I'll just shoot you. Easier that way. No loose ends. Anyway, one thing at a time.'

Tracy folded her arms and shrank into her seat. *White slavery*. It sounded silly when she put it that way, such an old-fashioned term, but it still sent a shiver of fear through her. It wasn't quite as far fetched as it sounded. She had heard and read things in the papers recently about white girls sold into sexual bondage overseas, and her father had worked on a people-trafficking case not so long ago involving girls being smuggled from eastern Europe. He didn't discuss his cases in any detail with her, but he had let slip one or two disturbing facts about the way these things were done.

'And just in case you get any clever ideas about trying to escape when we're among people again, you can forget it. If I'm close to being caught because of you, and I think it's all over, anyway, I'll shoot you without a second thought. If I think I can get away, I might not shoot you in public, but I *will* catch up with you, or my friends will. We have long memories. Every car that passes you on your way to work in the morning, every suspicious-looking person you see lurking on the street . . . Get the idea? You'll never know. You'll never see it coming. Then one day, the hardly felt needle-prick, and when you wake up you're in a stinking metal container on the way to some shithole country you've never heard of where rich men will pay unimaginable sums of money to do things so filthy to you you'll wish you were dead. So don't even think of trying to escape.'

Soon they were on the M621 under the sodium lamps. When Tracy closed her eyes, she couldn't prevent the images of Annie's shooting from running again in her mind, the shock in her eyes and the way she fell among the crockery, breaking the glass table. She thought about what Jaff had just said, wondering whether he was simply trying to scare her or not, and she felt herself on the verge of panic. Maybe he was laying it on a bit thick, but no amount of reason could hold at bay the images that now tormented her. She had never been so frightened in her life, had never wanted her father so much, had never felt so far from home.

Jaff turned off the motorway into Beeston.

14

'This *is* an unexpected pleasure. Do come and join me in the den, Mr Banks, and Ms . . . er?'

'Jackman. DS Winsome Jackman.'

'Winsome. What a delightful name. And one that, might I say, most certainly does you justice.'

Banks glanced at Winsome, and he could tell by her expression that she was wishing she hadn't told Fanthorpe her first name. As Fanthorpe led the way, she put her finger in her mouth and mimicked vomiting. Banks smiled.

The den was an unabashedly masculine room, from the dark wainscoting and the rosewood and mother-of-pearl chessboard, with its intricately carved ebony and ivory pieces, to the mounted brass telescope by the bay window, the mounted stag's head and the framed racing scenes on the wall. Four maroon red-leather-upholstered armchairs were arranged around a solid oak antique table at the centre. Mozart's *Eine kleine Nachtmusik* played from hidden speakers.

The Farmer walked over to the cocktail cabinet and brought out three crystal tumblers and a decanter. He was wearing baggy brown cords and a cable sweater knit from Swaledale wool. With his round shoulders and jaunty walk, spare tyre and mass of curly grey hair, he reminded Banks of a leprechaun on steroids. 'Drinks? I do hope you'll join me. I have a rather fine old malt.'

'It's not a social visit,' said Banks, settling into one of the chairs. It was so comfortable that if he took Fanthorpe up on his offer of a drink, he thought, he would probably curl up and go to sleep. Winsome crossed her long legs and took out her notebook.

'Pity.' The Farmer poured himself a large measure, sat down and smacked his lips. 'It's Ardbeg Airigh Nam Beist. That's Gaelic for "Shelter of the Beast", in case you don't know. So what can I do for you?'

Banks caught a strong whiff of the peat and iodine. He was getting used to it more and more, and was rediscovering his taste for Islays, but he wouldn't be sampling any of Fanthorpe's wares, even if he weren't so tired. The Mozart ended and was followed by Beethoven's *Für Elise*. A Classic FM collection of the Great Composers' best bits, if Banks wasn't mistaken. 'We're looking for an employee of yours,' he said. 'Name of Jaffar McCready, or Jaff. Any idea where we can find him?'

'Jaff? I'm afraid I have no idea. He just does odd jobs. I'd hardly call him an employee.'

'Casual labour, perhaps, then? How do you get in touch with him if you need him?'

'By telephone, of course.'

'Mobile?'

'Home number.'

That was no use; Banks knew it already. If Jaff had a mobile, it was pay as you go, unregistered and untraceable. 'Exactly what sort of odd jobs does he do for you?'

'Jaff's a Jack of all trades. Or should that be a Jaff of all trades?' Fanthorpe laughed, but neither Banks nor Winsome joined him. He cleared his throat and sipped some malt. 'Sure you won't join me?' he asked, holding up his glass. 'It truly is magnificent. Goes down like prickly silk.' By the sound of him, Banks reckoned he'd had a few already.

'Can you be a bit more specific about the nature of Jaff's employment?'

'Well, he doesn't muck out the stables, if that's what you mean. Bit of courier work, the occasional security duty, when necessary.'

'And when would that be necessary?'

'You might not realise this, Mr Banks, but racehorses can be valuable properties, very valuable indeed. And they're vulnerable. Sadly, there are some unscrupulous people in the business. One has to be careful.'

'I've read Dick Francis,' said Banks.

Fanthorpe smiled. 'Then you'll get the picture.'

'Strong-arm stuff?'

'Hardly, Mr Banks. I have no call for that sort of thing in my business.'

'I thought you said there are some unscrupulous people around?'

'Yes. But actual violence – strong-arm stuff, as you call it – is a rarity. They have more subtle ways of making their needs known.'

'What, exactly, is your business?' Banks asked. 'I understand about the horses, but that's merely the tip of the iceberg, isn't it, a hobby almost?'

'I suppose you could say that.' Fanthorpe turned the crystal glass in his hands. It caught the light from the shaded desk lamp and different colours flared and sank in its facets. 'Bit of this, bit of that. Mostly dairy farming and production – we own a cheese factory, my wife and I – the stables and horse training, of course. I also part-own a couple of thoroughbreds. Doing very well, they are. If you ever want a tip for—'

'Drugs?'

'Mr Banks! Wash your mouth out.'

'Only I heard you're quite a mover and shaker in the local coke trade. It seems to be having quite a renaissance these days, in case you haven't noticed.'

'I wouldn't go around making unfounded accusations like that if I were you.'

'Why not? Pal of the Chief Constable, are you?'

'As a matter of fact, we have been known to play the occasional round, bring home the odd brace of grouse. I own quite a nice stretch of moorland up—'

'Let's cut the bollocks, Fanthorpe,' said Banks, leaning forward. 'I'm looking for Jaffar McCready. Simple as that. To be honest, I don't give a damn about your dairy farms, thoroughbreds and coke business right now, except in that they relate to Jaffar McCready. You may or may not be aware of this, but he's wanted in connection with the shooting of a female police officer.'

'Friend of yours, was she?' Fanthorpe's eyes glinted with cruelty. 'Something a bit personal, is it? Girlfriend, even? I thought that sort of thing was frowned upon in your line of work?'

'If you'd just stick to the point, sir,' said Winsome. She picked up her briefcase and passed over Rose's sketches of Ciaran and Darren and a glossy photograph of Jaff they had got from Erin Doyle's Laburnum Way room. 'Do you recognise any of these men?'

Fanthorpe picked up each one in turn, made a show of scrutinising them, then passed them back to her. 'That's Jaffar McCready,' he said of the photograph, 'and that's Ciaran, and that's Darren. But you know that already.'

'Just need to make certain, sir,' Winsome said, slipping the pictures carefully back into her briefcase.

Banks gripped the arms of the chair and let his anger abate. He was thankful for Winsome's timely interruption, and for the breathing space the pictures had afforded him. He might easily have said or done something stupid otherwise. He still might, if he didn't get a grip.

Fanthorpe turned his gaze to Winsome. 'I had a mate owned a sugar-cane plantation in Jamaica once,' he said. 'Wanted me to go into business with him. I told him I couldn't stand the climate, though. Or the people. Lazy sods, the lot of them.' Then he eyed Winsome up and down. 'Seems things have come a long way since then.'

'Yes, indeedy, mastah, sir,' said Winsome. 'They even give us darkies warrant cards and let us arrest criminals.'

The Farmer laughed. 'Cheeky with it. I like that.'

'Where's McCready?' Banks cut in.

'I wish I knew.'

'Oh? Why's that?'

'He owes me money.'

'The bonds? Is that why Ciaran and Darren are looking for him?'

Fanthorpe swirled his whisky in the glass. 'You can draw your own conclusions. You will, anyway. I don't know anything about any bonds. I don't know where you got that from. All I'm saying is that McCready owes me money, and I want it before he disappears into a cell and it all ends up in a copper's pocket.'

'McCready was already on the run before he shot Detective Inspector Cabbot. We were wondering if that had anything to do with you.'

'Me? No. Something to do with a gun, I heard,' said Fanthorpe. 'It was all over the news.'

Winsome made a note and spoke up again. 'Jaffar McCready was never mentioned in connection with the gun Juliet Doyle handed in to us,' she said. 'We didn't tell the press that, and they didn't broadcast his name.'

'So how did you know?' Banks asked Fanthorpe.

'Oh, you think you're so bloody clever, don't you, the both of you? Do you think I don't have my sources? A man in my position? Do you think I don't know what *doesn't* go into the newspapers or on the telly? Come on. Grow up.'

'Chief Constable tell you, did he? A brief chat at the ninth hole?'

'For crying out loud.'

'Does this gun mean anything to you?' Banks asked. 'It's a nine-millimetre Smith & Wesson. Is there some reason that its falling into our possession disturbs you?'

'Not at all. I have nothing to fear.'

'So you think you're clean on the gun? OK. What does McCready have of yours? Drugs? Cash?'

'I told you. He owes me money.'

'Apparently, he told someone he was carrying bonds.'

'Rubbish. He was just trying to make it all sound legit, like he's some sort of high-powered business broker. He stole from me. Cash. Simple as that.'

'Drug money?'

'I told you, he does occasional courier duties. Sometimes that involves carrying and banking large sums of money. He happened to have just such a sum in his possession when he disappeared.'

'When Jaffar McCready disappeared,' Winsome said, 'he'd just returned from a business trip to Amsterdam and London, or so he said. How did he end up with so much of your money in his possession?'

'If you think I'm going to divulge my private business transactions to you, you've got another think coming, Ms Winsome.'

'Do you usually use your farmhands as debt collectors?' Banks asked.

'Ciaran and Darren are men of many talents. Limited intelligence, but many talents. Their appearance can be rather . . . intimidating, as I'm sure you remember. Sometimes their mere arrival on a scene encourages people to do as they ask. It can be important when large sums are at stake.'

'I'll bet it can. So far they've terrorised an innocent twenty-four-year-old girl and tied up and threatened with torture a young man. Real tough guys. Ever heard of a Victor Mallory?'

'Can't say as I have.'

'He's an old university and public school pal of McCready's.'

'The old boys' network? Well, Jaff always did move in rarefied circles. A bit too rich for my blood. Cambridge does that to people, you know. I came up the hard way, sheer graft, hard work, getting my hands dirty. I never went to university, and West Leeds Boys High is hardly a public school, so I wouldn't know about all that. Wouldn't know this Mallory, either. Jaff has a lot of friends I don't know about and don't want to know about. There's a big age difference, for a start, then the employer–employee relationship. Hardly conducive to friendship. I should imagine Jaff's friends are more his own age.'

'Do you know what information Ciaran and Darren wanted from the people they threatened?'

'Enlighten me.'

'They wanted to know where Jaffar McCready is heading.'

'Well, then, we're back to square one, aren't we?' Fanthorpe spread his hands. 'That's exactly what I'd like to know. Except nobody yet has mentioned the elephant in the corner of the room.'

'Meaning?' said Banks, though he had an inkling of what Fanthorpe was getting at, and the thought chilled him like a shadow crossing the high daleside.

Fanthorpe stood up, poured himself another generous shot and pointed at Banks. 'Your daughter, Banks. Tracy. Nobody's mentioned her part in all this yet, have they?' He leaned against the wall and grinned. 'Now, if you ask me, you're a man in a lot of trouble, Mr Banks, a lot of grief and trouble. I have daughters, too. I can understand that. Who knows, if we put our heads together, then maybe we might even be able to help one another? What about it?'

Jaff left the van behind a doorless Mini on blocks in a street of dirty red-brick terraced houses not far from Beeston Hill Cemetery. The tall pre-war houses seemed to Tracy to loom menacingly over them in the growing dark as they walked away, watched closely by a gang of hooded youths congregating at the end of a ginnel, looking shifty and threatening by turns. There was a mosque on the corner with an ornate mosaic dome. Televisions flickered behind moth-eaten curtains. Canned laughter spilled out into the street and mingled with the beat of a distant pub band. The street lights had just come on, a jaundiced yellow in the late twilight purple, and they were surrounded by haloes of haze. A hint of exotic spices filled the night air. Behind the high-pitched slate roofs, roiling dark clouds parted now and then to allow a lance of moonlight to break through. There was an edgy feel to the night, Tracy sensed, and the sky seemed to echo it. Perhaps a thunderstorm was on the way. Anything could happen.

One of the youths turned and called out something after them. Tracy couldn't make out the words. She could see that Jaff had one hand in his bag, though, and a grim smile on his face. A 'just let them try something' smile. Tracy felt her pulse quicken with her footsteps. But nobody followed them. Nobody threw anything. When they got to the well-lit arterial road with its people, pubs, hairdressers, Asian shops and curry houses, Jaff relaxed his grip and removed his hand from the bag. They caught the first bus into the city centre and sat upstairs at the front. There were hardly any other passengers at that godforsaken time of the evening, well after office hours and before closing time.

'Isn't it dangerous, going to a hotel?' Tracy said. 'I told you, they'll be looking for the two of us together.'

Jaff gave her a sideways glance. 'I'm not letting you go, so don't start that again. We'll be fine. I suppose you just want to go home to Daddy?'

Tracy said nothing. She did.

'Well, that's not going to happen, so you'd better make the best of things. Don't forget what I said back there in the van. I mean it.' He looked her up and down. 'At least you're reasonably presentable now. You'll just about pass muster. Just. How about me?'

Jaff looked fine. Immaculate as usual. 'You'll do,' she said.

'It's a nice hotel I've got in mind,' Jaff said. 'Not some fleabag place. We'll be able to have a shower, get room service, minibar, the lot.'

The bus lumbered on, around corners, across intersections, and finally made its way into the city centre.

'What about the CCTV cameras?' Tracy asked, as she saw the familiar landmarks of the Corn Exchange and Kirkgate Market ahead.

'They're only useful if someone's watching them and knows what to look for,' said Jaff. 'If you think how many of them there must be, you've got to realise that there can't possibly be enough people to watch them all, or we'd all be watching each other all the time. Real *Big Brother*. It's a risk, but a minor one. Especially here. Like I said, no one's going to expect us to come back here. And by the time anyone gets to checking all the CCTV footage, we'll be sunning it up on the Costa del Sol. At least, I will.' He grabbed the chrome rail. 'Come on. Our stop.'

'Help one another? Where do you get that from?' said Banks.

Fanthorpe sat down and cradled his fresh drink, a superior grin on his face. 'I would have thought it was obvious,' he said.

Winsome cast Banks a puzzled glance.

'Go on,' Banks said. 'Enlighten me.'

Fanthorpe sprawled in his chair. 'We both know that Jaff McCready's on the run with your daughter Tracy. I haven't the least interest in her, but I do have a very strong interest in young Jaff. Like I said, he's got something of mine, and I want it back.'

'So it's I scratch your back and you scratch mine, is that it?'

'Something like that. I can guarantee your daughter's safety, Banks – that is, if she's still in one piece when Ciaran and Darren find her. Can you do that, with all your protocols and procedures and red tape? Can you?'

'Go on.'

Fanthorpe leaned forward. 'I thought you'd be interested. My proposal is a simple one. Leave me to find Jaff and Tracy. When I do, she's yours. Unharmed. As I said, I have daughters, too. Believe me, I understand how you must be feeling.'

'You understand nothing. Don't try to tell me you give a damn about saving my daughter's life. All you want to do is carry on making your illegal fortunes.'

'I can't help it if I make a good living.'

'Off other people's misery.'

'Giving people what they want.'

'Selling them drugs?'

'However you look at it, you can hardly say that *you've* made a hell of a lot of people happy in your life so far, can you? I mean, how many of the petty villains you banged up got rogered so often in prison that their arseholes turned black and blue? How many scared young kids got stabbed by makeshift shivs in the showers? You hardly go around spreading joy and sunshine, mate, so don't give me that holier-than-thou shit. I'm giving you a chance here. A chance to save your daughter's life. Don't you throw it back in my face. I never make an offer more than once.'

Banks felt sick. The Farmer's offer was tempting, way too tempting, and he could do as he said; he could deliver with a lot more chance of success than any police intervention could offer. You only had to look at the Patrick Doyle case to know that. Then Banks would have Tracy back and Jaff . . . well, Jaff was a waste of space, anyway. Who cared?

But it would mean ending up in Fanthorpe's pocket. It wouldn't stop there, either, with Tracy's safe return. There would be more demands, a little insider information, a tip here, a tip-off there, polite requests to turn a blind eye, payments made. Before long, Banks wouldn't be able to bear looking at his reflection in the mirror. And Winsome was here, too, his moral compass: a witness to it all. She would never agree, and she wouldn't lie for him, no matter how rude the Farmer had been to her earlier.

'And Jaff?' Banks said. 'What happens to Jaff?'

Fanthorpe looked away. 'What do you care? I can't imagine why that would matter to you. I have no real interest in harming him. I just want my money back. Of course, it's always possible that Darren and Ciaran might see fit to teach him a lesson. What he did reflects on all of us, you see. I won't lie to you. What Jaff has done can't go unpunished, and Ciaran doesn't always know where to draw the line.'

'I do see,' said Banks. 'They're going to kill him. Or they're going to take him somewhere where you can kill him.'

Fanthorpe laughed. 'Now, don't be silly. I wouldn't harm a fly. Besides, it's nothing as extreme as that.' He sipped some whisky. 'A short period of hospitalisation, perhaps, a while before he can get back in the saddle, so to speak. A mere slap on the wrist. Surely even you can see the poetic justice in something like that. I mean, look what he did, shooting that policewoman. Bit of a goat, too, is Jaff. Your daughter—'

Before Winsome could step in again, Banks held his hand up, palm out. 'Don't,' he said quietly. 'For all our sakes, don't follow that line of thought any farther.'

'Fair enough. I can see how you might find it painful. As you say. I simply thought you would approve of my intentions, that's all. If not, I can't be in any way responsible for your daughter's safety.'

It felt like time for the 'if you harm a hair on her head

I'll rip out your spine and shove it down your throat' speech, but Banks didn't see the point. He was sure that he and Fanthorpe understood one another already. Instead, he said, 'People like you can't let others steal from them. You have to show your power. Exercise it. You have to make examples. Jaff will be executed, no doubt in a slow, painful and terrible way, and everyone you deal with will know it. They will know what happened and why and who did it, will know that they stray at their peril. What you do to Jaff will keep your troops in order till the next time some Jack the lad thinks he can put one over on you. I can't be a part of that.'

'What does it matter? We're splitting hairs. What do you care about Jaff McCready, especially after what he's done to your daughter and your colleague? For Christ's sake, Banks, you must want him d—'

'I told you not to take that route.'

Fanthorpe stopped in mid-sentence and sighed. 'Well, come on,' he said. 'Isn't it about time you woke up and saw what was happening? What you're really dealing with here.'

Fanthorpe's face had flushed as he talked, with anger and with drink. Banks wanted to hit him. Plant a hard, heavy fist smack in the middle of his face and watch the claret flow. 'And assuming I went along with this plan of yours?' he said. 'Just what would I have to do?' Banks could sense Winsome looking agape at him, but he ignored her. She would find out where he was going soon enough.

'Why, nothing! That's the beauty of it.' Fanthorpe's grey eyes glittered. 'A mere slap on the wrist, as I said. You simply have to leave it to me.'

'To Ciaran and Darren, you mean?'

'They've got a head start. And I'll bet you anything my

contacts are better than yours, that I can find out where Jaff and your daughter are going sooner than you can.'

'That may be true,' Banks agreed. 'So why don't you just share that information with me, and we can do this all legal and above board. That should make everyone happy. It'll keep Ciaran and Darren from facing a murder charge and life imprisonment, too. And you, if you're implicated.'

Fanthorpe shook his head. 'You just don't get it, do you? You just don't get it. And have what's mine disappear from the evidence room, or get tied up in judicial red tape for the next twenty years? No way.'

'That must be some dodgy fortune you're after getting back. Or maybe it's a nice kilo or two of coke? If that's the case, we'll definitely be hanging on to it.'

'That's none of your business. What *is* your business is that Ciaran and Darren don't know to leave Tracy alone. Focus on that.'

Banks felt a chill run through him, immediately followed by the raging impulse to hurt Fanthorpe. 'What do you mean by that?' he asked, though he knew full well the meaning of Fanthorpe's threat. He could sense Winsome's empathy, and her determination to hold him back if he suddenly snapped. She was poised, ready. But he wasn't going to snap.

If there was one part of the job Banks hated more than any other, it was that feeling of impotence and ineffectiveness he so often felt by having dedicated himself to upholding the law, following the rules. He cut corners from time to time, like everyone, had occasionally acted rashly and even, perhaps, illegally, but on the whole, he was on the side of the virtuous and good. There was no way he would go along with what Fanthorpe was suggesting. He was going to get Tracy back, and he was going to take Jaff down. Fanthorpe,

Ciaran and Darren along with him. He was as certain of that as he had been certain of the way things really stood in his life that night out in the Nevada desert. He just didn't know how he was going to achieve it all yet.

'I should have thought my meaning was obvious,' said Fanthorpe. 'As far as Ciaran and Darren are concerned, Jaff and your daughter are one and the same. My enemies. Tarred with the same brush. However you care to put it. They're in it together. If I let my men know otherwise, then all will unfold as I promised. Your daughter will be rescued unharmed, and Jaff will take his punishment like a man.'

'And if I don't?'

'That's asking for trouble. Events would take their course. Why would an otherwise intelligent man like yourself want to take the moral high ground here?'

'Because I'm a policeman, Mr Fanthorpe. And as a policeman I could hardly turn a blind eye to murder, could I? Because, however you whitewash it, that's what it would be. What you're basically telling me is that you'll make sure your men hurt my daughter if I don't let you have your drugs or your drug money back and leave you free to do what you want with Jaffar McCready, including killing him? Well, he might be a criminal, it's true, but if I do as you say, I become like you. Nothing more than some twopenny-ha'penny gob of slime who's managed to raise his greedy maw a few inches out of the gutter at feeding time.'

The Farmer spluttered on his whisky and dribbled some down his jumper. 'Hey, steady on. Bloody hell, that's a bit strong, Banks,' he said, pointing his finger. 'You'll regret that. Whatever happens, you'll regret that. Ciaran and Darren are in London already, awaiting my instructions.'

'Well, why don't you call them? We're not stopping you.

But you don't have any orders to give them yet, do you? You don't know any more than we do. Probably less.' He looked over at Winsome, who smiled and shook her head.

Fanthorpe stared at Banks for a long moment. 'I don't understand you,' he said finally. 'I just don't understand. I propose a simple deal. I get my money back. I give the thief a slap on his wrist. You get your daughter back unharmed. Where's the problem?'

'That's exactly the problem,' Banks said, gesturing to Winsome that they should be going. 'That you don't see it as a problem. We'll trouble you no more tonight. No need to see us out.'

'Was that wise?' Winsome said as Banks got into the passenger seat beside her. 'Winding him up like that?'

'Perhaps not,' said Banks. 'I don't know. But Fanthorpe's not the answer. If I could arrest him, I would, but we've got nothing on him. Not yet. It wouldn't even do any good to take him in on sus and sweat him in an interview room for a while, either, much as I'd enjoy the opportunity. First off, we don't have a while and, second, he's too canny for that. He'd have his team of high-priced lawyers down there like a shot. No, we'll get the Farmer when the time is right. For the moment, I'll ask the locals to keep an eye on his movements. At least we know now that Ciaran and Darren are in London because that's where they think Jaff and Tracy are heading.'

'Can we put a tap on Fanthorpe's phone? Their mobiles?'

'Not enough time,' said Banks with a wistful grin. 'Besides, he's bound to have a throwaway. I suppose we could try hanging him upside down or beating it out of him, or maybe pulling his fingernails out with pliers, but that relinquishes the moral high ground petty damn quickly, doesn't it?' Banks gestured towards Winsome's briefcase. 'And at least we've got his fingerprints.'

'I didn't think you'd noticed.'

'I'm not *that* tired. Well done. They might come in useful, and we don't have them on record.'

'Well, he's never done anything illegal, has he?'

'He certainly hasn't been caught.'

'What next?'

'Back to the station. Regroup. Don't forget, we've got Justin Peverell's surname and the Farmer doesn't. We're not without our contacts, either. I'm still willing to bet that our resources are better than Fanthorpe's. I also have a sneaking suspicion that Jaff and Tracy are nowhere near London yet. Wasn't it you who told me that the van they stole was an old clunker? Wouldn't go more than forty miles an hour? Isn't that what you said?'

'Yes.'

'Fanthorpe doesn't seem to know that, either. It buys us time. Let's go see if Madame Gervaise and the rest have made any more progress with Ian Jenkinson and this Quisling bloke.'

As soon as Tracy watched Jaff walk up to the hotel reception desk and start talking to the pretty young blonde receptionist in his best posh accent, offering his corporate credit card, the one that couldn't be traced back to him, her heart sank. He could do no wrong. Judging by the girl's smile and her body language, she was practically in bed with him already.

Tracy seriously considered making a run for it at that very moment, but Jaff's words and threats came back to her, and the images he had evoked – a car door opening, and someone dragging her inside the dark interior, or tossing her into the boot, smothering her with smelly old blankets, the threat of the unseen pinprick in the thigh or hip, waking in an unfamiliar country, standing on a sort of makeshift stage with other girls, dressed only in pink diaphanous chiffon fluttering in a breeze from nowhere, the leering eyes of the men on the front row crawling all over her. She realised it was a ridiculous image, of course, but it kept her sitting where she was, only a few feet behind him as he made the booking, glancing occasionally back at her and grinning, but giving most of his attention to the blonde.

He had the clothes, the voice, the gift of the gab, the air of superiority, all he needed to succeed, despite his mixed-race heritage, the golden colour of his skin. He was public school and Oxbridge, establishment through and through, and, vicious criminal or not, he acted just like one of them, cocksure, certain of his place, of his due, of his worth, sure of his position, a member of the right class. To the manor born. There was no way anyone in this jumped-up provincial hotel, pretentious as it was, was going to deny his demands, let alone mistake him for a dangerous criminal on the run, or associate him with someone wanted for murder. *If* Annie was dead. Tracy had no way of knowing, as she hadn't seen or heard any news since they left the cottage. Her heart sank as she watched Jaff, yet she couldn't help but admire the performance, if performance it was. There were many sides to him, she suspected, and this was just one of them.

He turned back to her, a key in his hand and a smile on his face, and gestured for her to follow him to the lift. They went up to the fourth floor in silence and walked along the deserted corridor, trays of empty bottles and glasses outside some of the rooms, the remains of half-finished steaks and prawn shells scattered on plates.

No one saw them as they entered Room 443. The view was nondescript, a backstreet so narrow you couldn't really see anything but the low slate roofs opposite, and beyond them, the windows of an office tower, empty for the night, though one or two lights still burned in the chequerboard pattern of windows.

The thunderstorm hadn't come yet, but the sky still looked as angry as a boil ready to burst. Jaff drew the heavy curtains. Their closing made Tracy feel claustrophobic. Somehow, at least having a view, however mean, gave her some hope, some snatched glimpse of a part of the world that was being kept from her, a place she might never enter again. She told herself to stop being so maudlin, that the fears Jaff had planted in her mind had taken too strong a hold and made her jittery.

Jaff tossed his grip on the bench under the window, then fumbled inside it and brought out the small plastic bag he had prepared for himself. He held it up to her and raised his eyebrows. Tracy shook her head and sat on the edge of the bed, hunched in on herself. Jaff shrugged and laid out a couple more lines on a mirror. When he'd snorted them, he used his untraceable mobile, and Tracy guessed he was calling Justin in London.

'It's ready? Great . . . terrific . . . Hey, that's a bit steep . . . No, all right, I'm not arguing . . . Yeah, I understand . . . OK. Look, Jus, we won't come around to your place, if that's all right with you, just in case, you know, yeah, in case we're being followed or something . . . Yeah. Right . . . How about we meet somewhere . . .? The Heath . . . that's cool . . . Highgate Pond. 'Course I can find it. No problem. We'll have wheels in the morning . . . Yeah, early afternoon . . . I'll give you a bell . . . See you then, mate. You're a lifesaver.'

He ended the call, dropped the phone on the bed, then clapped his hands and raised his fist in the air. 'We're away!' he said. When Tracy didn't react, he turned on her. 'We're off to London in the morning and then . . . points exotic. Who knows? Well, at least I am. What's up, misery guts? Are you planning on sulking like this from now on? I mean, it's a difficult enough situation we're in already, without you sitting there with a face as long as a wet weekend in Blackpool.'

'Jaff,' Tracy said. 'I'm tired and I'm scared. I'm not here to cheer you up or amuse you. I'm your prisoner, remember? All I want is to go home. Please, just leave me alone.'

'Same old bloody record, isn't it? Can't you change your tune? You should do some coke, have some fun while you can.'

'I don't want any.'

'Have it your way. We've got all night.'

Tracy shuddered at the thought. She didn't think Jaff noticed. The room was spacious, but it was impossible to ignore the fact that it was dominated by a king-size bed. Tracy was quite happy to sleep in the bath, if in fact she could sleep at all, but she doubted that was what Jaff had in mind. He wouldn't want her out of his sight, for one thing. 'Can we have the TV on?' she asked.

'Why?'

'I want to see the news. They might say something about . . . you know.'

'They can't tell us anything we don't already know,' said Jaff. 'Are you hungry? Shall I call room service? What do you fancy?'

'I don't know. Whatever you want.'

'Whatever I want?'

'Yes.'

'OK. How about pizza?'

'Pizza's fine.'

'What do you want on it?'

'I don't know. I don't mind.'

'Mushrooms? Onions? Olives? Hot Italian sausage. Anchovies? Pineapple?'

'That's fine.'

'Right. And a bottle of wine. I'll order a bottle of red wine, too, shall I?'

'If you want.'

'If I want. It's not just me, Francesca, you know. Will you give me a little help and encouragement here? What do *you* want?'

'A bottle of red wine is fine.'

'Right. I'll order pizza and a bottle of red wine. Anything else?'

'Not right now, no.'

'Maybe some bottled water, too, eh? Can't be too careful. Fizzy or still?'

'It doesn't matter,' said Tracy. 'Tap water's fine with me.'

'Fizzy,' said Jaff. 'Right. Good. Good.' His leg was twitching from the coke now, and he made no move towards the telephone. 'What about Madison?'

'Madison?'

'Yeah. The blonde girl on the desk. She's American. I bet she'd be game for it. Shall I see if I can get her to nip up too for some fun and games? A threesome?'

'Don't bother on my account. She's probably busy, anyway.'

'I suppose so.'

'Look, do you want me to call?' Tracy asked. She stood up and walked towards the telephone. 'I'll do it, if you like.'

Jaff wagged his finger as he swiftly intercepted her. 'Clever try,' he said. 'No doubt there's some secret code you can use to communicate with Madison and get her to put you through to your father. You like your father, don't you? Love him, even. I hated mine. No way. I'll do it.' He went over to the phone and ordered a pizza with green peppers, pepperoni and chicken, and a bottle of Chardonnay, then hung up, licked his lips and walked over to her, coming a little too close for comfort. Tracy started to back slowly away. 'While we're waiting, though,' he said, 'why don't we . . .? I mean, it has been a while. Work up an appetite. Know what I mean? Even if it is just the two of us.'

'You mean sex?' Tracy said, hoping she didn't sound as incredulous as she felt. 'After everything that's happened? You want sex? You're sick, you. You must be joking.'

But the expression on his face said not. 'I'll show you how sick I am,' he said. 'And how much I'm joking.'

Tracy felt his hand grasp her throat and push her towards the bed behind her. The backs of her knees hit the edge of the mattress, and her legs buckled, causing her to fall back. She knew then that he wasn't joking.

15

Annie Cabbot felt as if she were dragging herself up from the depths of the ocean, huge shadows circling her in the dark green mist, slimy fronds of underwater plants undulating in the water, wrapping themselves around her arms and legs to immobilise her as she tried to float to the surface, pulling her back. She struggled in the grip of invisible tentacles that wouldn't let go, no matter how much she kicked and thrashed. The pressure of the water pushed down on her chest, into her lungs, so she couldn't breathe but only flail uselessly as the tentacles hauled her down. She opened her mouth and breathed in deep gulps of salt water, and suddenly she was floating free, calm, wrapped in a warm cocoon, rising up, up. Just as she was about to give in to the drowsy warmth that was spreading through her body, she burst to the surface and her lungs were suddenly filled with cool air.

Annie's first sensation was of pain; her second was panic. There was something stuck down her throat, and she felt as if it was choking her. As she fought to control her racing heart, she could hear the buzzing and beeping of the machines surrounding her. OK, she told herself, opening her eyes and slowly adjusting to the dim light. Be calm. You're in hospital. Hooked up to machines. She had thought someone was with her – Ray, her father – but she soon realised that she was actually alone.

She couldn't remember how she had got there, and she only had the poorest recollection of why, but she was alone in a room, her bed slightly raised, propping her at a thirty-degree angle. There were tubes coming out her chest as well as the one down her throat, and IVs hooked up to a catheter on the back of her hand. Pouches of blood, plasma and clear liquid hung on stands beside the bed. Beyond them was an illuminated screen which told her that her blood pressure was 125/91 and her heart rate 102. Even as she watched, the automatic sphygmomanometer strapped to her upper arm activated itself. Her BP was now 119/78, heart rate 79. She tried to relax. That was better, she thought. Not bad at all. But her throat still hurt and her breathing felt the same way it had under the ocean in her waking dream.

As she took stock of herself and her various aches and pains, needles and machines, she realised that one thing struck her above all others: she was still alive. Maybe she was dying, a machine doing her breathing for her, or maybe she had even died and been brought back, but right now she was alive. Her brain felt slow and heavy, as if it were stuffed with warm cotton wool, and her memory felt tenuous and flimsy, but it still worked. Her nose also seemed to be in the right place, ears, arms, legs and torso, too. What really hurt most of all were her chest and her back. Painkillers dulled some of it, but not enough. From her neck down to her stomach, front and back and inside, she felt as if she had been beaten black and blue by a giant cricket bat. Maybe she had been. Maybe that was why she was here. She could feel her toes, though, even wiggle them; and she could clench and unclench her hands, so she knew that neither her neck nor her back was broken.

Annie had a hazy sense of people going about their business outside her room, of muffled conversations, laughter and tannoy messages, but there was no clock, and she didn't know where her watch was, so she had no sense of time, day or night. She lay there trying to calm the images of fear and panic that had first crowded her mind on her trip back from the underworld. She felt dreadfully thirsty and noticed a plastic cup of water on the bedside table, complete with a bendy straw; then she realised she couldn't drink anything with the tube down her throat. Nor could she call out. Feeling the panic rise again, she looked for a bell or a buzzer, and finding a button, pressed it, but even as she did so, she became aware of people dashing into the room, and there was no doubt that one of them was Ray, bearded and dishevelled as ever. She couldn't speak, but her heart ached with love for him, and she was sure the tears streamed down her cheeks as she lay back, exhausted with her efforts, and waited for the doctor and nurses to take out the tube that was choking her.

Everyone in the boardroom at close to midnight that Thursday night was tired, but none of them would entertain any ideas of sleep until Annie's shooter had been brought to justice, and until Banks's daughter was safe. Banks and Winsome were present, along with Gervaise, and Doug Wilson, Geraldine Masterson, Vic Manson, Stefan Nowak and several of the uniformed officers from traffic, patrol and communications. They had already been cheered by the news that the fingerprints Vic Manson had taken from the photograph the Farmer had handled matched those on the magazine of the Smith & Wesson automatic found in Erin Doyle's possession. It confirmed the link they already suspected between the Farmer, Jaff McCready and the murder of

Marlon Kincaid. But there was no sign of Justin Peverell on the electoral rolls.

'I think we're getting to the stage now where everyone's feeling just a bit twitchy,' Gervaise said, when Banks and Winsome had finished telling everyone about their visits to Victor Mallory and the Farmer. 'There are just so many factors in the equation.' She glanced at Doug Wilson and Geraldine Masterson. 'What did you get from West Yorkshire Homicide and Major Enquiries?'

Wilson indicated that Geraldine Masterson should do the talking. 'Not a lot, ma'am,' she said, clearly nervous to find herself performing in front of such a distinguished audience for the first time. 'Detective Superintendent Quisling was able to confirm that the body of Marlon Kincaid was discovered beside a bonfire close to Woodhouse Moor, Leeds, in the early hours of November sixth 2004.'

'By a jogger?' Banks asked. 'A dog walker?'

'No, sir. Someone had to douse the flames, make sure the fire was out. Health and Safety.'

'So Health and Safety turn out to have their uses after all,' said Banks. 'Miracles will never cease. Carry on.

Geraldine Masterson gave him a nervous smile and continued. 'The body was partially burned, but examination at the scene soon showed he'd been shot. Twice. You already know about the bullet and casings matching. Mr Quisling said it was hard to track down everyone at the bonfire. It had been quite a large party, apparently, with live music, dancing, lots of drink. At first, the people putting out the fire thought it was just some unfortunate drunk who had fallen down in the wrong place.'

'Drugs were involved, too, no doubt?' Gervaise suggested.

'Yes, ma'am.'

'Was Ian Jenkinson any more forthcoming than Mr Quisling?'

Geraldine Masterson cast a sideways glance at Doug Wilson, who was looking more like Harry Potter than ever tonight, wearing what looked like his school tie and blazer. With her long red hair, green eyes, high forehead and pale skin, Geraldine Masterson could easily have passed for one of his fellow Hogwarts pupils, but she hadn't been around long enough to be given a nickname yet. Annie Cabbot, who knew about these things, had once suggested that she resembled Elizabeth Siddal, the famous pre-Raphaelite beauty and artists' model, immortalised by Dante Gabriel Rossetti and other painters, but that was hardly nickname material.

Doug Wilson adjusted his glasses and picked up the story. 'Believe it or not, Ian Jenkinson is studying for the ministry at the moment. Wants to be a vicar. C of E. Gone quite religious. Not a fanatic or anything, but it's a bit of an about-turn from his past.'

'I suppose we should thank heaven that there is such a thing as rehabilitation,' said Gervaise. 'Go on.'

'According to Jenkinson, who went down from Eastvale to the bonfire and who knew the victim, Marlon Kincaid was bragging a bit that he'd been warned off the territory by some bloke called the Farmer, but he wasn't planning on paying any attention to any country bumpkin. Marlon wasn't a big player, apparently, just sold a bit of pot and E to the student population now and again, but he thought it was his patch. Word had reached the Farmer, who'd been assuming he had the whole scene locked up and under control.'

'So he wanted to make an example of Kincaid?'

'I guess so, ma'am.'

'Did Jenkinson witness the shooting?'

'He says not.'

'Do you believe him?'

'Yes, ma'am. It's not just the churchy bit. He really does seem to genuinely regret his past, the drugs, the dealing. There were a lot of loud fireworks going off that night, he said, a lot of loud music, and a lot of drunkenness. People passed out and fell asleep right there on the ground. There was a good chance that nobody would have either heard the shot or noticed that Kincaid was dead.'

'Terrific,' said Banks. 'Does Jenkinson know Jaff McCready?'

'He says not, but he *did* say that he saw a young Asian bloke slinking away at one point in the evening, quite late on. He was wearing a black leather jacket, and he had one hand inside the front of it, you know, like Napoleon, as if he was carrying something he was trying to hide.'

'Like a gun,' said Banks. 'Did he tell this to Detective Superintendent Quisling and his team at the time?'

'No. He says that, in the first place, it was all very vague – he was far from sober himself at the time – and in the second, the last thing he wanted was the police following up on his accusations and bothering him again. He was worried we'd frame him or harass him or something. He just wanted to give his statement and get back to Eastvale.'

'Hmm,' said Banks. 'He never mentioned it when I talked to him in Eastvale, either, though he did hint at this feud between the Farmer and Kincaid. That's how I first came across the name. When I pressed him, he maintained he had no idea who the Farmer was, or even whether it was a name or a nickname. Jaff McCready wasn't even on the radar then.'

'If the Farmer's fingerprints are on the magazine,' said Gervaise, 'and if McCready was possibly the shooter, then Fanthorpe must have given the gun to McCready and sent him to do the job. A trial or an initiation ritual. Something like that? Prove himself.'

'It's possible,' said Banks. 'And now we're caught up in falling-out among thieves precipitated by Erin Doyle's actions.'

'Maybe McCready was using the gun as some kind of hold over the Farmer?' Gervaise suggested.

'I doubt it,' said Banks. 'The Farmer's not the kind of villain to sit around and let something like that happen. No, if McCready had tried it on with him, he'd have had Ciaran and Darren round to his flat before you could say abracadabra and McCready would have ended up in bits and pieces in the canal. You can be sure that if the Farmer did give McCready the gun to shoot Kincaid, he had no idea that he was still holding on to it.'

'Then why?' Winsome asked.

'Insurance?' Banks said. 'Or sheer bloody-mindedness? McCready and his pal Mallory liked guns. It was a hobby of theirs. And West Yorkshire's still trying to find Mallory's drug lab. The odds are that when they do, they'll find a cache of Baikals as well. The Smith & Wesson's a nice gun. The Farmer no doubt told McCready to dump it when he'd finished the job, but the cocky young bastard decided to keep it. He would have known that Fanthorpe's prints were still on the magazine, once he'd wiped the gun clean of his own. Maybe it gave him a feeling of power or security?'

'Makes sense,' said Gervaise.

'Anyway,' Banks went on, 'we've got a lot of scraps of information, and they seem to be making some sort of a pattern, but most of all, if we're to bring an end to all this, we need to know Justin Peverell's bloody address in Highgate. It's a waiting game. And nobody enjoys that when the stakes are so high. We need to step up our road surveillance. If their van's held out, there's a good chance they're still chugging along in the slow lane somewhere on the M1.'

'And if not?' said Gervaise.

'Then they've holed up somewhere en route, and McCready's thinking furiously about how to get hold of another vehicle.'

'We've already got all the motorway patrol cars keeping their eyes open for a slow white van heading for London,' said Gervaise. 'And if they have stopped for the night somewhere on the way, it gives us even more time to trace this Justin. He's the key. Once we know where he lives we can stake out his house.'

'True,' said Banks. 'But McCready won't want to linger. One way or another, he'll be back on the road as soon as he can be. McCready needs Justin, or needs what he can get from him. Then he'll disappear like smoke. Or so he thinks.'

'And Tracy?' asked Gervaise.

'I don't like to think about that,' said Banks. 'I can't see as it would be in his interests to hurt her. Or Darren and Ciaran's, no matter what Fanthorpe said. On the other hand, when McCready has got what he wants, I can also see that Tracy would become an unnecessary burden. That's why we have to get to them first.'

'We've got Armed Response Units across the country on call,' said Gervaise.

Banks managed a grim smile. 'Now, why doesn't that make me feel a whole lot better?'

'Should we bring in the Farmer right away?' suggested Gervaise. 'Now we know those prints of his you got on the photos earlier are a match with those on the magazine of the Smith & Wesson, we might be able to put a bit of pressure on him.'

'I don't think it'll do any good,' said Banks. 'He won't tell us anything, and the lawyers will spring him in minutes. All it means is that he handled the magazine at some point. There's no proof he shot the gun that killed Marlon Kincaid. In fact, he most likely didn't. I'm certain he was never at the bonfire. He'll have a perfect alibi.'

'But you said yourself that the Farmer's name came up in that investigation,' said Winsome.

'From Ian Jenkinson, who didn't really know what or who it referred to. We've still nothing to arrest him for—'

'Perverting the course of justice? Wasting police time?' suggested Gervaise.

'We'd be better off waiting till we get something a bit more serious than that. Best just keep a close eye on him. We do hav—'

'Don't worry, Alan. Ripon are keeping a close watch on him. He's not going anywhere.'

'He doesn't need to. He can do all he needs from the comfort of his cosy little den. Anything on Darren and Ciaran?'

'We can hardly check all the London hotels,' Gervaise said. 'Besides, they could be staying at a private house. All we know is what you told us, that they're in London somewhere waiting for orders.'

'Have you checked Fanthorpe's holdings?'

'Yes. No London property. At least, not under his own name, or any of his companies that we can find.'

'Damn. So it's back to the waiting game.'

'At least *we* know there's a connection between Fanthorpe, the gun, McCready and an unsolved murder,' said Gervaise. 'A few more missing pieces and we ought to be able to put something together.'

'And the Met are on Justin Peverell's trail,' said Winsome. 'The Intelligence Bureau. They've got men out talking to their informers, people they've planted in the trafficking business. They're taking some risks. They're doing what they can.'

'I know,' said Banks. 'And I appreciate it. I'm not criticising. Just frustrated, that's all.'

'Why don't you go home?' said Gervaise. 'Or back to your digs. Put your feet up for a while, have a bit of a nap if you can. You're doing no good here. We've got the manpower we need for what we have to do. You never know, your eyes might close for a few minutes of their own accord. We'll keep everything ticking over here and call you the minute anything breaks.'

'The minute?'

'The minute.'

'I might just do that. And Annie?'

'Holding her own, last I heard,' said Gervaise. 'Her father's with her. Again, I'll let you know as soon as I have anything more.' She must have noticed Banks hesitate. 'Don't worry,' she went on, 'I'll hold the fort here. I'll be passing out TIEs and actions momentarily. Winsome, I want you to keep pushing on the London angle. Something's got to give. Somebody down there has to know this Justin Peverell.'

'Yes, ma'am,' said Winsome. 'I have a few irons in the fire already.'

'Good. And let's not forget, Ciaran and Darren are after

Justin, too, and I don't fancy his chances if they find him first.'

'Me neither,' said Banks. 'Or McCready's and Tracy's. Ciaran's been indulging in a lot of foreplay over the last couple of days, and he'll be just about ready to go all the way with someone.' He glanced sheepishly at Winsome. 'If you'll pardon the metaphor.'

Winsome said nothing.

A quick tap at the door was followed by the appearance of a PC with a yellow message note in his ham-like hand. 'Sorry to interrupt, ma'am,' he said, addressing Superintendent Gervaise, 'but it's important, and I thought you'd want to know as soon as possible.'

'What is it, lad? Give,' said Gervaise.

'It's about DI Cabbot. Message from Cook Hospital. She's regained consciousness.'

Gervaise turned to Banks with a smile. 'Alan? I imagine this will change your plans a wee bit.'

'Of course,' said Banks. 'Sleep can wait. You'll drive, Winsome?'

'My pleasure.'

The Farmer felt ill at ease after his visit from Banks and Winsome. Not that he was unduly worried by them. They had nothing on him, and they never would have. He never touched anything he sold, kept no paperwork, and anyone who did know his name was usually wise enough not to repeat it. Well, something had slipped out once, but that was a few years ago, and the surviving kid, Ian Jenkinson, hadn't known who or what he was talking about. The Farmer had heard that the young lad was training for the ministry these days. Good for him. He liked to keep tabs on people who'd crossed his path over the years, and you never knew when it might be useful to have a vicar in your pocket.

Besides, the kid had been a drug user. The Farmer didn't employ druggies any more. In this business, he had come to realise, it pays to keep a clear head on your shoulders, which means not indulging in your own merchandise, for a start. Like a pub landlord. Once you start sampling the produce, you're finished, and your pub could burn down around you while you sleep it off on a bench in the public bar after the punters have all gone home. No. Abstinence was a good policy. The only policy. The way it had to be. Which certainly didn't mean that he couldn't enjoy a nice malt now and then, he thought, topping up his glass.

This was also why Jaff had always been a bit of a worry. The Farmer knew that Jaff was a user, coke mostly, but the kid was so bright, so quick, so lethal and so ruthless that it somehow didn't seem to matter. There were people who had a great capacity for mind-altering substances, who functioned all the better, or at least as well as ever, under the influence, and Jaff was one of those. Or so he had appeared.

The Farmer had told him right from the outset that if he ever saw him obviously off his face on anything at all, he'd get his marching orders on the spot. And he hadn't. Whether Jaff had actually been stoned at any of their rare one-on-one meetings or not, Fanthorpe had no idea. All he knew was that Jaff's thought processes were always sharp and logical, and his contributions helped fill the coffers. The kid was cocky, and he liked to see himself as more of an equal partner than an employee, which, in a way, the Farmer supposed he was. He was certainly willing to let Jaff go on thinking so, up to a point.

But now things had gone way too far, and that point had

been passed. If he didn't act quickly and decisively, and do what had to be done to eradicate the source of his problem, he might as well hand over the reins. Sources, really, because the Banks girl was now part of the problem, when he had tried to make her part of the solution. Now she would have to suffer the same fate as Jaff, then all would be on an even keel again. Ciaran and Darren would disappear overseas for a reasonable period, operations would be slowed down to the absolute minimum necessary to keep things ticking over, like an animal's system in hibernation, and as soon as it had all died down, he would be back to normal again.

The Farmer lounged back in the soft embrace of his chair, sipped the Ardbeg and surveyed the gleaming wainscoting, the racing scenes, the crystal decanters and ornate cabinets. Classical music was still playing, though he had no idea what the piece was now. It was soothing and quiet, strings, wood-wind, no blaring brass, and that was what counted. He lit a Cuban cigar.

He would never understand cops. Not if he lived a million years. In the old days, when everyone knew where they stood, they beat confessions out of innocent men, even hanged some of them, took kickbacks, bribes, resold confiscated drugs and generally indulged in the madness and mayhem of power gone haywire. But you knew where you were with them.

PACE had tidied things up a bit, but no one could convince George Fanthorpe that these things didn't still happen, that suspects didn't get beaten to a pulp, or that coppers weren't on the take. And then you had someone like Banks, a known maverick, a bad boy, who wouldn't even lift his little finger to save his own daughter's life. Some world. Bizarre.

And Jaff . . . how he had turned. Fanthorpe remembered

their first meeting over six years ago in a posh restaurant in the Calls. One of his dinner companions had pointed Jaff out at the next table with two very attractive girls. 'So you're Jack McCready's lad,' Fanthorpe had said, offering his hand. 'Bless my soul. I've never met him, but I've lost a bob or two to your old man in my days.' Jaff had smiled at him, but the smile hadn't reached his dark, haunted eyes.

They had talked a little about racehorses, on which subject Jaff seemed knowledgeable enough, and soon it had been obvious to both of them that they were the same beneath the skin, though nothing was said there and then.

The Farmer had given Jaff his card; Jaff had given Fanthorpe one of the girls and a room key for the discreet boutique hotel across the road. What a night. They hadn't looked back. After that, contact had to be kept to a minimum for business reasons, but he always remembered that night and imagined Jaff thrashing the sheets with gorgeous women like that every night while he stayed at home and worried about the bills, his daughters' education and Zenovia's increasingly extravagant shopping trips. He knew he felt more than a little envious of Jaff, that he lived life vicariously through him. Perhaps, he had even once gone so far as to think, Jaff represented the son he had never had. Even in business, Jaff was perhaps the partner the Farmer could never quite acknowledge that he had.

And he remembered a few months after their first meeting, in this very same den where he was sitting now, handing the Smith & Wesson automatic to Jaff, putting in the magazine for him, identifying the target and telling him to make sure he dumped the gun in the river afterwards. Well, it appeared that he hadn't got around to that last part. But what did it really matter? the Farmer thought. So he'd been a bit sloppy once. So the cops might get his prints from the magazine. So what? Jaff wouldn't be talking; that was for certain.

The Farmer was lost in this line of thought when his private mobile rang, the one with the bell that sounded like an old telephone. He picked it up and barked his name. From the other end of the line came a name and an address followed by a click. It was all he needed, all he'd been waiting for. He keyed in the number of Darren's throwaway.

'Sir?' said Winsome on the way to the hospital.

'You don't need to call me that.'

'I know. I just feel more comfortable sometimes.'

'Oh? Does that mean you have a tricky question? A complaint?'

'Neither, I hope, sir. I just . . . well, I just wondered why you didn't take George Fanthorpe's offer.'

'I'm surprised to hear you, of all people, asking me that.'

'What if I hadn't been there?'

'You think I'd have gone along with him then?'

'No, sir, not that. But would you have done the same? After all, you could always have agreed, pretended to go along, and then when Tracy was safe, you could have made your move.'

'When you sup with the devil you need a long spoon, Winsome, and I didn't have time to go out and get one.'

'Sir?'

Banks sighed and glanced out of the window. Beyond the buildings, he could see lightning from a distant storm. Tracy had been scared of storms when she was a little girl, he remembered. He hoped she wasn't scared of them any more; she had enough to worry about. 'Right now,' he said, 'we're at a delicate stage of the game where Fanthorpe, Jaff, Ciaran

and Darren hold most of the cards. We're also at that stage
where things are tending towards chaos. The still point. It's
a bad place to be and an even worse place to make the sort
of gamble that puts one's daughter's life at stake.'

'I still don't understand, sir.'

'I'm tired, Winsome. There were many reasons – ethical,
personal, practical – why I didn't take the Farmer up on his
generous offer. But when you get right down to it, it just
wasn't that good an offer.'

'But why not?'

'Because Fanthorpe couldn't guarantee Tracy's safety.
Situations like the one Ciaran and Darren are entering into
right now are volatile by nature, full of uncertainty and
chaotic in the extreme. No one can predict what the outcome
might be. Anything could happen. A butterfly might spread
its wings in Mexico and change the world. My gambling on
Fanthorpe would have been exactly that. A gamble. And the
way things are now, I at least maintain a modicum of control,
and more than enough self-respect. And that'll have to do
for now. You can get quite a long way on them, actually.
We're here, aren't we?'

Tracy Banks lay awake in the dark. The ropes that secured
her hands and her ankles to the bedposts made her feel as
if she were on the rack every time she moved. Whenever
the thunder rumbled outside, she felt a deep and primitive
sense of unease ripple through her. Despite the stimulation
of the coke, Jaff had fallen asleep quickly and easily. She
could hear his gentle snoring beside her, see the outline of
his sleek naked body glistening in the darkness. Four twenty-
three. The devil's hour. Her spirits were low and she felt
used, abused, humiliated, worthless. And powerless.

Jaff had had his way with her, of course, after he had tied her up, and then he had turned the TV on when he lost interest, muttering something about ringing Madison, blaming Tracy for just lying there like a sack of potatoes. It could have been worse. He could have beaten her. But he hadn't; he had just shagged her routinely and fallen asleep watching TV. Worse things had happened after a night in the clubs and a drunken trip home with a stranger, awkward fumblings in the back of a minicab. But this time she hadn't been drunk or stoned, and Jaff wasn't a stranger, though in a way he was more unknowable than any of the predictable boys she had slept with before. And this time it *had* been different. This time it had been rape. He had tied her down and had sex with her against her will. That she hadn't screamed out or struggled changed nothing. She was his prisoner, and he had a gun.

She couldn't reach the telephone even if she tried; it was on Jaff's side of the bed. Even in his intoxication and his lust he wasn't stupid; he never lost sight of the practical realities. She wished she could at least get hold of the remote to turn off the bloody TV, which he had switched on just before falling asleep. It was an American football game, and it was driving her crazy. But the remote was on Jaff's side, too, of course.

Suddenly she sensed that he was awake beside her.

'Did you hear that?' he said.

'All I can hear is the bloody TV,' said Tracy.

Jaff ignored her tone, grabbed the remote and switched the set off. 'Listen,' he commanded.

Tracy listened. 'I can't hear anything.'

'Ssshhh. I thought I heard someone outside, in the corridor.'

'You're paranoid. It's just the thunderstorm. Or someone going back to their room after a night out.'

Jaff slipped out of bed. He was wearing only his white underpants. 'Paranoia is a form of awareness.'

'And whose words of wisdom are those?'

Jaff gave her a knife-blade of a smile. 'Charles Manson.' He pulled the gun from his bag and went over to the door, placing his ear against the wood. Then he looked through the peephole. A few moments later, he undid the chain and opened the door, checked both ways up and down the hotel corridor, and came back in.

'I could have sworn I heard someone out there.'

Tracy couldn't very well tell him not to worry and come back to bed. In her position, there wasn't much point in saying anything. She just kept quiet, hoping he would leave her alone and fall asleep again.

He did lie down beside her, but he didn't fall asleep. She could feel the tension emanating from his body, coiled on the bed beside her. But he didn't touch her, and she was relieved for that at least.

Time dragged slowly on, the storm abated and the dawn light started to show through the curtains. Tracy wondered how long they would stay here, how long before they headed out to the garage, where they would pick up a nice clean car and drive to London and . . . When did the place open? Seven o'clock? Eight? Nine? It didn't matter how many CCTV cameras recorded their journey if the car wasn't on the police's stolen list. Jaff was certain to obey all the rules of the road and to avoid speeding, no matter how much of a hurry he was in. Because for him the journey meant freedom, and for her it might mean death.

★

Annie still seemed a small and pathetic figure as she lay there against the white sheets, hooked up to the machines and tubes, but her return to consciousness seemed to have given her more presence, Banks felt. The tube was gone from her mouth, and she even managed a taut grin when she saw him walk into her room. He took her free hand and gave it a gentle squeeze. 'How are you doing?'

'I feel like I've been hit by a ten-ton lorry.'

'Two bullets from a Baikal nine-millimetre, actually.'

'Trust you to take all the romance out of it.' Banks smiled and felt Annie squeeze his hand. She wheezed. 'It's still hard to breathe sometimes. Could you pass me the water, please?'

Banks passed her the cup of water with the bendy straw. 'I don't suppose the morphine does any harm, either?' he said.

'Certainly not. Want some?'

'What would the doctor say? Besides, if I had anything other than tea or coffee right now, I'd probably fall right down in the bed beside you. I . . . er . . . I . . .'

The machines beeped into the silence that stretched between them.

Annie squeezed his hand again. 'That probably wouldn't be such a terrible thing,' she said, 'if it weren't for all these tubes and needles. We'd make an awful mess. But I don't suppose that's why you're here.'

'Believe it or not,' Banks said, 'I'm here because we just got the news you'd returned to the land of the living, and I wanted to come and see you with my own eyes. I'm here because I care, Annie, that's all. We all do.'

'Stop it, you'll make me cry.' She took her hand away for a moment to wipe her eyes.

'Where's Ray?' Banks asked.

'He's gone to get some sleep. Finally. It took a lot of persuading.'

'I'll bet. By the way, your girlfriend says hello.'

'Girlf . . . Ah. So you've met Nerys?'

'Yes. She's very smitten with you, you know.'

'She told me I wasn't her type.'

'I guess she just didn't want to risk driving you away.'

'And you know all about these things? You're the expert all of a sudden? Anyway, Nerys is all right. Tell her thanks. Don't you want to interrogate me about what happened?'

'Oh, I'd love to. Foremost thing on my mind. Seriously, though, if you feel up to answering a couple of questions . . . you know, seeing as I'm here . . .'

'Bastard.' Annie dug her nails into his palm. 'A real Mr Sensitive, aren't you? I don't remember anything, really, you know. Except . . .'

'Except what?'

'Except Tracy.'

'What about her?'

'Just that she was there, at Newhope Cottage. She opened the door. We were talking.'

'How did she seem? Do you remember?'

'Scared. She seemed scared. And nervous. Always looking over her shoulder, biting her fingernails.'

'As if she wasn't in control?'

'As if she was playing a part and someone was watching her and she knew she had to get it right. But she was off balance, a little stoned, I think, or drunk.'

'Did you see anyone else?'

'Jaff McCready, you mean? No, I didn't see him. Just a shadow. That's all. It happened so fast. After that, nothing.'

'Tracy may have saved your life,' Banks said. 'She phoned

it in. The 999 call. It cost her her mobile, her lifeline, and maybe even a beating, but she did it.'

Annie smiled. 'Tell her thank you from me.'

'I will.'

'What's wrong?'

Banks shook his head and stroked the palm of Annie's hand, looking down at the dry skin. 'I don't know where she is, only that she's in danger.'

'Jaff's still got her with him?'

'Yes.'

'Oh, Alan. I'm sorry.'

'We'll find them.' Banks patted her hand. 'Look, the doctor told me not to tire you out.'

'From where I'm lying, you're the one who looks the most tired.'

'Jet-lag,' said Banks. 'It's been a long day.'

'I suppose it's no good telling you to go home and get some sleep?'

'I can't go . . .' Banks let it trail.

'What? Oh, of course,' said Annie, and he saw the realisation dawn on her face. 'The shooting. I'm sorry, Alan, sorry I got shot in your lovely conservatory and turned your cottage into a crime scene.'

Banks was about to protest, say it was all right or some such silly retort, when he saw the mischievous smile curling at the edges of Annie's lips.

'You're winding me up.'

'Gotcha,' she said. Then she looked beyond Banks and her expression brightened even more. 'Winsome! Wonderful to see you.'

'You too,' said Winsome, hurrying over and giving Annie a gentle hug as best she could through the jumble of tubes.

She passed the mobile to Banks. 'You might want to hear this,' she said. Banks nodded, said he'd be back, and hurried out of the room.

The line was open, and Superintendent Gervaise was on the other end. 'Alan? How is she?'

'Stunning,' said Banks. 'Magnificent. What's the news?'

'Don't get your hopes up. Nothing on Jaff and Tracy's whereabouts yet, but we think we've found Justin Peverell. Or, rather, Winsome found him shortly before she drove you to Middlesbrough, only she didn't know it. We just got the call back. It was touch and go to get her contact to talk to *me*. I must say, he was rather rude.'

'Excellent news,' said Banks. 'I didn't mean about the rudeness. Sorry.'

'Yes, I'm sure. Anyway, the Met are none too happy about shutting Peverell down, according to a bloke called Burgess, apparently, Commander Burgess. Gave me a right earful. I believe he's a friend of yours?'

'I know him,' said Banks. 'What did he say?'

'Simply that his department, which he wouldn't name, by the way, had been watching Justin Peverell for some time, and he'd led them to identify a number of couriers and traders they hadn't known about before, in addition to a couple of routes and methods for smuggling in asylum seekers and sex-trade women that nobody had thought of. He didn't know they were watching him, and if we shut him down, all the good information goes with him, and the ones they've already identified scatter.'

'Can't he round them up before we take in Peverell? Put a rush on it?'

'Yes,' said Gervaise. 'Some of them. That was what I suggested, and that's exactly what he's doing. But he's not happy about it, and he wanted me to know it. You know the way it goes. There's always the hope of more. Peverell hasn't outlived his usefulness as far as Burgess is concerned.'

'There'll be plenty more where he came from,' said Banks. 'What next?'

'Burgess says he'll put a watching brief on Peverell's house in Highgate. They've been faxed Rose's sketches of Ciaran and Darren, along with photos of McCready and Tracy. They'll take note if anyone comes to the house, and there's another team to follow anyone who leaves.'

'Good,' said Banks. 'Let's hope we can catch up with McCready and Tracy before they get there, but it's good to know there's a second line of defence in place if we don't. The only thing that worries me is they can be a bit quick on the draw down there, if you know what I mean.'

'Commander Burgess has been fully apprised of the situation,' said Gervaise. 'He ... er ... he knows McCready has your daughter, and he asked me to pass on his sympathy. He said he wouldn't be telling me any of this if it wasn't for you. He also gave his word that he'll see to it she comes out unharmed. Can you trust him?'

'I can trust him,' said Banks. 'I don't necessarily trust the company he keeps, but I trust him, all right.'

'Best we can do for the moment, then,' said Gervaise. 'Get Winsome to drive you back to your flat. Have a little nap. I'll be in touch as soon as there's any news.'

Winsome wandered over and joined Banks just as he ended the call. 'The nurse came in,' she said. 'Kicked me out. Told me we should leave and let Annie rest. She said to say goodnight to you.'

'Winsome, you devil,' said Banks. 'Did you get in touch

with Dirty Dick Burgess behind my back? Was that one of those irons you had in the fire?'

Winsome grinned. 'Well, I had a bit of contact with him over your return. You remember, when we pulled you aside at Heathrow? He said to stay in touch, keep him apprised of what was happening. From what you'd told me about him, and from my own conversations with him, I thought he might be just the kind of bloke who would know something about the world we were investigating, so I phoned him.'

'He must have fancied you,' said Banks.

'Sir!'

'It's all right. There's no need to get your knickers in a twist. Burgess fancies anything in a skirt.'

'Charmed, I'm sure.'

'Any chance of a lift back to Gratly?' Banks said.

'Only if you apologise and promise there'll be no more such profane talk.'

'You drive a hard bargain, Winsome, but I think I can just about manage that.'

A slight figure walked up to the corridor towards them. 'Mr Sandhar,' Banks said, holding out his hand. 'I'd like to thank you.'

Sandhar shook hands a little shyly. 'You're welcome,' he said. 'Though I can hardly claim credit.' He cleared his throat. 'I wonder if we could have another quick word. Same place as before?'

Exchanging curious glances, Banks and Winsome followed Sandhar to the examining room.

'There's something else?' Banks asked, settling himself on the crinkly tissue of the examination table. 'A problem?'

'I'm afraid so, though I am extremely satisfied with Ms

Cabbot's progress. The broken clavicle is a problem, of course, and it may severely limit her future range of arm movement. Usually these fractures heal quite well after four to six weeks in a sling, but in this case, there was some fragmentation of the bone structure as well as of the bullet. We've removed the fragments, but recovery could take up to three months, and Ms Cabbot could experience considerable pain and discomfort. But it will heal. At the very least, though, it will require a great deal of physiotherapy before Ms Cabbot can play tennis or golf again, or bowl for the England Ladies' eleven, if, indeed, she ever can.'

That wouldn't be a problem, Banks thought. Annie didn't much like playing sports. She did love yoga, though, and the loss of flexibility would be a great blow to her. 'What about the bullet fragments?' he asked. 'Did they stray far from the entry?'

'They caused an additional amount of muscle and tendon damage we could have done without,' Sandhar said, 'which compounds the problem of the fractured clavicle, of course. That's what makes recovery an even slower and more painful process. But that isn't the worst of it.'

Banks swallowed. 'What is?'

'The other bullet. The one that didn't fragment. It pierced the right lung, as I said, and it lodged in the spinal column, close to T5, one of the central vertebrae, in the anterior thoracic area. Do you—'

'I understand what you're saying,' said Banks. 'Please go on.'

'There was no vertebral damage, and fortunately the bullets weren't hollow-points. But it is my opinion that Ms Cabbot will require further surgery, and with such a delicate procedure, there's a always a danger . . .'

'Of damage to the spinal cord?' Banks interrupted. 'Of paralysis?'

'Yes,' said Sandhar. 'But I want you to know that we have in this hospital perhaps the best trauma specialists, thoracic surgeons and spinal injury teams in the country, if not in all of Europe.'

'I know your reputation,' said Banks, with a wan smile. 'But there's still a risk she'll end up in a wheelchair?'

'To put it bluntly, yes. There's always a risk, even without the surgery. In fact some surgeons recommend *against* the operation. They argue that removing the bullet could destabilise the spinal cord.'

'But you don't think so?'

Sandhar shrugged. 'As I said. There's always a risk. A second opinion would be entirely acceptable, given the circumstances. Her father already knows about this and he's thinking it over. There are also many other factors, such as infections and blood poisoning, to consider, too.'

'I think the last thing we'd want is a doctor fight,' said Banks. 'When do you plan on performing this operation?'

'It's hard to say,' said Sandhar. 'We certainly can't go in until the damaged lung has healed and Ms Cabbot has fully recovered from the trauma she suffered. And we would like to see her recover from her other injuries. She's young, strong, healthy in every other respect, as she has already proved, so I don't foresee any serious problems there, but she needs to be stronger.'

'What kind of time period are we talking about?'

'If we operate, the sooner we do it the better. Scar tissue starts to form in, say, two weeks, and that makes the surgery more difficult. Of course, it may not be possible to do it that soon, depending on her general progress.'

'Will she have to remain in hospital during this period?'

'Oh, yes. She will also need to avoid unnecessary movement.'

'And for now?'

'We'll keep her under close observation. We'll also be keeping track of the lodged bullet, on the lookout for any movement, any slippage.'

'And if it does slip?'

Sandhar smiled. 'Not to worry too much, Mr Banks. We still have, as you say, a little wiggle room. Just not quite enough to risk operating until some of Ms Cabbot's other issues are resolved.' He stood up. 'I hope I've been helpful. Now you really must excuse me. I have patients to see.'

'Thank you again,' said Banks.

It was strange to be back in the old Steadman house, Banks felt, as he climbed the stairs to his upper flat. It must have been close to five years since he had lived there after the fire, when Newhope Cottage was under repair. He opened the door, walked into the hall and turned the lights on. The place smelled fresh, with a hint of some sort of lavender-scented air spray, and apart from the meagre furniture, it was empty, with nothing to show that anyone had ever lived there – no family photos, only generic landscape prints in Yorkshire Trading frames, no mess, no phone message light blinking. Nothing.

Not surprisingly, being there made Banks immediately think about his brother Roy, and that night he had wobbled back, a little drunk, from the Dog and Gun, puzzled as to why Penny Cartwright had turned down his dinner invitation, and found Roy's distress message waiting for him. That had set off a chain of events that took him down to London and deep into the shady world his brother inhabited. Burgess had been involved in that case, too, as he had in so many.

Banks dropped his suitcase in the bedroom, noticing that the bed was freshly made up, covered in a green candlewick bedspread, and glanced through the curtains. Nothing had changed. The room looked out over a tiny, disused Sandemanian graveyard, no bigger than a garden, and some of the tombstones leaned against the wall beneath his window. He had often enjoyed a feeling of tranquillity sitting on the window seat looking down over the graves on moonlit nights, listening to the gentle wind sough through the long grass, but tonight he didn't feel like sitting there. That night five years ago, he hadn't known just how closely death was to brush against him, but this time it almost had. Almost. Annie was alive, though she might lose the use of her legs, or even everything from the chest down. Tracy was alive, though her life was in danger. He was in no mood for memento mori.

Banks took his smaller carry-on into the bathroom, where he unpacked his regulation plastic bag of toiletries before settling down in the living room. Then he took out the bottle of ten-year-old cask-strength Laphroaig, all dutifully sealed and stamped, that he had bought at San Francisco airport duty free. He hadn't been certain when he bought it that he would want to drink it himself, but the little taste Burgess had given him at Heathrow had gone down very well indeed.

After he had poured a small measure into a glass he found in the kitchen, Banks opened the living-room curtains and lifted the window a few inches to let in some air. The room had a magnificent view north, from the thin ribbon of Gratly Beck glittering in the moonlight, past Helmthorpe church, with its square tower and odd turret attached, then beyond the lights of the small market town to the opposite daleside, peaking in the magnificent limestone curve of Crow Scar above the high pastures and drystone walls, still visible, white as bone in the silvery moonlight.

He carried a portable docking station to play his iPod in hotel rooms, and now he took it out and plugged it in. The sound wasn't great, but it was impressive enough coming from a unit the size of a paperback. He docked his iPod, selected Norma Waterson's solo album and turned out the overhead light as that beautifully forlorn voice started singing 'Black Muddy River', one of his favourite late-period Grateful Dead songs. He sat down and put his feet up, sipped Laphroaig, looked out towards Crow Scar and luxuriated in the music.

When he closed his eyes, the backs of his eyelids seemed to fragment in discs and chips of bright shifting colours, like a kaleidoscope. He rubbed them, but it only made them worse. He sipped some more whisky and tried to keep his eyes open. It was about three o'clock, and he didn't think much was likely to happen until morning. He felt so impotent, unable to do anything for Tracy, and he agonised again over getting in touch with her mother, his parents, or Brian. If anything happened to her, they'd never forgive him. But if she came out of it as he hoped she would, then they need never know. Her name hadn't been mentioned in the media yet.

Norma Waterson sang about how God loves a drunk, and Banks continued to follow the drift of his thoughts. He didn't know whether he even wanted to try to sleep or not. It had been so long, he feared that if he did drop off, he might not hear the phone, which sat on the chair-arm beside him, might never wake again. It seemed ages since he had woken up in Teresa's bed at the Monaco in San Francisco. Surely it couldn't be only two days ago? She would be back to her life in Boston now, and their encounter would start slipping slowly but surely from her memory, the way such things do without further contact. The flesh forgets.

When Banks finally became aware of the mobile playing the opening notes of Bach's Brandenburg Concerto No. 3, Norma Waterson had long finished, and an early morning mist was rising from the valley in wraiths around the church tower, like will-o'-the-wisps slithering up the opposite dale-side. Above Crow Scar, the indigo sky was tinted with the rosy hues of dawn.

He awoke with a start from a dream that scuttled away into the dark recesses of his mind, like some light-shy insect, but left him feeling unsettled and edgy. Reaching for the phone, he almost knocked it off the arm to the floor, but he managed to hold on and flip the case. 'Banks,' he mumbled.

'It's Winsome. Sorry for waking you but there's been developments. Madame Gervaise wants you to come in now. Shall I drive over and pick you up?'

'Please,' said Banks. 'Tracy?'

'No, no, it's not Tracy or Annie, but it is important. I can't tell you any more right now. Information's still coming in. I'll be there in twenty minutes.'

'I'll be ready.' Banks closed the mobile and ran his hand over the stubble on his chin. Twenty minutes just about gave him time for a quick shower and a shave, which might help make him feel more human. He'd brush his teeth, too; he could still taste the Laphroaig. As he moved towards the bathroom, he wondered what Gervaise could be in such a tizzy about.

16

Over two hundred and fifty miles away, and not much more than an hour earlier, Commander Richard Burgess, Dirty Dick to his friends, was equally discombobulated when his phone rang at an ungodly hour of the morning, and the officer commanding the stake-out team watching Justin Peverell's house requested his urgent presence there. The cheap lager Burgess had been drinking earlier down the pub had turned his stomach sour, and it rose up in a loud and tasty belch when he stood up. He glanced back at the bed to make sure he'd been sleeping alone that night. He had been. Then he pulled on yesterday's clothes, helped himself to three paracetamol, two Rennies and a large glass of water fizzing with Alka-Seltzer, grabbed a can of Coke from the fridge and headed out to the garage. If he had no time for coffee of a morning, he always found that Coke gave him the caffeine jolt he needed to get his brain into gear. These days, his body tended to lag a bit behind, but his work was rarely physically demanding. Getting up early was usually the hardest part of his day.

The traffic around Canary Wharf wasn't too bad in the pre-dawn light, and he was heading north-west, driving through the fringes of Limehouse and Bethnal Green, then through Hoxton and Holloway, in no time. His destination was just off Highgate Hill, past Junction Road, and all in all, it took him a little over half an hour.

The house they had commandeered for surveillance was on the opposite side of the street to Justin Peverell's semi, a few houses down. Luxury surveillance was one of the perks of Burgess's new position, which mostly involved counter-terrorism and not shutting down a valuable people-trafficking network for the sake of an old friend's daughter. Not for him a shitty old Subaru littered with McDonald's wrappers and a plastic cup to piss in. That national security was at stake was all they had to say these days. That covered a multitude of sins and opened a multitude of doors, including this one. They had packed the occupiers off to a cheap hotel for the night, moved in and made themselves at home. According to DS Colin Linwood, the surveillance team leader, the owners couldn't get away quick enough, visions in their minds of wild-eyed barbarians aiming portable missile launchers.

'So what's so bloody important you have to wake me up before dawn?' Burgess demanded of Linwood as he stormed into the house.

'They've gone, boss,' Linwood said.

Burgess scratched his head. 'Who's gone? Where?'

'French and Saunders, sir,' quipped DC Jones, who was now, in Burgess's mind, about to remain a DC for an unusually long time. 'Ciaran and Darren, that is.'

'Hang on,' said Burgess. 'Let me get this straight. I put you bozos on surveillance, and the first thing you tell me is that the men we're waiting to see arrive have left? Am I even close?'

'They must have been already inside,' said Linwood. 'There was no way we could have known.'

'Geez, I would never have thought of that.' Burgess flopped on to the armchair and swigged some Coke.

'Fancy a coffee, sir?' said Jones. 'They've got one of those fancy Bodum things and some of that nice Fairtrade Colombian.'

'Might as well,' said Burgess, putting the Coke can down on a smooth polished table, where it made a sticky ring. 'Black, two sugars. And strong.'

Jones disappeared into the kitchen. 'So what time did you lot arrive?' Burgess asked Linwood. 'Remind me.'

'Eleven fifty-four p.m.'

'And Ciaran and Darren left when?'

'Three thirty-six a.m.'

'That's a bloody long time. You sure you couldn't have missed them going in?'

'No way, boss. We've even got a man watching the back.' He smiled. 'Not quite as comfortable as we are in here, but . . .'

'Someone's got to get the short end of the stick.'

'Anyway, like I said, they must have been already in the house when we arrived.'

'Which means that their man in Yorkshire tipped them off as to where to find Peverell well before we did our little favour for our colleagues up north.'

'Well, boss,' said Linwood, 'in all honesty, they're pretty lucky we did it at all, given the circumstances.'

'So they were in there for over four hours?'

'Looks that way.'

'And you didn't clock anyone else coming or going?'

'No way.'

Jones came back with the Bodum and cups on a silver tray. 'We'll just let it brew a few minutes, sir, huh?'

'Where did they go from here?' Burgess asked.

'Ferguson and Wilkes followed them to a hotel on the Old

Compton Road. Mid-range. Nothing too ostentatious. Lot of tourists. Americans, mostly.'

'I don't need the pedigree of the fucking hotel,' said Burgess. 'I hope Fergie and Wilkes are sitting tight.'

'They are, boss. Nobody's going anywhere without us knowing.'

Jones poured the coffee and they all took grateful sips. 'Well done, lad,' said Burgess. 'Terrific coffee. We'll make a detective of you yet. The way I see it is like this. Brody and French were in there an awfully long time. Either Peverell wasn't in and they were waiting for him, or he was in and . . .'

'They worked him over, got what they wanted?'

'Something like that. Either way, soon as we've finished our coffee, we'd better get over there and suss out the situation.'

'It might be an ambulance job, boss,' said Linwood. 'If they were in there that long. Maybe we should go in right away.'

'After DC Jones has taken the trouble to make us this wonderful coffee? Peverell is a scumbag who helps smuggle in underage girls forced into prostitution,' said Burgess, ever fond of the crude American slang he picked up from TV and movies. 'Letting him bleed a few minutes longer won't do anything but good for the human gene pool. It's French and Saunders who'll lead us to McCready and the DCI's daughter now.'

So they finished their coffee in peace as the light grew slowly outside. A weary-looking shift worker got out of his car a few houses down. It was still a dull, overcast morning, and bedroom lights started going on as people got up to get ready for work. This was a decent neighbourhood, Burgess thought. People had worked hard for their little piece of England, and while they weren't rich, they were mostly comfortable in their middle age, despite the recent credit crunch. Perfect protective colouration for a smooth operator like Justin Peverell. Not that he'd be home all that often, anyway, in his line of work. But if Peverell was expecting McCready, and more to the point, expecting handsome payment for forged documents, then there was every chance he would have thought it worthwhile hanging around for a day or two.

'OK,' said Burgess, putting down his empty coffee cup and getting to his feet. 'Let's go. You got the door-opener, Col?'

'In the boot.'

First they picked up the battering ram on their way. They wouldn't use it unless they had to, a quiet entry being far more desirable than waking up the entire street. Then they would have to send for reinforcements just to keep the neighbours back if anything went awry, as things so often did when Burgess was around.

The door was maroon, with pebble-glass windows at the top. First, Burgess knocked gently and rang the doorbell. Nothing happened. He glanced over at Linwood, who shrugged, then tried the handle. The door opened. The three of them paused for a moment on the threshold, then entered.

They found themselves in the hall, with hooks for coats and a mat for shoes. Burgess calculated that the living room was off to the right, through another door. The front curtains had been drawn, so they hadn't been able to see inside from the street.

Burgess went in first and switched on the overhead light He stood transfixed and appalled for a split second, then he turned and stumbled into Linwood and Jones before he doubled up and vomited up last night's curry and lager all over the hall mat. The other two held on to him as he gasped for air and cursed. It was the first time he had ever been sick on the job since he'd been a cadet, and he had seen some things in his time.

When Burgess had regained his equilibrium, helped by a glass of water Jones brought from the kitchen at the back, he took a deep breath and led them in. The scene was so posed, so markedly surreal, that it took everyone a few moments to put the pieces together and work out exactly what they were looking at. Then Jones and Linwood staggered back, handkerchiefs over their mouths. The smell was awful. Piss, shit and fear desecrating a nice upper-middle-class London semi.

Two hardbacked chairs, the kind that had probably been at the dining table, faced each other about eight feet apart. In one chair sat what had once been a very beautiful woman. Probably Peverell's girlfriend Martina, Burgess guessed, long black hair trailing over her pale naked shoulders. Naked as the rest of her, as far as he could see.

From what Burgess could make out on a preliminary examination, it had taken her a long time to die, and it had been a very painful process. Grey duct tape covered her mouth and bound her hands to the chair behind her back, and one ankle to each front leg. It was hard to say exactly what had killed her. There were cuts and areas where the skin had been stripped, or peeled, from her flesh, blood between her legs. On her left hand, her index and middle fingers had been docked at the first joint, the flesh peeled off and the bone sharpened like a pencil point. One eye was wide open, dead and staring, but the other socket contained only the raw remains of an eyeball; a viscous trail streaked down her cheek like bloody, unset blobs of egg white.

There was more, much more, things the like of which Burgess had never imagined before and would remember till the day they put his body in the ground. He was crying, he knew, but he couldn't help it. Such beauty. Such pain and horror. Linwood and Jones weren't in any condition to notice his tears, anyway.

In the other chair sat Peverell, fully clothed, also gagged and secured with grey duct tape. At first glance, he seemed dead, too, nobody home behind the glazed eyes, but Burgess noticed that when he looked carefully, he could see Peverell's chest rising and falling. There wasn't a mark on him, but if Burgess had to choose, he couldn't for the life of him decide in which position he would rather be.

'Right,' he said, turning to his men. 'Stop staring at her tits, Jonesey. Get on to Fergie and Wilkes and tell them to bring French and Brody back here right now. Back here. Got it? I want a word with those bastards *before* we have to get the brass and the lawyers involved. And Col, the SOCOs will have our balls for this, but get a sheet from upstairs and cover the poor cow up, would you? Then somebody see if they can't find a bottle of decent whisky in the place.'

Tracy awoke with a start, Jaff shaking her shoulder, and realised that she must have dozed off in the early dawn light. Perhaps Jaff had, too. But now he was wide awake, fully dressed and looming over her, fiddling with the ripped sheet to untie her. 'Come on, wake up,' he said. 'Wake up. It's time to go.'

Tracy opened her eyes and moved her head groggily. Jaff was fresh out of the shower, but she hadn't heard a thing.

The curtains were open, and she could see people already at their desks in the office tower. She gathered the sheet around her and headed for the bathroom. 'What time is it?' she asked.

'Eight o'clock. Get a move on. You've got ten minutes.'

Tracy showered as fast as she could. There was no time to do anything with her hair except give it a quick rub with the towel. Luckily, it was short and it would dry quickly. She wished she had more clean underwear, but she was wearing the last of her new pairs of knickers. The best she could do was turn them inside out before she put them on. She binned her bra. She had always thought her breasts were too small, anyway, so she really didn't need one. The outer clothes she had put on last night in the van were still fine.

Before she could even finish brushing her teeth, Jaff was standing at the door. 'You ready yet?'

'Coming,' Tracy said. 'Coming.' She glanced desperately around the small bathroom for an escape hatch or a weapon of some sort. There was nothing. It would be no use, anyway, as Jaff hadn't allowed her to lock, or even to close, the bathroom door. Resignedly, she rinsed out her mouth and went back into the room. Jaff was just finishing off a line of coke, probably not his first of the day.

Everything went smoothly at check-out. There was a different girl on the desk this morning, a tanned brunette, but the smile was the same, the flirtatious body language. When he had finished, Jaff strode over to Tracy with that cocky, confident walk of his, holdall still in his hand, and nodded towards the door. She left with him.

Tracy had expected that they would take a taxi to the garage, but Jaff clearly had other ideas. Taxis could be traced, he explained, when she asked, and taxi drivers could be questioned. Caution, or paranoia, seemed to be his natural state of mind now. They walked all the way to the Corn Exchange among the hordes of city workers dashing to their little hutches for the day. How Tracy wished she were one of them. Everything seemed so normal, yet so completely unreal. At one point, she realised that she wasn't too far from Waterstone's, where she worked, and she wondered whether she should make a dash for it. Then she remembered the things Jaff had said, the threats of retribution he had made, and that she believed them. She couldn't live her life like that, always feeling scared, in fear, always looking over her shoulder. She had to go through with this right to the end. Whatever that end might be.

They caught a bus to Harehills and Jaff sat silently all the way, tapping his fingers on his knee and gazing out of the window. Soon they would be in a new car racing down to London, where Jaff would get his new identity, sell his wares, pack enough cash to start somewhere else, and disappear. Tracy didn't believe he would sell her into slavery, and she still couldn't believe that he would just kill her in cold blood, despite the evidence of his violence she had witnessed. With any luck, once he got where he was going and got what he wanted, he would simply lose interest in her, dump her and forget all about her. She hoped so.

'Next stop,' said Jaff, and they walked to the front. She could see him scanning the faces of the other passengers, processing them. They got off at Roundhay Road and Harehills Lane then turned a few corners. 'It's down here,' said Jaff finally, turning left.

The small garage was sandwiched between a sewing-machine repair shop and an Asian music imports emporium, from which some very odd sounds indeed were drifting out into the air. Tracy couldn't even recognise what instruments were being played. Next to the music shop was a greasy spoon with plastic chairs and tables. Dead flies lay scattered on the inside window ledge, and the mingled smells of cumin and coriander wafted through the door. Tracy liked curry, but she didn't fancy it for breakfast.

On the opposite side of the street stood a closed school, a late nineteenth- or early twentieth-century building, Tracy could tell, which was due for demolition. There were so many of them in Leeds, the old red-brick kind, darkened by years of industrial soot, like the houses around them, surrounded by high pointed metal railings embedded in a low concrete wall, weeds already growing through the cracked tarmac playground. Some of the windows were boarded up, others simply broken, and a liberal sprinkling of graffiti adorned both the boarding and the red brick. A faded sign said HAREHILLS PARK. Tracy couldn't see any park. The place gave her the shivers. A few yards past the school was a red-brick mosque.

Tracy was so busy looking at the school and the mosque that at first she didn't notice what had happened until she heard Jaff kicking at the garage door and yelling for someone to open up. Then she saw the GOING OUT OF BUSINESS sign half covered with pasted bills and graffiti.

'They're gone, Jaff,' she said. 'There's nobody here.'

Jaff turned on her. 'I can bloody well see that for myself. Why don't you stop stating the obvious and contribute something here?'

'Like what?'

'Like some ideas.'

'You seem to be forgetting I'm not in this with you. I'm not here to help you. I'm your hostage.'

'Whatever we're in, we're in it together. Make no mistake about that. Your fate depends on mine. So a little contribution wouldn't go amiss.'

'I've already told you what I think. Let me go, and you take off alone. Then you'll have a chance.'

Jaff shook his head. 'No. No way I'm letting go of my greatest asset.'

'Oh, really? I thought that was your gun.'

'Guns are just tools. You're a bargaining chip.' He paused. 'Goddamn, that's it!'

'What is?'

'You. I've been holding you in reserve all this time, and now it's time to use you. Of course! What a bloody idiot I've been.'

'What do you mean? You're scaring me.'

Jaff pulled out his mobile. 'What's your father's number? His mobile, not the fucking police station.'

'My father—'

'His mobile number. Now!'

Numbly, Tracy told him. She could see his hand shaking as he keyed in the numbers and mumbled to himself, then he put the phone to his ear.

'Are you alone?'

This wasn't the usual opening to a telephone conversation, and it alerted Banks to possible danger. 'Yes,' he lied, though he didn't recognise the voice. He was actually in the boardroom of Western Area Headquarters with Gervaise, Winsome, Geraldine Masterson, Harry Potter and Stefan Nowak, discussing the fate of Justin Peverell and his dead girlfriend Martina Varakova.

Burgess had just reported from the Highgate house again,

and Ciaran and Darren had finally been taken from their hotel in an ambulance under police guard. Ciaran had apparently broken his arm in two places while trying to escape police custody, as well as sustaining other minor cuts and bruises, including one groin injury that might impair his sexual performance for some years to come. Neither had given up the Farmer, but Banks planned on paying the bastard another visit soon, anyway, now he had a little more ammunition up his sleeve. And if they let Burgess into the interview room down south, anything could happen. Banks had never heard him sound so upset and enraged.

He excused himself from the conversation and went out into the corridor. 'Right,' said the voice on the phone. 'I've got a job for you.'

'And you are?'

'Never mind that. Here's someone you might recognise.' There was a brief pause, during which Banks could have sworn he heard sitar music in the background, then a girl's voice came on. 'Dad, it's me! Tracy. Please do what he says. If you don't he'll—'

'Tracy? Are you all right?'

But before she could reply, the other voice came back on again. Jaff's voice, Banks now knew. 'She's fine,' he said. 'And if you want her to stay that way, you'll listen carefully to what I have to say. We're in Leeds, in Harehills, outside a closed-down garage opposite a boarded-up school called Harehills Park. Got that?'

'Leeds. Harehills Park. Yes. If you so much as lay a finger on her—'

'I know. I know. You'll kill me. How long will it take you to get here?'

'About an hour.'

'Bollocks,' said Jaff. 'Forty, forty-five minutes max. But I'll give you one hour. Not a minute more. We'll be watching for you. Don't talk to anyone. Don't even think of bringing a friend or arranging a welcome party. Believe me, if I see any signs of police activity in the area, your daughter gets it. Understand?'

'I understand,' said Banks. 'What do you want from me?'

'I'll tell you that when you get here. You're wasting time. Get going.' And the connection was broken.

Banks popped quickly back into the boardroom and said that one of his informants had called, and he had to go out for a while. Gervaise nodded, and everyone got back to their conversation. For a moment, he was in two minds whether to tell Gervaise the truth, as he knew he should, and let her organise the cavalry, but he also knew from experience what the red tape was like, the necessary levels of approval, documents in triplicate. He also had the recent example of the Patrick Doyle fiasco if he needed any concrete reminder of what could go wrong. His daughter's life was at stake this time. He remembered Jaff's warning and believed it. He grabbed his jacket from the back of the chair, dashed down the stairs and out the back.

He had no trouble signing a car out of the pool. It was just after nine o'clock in the morning, and what passed for rush hour in Eastvale was already beginning to abate by the time he had negotiated the one-way streets and joined York Road. The weather was fine, the traffic running smoothly, and he made it to the Leeds ring road in about forty minutes. He didn't even put any music on. He didn't want any distractions. He needed a plan, needed to think.

Banks knew the general Harehills area, but not the back-streets, and it was one of those rare occasions where the satnav actually proved its worth. This time, he didn't end up facing a brick wall while being told he had arrived at his destination, nor was he in Guisborough when he had set the thing for Northallerton. The boarded-up school came into view on his right about a hundred feet ahead as he turned into the street, and opposite it stood the out-of-business garage and a greasy spoon. It was an odd place to arrange a meeting, and Banks guessed that Jaff had come to the area looking for something he had expected but hadn't found. The garage was the most obvious clue. If it came to it, he could find the owner's name and see whether he had any links to McCready or Fanthorpe. For now, though, he wanted to see for himself that Tracy was unharmed.

Banks came to a halt outside the garage, as instructed. He scanned the street in both directions but saw nothing out of place. A few men in traditional costume coming in or out of the mosque. A couple of women in black burqas chatting as they walked down the street carrying their shopping. A normal day in a normal street.

There were plenty of parked cars, facing in all directions, and most of them were in need of rust treatment and a new tyre here and there, but nothing stood out. A silver Honda hatchback had pulled into the street after Banks and parked on the other side, behind a yellow Fiesta with a dented door, but a youth in a dark blue hoody and black tracksuit bottoms got out and went into the sewing-machine repair shop without so much as glancing in Banks's direction.

In his rear-view mirror, Banks saw two figures emerge from the greasy spoon, huddled close together like lovers, one of them carrying a bulky holdall, the other a leather shoulder bag. The slighter one was Tracy, and his heart lurched in his chest at the sight of her. They got in the back of his car and the voice from the telephone said, 'Drive.'

Banks drove.

'Give me your mobile,' Jaff said, when they were on the main road. Banks took it out of his pocket and passed it back. He noticed Jaff switch it off. He was a tall, good-looking kid with long eyelashes, a burnished gold complexion and big brown eyes. Banks could see why women found him attractive. Tracy sat huddled as far away from him as she could get, on the edge of the seat, hunched in on herself, pale and frightened-looking. Banks wanted to tell her it was all right, Daddy was here, everything would be fine, but he couldn't force out the words in Jaff's presence. It had to be enough for him just to know that she was still alive and, apparently, unharmed.

Seeing her like this reminded him of the time she was twelve and finally confessed to him in tears that one of the girls at school had been bullying her and extorting her dinner money from her. Banks wanted to hug her, as he had then, and make all her pain go away.

'We're heading for London,' Jaff said. 'I suppose you know the way?'

Banks nodded. He also knew there was no point in going to London, that Martina Varakova was dead and Justin Peverell's reason had taken a hike, maybe for ever. And the fake documents were in the hands of the Metropolitan Police. But he wasn't about to tell Jaff that. Everything depended on Jaff believing he was on his way to freedom.

'Whereabouts?'

'King's Cross. You can drop us there, and I'll let her go in half an hour.'

Banks didn't like the sound of that, but now was far too

early to negotiate. By the time they got to King's Cross the balance of power might have shifted a little in his favour. They were probably not meeting at the Highgate house, Banks thought. That was why Ciaran and Darren had left after they had finished with Justin and Martina. They were going to lie in wait for Jaff and Tracy, but they hadn't said where. 'You've been causing us quite a bit of trouble, Jaff,' he said, without turning his head.

'It's Mr McCready to you. And you've only got yourselves to blame for that. Live and let live, that's what I say.'

'That what you said to Annie when you shot her?'

A sly smile spread over Jaff's face. 'She your girl, was she? I know it's a waste, a tasty morsel like that, but needs must. Just drive. I'm not in the mood for conversation.'

'Are you OK, Tracy? Are you comf—'

'I said just drive.' Banks felt a hard metallic circle push against the back of his neck, and he knew it was the Baikal's silencer.

'Shooting me right now wouldn't be a great idea,' he said.

'That's just to let you know that I'm still in charge. Besides, I could shoot her, not you. Maybe just in the leg or something. Or the gut. I said just shut up and drive. And don't draw attention to us by your driving, or you'll regret it.'

Banks drove east to the ring road, then turned right and followed it down through Seacroft, Killingbeck and Cross Gates to the M1 at Selby Road. He knew that he would show up on dozens of CCTV cameras but that no one would take the slightest bit of notice because his papers were all in order, the car wasn't stolen and he wasn't a wanted man. Unless someone flagged him as a stray and questioned Western Area as to where he was going, which wasn't very likely. The police drove all over the place in unmarked cars all the time.

'Put some music on,' said Jaff.

'What's to your taste?'

'Got any Beatles?'

'I have.'

'Yeah, well, I can't stand them. What about some jazz?'

Banks didn't often listen to jazz when he was driving, but he had plenty on his iPod. 'Anything in particular?'

'*Kind of Blue.*'

'No problem.'

'One of my mother's boyfriends in Mumbai used to play *Kind of Blue* all the time,' Jaff said, so softly he might have been speaking to himself. 'Every time I saw him, I used to say, "Play Miles for me, play Miles for me." My mother had a lot of boyfriends. I learned all sorts of things from them.' Then he lapsed into silence as Bill Evans's piano intro to 'So What?' started up, followed by the bass, and soon the music filled the car, Miles's trumpet, Coltrane's tenor. It was surreal, Banks thought. Here he was, hurtling towards the M1 and only God knew what fate, a desperate man with a gun holding him and his daughter hostage, and one of his favourite jazz albums of all time was blasting out of the speakers. Not a word was spoken. Banks chipped away at the edge of the speed limit, but never went so much beyond it that he would raise any unwanted interest. Occasionally, he would look in the rear-view mirror and see Tracy sucking her thumb with her eyes closed as she did when she was a little child, clearly not asleep, the tension still tight around her mouth, eyelids twitching now and again. Jaff was just staring out of the window, looking grim.

It wasn't until they had passed Sheffield that Banks became certain the silver Honda hatchback he had seen in Harehills was the same one that had been keeping a respectable distance behind him all the way down the motorway. And when he came to think of it, though he didn't want to appear prejudiced at all, it had seemed odd at the time that a person dressed in a hoody and a tracksuit bottom had gone into a sewing-machine repair shop in the first place.

Detective Superintendent Catherine Gervaise took off her reading glasses and rubbed her eyes. It had been years since she had stopped up practically all night, catching only a quick nap in her office between two and three, and she felt exhausted. Naps were all very well, but these days they often left her more tired than before. While she was proud of her origins as a street copper before she made the fast track, and she liked to let people know that she'd done many of the tough jobs they complained to her about, she had to admit that for the most part she'd been on training courses, studying for a university degree, sitting exams, transferring back and forth to uniform and, for the most part, she had become an administrator rather than a working detective. Now her eyes were sore, her brain slow and her body felt weak. She just wanted to go home to bed, but she had important decisions to make.

Gervaise sipped the strong coffee that Winsome Jackman had brought her, but it didn't seem to do much good. Now they were well into the morning, her tiredness was beyond coffee. Still, at least the taste and warmth of the dark liquid kept her at subsistence-level consciousness, though she still felt like one of those zombies out of the movies her son liked to watch so much. Winsome sat opposite her, on the other side of the large desk. She seemed fine, Gervaise thought; but then she was twenty years younger and far more used to the hours.

'I've just had Dirty Dick . . . I mean Commander Burgess on the phone, ma'am,' said Winsome.

'My, my, you two *are* getting familiar. Be careful. That man sounds like a walking toxic waste dump to me,' Gervaise said. 'What did he say?'

'Still nothing from the two suspects about the Farmer's involvement.'

'Well, I'm not surprised,' said Gervaise.

Winsome smiled. 'But the one thing they did give up – or rather, Darren Brody gave up – was the location for the meet.'

'Justin Peverell with Jaff and Tracy?'

'Yes. Hampstead Heath, near Highgate Ponds.'

Gervaise thought for a moment. 'That means McCready's probably still on his way. And he was being extra careful just in case someone had located Peverell's house.'

'But he can't have bargained for what actually happened.'

'No. I'm sure he doesn't know, or he'd be heading as fast as he could in the other direction. Maybe he is.' Gervaise shook her head. 'I don't know, Winsome. What the hell are we to do?'

'Commander Burgess suggested organising an armed reception committee for McCready at the Heath.'

Gervaise snorted. 'He would. What about Tracy Banks?'

'He said he thought he could keep it low key enough, that McCready wouldn't spot it was happening until they were on him.'

'I doubt it. We know how easily these things go pear-shaped. Where's DCI Banks, anyway? He's been gone ages.'

'I don't know,' said Winsome. 'He's not around here, that's for certain.'

Gervaise frowned. 'Where did he *say* he was going?'

'To meet with an informant, I think. I don't really know where. We were all so busy talking about what had happened to Justin Peverell and his poor girlfriend.'

Gervaise checked her watch. 'Whatever it was, it shouldn't have taken him this long. Especially given his concern over Tracy. Try his mobile, Winsome.'

Winsome keyed in Banks's mobile number. 'It's turned off, ma'am,' she said.

'That's not like him. Why would he turn off his mobile at the crucial point of an investigation that involves him personally?' Gervaise felt her brain springing to life, though it was a chaotic sort of life, sparks flying everywhere, but none of them lighting up the bulbs they should, or making the connections they were aiming for. Her thinking felt like a badly played game of pinball, but something was definitely happening. 'Help me out here, Winsome. What's going on?'

'I don't know,' said Winsome. 'Unless . . .'

'Unless what?'

'Unless DCI Banks was . . . *lying* about the informant.'

'Don't sound so horrified at the thought. People do. Sometimes for good reasons.'

'Yes, ma'am,' said Winsome, tight-lipped.

'So, if Alan was lying, or making an excuse – he did go into the corridor to take the call – then perhaps it was Tracy. He would certainly lie for her.'

'It could have been McCready.'

'Either way, he might be in trouble.'

'It's McCready I'd be worried about,' said Winsome. 'He's had a lot of trouble with transport. Perhaps he needs DCI Banks to drive him to Hampstead.'

The neurons were firing a lot better now, and the pinball score was racking up. 'Look,' said Gervaise, 'let's find out which car Alan signed out from the pool and see if we can access Automatic Number Plate Recognition control, find out where he is. If you're right, he'll be on his way to London, to Hampstead Heath, and we should be able to track his progress.'

'Should we alert all the motorway patrol units?'

'Not yet. We don't want a car chase on our hands. Not if Alan and Tracy are in one of the cars with McCready armed. Let's keep it low profile for now, until we know what's happened. If they're still on their way to Hampstead we've got a while yet to work something out. Get on to Burgess again, too. Try to persuade him that softly, softly's the way to go for now.'

'Do you have a plan, ma'am?'

'I wish to God I did, Winsome. I wish to God I did.'

Banks was also desperately trying to work out a plan as he drove down the M1 with his silent passengers and loud music. He had already figured out that Jaff's mood shifts were volatile. Perhaps the pressure of being on the run was getting to him, and he had also been snorting cocaine in the car. So much had gone wrong so far that he had to be becoming increasingly worried about making it. Whatever plan Banks came up with, he knew he would have to take great care and choose his moment.

Separating Jaff from his gun was the key. Without that, he was nothing. The gun was in the holdall; of that Banks was certain. There was something about the way Jaff held it close to him all the time, often thrusting one hand inside it for a while, gripping something that gave him comfort and confidence, that made it obvious. It wouldn't be easy to get it away from him, and there was no way it was going to happen if he dropped Jaff and Tracy off at King's Cross. He couldn't let that happen.

'I need to go to the toilet.'

It was Tracy, speaking up from the back. Banks turned the music down. More Miles: *Someday My Prince Will Come.* 'What was that, love?' he asked.

'Well, you can't,' Jaff cut in. 'We're not stopping.'

'It won't take five minutes,' Tracy argued.

'I told you. We're not stopping.'

'What do you expect me to do? Piss in the car?'

'I expect you to wait.'

'I *can't* wait. I've been crossing my legs for the past half-hour. I can't wait any more. There's a services coming up soon. I need to go to the toilet.'

Jaff's hand dug deep inside his holdall. 'I told—'

Tracy turned to face him. 'What kind of a person are you? What harm's it going to do? Do you think I'm going to make a run for it across the car park after you've told me what you'll do? When you've got my dad here, too? Do you think I'll run away if you've got your gun on him? What are you scared of? What do you really think I'm going to do? Start shouting out that you've got a gun so you can shoot a few more innocent people? For Christ's sake get a grip, Jaff. I need to go to the toilet. Simple as that.'

There was a short silence after Tracy's outburst. Banks held his breath, admiring his daughter for her guts, but uncertain about which way it would tip Jaff's erratic brain.

'Fine,' Jaff said eventually. He tapped Banks on the shoulder. 'I could do with a cup of coffee, myself. You heard the lady, James. Next services.'

Banks thought furiously. Could this be his best opportunity? How could he do it? Throw a cup of hot coffee in

Jaff's face, snatch the holdall, toss it to Tracy, take on Jaff hand to hand? It was a possibility, maybe the only one.

Jaff stared out of the window, tapping his fingers on his thighs. He was working it out, Banks knew, figuring out every angle, every moment, every move that could possibly go wrong for him, as so many had before. He would be at his edgiest, his most unpredictable and dangerous, from the moment they left the car. As Banks turned on to the slip road, he looked for the silver Honda hatchback in his rear-view mirror, but he couldn't see it. Maybe he'd been imagining things.

The car park was only about half full. As soon as Banks had pulled into the spot Jaff had chosen for him and turned off the engine, he opened the door and felt the wind on his face. It had just started to drizzle.

'Not so fast,' said Jaff. 'We need to set a few ground rules before we go anywhere.'

Banks closed the door again.

'Hurry up,' said Tracy. 'It hurts.'

'We stick together, right?' Jaff said. 'Tracy by my side, you in front. And I'll have my hand on the gun the whole time, so don't even think of making a break for it. And both of you remember this. If one of you's out of my sight, the other isn't.'

Banks wanted to question Jaff on whether he would really start shooting in a public car park, but he didn't bother. First of all, Tracy was desperate, and Banks wanted them all out of the car as quickly as possible to increase his chances of taking control of the situation. Second, he suspected that at this point Jaff was so wired that he probably *would* start shooting. Banks had noticed him snorting more lines of coke in the back of the car, seen how twitchy he was becoming.

'It's your call,' said Banks, pulling the door handle again.

They all got out and started moving across the car park and the open space to the toilets and restaurant. There were a few amusement machines near the entrance, and a convenience store opposite. Next to the store were the ladies' and gents' toilets.

'So how are we all going to stick together now?' Banks asked, looking at the flow of people coming in and out of the toilets.

'Don't be a clever bastard. Obviously we can't. Francesca goes in. We stay here.'

'But I need to go, too,' said Banks. 'And her name is Tracy.'

'I know that. I prefer Francesca. You can wait your turn. Go on, Francesca. And no tricks. Don't try borrowing anyone's mobile or trying to pass any messages. Remember what I told you. Your dad's out here with me.'

Tracy dashed inside the ladies'. Jaff stood close to Banks, with his hand inside his holdall, eyes on stalks, twitching in all directions.

'You're not going to get away with this, you know,' Banks said casually, trying to discover just how far he could push Jaff.

'What do you know?'

'You could stop it now. It would count for you in court.'

'Rubbish. I shot a copper.'

'But you didn't kill her.'

'I can't do time in prison. I'd never survive.'

'There's no way around that.'

'So we just do as I say.' He glanced at his watch. 'She's taking a long time.'

'She's a woman,' said Banks.

Jaff actually laughed. It was a slightly mad laugh, and one or two passers-by glanced curiously at him. Luckily, Tracy came out immediately after the comment, and Jaff gave her instructions to wait exactly where she was while he and Banks went. When they came out, she was still there, rooted to the spot.

'So far, so good,' said Jaff. 'Let's get something to eat.'

They went upstairs to the takeaway section and bought coffee and sandwiches, which Jaff directed Banks to carry, no doubt so he could keep a firm grip on his gun. The food was in a bag, which would make it more difficult for Banks to remove the top from the coffee unseen and toss it in Jaff's face. But it was a long walk back to the car. Banks had had no time to talk to Tracy alone, to make her aware of what he might try. He had to depend on her survival instinct and her quick grasp of the changing situation. She would have to follow his lead.

Slowly they walked back, Banks slightly ahead, as he had been told, Jaff with his hand in his holdall, Tracy beside him. Banks didn't like walking blind to his adversary's exact position and movements, but he thought he could shield the bag slightly with his body as he reached inside with his free hand and felt for the top of the coffee container. He knew that some of it might splatter on Tracy if Jaff was sticking close to her, but that couldn't be helped. He would try to be as accurate as possible given the circumstances.

They made their way through the parked cars, sometimes having to walk in single file through a narrow space, getting closer and closer. Banks got the top off, and the hot black coffee scalded his fingers. He grimaced in pain but managed to avoid shouting out. He must have stumbled a little, though, because Jaff told him to turn around. There weren't any people near by, though Banks could hear the cars whizzing by on the M1 and wondered whether that was the last sound he would hear.

He turned, the coffee cup in his hand, spillage burning the stretched webbing between his thumb and forefinger. Jaff had the gun out of his holdall now, and he was pointing it at Tracy's head. As Banks released his grip on the coffee, and let the whole bag of food fall to the ground, a woman shepherding her two kids back to a car about four rows away screamed. Jaff turned to face the direction of the sound, but she had already dragged her children down behind their parked car.

Jaff turned back to Banks and pointed the gun towards him, his arm around Tracy's neck. There were more screams, the sound of people running, car doors slamming, engines starting. Jaff's face contorted in anger and confusion. He was losing it, Banks thought; he was going to shoot.

As Banks steeled himself to take the bullet, the upper right quadrant of Jaff's head disappeared in a reddish-grey mist. The gun clattered to the tarmac. Jaff shuddered like a marionette out of control, spread his arms wide and lost his grip. Tracy threw herself forward into Banks's arms. Banks dropped to his knees and held her close to his chest, shielding her from the sight behind her. He felt her arms around him, clinging on tightly for dear life, her face buried in his shoulder, her little voice crying Daddy, Daddy, Daddy, how sorry she was, through her tears.

17

There wasn't one smiling face among the six people sitting around the polished oval table in the boardroom, under the equally unsmiling portraits of Yorkshire wool barons in their tight waistcoats, with their roast-beef complexions and whiskery jowls.

Banks was beyond tiredness now. He didn't even know what time or day it was, except that it wasn't dark. But it was getting there. It had been a long, long day since the incident that morning at the motorway services. Tracy was out at Banks's temporary accommodation, sleeping under a mild sedative administered by the police surgeon – at least he hoped she was – with Winsome watching over her. But there was dirty business to be done behind closed doors at the Western Area Headquarters. At one time, Banks would probably have been worried about the outcome, but now he didn't care what happened. He just wanted it to be over so he could get on with putting his and Tracy's lives back together.

'What the hell did you think you were doing, Officer Powell?' asked Mike Trethowan, Firearms Cadre superintendent, and Nerys's immediate boss.

'Using my initiative, sir,' said Nerys Powell. She had changed from the tracksuit bottoms and hoody top into jeans and a crisp white blouse and black windcheater, and she was managing to put a brave face on things so far, Banks thought.

She looked scared, but she been unshakeable in her conviction that she had done the right thing. If she had to go down, she might try to take a few of the enemy with her.

Chambers gave a 'God save us all from initiative' sigh. 'All right,' he said. 'Why don't you just start from the beginning?'

Nerys glanced at Banks, who tried to keep a neutral expression on his face. 'I overheard DCI Banks taking a call on his mobile, sir,' she said. 'When he was out in the corridor. I was in one of the empty offices opposite, just hanging around and waiting.' She gave Chambers a dirty look. 'There's been a lot of pointless hanging around with this investigation going on. You never know when they're going to call you back in to go over some minor detail again. They never tell you anything. Anyway, I couldn't hear what the person at the other end was saying, but DCI Banks mentioned his daughter's name and repeated the name of a school in Harehills, and he seemed nervous and furtive. DCI Banks, I mean, sir. He seemed upset, and at one time he threatened the caller. I knew that his daughter was missing, and that the man suspected of abducting her was armed.'

'Did you know the location of this school? Did it mean anything to you?'

'No. But I grew up in Leeds. I know where Harehills is.'

'Yes, yes, we know where you grew up,' said Chambers. 'Go on.'

'DCI Banks left hurriedly, and I suspected he might have made some . . . er . . . private arrangements to help his daughter. Not that I'm blaming you, sir,' she said to Banks.

'I'm relieved,' said Banks drily.

Nerys narrowed her eyes at him, as if she couldn't make up her mind whether he was acting as a friend or an enemy. Banks wasn't too sure himself. He needed to listen to all this, Nerys's side especially, before he planted his feet down firmly anywhere. 'Anyway,' she went on, 'as I said, I knew that Jaffar McCready was armed and DCI Banks wasn't. I also knew that DCI Banks wouldn't call in the FSU because of his daughter, that he'd want to try and settle this himself, somehow try to take advantage of the situation, overpower McCready, if possible. I thought it involved an incredible risk, sir, so I . . . well . . .'

'You decided to ride shotgun,' said Trethowan.

Nerys glanced from Chambers to her boss. 'I suppose so, sir.'

'What do you mean, you suppose so? How else would you describe what you did?'

'Well, sir, I was following my gut instinct, taking an initiative. Here was an unarmed man, a fellow police officer, going up against someone we already knew had no qualms about pulling the trigger on a cop.'

'This wasn't anything to do with revenge for what happened to DI Cabbot, was it, Officer Powell?' Trethowan asked sternly.

Nerys blushed deep red. 'I resent that, sir.'

'Whether you resent it or not isn't the issue. Was DI Cabbot on your mind at all when you went chasing after DCI Banks?'

'I won't say I didn't think of what McCready did to her. But you've got no—'

'If your sexual feelings for Annie Cabbot clouded your judgement,' said Chambers, with obvious relish at the image, and a hard glint in his piggy eyes, 'then we have every right to question your actions and motives. You had a crush on her, didn't you?'

'Ladies, gentlemen,' said ACC McLaughlin, holding up his hand, 'this line of attacking Officer Powell on the basis of her sexual preference will get us precisely nowhere in our unofficial adjudications, and nor should it. Whether the officer in question had feelings for DI Cabbot or not isn't the issue here, nor is the nature of those feelings. The issue is what she *did* and what we're going to do about it. Carry on, PC Powell.'

'Thank you, sir,' said Nerys. Sufficiently chastised for the moment, Trethowan and Chambers slumped into a sullen silence as she took a sip of water and went on. 'I followed DCI Banks to Harehills, and there I observed his daughter Tracy and Jaffar McCready get into the back of his car. It seemed as if McCready was clutching a gun in a holdall he was carrying.'

'But you couldn't actually see the firearm?' asked Trethowan.

'Not at that point, no, sir. But I knew he was—'

'Very well. That's all I need to know.' Trethowan looked to Chambers. 'Go on.'

'How did you know who they were?' Chambers demanded.

'Well, I didn't think he was picking up hitchhikers,' said Nerys.

Chambers reddened.

'That'll be enough of that,' said Trethowan.

'Yes, sir. Sorry, sir.' She glared back at Chambers, who was the first to avert his gaze.

'Did you have any idea at this point what you were going to do?' asked Detective Superintendent Gervaise. 'Had a plan of any kind formed in your mind?'

'No, ma'am. All I knew was that McCready was armed, that he'd shot Ann— DI Cabbot, and that he had DCI Banks and his daughter hostage.'

'And wouldn't it have made perfect sense right then and there to call me?' said Trethowan. 'Or someone in authority?

There are procedures to be followed, you know. Protocol. Why didn't you call me, or Superintendent Gervaise, with your suspicions about DCI Banks's course of action?'

'I know I should have done, sir,' said Nerys, 'and I have no excuse. But sometimes you just have to think on your feet, and think fast. In my judgement, there wasn't time for protocol, for getting the necessary wheels in motion. I didn't have my mobile, for a start, and I would have lost them if I'd stopped to fill in all the necessary forms. Calling in the cavalry would have alerted McCready that we were on to him. I considered him armed and dangerous, and the last thing he needed was to feel that he was surrounded by armed police. There was always a chance that drugs were involved, too. They tend to make people jittery and unpredictable, as turned out to be the case.'

'He'd been snorting cocaine on the journey,' said Banks.

'So you discharged your weapon in a public car park,' said Trethowan, ignoring Banks. 'A motorway service station. Risking injury to God knows how many innocent men, women and children.'

'I targeted Jaffar McCready, sir. I'm a good shot. The best in the unit. You know I am. And my weapon is accurate up to nearly a thousand yards. I was only three hundred yards away, at most.'

'And after you hit your target? Did you have any idea where the bullet would end up?' Chambers asked.

'I was at the top of a hill. From the angle of my shot, sir, I judged it would lodge itself in the body of the car behind McCready, which it did. Do you want to charge me with damaging private property, too, now, sir? I'll see if my insurance will cover it.'

Trethowan thumped the table. 'I've told you, Officer

Powell. That's enough of your bloody insolence. This is a very serious matter. Your career's on the line. You're not doing yourself any favours. Sarcasm won't get you anywhere. Not with me and not with Superintendents Chambers and Gervaise or ACC McLaughlin. And we're the ones holding your fate in the balance. Remember that. One more remark like that, and I'll have you on disciplinary charges no matter what the outcome here this afternoon. Do you understand?'

'Yes, sir,' Nerys mumbled, head down.

'What happened when you got to the services car park?' Gervaise asked, pouring oil on troubled waters.

'I parked my car, ma'am. I'd checked out the surrounding area as best I could on my way in, and there was a slope just across the slip road. I could lie down just behind there unseen and get a direct line on DCI Banks's car, and a good line of shot if it came to that. I wasn't planning on shooting anyone. I didn't want to alarm the public.'

'So that's where you went?' asked Chambers. 'The grassy knoll?' He beamed at his little joke, but everyone else ignored it.

Nerys bit her lip. 'Yes, sir.'

'With the intent of shooting Jaffar McCready as soon as you thought you had a clear shot?'

'With the intention of protecting the lives of DCI Banks and his daughter, sir, should the DCI make any foolish or desperate moves. I could tell McCready was wired when they first got out of the car.'

Banks raised his eyebrows.

'I'm not saying that making foolish moves isn't entirely out of character for DCI Banks,' said Chambers with a self-satisfied grin, 'but how could you know that he would do such a thing in this instance?'

'I didn't. Not for certain. But I would have done, if I were him. It was his best chance at McCready. Out in the open. If he was going to try anything, I calculated that would be his opportunity.'

'With other people around?'

'His daughter's a person, too, sir. So is DCI Banks himself.'

'I'm quite aware of that,' said Chambers.

'Let's move on,' Gervaise interjected.

Chambers seemed exasperated, but he went on, 'Are you saying you knew DCI Banks was doomed to failure if he acted?'

Nerys shrugged. 'I knew there was a possibility of failure. And that McCready had a gun he wasn't afraid to use. I just wanted to be prepared, that's all, to give the DCI an added advantage.'

'I suppose now you're going to tell us that it all happened so fast you don't remember the details, that you're not responsible for your actions?' said Chambers.

'On the contrary, sir. Time slowed right down. I knew exactly what I was doing. I took my time pulling the trigger, squeezed it slowly, making certain of the accuracy of my shot, and I take full responsibility for my actions. I stand by them.'

That reduced Chambers to a reluctant silence, and Gervaise gently picked up the slack. 'Tell us what happened.'

'They were walking back to the car, the three of them. DCI Banks was in front, and I could see him fiddling inside the food bag. I couldn't know at the time exactly what he was doing, of course, but it seemed suspicious, like he was preparing to do something, and it would certainly look suspicious from behind, to McCready, who was already acting jumpy as hell.'

'So you saw DCI Banks fiddling with the paper bag?'
Gervaise went on.

'Yes.'

'And what did you do next?'

'Nothing, ma'am. I watched and waited.'

'Through the sights of your gun?' asked Chambers.

'Through my scope, yes.'

'The sniper's rifle you just happened to be carrying with
you?' He glanced down at his notes. 'A Parker-Hale M85,
if I'm not mistaken. Not exactly standard issue. Where did
you get it?'

'It was my father's, sir. I keep it locked in a special compartment in the boot of my car. I practise with it sometimes. In
my opinion, the Park—'

'Is that where you're supposed to keep your weapon,
Officer Powell?' asked Trethowan. 'In the boot of your car,
like some American redneck?'

Nerys turned away. 'No, sir. The Firearms Cadre has proper
storage facilities, as do our transport vehicles, but—'

'Carry on,' said Trethowan. 'We'll deal with that infrac-
tion later.'

Nerys swallowed again, as if her mouth were dry. She still
had a glass of water in front of her, Banks noticed, but this
time she didn't touch it. She probably didn't want them to
see her hand shaking. 'I was watching them walk towards
the car. DCI Banks pulled a face and flinched. I thought
maybe he'd burned himself or something. That gave me an
idea of what he might be about to try.'

'And?' asked Gervaise.

Nerys looked directly at Banks. Her gaze was unnerving.
'In my opinion, he wouldn't have succeeded, ma'am. His
awkward movements had already alerted McCready that

something was going on. DCI Banks was going to try and throw hot coffee in his face, but he must have burned himself getting the lid off, and he flinched. McCready noticed, knew something was wrong.'

'Is this true, Alan?' asked Gervaise.

Banks nodded.

'What did McCready do then?' Gervaise asked Nerys.

'He took the gun – the Baikal with the silencer – out of his holdall. He'd had it in his hand all the time they were walking, but now he pulled it out into full view. One or two of the people around them in the car park noticed and screamed. I could see that if it went on like that there was going to be a panic, and that would only make McCready more volatile. But at that moment, there weren't many people in that particular area, certainly nobody really close.'

'Where did McCready point the gun?'

'First he pointed it at Tracy Banks. At her head. I surmised that he was threatening her father that he would shoot her if he tried anything.'

'And then?'

'McCready was edgy, ma'am. Erratic in his behaviour. He said something to DCI Banks, and then pointed the gun directly at him.'

'By this time DCI Banks had turned around?'

'Yes. He was facing McCready, who was using Tracy as a shield.'

'And how did you respond?' Chambers cut in.

'I shot McCready, sir,' Nerys said dispassionately. 'In the head. It was the best shot I could get. Luckily, he was quite a bit taller than DCI Banks's daughter.'

'You killed him,' Chambers said.

'Yes, sir. A head shot is usually . . .' She noticed the storm brewing on Trethowan's face, then turned back to Chambers. 'Yes, sir.'

'Then you fled the scene.'

'Then I returned to Western Area Headquarters. I handed over my weapon to Detective Superintendent Gervaise, told her what happened, and you know the rest.'

'Why didn't you remain at the scene?' Gervaise asked.

'There seemed no point. McCready was dead. DCI Banks and his daughter were safe. The services would be swarming with police in no time at all.'

'And you might have found it rather difficult to explain yourself?' suggested Chambers.

'Yes. I'll admit that crossed my mind, too. And if other armed officers arrived on the scene, my presence could have caused a serious danger to the public.'

'How public spirited of you,' said Chambers. 'Do you know how long those officers spent questioning people, looking for clues to the identity of the shooter?'

'Do you want to add leaving the scene of the crime to the list of charges against me?' Nerys said.

Trethowan just shook his head. Chambers spluttered and tossed his pencil down. 'I told you this would be a waste of time, Catherine,' he said to Gervaise. 'She needs to be suspended from duty right now, without pay, and we need to bring in an outside team.'

'I'll be the judge of that,' said McLaughlin.

'I don't think it was a waste of time, Reg,' said Trethowan. 'Officer Powell's cheap repartee aside. Not when one of my officers is involved in a serious incident such as this. And not if we can contain the fall-out.'

'Nor do I, for what it's worth,' said Banks, speaking up with a contemptuous glance towards Chambers. 'I don't think it was a waste of time at all. One thing you all seem to be forgetting in all this mud-slinging is that Officer Powell here saved my life. And my daughter's.'

'It's a long time since I've been here,' said Tracy the following lunchtime in the Queen's Arms.

Banks studied the drab decor. The red plush on the benches was worn, the stuffing coming out here and there, the dimpled-copper tables were wobbly, and the wallpaper was peeling in places where it reached the ceiling. The whole place could do with a lick of paint, too. Still, it was familiar, and it was comfortable, and those were qualities, Banks felt, that both he and Tracy needed right now. It was also still hanging on, when so many pubs were closing down for good. And the food wasn't bad.

Tracy picked at her chicken and chips in a basket, and Banks tucked into his giant Yorkshire pudding stuffed with roast beef and smothered in onion gravy. He had slept on his living-room couch at the rented flat the previous night and let Tracy have the bed, but he hadn't slept well. The jet-lag was still with him, and he kept experiencing waves of tiredness and dizziness at the oddest of times. But he could live with that. It wasn't so different from when he'd had to work shifts.

'It's a while since I've been here, too,' said Banks between mouthfuls. He sipped his Black Sheep bitter. The Queen's Arms wasn't overly busy for the time of day, and their table by the window was a little island unto itself. Sunshine filtered through the red and blue diamonds of stained glass. A couple of young lads were playing the noisy machines in the passage to the gents', and the usual oldies played on the radio, or whatever it was Cyril had rigged up as his source of music instead of the old jukebox. 'Substitute' by The Who was playing at the moment. 'I understand you called yourself Francesca,' Banks said.

Tracy blushed and stared down at her plate. 'That was silly. I'm sorry.'

'We never gave you a middle name. I'm sorry for that.' Banks smiled. 'We couldn't afford one for you at the time.'

Tracy laughed, and he saw an image of the daughter he knew and loved behind the attitude and the new look. Not that he cared how she did her hair or dressed, as long as she was happy. But she hadn't been happy; that was becoming apparent enough. 'I don't have one, either,' he went on. 'When I was young I called myself Davy, after Davy Crockett. I must have seen *The Alamo* a hundred times.'

'You didn't!'

'I did. You know,' Banks went on, glancing at her sideways as he cut off some more beef and Yorkshire pudding, 'it doesn't really matter about your exams. I mean, I know you're disappointed, and I can't do anything about that, but you don't have to feel you let me or your mother down. You worked so hard. We're proud of you. I honestly didn't know you were beating yourself up so much about the results.'

'But you expected so much more,' Tracy said. 'Me too. And I do feel as if I've let everybody down. I mean, look at me now, telling people where they can find the latest Katie Price or Dan Brown, while Brian is playing to sell-out crowds in Nagasaki or wherever. He's the big success in the family.'

'I love both of you. It's not a competition. I tried not to favour either of you.'

'But you did, didn't you? I mean, I'm not blaming you. It's only human nature. Parents can't help it. People can't help it.'

'If I did, it was always you I favoured.'

'Until Brian made it big.'

'That's not true,' Banks said. 'I spent half my time trying to keep Brian in university. I wanted him to finish his degree, get a real job. If anything, I discouraged him from making music a career. If he succeeded, it's despite of me, not because of me.'

'But you had so much in common. You bought him his first guitar.'

'You can't blame a man for loving music. With you I . . . I tried. I just couldn't communicate so easily with you. I didn't know how to reach you. How to talk to you about boyfriends and girlie stuff. Even the thought of you with a boy made my blood boil. And the music . . . I mean, you liked Take That and the Spice Girls, while Brian was into Led Zeppelin and Bob Dylan. I'm sorry, but it was no contest musically.'

Tracy stared at him in disbelief for a moment, then she burst out laughing. 'Oh, I'm sorry, Dad. You do say the strangest things. Anyway, I like the Unthanks, Smoke Fairies, Regina Spektor and Noah and the Whale these days. And the Kings of Leon.'

'That's an improvement. Anyway, I felt awkward with you when you were growing up, not Daddy's little girl any more. Not having your mother around didn't help, either.'

'But that was years ago. Maybe you just didn't try hard enough?'

'Maybe I didn't.' Banks scratched his scar. 'I'd be the first to admit that I put my job first too much of the time. And I suppose I had a few personal problems of my own, too.'

'Have you got a girlfriend at the moment?'

'No,' Banks said. 'No one.' He thought about Teresa, but

she wasn't his girlfriend. He probably wouldn't even see her again. And he certainly wasn't going to tell his daughter about a one-night stand in San Francisco. He thought of the email with the attached JPEG he had received from Teresa that morning: the two of them standing in Burritt Street looking at the plaque that said, ON APPROXIMATELY THIS SPOT MILES ARCHER, PARTNER OF SAM SPADE, WAS DONE IN BY BRIGID O'SHAUGHNESSY.

'What about Annie?'

'Annie? It's . . . complicated.'

'Why? She's in love with you.'

'Stop it. Don't be ridiculous. It's not as easy as that.'

'She is. A woman can tell these things.'

'But you're just a girl.'

'Really? I'm twenty-four. And still waiting for my latest birthday card, by the way. Anyway, let's just put it all behind us, shall we? Start afresh.'

'That's OK with me,' said Banks. 'But we do need to talk.'

'I know. I know. And I've been dreading it. I've had enough of that.' She pushed her basket aside.

'You used to like it.'

'When I was "just a girl".' Tracy sipped her white wine. 'Around the same time I used to like McDonald's and Take That.'

It was true, Banks realised. His daughter was a young woman now, and it was about time he accepted that and learned how to deal with it. 'Do you want to tell me what happened? From the start.'

Tracy rested her elbows on the table. 'I knew this was coming,' she said. 'I've been dreading it.' She wasn't wearing any make-up today, and Banks thought she looked quite beautiful. Even the piercings beside her eyebrow and below her lip couldn't detract from it. Her skin was naturally pale, her pink lips well defined and shapely, and she had her mother's eyes. The short hairstyle suited her, too. But then he was biased.

'Take a deep breath and plunge right in.'

'OK,' Tracy said, and inhaled. 'But you already know most of it.'

'Humour me. How did you meet Jaff?'

'Through Erin. They met at that restaurant she worked in, down the Calls. I didn't know him well at all, but he sort of hung out with us sometimes at the clubs and whatever.'

'And you found him attractive?'

'Hard to believe, isn't it? But at one time I suppose I did.'

'Oh, it's not so hard to believe. He was handsome, and I'm sure he was charming enough,' said Banks. 'And he was a bad boy. It's quite a heady combination.'

'That's Erin's thing, not mine. He was *her* boyfriend.'

'Did you know he was a criminal, a drug dealer?'

'No way!' said Tracy. 'If I'd known any of that I would have stayed well away. Like I said, it was just a superficial relationship at first. We danced sometimes, chatted about music and stuff. It was just fun . . . you know . . . a laugh.'

Banks sensed that Tracy might be avoiding the whole issue of drugs, and he didn't want to push her on it. He didn't imagine for a moment that she was a total saint. He assumed that, like a lot of kids who go clubbing, she probably took E now and then, the way people smoked pot or dropped acid in his day. Maybe she did that, too. He just hoped she was careful about what she did and didn't use anything harder, like coke or heroin. But there was no gain in opening that route right now. 'What changed things?' he asked.

'One night he kissed me on the dance floor. I know it

sounds like a cue for a tacky old song, "And Then He Kissed Me" or something, but it's true. And it *was* a bit romantic.' Tracy blushed. 'Pity the romance didn't last,' she said.

'What happened?'

'Well, him and Erin had a blazing row right there in the club. It was so embarrassing, even if the music was so loud nobody could hear. She called me some names, then stormed off. Fast-forward to me coming home from work a few days later, and Rose telling me the police had searched the house, then all the stuff on the news later, about Mr Doyle, the gun . . . police all over our old street . . .'

'Slow down. Why did you dash over to Jaff McCready's flat immediately?'

'To tell him what had happened. He was still Erin's boyfriend. Something had happened to her. Something was dreadfully wrong. I mean, I know there'd been a misunderstanding, a row, but it was just a kiss. Honest. I mean, we didn't sleep together or anything.' Her lower lip trembled. 'Not . . . not then.'

'One thing at a time,' Banks said, putting his hand on her forearm. 'Take it easy.'

Tracy held her glass up and tried to smile. 'I could do with another one of these. Dutch courage.'

Banks went to bar and got them both refills. 'Daughter?' said Cyril, the landlord, nodding over in Tracy's direction.

'Yes.'

'That the same young lass you used to bring in here for a Coke and a burger years back, when you lived just down the road?'

'One and the same.'

'Haven't seen her for a long time. She's grown up into a fine-looking young lass.'

Banks looked over at her. 'Indeed she has. Thanks, Cyril.' He paid for the drinks and went back to the table. Paul Jones came on singing 'I've Been A Bad, Bad Boy'. These oldies were making him feel sad. He had almost forgotten that one.

'What happened when you went to Jaff's flat?' Banks asked, when Tracy had sipped some wine.

'He went berserk,' she said. 'He scared me. First, he went into his bedroom and came out just raving, calling her a stupid bitch and God knows what. I didn't know at the time, but he'd been looking for the gun she took.'

'How did you feel about that?'

'I was frightened,' said Tracy. 'I mean, I thought he was nice, but suddenly he seemed so angry, so unpredictable. I didn't know what he was going to do. I was only the messenger.'

'What happened next?'

'He grabbed me and said we had to get out of there.'

'We?'

'Yes.'

'So you were already a hostage, right from the start?'

'I suppose so. I don't know what he was thinking. All I know is that he needed a place to go and he was taking me with him.'

'How did you end up at my cottage?'

Tracy turned away. 'He . . . he made me take him there. He said he'd got nowhere to go, and he needed to be some-where nobody could find him for a while, till things got sorted out. He asked me if I knew anywhere. I was really scared. It was all I could think of. I thought he might hurt me if I said I didn't know anywhere.'

'Did you feel that you were free to leave him at this time?'

'No. I don't know. It all happened so fast. I mean, I wasn't tied up or anything, but he had hold of my arm, and he was hurting me. I thought of your cottage. I knew you were on holiday. I'm so sorry. I . . . Look, I'm confused. You're interrogating me just like one of your suspects. I don't know why it all happened the way it did. I look back and it all seems like a blur, a terrible nightmare. All I know is that I'm the victim here.'

'Calm down, Tracy,' Banks said. 'I know this is difficult for you.' Tracy wiped her eyes and sipped more wine. One or two people were looking over, but Banks ignored them. The machines were still making enough noise to drown out their conversation, and 'Be My Baby' was playing. Banks kept his voice down, all the same. 'I'm not interrogating you,' he said, 'but I have to ask these questions. OK?'

Tracy nodded. 'OK.'

'On the way out of Leeds, Jaff stopped at Victor Mallory's house. Why?'

'To change cars. Jaff was worried that the police might be looking for him in his own car.'

'So you knew about the gun by then, right?'

'No. He didn't tell me about that until we got to your cottage, otherwise I might have been more concerned about getting away. He just seemed in a desperate hurry to leave Leeds. I thought maybe . . . you know . . . he was worried about getting busted for drugs.'

'You said you didn't know he was a dealer.'

'I knew he had stuff from time to time. Just not a dealer like you mean.'

'Why didn't he head straight for London?'

'Because he said he needed to make some phone calls, set up some deals. I didn't know what he meant at the time, what he was talking about, but now I think he meant about selling the coke – there was a lot of it – and getting a phoney passport and all that. He said it would take time, and he needed to lie low. He was on his mobile a lot.'

'But you didn't know why was he running?'

'Not at that time. Not when we stopped at Victor's, no.'

'Did you go inside Victor Mallory's house with him?'

'No. Jaff told me to wait in the car.'

'Were you restrained in any way?'

'No.'

'So you could have simply got out and walked away at this point?'

'I suppose so. I wish I had, now. But I was confused. He told me to wait. He needed me to direct him to your cottage. He didn't know the countryside. He'd never even heard of Gratly. But if I'd known what . . . I'd have got out and run as fast as I could.'

'It's OK,' said Banks. 'I'm not saying you did anything wrong. I'm just trying to get things clear, that's all. How long was he in there?'

'I don't know. Five or ten minutes. Fifteen at the most.'

'Do you know Victor?'

Tracy shrugged. 'I'd met him a couple of times at the clubs. He seemed OK.'

'What happened next?'

'We switched cars and drove to Gratly. I'm sorry, Dad, sorry for leading him to the cottage. I really didn't know what he was like, what he would do.'

'What do you mean?'

'Your CD collection. You mean you don't know?'

'I haven't been allowed home yet. The SOCOs have just about finished, and Superintendent Gervaise says she'll arrange to send in a clean-up team after them, then I can go back. Maybe tomorrow or the day after.'

'He made a bit of a mess, that's all, chucking CDs around, breaking some of the cases, spilling drinks.'

'Don't worry. That's not your fault. How did you find out about the gun Erin took?'

'We saw the news. They didn't mention it specifically, but someone said they'd seen the police bring out a gun-shaped object wrapped in a tea cloth. He knew that's what it was, that it had been missing from his bedroom and Erin must have taken it to get at him. That's when he first told me what was going on.'

'Did he tell you why he was so upset about the police having it?'

'No.'

'What did you say?'

'I didn't say anything. I just asked him why he needed a gun, and why Erin had taken it. He said that now I knew about it, I should see that he couldn't let me go, that I had to stay with him to the bitter end.'

'He said that?'

'Yes. Please, Dad. You're interrogating me again. Don't you believe me?'

'Of course I do,' said Banks, though he was starting to have some misgivings about Tracy's version of events. 'And I'm sorry if I'm making you uncomfortable. I just want to get it all clear in my mind.'

'It's not even clear in *my* mind.'

Banks sipped some Black Sheep. 'I understand that. That's the reason for the questions. They're supposed to focus you, not make you feel as if you're being interrogated.'

'I'm sorry.' Tracy twirled her glass. 'He opened your

wine. Drank some of the really good stuff. And your whisky.'

'That's all right,' Banks said, wondering just what sort of a mess McCready *had* made, and what he would find missing when he got home. 'Telstar' started playing. It took Banks right back to when he was about twelve and used to listen to Alan Freeman's *Pick of the Pops* every Sunday afternoon on a transistor in the park with his friends, looking at the girls who walked by, so pretty in their Sunday summer dresses, blushing and flirting. Graham Marshall always used to be with them, until he disappeared one Sunday morning during his paper round. Years later, Banks had helped to uncover what had happened to him. Graham's face flashed before his mind's eye as the music played. They had all liked that weird organ sound on 'Telstar'.

Tracy lowered her voice and leaned forward. 'And he had drugs. Some pot. Cocaine. A lot of it, in big plastic bags. Kilos. But he filled a little plastic bag for his own use. He was taking it all the time. He was crazy.'

'Yes. Our men found it in his holdall along with about fifty thousand pounds. Know where that came from?'

'No. He had it from the start, I think, from his flat. At least, he had the holdall, and it seemed heavy. I didn't take any of the coke. Honest, I didn't, Dad.'

'It's all right. I believe you. So he drank some wine, drank some whisky, smoked some marijuana, snorted some coke. A right old knees-up, by the sound of it. Where were you while all this was going on?'

'Just sitting there watching. There was nothing I could do to stop him. He was much bigger and stronger than me.'

'I understand that. Did he . . .?'

'Rape me?' Tracy looked directly into Banks's eyes and nodded. 'Yes. He did. Later. When he found out who I was.

He took me upstairs, to *your* room. I tried to fight, tried to resist him, but it was no good. He was so much stronger. He threw me down on the bed and—'

Banks felt his throat constrict and his heart beat fast. 'It's all right, Tracy. I don't need to know the details. You say all this happened *after* he found out who you were, that you were a policeman's daughter?'

'Yes. He found a letter or something with your name and rank on it. He found out you were a police detective, a DCI.'

'And how did he react?'

'It made him really angry at first, then he said it meant I might come in even more useful than he'd imagined. He was still furious at me for not telling him before. And he didn't like the police. He became more aggressive. That's when he raped me. He thought it was really cool, something special to do it to me in *your* room, on *your* bed, like he was getting at you personally, or violating you in some way.'

Banks certainly *felt* violated, and if McCready had still been alive at that moment, he would cheerfully have strangled him with his bare hands. 'What happened when Annie came?' he asked.

'He was hiding behind the entertainment-room door. The gun was in his holdall in the breakfast nook in the kitchen. He told me to get rid of her as quickly as possible or he'd shoot her. I tried, Dad, I really tried. But you know Annie. She just wouldn't stop, she wouldn't give up, wouldn't go . . .'

'She didn't know the danger she was in,' Banks said. 'She thought she was helping you. And she's nothing if not persistent.'

'She knew something was wrong, that I was there under duress. I know she was trying to help me, but she just wouldn't take no for an answer, and then Jaff appeared and . . .'

'Tracy, you know you probably saved Annie's life, don't you? That mobile phone call you made.'

'She was bleeding. I thought she was going to die. What else could I do? He was so angry when he heard me phoning for an ambulance. I thought he was going to kill me, too, then, but I guess I was still too valuable to him. So he crushed my mobile.'

'And after that?'

'The car broke down on the moors. We were on foot, on the run. It was one misfortune after another. I have to say, if he was a master criminal, he wasn't very good at it.' Tracy managed a grim smile.

'Lucky for us,' Banks said. He glanced at his watch, then over at the door. 'Want another?'

'I shouldn't,' Tracy said. 'I'm already feeling a bit tipsy.'

'Coffee, then?'

'That'd be good.'

Banks was just about to go and get Tracy a coffee and himself another pint when the door opened, and Erin and Juliet Doyle walked in. Tracy gaped at Erin, then at Banks. 'Did you arrange this, Dad?' she said.

'I told them we might be here until about half-one, that's all.'

The two girls just stared at each other for what seemed like an age, then Tracy got up from the table, walked over to Erin and threw her arms around her. Erin hugged her back. The tourists gawped. Banks caught Juliet Doyle's eyes beyond Erin and Tracy. She just gave a curt nod. Banks breathed a sigh of relief. He had thought Tracy was going to thump Erin and that Erin and Juliet would never speak to one another again.

18

Banks could hear the strains of the adagio from Beethoven's 'Moonlight' sonata as Françoise, the au pair, led him across the Farmer's cavernous entrance hall towards the living room. Whoever was playing hit a wrong note, then hesitated and stumbled before picking up the melody again.

'The family is watching television,' Françoise explained in precise, unaccented English. 'And Miss Eloise is practising for the piano examinations in the next week.' She opened the door and announced Banks and Winsome formally. The uniformed officers were awaiting instructions in their cars outside.

Banks had never seen Fanthorpe's wife before. She was a beautiful woman, a good few years younger than her husband, with a figure sculpted by daily workouts, long, silky brown hair, and a complexion that can only be achieved either through the blessings of nature or the right combination of chemical emollients. She gave her husband a puzzled look. The little girl with the long ponytail sitting next to her didn't take her eyes from *Strictly Come Dancing* on the forty-two-inch TV screen.

'I see I've interrupted a family tradition,' said Banks.

Fanthorpe got to his feet. 'What do you want this time, Banks? I've had just about enough of this. This is too much. I'm going to ring my solicitor.'

'Maybe you can ask him to meet you at Western Area Headquarters,' Banks said. 'We've got a custody suite waiting for you there.'

The woman was on her feet, too, now, swiftly uncurling like a cat. 'What is this, George?' she asked, with a slight eastern European accent. 'Who are these people? What are they doing in my house? What's going on?'

The Farmer put the phone down and went to rest his hands on his wife's shoulders. 'It's all right, Zenovia. Just calm down, love. I'll handle this.' He strode towards the door and turned to Banks. 'Come on. We'll go into the den.'

'If you like,' said Banks, following him across the hall into the room where they had talked the previous week.

'This is an outrage,' said Fanthorpe, pouring himself a large whisky and not even bothering to offer Banks one this time. He might actually have taken it. 'It's police harassment. It's persecution. It's—'

'All right, all right, I get the message,' said Banks. 'Let's just all sit down and have a nice quiet little chat before I bring the lads in.'

'Lads?'

'The search team.' Banks took some papers from his pocket. 'I have here a search warrant signed by a local magistrate empowering us to conduct a full and thorough search of your premises.'

'Search my house?' Fanthorpe spluttered. 'You can't do that! You can't just—'

'We can and we will. But first things first. I'd like to let you know just what deep shit you're in.'

'What are you talking about?' Fanthorpe flopped into his leather armchair. He slopped a little whisky on the front of his cable-knit jumper as he did so, and dabbed at it with a handkerchief he took from the pocket of his brown cords.

Winsome sat opposite him and took out her notebook and pen.

'If you think I'm going to say anything incriminating,' said Fanthorpe, pointing his finger at her, 'then you've got another think coming.'

'It always pays to be prepared, sir,' said Winsome. 'Don't you find?'

'What do you know about the shooting of Marlon Kincaid on November fifth 2004?' Banks asked.

'*Marlon Kincaid*? Do I look like someone who'd know a person called *Marlon Kincaid*?'

'Why not? He was a student at Leeds Polytechnic University. Well, technically, he'd just finished his studies but he was still hanging around the student pubs in the area, the way some people do, selling drugs. Couldn't seem to let go of the old college life.'

'What are you talking about?'

'Marlon Kincaid. Art student. His dad was a big fan of Marlon Brando, apparently, which is how he got his name. Marlon was building quite the little business for himself, selling coke and various other illegal substances to the Leeds student population at parties and in the pubs and clubs.'

'So?'

'He had his own suppliers, and you weren't one of them.'

'I don't know what you mean.'

'You couldn't allow that, could you? You were well on your way to being the local drug kingpin, and along comes some skinny, long-haired upstart and cuts right into your market. Not only that, but he makes fun of you and it gets back to you. What did you do first? Warn him? Send Ciaran and Darren to administer a beating, perhaps?'

'This is rubbish.'

'But you had another weapon waiting in the wings, didn't you? A young lad called Jaffar McCready who was fast proving himself indispensable. And dangerous. He needed to prove himself, and you needed him to do it. That one final act of outrageous loyalty that binds for ever. You gave him a gun. You loaded it for him. Perhaps you even showed him how to fire it. And Jaffar McCready shot Marlon Kincaid. What he didn't know was that he'd been seen. A most unreliable witness, for sure, especially at the time, but he's scrubbed up quite nicely since then, soon to be a member of the ministry, actually, and his memory seems a lot clearer now, especially given everything we've found out since.'

'What does any of this have to do with me?'

'What you didn't know was that, for reasons of his own, McCready kept the gun. A trophy. A souvenir. Call it what you will. You no doubt told him to get rid of it at the time, and you probably thought he had. After all, why would he want to keep an incriminating gun around? Maybe he was just sentimental. His first kill. Or perhaps he liked the idea of having something on you? Whatever the reason, he kept the gun. Then one night he had a row with his girlfriend. To spite him, to piss him off, she took the gun and ran off, went to stay with her parents in Eastvale. Her mother found it. Maybe she just was cleaning up her daughter's room, the way mothers do, or maybe she was curious, wanted to see if she could find anything that would explain her daughter's unusual silences, her odd behaviour, her strange cast of mind since she'd come home. Either way, she found the gun. And that's when things started to go wrong. But that doesn't really matter here and now. What matters is that we found a clear set of fingerprints on the magazine inside the gun. Those fingerprints are yours. Can you explain how they got there?'

Fanthorpe frowned and sipped his whisky. 'I don't have to. You can talk to my solicitor about it.'

'I will. But there's really only one way they could have got there, isn't there? You handled the magazine at some time.'

'So what? You didn't find any of my prints on the outside of the gun, did you? On the trigger guard?'

'How do you know that?'

'Oh, very clever, Banks. Is this where I say, "Because I wiped them off," then put my hand to my mouth and admonish myself for making such a gaffe? It's not going to happen. The fact that you found my fingerprints on the magazine *inside* a gun proves nothing except that at one time I touched that magazine. It certainly doesn't prove that I ever fired the gun. I don't need a solicitor to prove that. You're fishing.'

'Do you often go around handling the magazines of prohibited weapons?'

'I can't say as I ever remember doing such a thing. There are any number of ways it could have happened. Perhaps a vet used it to put down a sick animal.'

'A nine-millimetre Smith & Wesson automatic?'

'Maybe a copper passed it over to me once and asked me what I thought?'

'Pull the other one,' said Banks.

'And just how did you get my fingerprints for comparison in the first place? I've never been fingerprinted in my life. There's no way I'm in your system.'

'That's a terrible oversight, and I promise we'll put the record straight as soon as possible. You did, however, handle a photograph of Jaff McCready that DS Jackman passed you the last time we were here. That glossy photographic paper has a wonderful sticky surface for fingerprints.'

'That's entrapment! You've fitted me up.'

'Don't be silly. It might conceivably be entrapment if they were forged documents, or a murder weapon. But it was only a photograph. It means nothing in itself.'

'I guarantee they'll laugh you out of court.'

'Do you really? Because I don't think so. And I'm very glad to hear that you agree with me that it *will* get to court. These days the Crown Prosecution Service is very picky about the cases it allows to go to trial. They don't like losing. They tend to choose dead certs.'

'Well, on the evidence you've got, there's always a first time.'

'Then there's the little matter of Darren Brody.'

'Darren Brody?'

'Yes. Come on. You know Darren. Your farmhand-cum-enforcer. For some reason, neither Darren nor Ciaran was involved with the Marlon Kincaid killing. Perhaps they were on another job, mucking out the stables or something. Or perhaps you just needed McCready to get his hands dirty, a blooding, like the kid's first foxhunt. But Ciaran and Darren have been doing quite a lot of overtime for you lately, haven't they?'

'What do you mean?'

Banks shook his head. 'Ciaran's seriously deranged. You should know what a liability it is to have someone like him on your payroll.'

'Ciaran would never say a thing against me.'

'You're right about that. Ciaran's a vicious psychopath who enjoys hurting people. But he's loyal. He probably thanks you for the opportunity. He hurt Justin Peverell's girlfriend, Martina Varakova. Killed her, in fact, very slowly and very painfully, while Justin was tied up and made to watch. Justin is catatonic now. The doctors aren't holding out a lot of hope of his making a full recovery. Well, you wouldn't after something like that, would you? Imagine someone doing that to your lovely wife.'

'Why are you telling me all this? What's it all got to do with me?'

'Jaffar McCready had something of yours – two kilos of cocaine, fifty thousand pounds and a hot gun, to be exact. We have it all now, locked up safely in our evidence room.'

Fanthorpe sneered. 'Safely? I'll bet.'

'You wanted it all back. Naturally. You even told me you wanted it back. DS Jackman here is a witness to that.'

Winsome looked up from her notebook and smiled at Fanthorpe.

'You just never told me what it was,' Banks said.

'But you think you've worked it out for yourself?'

'It wasn't that difficult.'

'I'm afraid you've come to the wrong conclusion. If that's what you found, then I was obviously mistaken, and Jaffar didn't have what I thought he had. None of that belonged to me.'

'Darren Brody has been working with Ciaran French for a few years now. He knows what Ciaran's like, has seen him getting progressively more violent and cruel. It's all right with him when it's worked as a threat and people talk, then usually go away with only a few cuts and bruises. But this time it got out of hand. Way out of hand. My guess is that

Ciaran had built up such a lust for bloodletting that he couldn't hold it back any longer. Victor Mallory. Rose Preston. Teasers. However it happened, Darren was with him, and Darren couldn't stop him, but he didn't like what he saw.'

'Darren's just trying to save his own skin. They're both psychos.'

'We'll leave the question of why you would employ a couple of psychos aside for the moment. Jaffar McCready certainly wasn't one. He was a greedy, cocksure, ambitious, intelligent young man with a tendency to violence when necessary. He wanted to be a player. He didn't especially like killing. He wasn't even particularly good at it. He had so many chips on his shoulder he could have given Harry Ramsden a run for his money. Anyway, the point is that Darren has had enough. He had to watch Justin's face while Ciaran sliced up Martina Varakova in front of his eyes. I doubt it was a pretty sight. Darren's a bit tougher than Justin, and he still has his faculties, but a strange thing happened to him that night. They'd found out what they wanted to know, that Justin was meeting Jaffar and Tracy on Hampstead Heath, near the Highgate Ponds, but Ciaran had already gone too far to stop. He couldn't. Because of that, while Darren was watching him, he was suddenly struck, like Saul on the road to Damascus, with a revelation. He asked himself, Why? Why was he watching this? Why was he participating in this? True, the people Ciaran was hurting were a couple of toerags who didn't give a damn about people's lives themselves. But this was too much. How on earth could Darren ever extricate himself from his complicity in Ciaran's actions, though those actions horrified and disgusted him? And do you know what? He found a way. It's called cooperating fully with the police in their enquiries.

Darren talked. In fact, he sang like the three tenors all rolled into one. The complete performances. Boxed set.'

The Farmer had turned pale now and seemed to shrink in his armchair, the whisky left untouched for several minutes beside him.

'You've still got no proof,' he said, rallying. 'It's his word against mine, and who do you think the court will believe? An uneducated thug, or an upstanding pillar of the community?'

'Darren is no more an uneducated thug than you are a pillar of the community,' Banks said. 'I reckon he'll make a very good impression on a jury. Reformed sinner and all that. Atonement. Juries love a good redemption story. He knows where all the bodies are buried. He also told us a few places we should be looking if we're after evidence of some of your shadier dealings and contacts, so we're executing these warrants simultaneously for this house and your business premises, including the mailboxes on Grand Cayman and Jersey. Winsome?'

Winsome excused herself and went to the front door, where she put her fingers to her lips and whistled loudly. Banks had always wished he could do that. Within a few moments, six uniformed officers had entered the house and spread out. DS Stefan Novak and DS Jim Hatchley were in charge of the search operation, and Banks said hello to both of them as he and Winsome escorted Fanthorpe, now in handcuffs, out to the car. Eloise was still practising the adagio to the 'Moonlight' sonata in the piano room, and Zenovia was screaming and waving her arms at the search team. The other young girl frowned and turned up the volume with the remote as she tried to concentrate on *Strictly Come Dancing* amid the chaos all around her.

As they walked to the car, Banks looked down the cinder path with the topiary hedges, towards the pond and fountain. 'A young boy pissing,' he said to the Farmer, shaking his head. 'That just about says it all, doesn't it? A young boy pissing.'

Banks walked along the now familiar corridors of Cook Hospital early the following week, saying hello to a couple of the nurses and general staff he had come to recognise. He had driven straight from Newhope Cottage, and while he was certainly glad to be home in some ways, he couldn't help dwelling on what had happened there. Superintendent Gervaise had arranged for a cleaning crew after the SOCOs had finished, so he hadn't had to face any blood, or the mess Tracy had told him about – except for a few damaged CDs and broken cases – but he knew where Annie had been shot, and he couldn't sit comfortably in the conservatory any more. Maybe he would get over it. If not, he would have to move. He couldn't go on living there feeling the way he did. Newhope used to be a joyous place, but since the fire, and now this, Banks was beginning to wonder.

He found Annie propped up on her pillows, fewer tubes than on his last visit, he was certain, and looking a lot better. She was flipping through the pages of one of the Sunday newspaper supplements.

'A bit dated, isn't it?' said Banks, pecking her on the cheek and sitting in the chair beside the bed.

'It's about all I could scrounge since I've been alert enough to read,' Annie said.

'Well, this is your lucky day.' Banks opened the large holdall he had brought with him and passed over a WHSmith's bag full of women's magazines he had seen her reading in the past, along with the latest Kate Mosse and Santa Montefiore paperbacks. 'These should keep you busy for a while.'

'Thank you,' Annie said, searching through the bag. 'That's great. I thought I was going to end up being bored to death. It's still a bit hard, reading with only one hand, though.'

'For when your arm gets tired,' Banks added, reaching into his pocket, 'there's this.'

'But it's your iPod.'

'I got a new one in San Francisco. This one's nearly full. I'm sure you'll find some music you like, there's a quite a bit of classical, and there's a few books on it, too, mostly classics – Jane Austen, Chekhov's short stories, Trollope, Tolstoy, the Brontës – and some non-fiction, history and biography. It'll help pass the time.' He glanced around furtively then stuck his hand inside the holdall again and brought out a bottle of Australian red wine. 'I know you prefer white,' he said, 'and the review of the Santa Montefiore book suggested it would go well with chilled Prosecco, but I don't think they'd exactly put it on ice for you here. I've seen you drink red. And the screw-top seemed important. It's no longer a mark of poor quality, you know. This is good stuff.'

'I know,' said Annie. 'I've had it before. And it's perfect. Put it down in the cupboard while no one's around, would you. I can already imagine midnight drinking sessions with one eye on the door.'

'The way I used to read books with a penlight and listen to Radio Luxembourg through an earpiece when I was a kid,' Banks said. 'One more thing.' He brought out a small bag of treats from Lewis & Cooper, the Northallerton gourmet food shop. 'There's a few different cheeses, vegetable pâté, potted shrimp, just in case you feel like being really naughty, and water crackers, figs, olives. Only the best.'

Annie laughed and put her hand to her face. Banks could see she was crying, too. 'Oh, thanks, Alan. Come here.'

He bent over her, and she held him with her good arm. He felt the warm, damp skin of her cheek against his and thought he should have shaved that morning, then he smelled her hair, smelled *her*. 'You shouldn't have.'

'Of course I should.' Banks moved away but held on to her hand. 'I'm afraid that's it,' he said. 'How is the food here?'

'As you'd expect. Not that bad,' said Annie. 'Though being a vegetarian is a definite liability. I must say, Ray's been wonderful, though.'

'Where is he?'

'He had to go to London. There's a gallery putting on a show of his work down there. He didn't want to, said he thought he should stay with me, but I made him go. He'll be back tomorrow.'

'Say hi from me,' said Banks. 'So how are you feeling?'

'Good days and bad. I'm on the mend.'

'Your breathing sounds a lot better. Have you talked to the doctor?'

Annie turned her head. 'Yes. Mr Sandhar and I had a good long heart-to-heart late last week. He told me about the operation, explained all the details, the ins and outs, the risks.'

'And?'

'I'm scared.'

Banks tightened his grip on her hand. 'It'll be fine. You'll see. You couldn't be in better hands.'

'I know that. It's just . . . you know, it's always been one of my greatest fears, being unable to walk, unable to move, confined to a wheelchair. Remember Lucy Payne? What a monster she was? I even felt sorry for her. I thought it might have been easier if she'd just died.'

'It's not going to happen to you. You'll be back to normal in no time.'

'He certainly didn't downplay the dangers.'

'He wouldn't. He's a realist.'

'Maybe a little kindly lying wouldn't have gone amiss.' Annie winced.

'What is it?'

She put her hand to her chest. 'Sometimes when I breathe in I still get a sharp pain in my chest. The doctor says it's my lung healing. My bloody shoulder still hurts like the dickens, too. Keeps me awake at nights.'

'It's a nasty wound.'

Annie paused. 'Tell me, Alan, is he really dead? Jaff McCready?'

'Yes.'

'Poor kid. I can't say I'd have wished that on him.'

'After what he did to you?'

'I'm not saying he didn't deserve punishment. Severe punishment. But . . .'

'It was quick,' said Banks. 'He didn't even see it coming.'

'I suppose not.'

'Don't feel too sorry for him, Annie. McCready was no innocent.'

'I know. You were there, weren't you?'

'Yes. I didn't see it coming, either.' Banks had brought a Starbucks grande latte with him, and he took a sip then set it down on top of Annie's side cupboard. As he did so, he realised that he had forgotten the flowers. He mentally kicked himself. *Idiot*. Next time. No, he'd have some delivered, with a note, as soon as he left. 'We recovered his gun, by the way.

McCready's. A Baikal, as we thought. It had a silencer, and I think that's what saved your life. Apparently, with a silencer, it loses a third of its power and is far less accurate.'

'Well I never,' said Annie. 'What's happening over the McCready shooting business?'

'About what you'd expect. They're all back-pedalling like crazy. In the end, it all comes down to spin, of course. The media don't have many facts, but there's been plenty of speculation about my presence there, and Tracy's, not to mention a "rogue" AFO. Mostly, the brass has being trying to quash those rumours, or at least deflect the worst of them. We've had a few more meetings, without PC Powell's presence this time. Even the Chief Constable himself was at one of them. Everyone has ended up bending over backwards, so the media reports it as all going according to procedure. An unfortunate necessity, but an officer's life at risk, a proven police shooter, a dangerous criminal on the run, unstable behaviour, hostages involved, official operation, judgement call, no choice in the matter. Blah, blah, blah. Take your pick.'

'You disagree?'

'Not at all. It's just – barely – possible to argue it that way. We even had civilian witnesses to bear out the evidence that my life and Tracy's were at immediate risk, and that the police sharpshooter acted appropriately, with all reasonable regard for any members of the public in the vicinity. All of which is true. The fact that she was there unofficially, under her own steam, and with an unofficial weapon . . . well, we just tried to sweep all that under the carpet. There are still bits sticking out, of course, but . . . ACC McLaughlin told the press that we hadn't been able to authorise any sort of large or visible Firearms Support Unit operation because of time constraints, the delicacy of the situation and the danger to the hostages, not to mention the public at large. He wasn't lying. We'll take a lot of flak, and Chambers is still on the warpath, but what's new? Cooler heads might prevail this time.'

'And Nerys?'

Banks sipped a little more of his latte and said, 'I'd say her career's effectively over, wouldn't you? I mean, not because of the taser business with Warburton. That's dead in the water. Even Chambers realises that. Ironically enough, it was partly your shooting that knocked it off the front page. Cop shootings do get us a lot of public sympathy.'

'Glad to be of help.'

Banks smiled. 'There may be a few slapped wrists for a less than full assessment of the situation at the Doyle house. Chambers and his lads from Greater Manchester will continue to conduct their inquiry, and they'll want their pound of flesh, or at least a couple of ounces in compensation, but I'd guess the result's a foregone conclusion.'

'Cover-ups all round, then?'

'Not really. Certainly not the taser incident. The whole thing *was* an unfortunate accident, and luckily the media's quite happy to view it that way – until the next time. But Nerys? The McCready shooting? That's a little different. Nobody wants wild headlines in the papers about rogue cops shooting people down in motorway services car parks, so we'll put a slightly more heroic spin on her actions. Even so, it won't be easy for her. There's the rifle, for a start. She shouldn't have been carrying it around. She's damn lucky not to be going to prison after what she pulled. They'll make her see a shrink, too, of course. I must say, you do pick them, Annie.'

'You can talk. Besides, I didn't pick her. She picked me. And how can you say that? Why are you so ambivalent about her? She saved your life.'

'I know she did. And I'm grateful for that. But she's still bloody lucky to get off without serious criminal charges, in my opinion. Lucky no one needs a sacrificial lamb right now. And I'm ambivalent because I'm not convinced of her motives.'

'What do you mean?'

'I think she did it as much for herself as for me.'

'Where do you get that from?'

'I can't prove it, but I'll bet you a pound to a penny that it was you she was thinking of, and what Jaff had done to you, when she pulled that trigger. She was shooting him for what he did to you.'

Annie reddened. 'Well, we'll probably never know, will we?' She let go of Banks's hand for a moment and reached for her water. Banks saw her grimace in pain as she turned, so he passed it to her. 'Thanks,' she said.

'We won't know unless she tells us, which I doubt she ever will,' said Banks. 'Why should she? I'd be the first to admit that it probably doesn't even matter to anybody but me, and to people like Chambers and Trethowan, who seem to want to make her lesbianism an issue here.'

'And you don't?'

'I don't care whether she did it for a man or a woman. What matters is that she didn't do it for the reasons she said she did. She did it for revenge. It was personal.' Then Banks rubbed his hand over his eyes. 'But it was personal for a lot of us, so I'm not saying she should be crucified for it.'

'And she saved your life.'

'Yes.'

'And there was no other way?'

'No. Look, I know I'm not making a lot of sense. I'll get it all sorted out in time.'

'So what happens to Nerys?'

'If she has any sense, she'll get out of North Yorkshire as fast as she can, lie low for a while, then she might well make some clandestine counter-terrorism squad or other. They're not always so fussy about who they take on, depending on the level of threat, and she *is* a good shot. She won't go to waste. Who knows, maybe even the Americans will take her? She suits their style.'

'Don't you think that's a bit harsh?'

'On whom? Nerys, or the Americans?'

Annie laughed. 'Touché. What about the Farmer?'

'Who knows?' said Banks. 'We're building a case. The CPS in enthusiastic. But he's got good lawyers. Still, there's some interesting stuff in his Jersey and Cayman Island files. We got Victor Mallory, too, by the way. Found his lock-up with the lab and cache of Baikals. The clever bastards were using one of McCready's father's old shell companies. That's why it took so long to track down.'

'What's going to happen to Erin?'

'I've recommended a good solicitor. She'll plead guilty, with extenuating circumstances. I think that given her previous good character and the circumstances surrounding the whole affair, she'll probably get away with a suspended sentence. At least, that's what the solicitor says.'

'And Tracy? How's she doing after her ordeal?'

Banks sipped his latte. 'She's young, resilient. She'll recover in time.'

'You sound uncertain. What's wrong?'

'It's nothing,' said Banks. 'She was raped, you know. McCready raped her.'

Annie said nothing at first. Banks wondered whether she was remembering her own experience of rape, several years ago, before she came to North Yorkshire. 'Good God,' she said finally. 'I'm so sorry, Alan. If I can help in any way . . . If you want me to talk to her, just let me know. I do wish I could remember more about what happened before the shooting, how she was, what she said. I just can't. All I have is the impression that she was scared and she was trying to get rid of me quickly.'

'Well, that would make sense if McCready was waiting in the wings, wouldn't it? She wanted you out before he hurt you. She knew how unstable he was by then.'

'Not before?'

'Annie, I don't really know how to say this, but I think Tracy was lying to me when she told the story from her point of view. Believe me, I've had plenty of experience listening to people lie. There are just too many inconsistencies.'

'Did you challenge her on them?'

'Of course not. It's nothing, really, but she just seemed to shade everything so she came out sounding like the victim all the time.'

'She *was* the victim.'

'I know. But I don't think McCready forced her to go with him. I think she fancied him and she went willingly, *and* suggested my cottage as a place to hide out. I think it was an adventure to her at first, maybe a form of rebellion, of payback . . . I don't know . . . We haven't been very close lately. She may blame me. She felt that I favoured Brian and that I was disappointed by her exam results and her lack of a promising career. I don't like to be suspicious of my own daughter, Annie, but . . .'

'Alan, if Tracy was playing down her role, she was doing it because she was feeling guilty and ashamed of what a fool she was, and the last thing she'd want is for you to think even more badly of her. Don't you see? She's afraid of your judgement. You're not just her father, you know. You're a policeman, too. You have no doubt that she became a victim and hostage later on, do you?'

'No. I think there came a point when the relationship changed. Maybe when you got shot, or even before.'

'Well then. She might have gone along with McCready in the first place for some sort of misguided romantic reason. She's young. But she didn't pull the trigger. She didn't steal the coke and the money. McCready did all that. Just give her time to heal. Build some bridges. Try to understand what she must be feeling. She'll tell the truth when she's ready.'

'You think so?'

'I do. Where is she now?'

'She's staying in London with her mother for a while. I'm so deep in the doghouse with Sandra now that even my feet aren't sticking out.'

Annie laughed at the image. 'For not telling everyone what was going on?'

'What do you think?'

'What a mess.' Annie shook her head slowly and took his hand again. 'I was so scared when I realised what was happening. There on the floor, in your conservatory, before it all went dark and I could hardly catch my breath. I was convinced I was going to die. I missed you so much at that moment, Alan.'

Banks swallowed and squeezed her hand. 'I missed you, too. You'd have loved it over there. The desert nights. The Grand Canyon. The Pacific Coast Highway. Fisherman's Wharf. The Golden Gate Bridge. Magic.'

'I wish I'd been with you, but it sounded like the kind of trip you had to take alone.'

'It was,' said Banks. 'This time. But who knows? One day . . .'

'If I can still walk.'

'You'll walk.'

'You know,' Annie said, 'you've told me plenty about Nerys and Tracy and what happened and all that, but what about you?'

'Me?' Banks shrugged. 'What about me? I've had plenty of practice being in the doghouse where Sandra's concerned. And it matters a lot less when she's a couple of hundred miles away.'

'No. I didn't mean so much about your family. I meant the other stuff. Job. Career. Future.'

Banks finished his latte and dropped the cup in the waste-basket. 'Well, Chambers is out for blood and I'm right in his sights. He'd love to throw me to the wolves. I broke every rule in the book, probably more even than poor Nerys, and he knows I'd do it again in the twinkling of an eye.'

'But?'

'I still have a few friends in high places. They're pushing for a spell of gardening leave until I sort out my "personal problems". Emotionally distraught father, understandably over-tired, daughter abducted, that sort of thing. The saving grace is that if the powers above did throw me to the wolves, most of them would have to fall on their own swords for allowing the situation to arise in the first place. Cold comfort, I suppose, but there you go. In the end, they'll either sack me, put me in the nuthouse or promote me to Area Commander.'

Annie laughed. 'But what will you do? Aren't you worried? Seriously. You don't sound too concerned.'

'I'm not.' Banks looked at the beeping machines with their wavy lines and numbers, then back to Annie. 'Maybe the trip put a few things in perspective for me. What will I do? Seriously? I don't know. Come back and fight another day, like I always do, I suppose. But sometimes I think I've had enough. I'm getting a bit tired of it all, to be honest. You?'

'I don't know, either. I suppose I'm on hold till after the operation. Then I'll re-evaluate my situation, as they say.' She laughed. 'We're a right pair, aren't we?'

Banks glanced towards the door, reached for the wine and a couple of plastic cups from Annie's cupboard, and smiled. 'We are indeed. Shall we drink to that?'

Acknowledgements

Many people contributed to this book and I would like to begin by thanking those who first read and commented – my wife and invaluable first reader, Sheila Halladay, my agents Dominick Abel and David Grossman, and my editors Carolyn Mays, Francesca Best, Carolyn Marino, Wendy Lee and Dinah Forbes. A special thanks to Dinah for collating all the comments into one manuscript and making my life a lot easier. I would also like to thank all the copy editors and proof readers at Hodder, Morrow and McClelland & Stewart, whose job it is to ensure that the book you read is free from grammatical, typographical and factual errors.

A number of professionals helped me with the police procedural and forensic aspects, and I would especially like to thank Detective Inspector Kevin Robinson, of West Yorkshire Police, and Julie Kempson for information about the approach to firearms. Any errors I have made are entirely my own. I would also like to thank Deputy Chief Constable Phil Gormley and Detective Superintendent Claire Stevens for their continued support and advice.

Thanks must also go to my publicists Sharyn Rosenblum and Nicole Chismar at Morrow/HarperCollins, Kerry Hood and Katie Davison at Hodder, and Ashley Dunn at McClelland & Stewart. Last but not least, this book wouldn't be in your hands today if it weren't for the sales reps and the bookshop employees, so a hearty thanks to you all.

Coming soon, a brilliant new standalone novel by

PETER ROBINSON
Before The Poison

Through the years of success in Hollywood composing music for the world's most lauded films, Chris always promised his wife they would return to the Yorkshire Dales one day. Now, after his wife's death, Chris feels he must not forget his promise.

Back in the Dales, he rents an isolated house that will allow him the space to come to terms with his grief and the quiet to allow him to compose his piano sonata. But when he finds that the house was the scene of a murder in the 1950s, and that the convicted murderer was one of the last women hanged in England, he finds himself increasingly distracted by the events of sixty years before . . .

Out in hardback in August 2011

To find out more about Peter Robinson, visit his website at
www.inspectorbanks.com.

HODDER &
STOUGHTON

NAME: Alan Banks.

RANK: Detective Chief Inspector.

DEPARTMENT: Major Crimes.

LOCATION: Western Area Headquarters, Eastvale, North Yorkshire.

BIRTHDAY: May 24.

AGE: Mid-fifties.

PLACE OF BIRTH: Peterborough, Cambridgeshire.

MARITAL STATUS: Divorced from Sandra, who has now remarried and has another child.

CHILDREN: Son: Brian, lead guitarist in successful rock band, The Blue Lamps.
Daughter: Tracy, a recent history graduate now working in a bookshop.

FATHER: Arthur Banks, sheet metal worker made redundant in the early 80s.

MOTHER: Ida Banks, retired cleaning woman.

temples; dark blue eyes; scar beside his right eye. At just over five foot eight, he is a little short for a policeman. He's not especially handsome, but women find him attractive. A casual dresser, he hates wearing a tie, and if he has to wear one, he will tie it loosely and leave his top shirt button undone.

POLITICS: Not a political creature but he is a moderate socialist and liberal humanist.

RELIGION: Cautious agnostic.

MUSIC: Fanatical about it. He appreciates almost all genres – opera, chamber, vocal, orchestral, jazz and rock – but is less fond of country and western, funk, fusion, operetta or hip-hop. Likes to listen as he drives. Started with a portable cassette player, then switched to CDs and now has an iPod.

FILMS: His favourites are war films, James Bond, historical epics like *Doctor Zhivago* and *Lawrence of Arabia*, espionage and thrillers. He's not much interested in horror, science-fiction, romantic comedies or art cinema. Likes old black and white noir films such as *The Third Man* and *Touch of Evil*, and the old Ealing Comedies.

FAVOURITE ACTOR: Alec Guinness.

FAVOURITE ACTRESS: Julie Christie.

BOOKS: Largely self-taught in the field of literature, he enjoys espionage writers such as Graham Greene, Eric Ambler, Len Deighton and John le Carré. Not much of a crime fiction reader, other than Sherlock Holmes, and has many more books on his 'should read' list than he will ever get around to reading.

VACATIONS: Prefers exploring a new city on foot or driving around an interesting region rather than lounging on a beach in the sun.

ALCOHOL: Enjoys a pint of bitter, especially Tetley's or Black Sheep. He also enjoys single malt whisky, especially Laphroaig, but recently has switched to red wine. He rarely drinks to excess, but stress can sometimes push him there. It's more likely to be emotional stress, though, rather than the stress of his job. He is slowly starting to regain his taste for Laphroaig.

HOME: After his divorce from Sandra, he moved from their semi-detached house in Eastvale to a small cottage in the hamlet of Gratly, isolated at the end of a cul-de-sac by the waterfalls and the woods. The house has recently been restored after a fire.

FEARS: Blindness over more than deafness, despite his love of music, loss of to slapstick, but he is equally fond of verbal humour. His favourite comedians are Peter Sellers, Spike Milligan, W.C. Fields, and his favourite comedy shows are *Monty Python, Fawlty Towers, Blackadder, Have I Got News For You, That Mitchell and Webb Look.*

CHARACTER:

Banks is a bit of a maverick in that he likes to get things done his own way, but he doesn't bend the rules to breaking point. He doesn't respond well to authority unless he respects the person behind the rank. He's empathetic, interested in people and curious about their motives, saddened and angered by murder. His mind is agile and he is eager for new experiences – new music, new books. Though he is a man of reason, he is not afraid to use his intuition. Since his divorce he has had a couple of romantic relationships but has been unable to sustain them and is often baffled by the whole relationship 'thing'. He loves women, though, and has many female friends. Normally even-tempered, he can become very frustrated if he feels he is not making progress in a case, and can sometimes be abrupt or sarcastic with people.

MOST DEEPLY KEPT SECRET:

That would be telling!

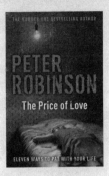

PETER ROBINSON
All the Colours of Darkness

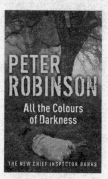

The Final Act

The death is clearly suicide. And even when the second body is found, it seems a straightforward case: a jealous man has killed his lover and hanged himself. Hardly worth DCI Alan Banks cutting his weekend short.

But when Banks is pulled off the investigation soon after he discovers that the murder victim wasn't all he appeared to be, his alarm bells start ringing.

This case is far from closed, and Banks will risk everything to get to the truth.

Out now

PETER ROBINSON
Friend of the Devil

PETER
ROBINSON

Friend of the Devil

THE NEW CHIEF INSPECTOR BANKS

A Maze of Murder

The victim is no older than Banks's own daughter. Just 19,
she's found raped and strangled in the dark tangle of
cobbled alleyways they call The Maze.

There's no shortage of suspects, and Banks finds himself
missing DI Annie Cabbot. Their personal problems aside,
he could do with her sharp instincts on this case.

But Annie has troubles of her own. On loan to the Eastern
Area, she's been called to investigate the cold-blooded
killing of a woman in a wheelchair.

On the face of it, the two deaths have nothing in common. But
as Annie digs deeper, she finds something disturbingly familiar
in the case. Perhaps she and Banks will find themselves
working together again a lot sooner than expected . . .

Out now

HODDER

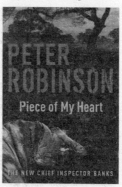